Praise for Fiona Buckley ... er
Ursul...

TO SH...

"A lively mystery s... ...irst mystery, former jou~~rnalist and editor~~ Buckley shows a deft hand with strong characterization and creates a plot that spins merrily and wickedly through palace, manor house, and intensely beautiful countryside. Ursula is a force to be reckoned with. . . . Her relationship with the young Queen is just one of the elements that makes this a promising series debut."

—*Publishers Weekly*

"*To Shield the Queen* is an exciting historical mystery that brings alive the early reign of Queen Elizabeth I. . . . The cast brings color and pageantry to the exciting story line....With the first Blanchard novel, Fiona Buckley has opened up an auspicious new series."

—*Feminist Mystery Corner Reviews*

"The debut of Ursula Blanchard, young, widowed lady of the Presence Chamber at Elizabeth I's court, combines assured storytelling and historical detail to present a credible interpretation of the events surrounding the 1560 death of Lord Dudley's neglected wife at Cumnor Place. . . . A terrific tale most accessibly told."

—*The Poisoned Pen*

"A lively debut that's filled with vivid characters, religious conflicts, subplots, and power plays. . . . High suspense throughout."

—*Kirkus Reviews*

"Buckely achieves the difficult effect of working historical detail into the action smoothly."

—*The Charlotte (NC) Observer*

BOOKS BY FIONA BUCKLEY

To Shield the Queen
The Doublet Affair

Available from POCKET BOOKS

THE
DOUBLET
AFFAIR

Fiona Buckley

POCKET STAR BOOKS

New York   London   Toronto   Sydney   Singapore

This book is a work of fiction. Names, characters, places and incidents are products of the author's imagination or are used fictitiously. Any resemblance to actual events or locales or persons, living or dead, is entirely coincidental.

 A Pocket Star Book published by
POCKET BOOKS, a division of Simon & Schuster Inc.
1230 Avenue of the Americas, New York, NY 10020

Copyright © 1998 by Fiona Buckley

Originally published in Great Britain on 1998 by Orion
Previously published in hardcover in 1998 by Simon & Schuster Inc.

ISBN: 0-671-01532-X

First Pocket Books printing December 1999

10 9 8 7 6 5 4 3 2 1

POCKET and colophon are registered trademarks of Simon & Schuster Inc.

Cover art by Harry F. Bliss

Printed in the U.S.A.

This book is for
Gwyneth Rowlands
with affection and gratitude.

ACKNOWLEDGEMENT

My thanks go to Selfridges Ltd., who kindly allowed me to visit their gift department and peer into the insides of the musical boxes on display.

CHAPTERS

THE
DOUBLET
AFFAIR

CHAPTER 1

Unlocking Secrets

"Gently, now, gently. That's the way. Let's take our time. Let there be nothing rough or crude, but only care and delicacy. Let us *see* with our fingertips. Aah! The word one might use," said Master Alexander Bone, creased face rapt, eyes closed, "is *exquisite*."

His movements were all finesse, his hands as tense and sensitive as a pair of pricked ears. Those same hands were also old and worn, with liver spots and prominent veins. Alexander Bone was old and worn altogether. His dust-coloured woollen gown was mended in several places and deplorably marred by foodstains, and the grey hair which straggled round his ears was in sorry need of trimming. He smelt musty. I didn't like being so close to him. Not for the first time, I asked myself what I was doing here with the likes of Master Bone. I would so much rather have been somewhere else. With somebody quite different.

There was a faint click from inside the little pewter casket he was holding, and he opened his eyes. Carefully, he drew out the wire device with which he had been picking the lock, and raised the domed lid.

"There!" he said. "There you are, Mistress Blanchard. Sweet as you please. You can lock it again—" he demonstrated—"as if nothing had ever happened." Master Bone gave me a grin which went further up one side of his face than it did the other. He handed me the wire lock-pick. "Try again. Remember: feel your way and go slow. You can't see the mechanism with your eyes, so close them. Work through your fingers. They'll make pictures in your head if you let them. They'll know when the lock-picks find the spring. Then you push it aside. It should resist first, and then yield to pressure. Press against it, steady and smooth."

It was February, and cold. Beyond the window, the Thames flowed sullenly under a leaden sky. The little room off Sir William Cecil's study in Whitehall Palace had thick curtains over the doors to keep out draughts, but although they made the air stuffy they didn't make it warmer. My waiting woman, Fran Dale, who was sitting in a corner of the room, had mittens on. My fingers were chilled and slow and I paused to rub them before I slipped the wire into the keyhole and made a fresh attempt to coax the lock to turn.

It would be interesting, I thought, to know where on earth the highly respectable and well-bred Sir William Cecil, Secretary of State to Queen Elizabeth, had found Alexander Bone. The man clearly had some education, and was an expert locksmith who, according to Cecil, had a shop in the City of London near London Bridge, yet Bone's acquaintance with wire lock-picks strongly suggested criminal connections. As I came to know Cecil better, however, I had learned that he had contacts in many unlikely places, acquired over the years as a provident farmer might acquire useful tools—not despising battered third-hand items but repairing and burnishing them for future use.

I couldn't imagine why a skilled man like Alexander Bone should ever have sunk into the underworld in the first place, but he might well have been offered a financial leg-up back into the realms of virtue, in exchange for teaching Cecil's growing network of agents and informers how to get at the private correspondence of people suspected of plotting against the Queen.

It was a fact that there were those who wanted to end our peaceful Protestant days and turn back the clock to the time when all must be Catholic, or die most horribly. Some of them believed that Elizabeth was not legitimate and that Mary Stuart, Queen of Scotland and also of France until her husband's recent death, should be on our throne instead. There was also one who wished to marry Elizabeth, and who was willing to invite a foreign army on to English soil to support him if the people of England rose against a king consort they disliked.

Thinking of that almost made me lose my grip on the wire because it made me so angry. Angry enough, in fact, to forget for a moment that if I had my way, I would be far away from here, in the company of my husband, sharing his home, leaving matters of state and the welfare of the Queen to men like Cecil, whose natural business such things were. Well, I had little choice about that. I had given up hope of hearing from Matthew again. I must perforce continue to make my living in my curious and unwomanly profession.

As it happened, I was the one who had found out

what Sir Robin Dudley, the Queen's Master of Horse, was up to. I hadn't needed any illegal wire keys, either. While attending royal functions, the Spanish ambassador, Bishop de Quadra, sometimes changed his clothes at court and left his portable document case in the robing room, not realising that it had an unreliable attendant. Unreliable as far as Spanish ambassadors were concerned, that is. The attendant was loyal enough to England, and besides, I had arranged for him to be well paid to let me have a glimpse of that case whenever it was in his care. Usually, its contents were harmless and dull, but there came a day when the bishop was careless enough to leave something more interesting in it: a memorandum, in fact, of Robin Dudley's quite incredible plan.

Quadra's seeming carelessness probably meant that he didn't take the notion seriously, but Cecil and I were sure that Dudley himself did. The very thought of it gave me wild fantasies of seeing Dudley led to the block; even of wielding the axe myself, which was absurd. I, Mistress Ursula Blanchard, aged twenty-six, was no more than middle height, and slender, even though I had borne a child. I probably couldn't even lift a headsman's axe, let alone make an accurate swing with it. Private rage was replaced for a moment by private amusement.

Laughter, even when silent, is no more of an aid to efficient lock-picking than indignation. The wire in my hand shook, scratching uselessly at the invisible entrails of the lock, and Master Bone clicked a disapproving tongue. I steadied myself. Concentrating with narrowed eyes, I at last felt the firm resistance I sought and pressed against it. Despite the cold, I was sweating, and the linen ruff at my neck prickled annoyingly. Which way did the invisible assembly inside want to move? As bidden, I tried to picture in my head the mechanism which Master Bone had shown me. Then, softly, satisfyingly, came the click I was waiting for. I relaxed. "I think that's it."

"Not bad, Mistress Blanchard, but you got flustered, didn't you? It's no good, getting flustered. As I said last week, you need practice. I've brought you some boxes, with various kinds of lock. You can keep them to practise on. Here they are." He picked up a leather sack from the floor and put it on the table. "I advise you to work with them for an hour each day. Keep the lock-picks, too. I brought this set for you."

I thanked him, and he gazed at me wistfully.

"I'll come again if I'm wanted," he said in hopeful tones. "Any time. You tell Sir William. I'm always ready to help. All this must seem very strange to a lady like you."

"It certainly wasn't in my education when I was a child," I agreed, wondering what Aunt Tabitha and Uncle Herbert, who had brought me up, would have said if asked to include this unusual subject in my curriculum. My aunt's remarks would have been especially interesting. There was no more upright and virtuous woman in the realm than my Aunt Tabitha Faldene.

Bone was being paid by Cecil, but I realised that he was probably hinting. "Dale," I said. "My purse, please. Have a drink or two on me, Master Bone. Something to keep the cold out." I gave him a silver crown, which he seized gratefully.

"That's kind of you. Money never goes as far as it ought. Things were better long ago, when I was a boy. My thanks, Mistress Blanchard. Though drink's not my demon," said Bone. He looked round for his cloak, which Dale took from the back of a spare chair and handed to him. He wrapped it round him, over his disreputable gown. "There's a cockfight planned this afternoon, near where I live. I'm a man who just can't say no to a wager and that's the truth. That's where your crown'll go, and I'll hope to double it."

"I wish you luck," I said, ignoring the fact that he was still gazing longingly at my purse. If I had any more spare coins, I preferred to spend them on my little daughter.

"I'll be away to see the feathers fly, then," said Bone, accepting defeat. "I'm leaving my shop shut for the whole day, to come here and then attend the cockfight, so I hope I do a bit of good."

And that, I thought, as Master Bone took his leave, no doubt explained why a qualified craftsman had needed to get involved in crime. Gambling debts, for sure. Well, Cecil was making good use of the outcome. If Bone had stayed respectable, his skills with pieces of wire might not have been so polished.

I liked Cecil as a man, but he had his ruthless side. He did indeed collect people to use as tools. In the service of Elizabeth, he would use any tool that came to hand.

And that included me.

When Master Bone had gone, I made haste to return through Whitehall Palace to the small chamber which I shared with Dale five nights a week. On the other two nights I sent her to be with her husband, my manservant Roger Brockley. My quarters were not in the same building as Cecil's office, and Brockley, my stocky, reliable, dignified Brockley, was waiting in the porch to escort us back. He was well wrapped, with a stout felt hat pulled down over his ears, and a thick cloak drawn round him, but he looked cold. I wasn't sure of his age, but from what he had told me of his past life, and from the silver hairs mixed with the brown at his temples, he must be in his forties. Today, his high, intelligent forehead, with its sprinkling of pale gold freckles, was a little puckered as if with the discomfort of the weather.

"Brockley, you should have come inside and found a fire to stand beside. There's one in the servants' room downstairs."

"I might have missed you if I left the porch, madam." Brockley spoke good, almost prim, English in a country accent. "And you should have an escort in this warren of a palace," he said. "Palace! It's more like a town!"

This was true enough. Whitehall, Her Majesty was wont to inform us proudly, was the biggest royal palace in the whole of Europe. It was a maze of halls and galleries, staircases and courtyards, lodgings, guardrooms, outbuildings and gardens, with a road going through the middle as though it were indeed a small town instead of a residence. In wet weather, people who hadn't set foot beyond the palace precincts often arrived drenched for meals or meetings.

To reach my quarters, we had to cross two courtyards, climb two staircases and go down one, and then cross a public thoroughfare, where Brockley stepped in front of me and grabbed Dale's arm just in time to keep us out of the way as a couple of satin-clad horsemen with feathers in their hats and huge rowelled spurs on their boots, clattered by, riding far too fast.

"A fine sort of house," said Brockley disparagingly, "where folk can be ridden down *inside* the gates! By the way, madam, did your—er—lesson today go well? I understand from Fran that you are learning to open locks."

His voice was carefully bland. I smiled. Brockley did not approve of the means by which I kept myself dressed and jewelled as befitted a Lady of the Queen's Presence Chamber, provided extras for my small daughter, paid Brockley's salary and that of his wife, and maintained the two horses which I kept for us.

"The lesson was most successful, thank you, Brockley. I need practice now, that's all, and the gear for that is in the sack that Dale is carrying."

Blue-grey eyes as expressionless as his voice, Brockley said, "And what's it all for, madam? May we know?"

"I wish I knew the answer to that myself," I said, "but I shan't find out until I take dinner with Sir William Cecil and his wife tomorrow. Meanwhile, both of you, I am due to attend on the Queen. I must hurry!"

Brockley left us at the foot of my staircase and Dale followed me up to my tiny room. Sprawling Whitehall had enough little cubbyholes, hollowed out of the thickness of old walls or created by partitioning bigger chambers, for many of the Queen's ladies to have their own rooms, or at least cubicles. I had a patch of floor in what had once been a big anteroom, now divided by faded tapestries which had been retired from the royal apartments. I had just space enough for my bed, Dale's truckle bed, a clothes press and a toilet stand. I hurried in ahead of Dale and then stopped short in surprise, for awaiting me, seated on my bedside stool, was the plump, beruffed and brocaded figure of the Queen's principal lady.

"Mistress Ashley!"

"I will not ask where you have been," said Kat Ashley severely. "I understand from Her Majesty that you undertook an errand for her today and that I need not question you. However, you are supposed to be on duty and it will cause talk if you don't present yourself promptly. Her Majesty's errands shouldn't become subjects of curiosity and gossip."

"No, quite. Of course not." I thought with amusement that Kat Ashley would know all about curiosity and gossip. She kept the Queen's secrets, or anyone else's if Elizabeth so ordered it, but the fat little paws now hidden in the folds of her plum and silver brocade nevertheless belonged to a woman who loved to dabble her fingers in other people's business. Her protuberant blue eyes were at this moment avid to know what I had been doing and why. For all her dignity and her exalted position, there was something incurably blowsy about Kat. Not that I disliked her: I had a fair share of curiosity in my own nature. She and I understood each other.

"I didn't realise I was so tardy," I said, while Dale put the sack she was carrying quietly out of sight. "I am sorry that you had to come in search of me."

"Oh, I didn't come on account of your lateness," Kat Ashley said, "but while you were—wherever it is you've been—somebody came looking for you, from outside. A ship's boy, sent by a Captain Sutton—a sea captain, apparently."

"A sea captain? Sutton?" I said in bewilderment.

"Just docked in the Thames, over from Calais, according to the boy who came asking for you at the river gate. The gatekeeper sent for me. The lad had a letter for you," said Kat Ashley. Her right hand had been hidden in her costly skirts, and now she withdrew it and held out to me a doubled sheet of paper, sealed.

"The reason the gatekeeper didn't know at once who you were, was that the boy didn't ask for Mistress Blanchard," she said. "He asked for Mistress de la Roche, one of the Queen's ladies. You would do better," said Kat, "to let your French correspondent, whoever he is . . . ?" She waited to see if I would tell her, but although I knew she had seen how my eyes were shining, I said nothing. ". . . Better tell him," said Kat disappointedly, "that here, you still go by the name of your first husband. Here you are."

Kat was among the few people who knew of my second marriage. It was one of the secrets she had been allowed to know because of her position in authority over me, but had been ordered to keep to herself.

Taking the letter, I saw my name, my legal name, Mistress de la Roche, written on it in strong black ink. The writing was masculine and elegant, a little ornate; the seal showed the letter M within a circle. I knew the hand and I knew the seal, from notes sent to me in the past, millenia ago—was it really only last year?—when Matthew de la Roche paid court to me.

"You bade me make haste," I said. "Please leave me now. I will be with the Queen in a few minutes."

Kat Ashley sighed, and heaved herself to her feet with a grunt. "Too many stairs for my liking, to get to these rooms. You're spryer than I am, and just as well. You have ten minutes at most, Mistress Blanchard."

I sat down at my toilet table. "Do my hair, Dale. Quickly. While you're doing it, I'll read this."

"Oh, ma'am! Is it from your husband? I know you said you'd written to him. And quite right too, in my view. A woman should be with her husband. Even if she doesn't agree with everything he says or does, she still ought to be with him. I'd be lost without Brockley, now that we're wed."

I met her eyes in the mirror, and smiled affectionately. Dale, like Brockley himself, was over forty, and she was not beautiful, any more than he was conventionally handsome, but she had regular features which were pleasant in their own way. If she had a few pockmarks from a childhood attack of smallpox, this was a common misfortune, and Dale's pocks were not so very obvious. They had somehow grown less noticeable, and her features softer since she and Brockley married. Her correct name now, of course, was Mistress Brockley, but I was used to calling her Dale and she was used to being thus addressed, so we had gone on with it.

Brockley had done well by her, I thought. If not an Adonis, he was still well looking, with the co-ordinated movements and air of strength which can be more impressive than facial planes. He was resourceful, the kind of man whose wife can rely on him. He had been a groom before I took him on, but he had also been a soldier, in the days of King Henry, and had been to war in Scotland and France. He knew the world.

Dale, when I first knew her, had been inclined to complain too much, but she had improved since her marriage, although I had never been easy to work for, and this had certainly *not* improved.

For one thing, I was often short tempered out of sheer envy, because Dale had the company of her husband whereas I had parted from mine. My reasons at the time seemed good and honourable, but I had learned, through lonely nights and long days of empty busy-ness, that virtue is not only its own, but its only reward. No matter how often I told myself that I had been right to put the welfare of the Queen and the safety of the realm before my own private happiness, it could not comfort my longing or heal my grief. I wanted Matthew.

In the end, after much secret crying in the darkness, I had put my need into words and found a messenger—a merchant travelling to the Loire valley where I believed that Matthew now was. I hoped to God that my letter would reach him, that it would bridge the chasm between us and that he would answer.

Until now, my only answer had been silence. I had tried to tell myself that my letter hadn't reached him, but it was all too probable that he didn't want me any more, and who could blame him? I had vacillated over writing to him again. Now, after all, the reply was here.

Though I did not yet know what was in it. As Dale took my hair, which was long and thick and very dark, out of its silver net and set about brushing it, I sat turning the letter over in my hands. When I first recognised Matthew's handwriting, I had been filled with joy, but it had now occurred to me that it was as likely to contain bitter rejection as impassioned invitation.

As I broke the seal, I was afraid.

CHAPTER 2

Delicate Mechanisms

As I unfolded the letter, I wondered just where and when he had written it. At what time of day? Morning, noon, evening? Looking out, perhaps, on the Loire? He had described the river to me: its beauty, its moods. Had it been sunlit or pocked with rain? Or had he sat down late at night to write by the light of lamp or candle? Had he been pensive, or unhappy, or angry? Had his pen raced swiftly, the words pouring from his heart, or had it travelled slowly, while he weighed every word before inscribing it?

What had he said? Well, Ursula: read it. Then you'll know.

The letter was in French. It began brusquely, without endearments.

Ursula. I have received your letter, asking if I still care for you and if I will take you back as my wife. What am I to say? Half of me rejoices to hear from you, and wants to call you my beloved Ursula and summon you to me. The other half, to say the least of it, feels otherwise. That half wants to fling your letter in the fire and forget you. How could you abandon me like that? You write saying that you had honourable reasons to do what you did. You say you had a duty to the Queen. What of your duty to your husband who had promised to love and protect you always? What of the love you said you felt for me? Do you remember how we lay in each other's arms? Do you remember how I said I loved your salty tongue, and how I nicknamed you my Saltspoon? You wish to come to me if I will have you, and if I will give a home also to your daughter Meg. Meg I would receive gladly, for she is a child who has done me no harm. But you? No, I do not know what I should say.

Yes, I do, for there is only one thing I can say. I still love you, although, God knows, there was a time when I could have killed you. If you mean what you say, then come to me and bring Meg. I live in a house called Château Blanchepierre, a few miles west of Saumur, beside the River Loire. I am sometimes away in Paris but my household would make you welcome while they sent word to me. You need not be afraid of them, although they know what you have done. Madame Montaigle was very shocked, but if I command it, she will put the past behind, as will I. Send me an answer, if you can find a messenger. Or simply come. Yes—after all, I send my love to you, my Saltspoon.

Matthew.

Tears burned my eyes. Dale was urging me to stand, so that she could brush down my clothes—a bodice of cream satin criss-crossed with tawny embroidery, a small farthingale and a tawny damask overdress open in front to reveal a kirtle which matched the bodice. I rose to my feet, blinking the tears away. As Dale began to brush, I folded the letter and pushed it into a pocket just inside the open skirt.

"Hurry, Dale. I must go. Oh, Dale!"

"Ma'am?" said Dale.

"Dale, if I go to France, will you and Brockley come with me?"

"You'll have to ask Brockley yourself, ma'am, but . . . well, I wouldn't say no." In the mirror I met Dale's eyes again and saw that hers, a lighter blue than Kat's, were bright with pleasure for me. She finished brushing and stepped back.

"Oh, *Dale!*" I said again. I wanted to run, then and there, to the Queen to tell her that I wished to leave her service and go to join my husband, but of course I could not. Such an interview would have to be formal, set up through Mistress Ashley. For the moment, I must wait, clasping my precious secret to me.

"Matthew had a nickname for me," I said huskily to Dale. "Because of my sharp tongue. He called me Saltspoon. He reminds me of it in the letter. It brings him back so. I can hear him saying it!"

My ten minutes were up. I must put on a calm face and make haste to attend upon the Queen. I would not wish to irritate her by any lack of promptness. Without her consent, I could not leave the country or take my daughter out of it. I needed her goodwill.

Elizabeth had been to a council meeting and had as usual retired to her private rooms afterwards, to deal with any matters of business arising from the council. As a Lady of the Presence Chamber, I held a privileged position, but I was still not one of the high-ranking Ladies of the Privy Chamber and the Bedchamber, who attended on her in private. I could only pass through the private door by special invitation. Now, I merely joined the throng who were waiting for her to emerge into the public anteroom.

I was just in time. Barely had I taken up my position, when the Queen's door opened, the trumpeters blew their fanfare, and out swept Elizabeth, amid a cloud of ladies, including Kat Ashley, and a bevy of favoured gallants. Sir Robin Dudley, the Master of Horse, splendid in a red doublet slashed with gold-embroidered azure, his gipsy good looks polished by expert barbering, was at her side and she was saying something to him with laughter in her voice.

In that year of 1561, I was still young and so was Elizabeth, for we were near in age. I have seen her change greatly over the years but one thing has never changed in the least, and that is the impact she makes whenever she comes into view. It is colossal, even on people who are used to her.

But it isn't always the same impact. Her mood goes ahead of her like the bow wave of a ship, and her moods change. You never know beforehand which version of Elizabeth is about to burst upon you. She may be majesty personified, or wrath incarnate; she may be all merriment, or all pensive sadness, or all mischief.

This time, it was mischief. I saw instantly that my queen and liege lady was as dangerously playful as a cat when its fur is full of sparks and it is ready to pounce on anything that moves, from a mouse to a piece of trailed cord to an incautious human hand, and stick all its claws in. Her eyes sparkled in her pale, shield-shaped face; even the pearls in her hair and the silver embroidery on her white satin dress seemed to have an extra glitter. I curtsied, along with the other ladies, and stood up again, with a sense of misgiving. I must arrange my interview soon, and the royal mind was not in its most favourable condition.

Elizabeth's bright gaze collected us all up. "We are bound for the River Chamber to give a private audience," she informed us. "An English craftsman wishes to make us a gift of a clever device, his own creation, or so my good Cecil tells me. We understand the man is already here and waiting, so it behoves us not to be late ourselves. Come!"

Away we went, crowding in the royal wake, heralded at every turn by the trumpeters, surging through a series of galleries, collecting more people on the way, among them the Spanish ambassador, Bishop de Quadra. Elizabeth set the pace, walking as fast as anyone well could without breaking into a run. The Queen had moments of exhaustion, but the rest of the time did not scruple to wear us all out with dancing and walking and riding (frequently at a headlong gallop, in all weathers. Several of her ladies pretended that they couldn't ride except on a pillion, simply to avoid what they considered a suicidal form of exercise). Her notions of dancing and walking were no less energetic. We reached the River Chamber in a remarkably short space of time.

The River Chamber was long and light, with tall windows overlooking the Thames, and a polished oak floor. On a dais at one end was a high-backed chair with a soft fur rug thrown over it, and a little table alongside. In the hearth halfway along the room, a wood fire burned, giving off a sweet smell.

Elizabeth settled herself in the chair, and Lady Katherine Knollys, who was related to the Queen and was one of her favourite attendants, arranged her wide skirts for her. Kat Ashley placed the rug over her knees. The crowd of courtiers clustered on either side of the dais and straggled down the sides of the room. Dudley and de Quadra, and some of the ladies including myself, had places on the dais, near the queen. Pages hovered, ready to undertake errands. Elizabeth pointed a jewelled forefinger at one of them and despatched him to tell Sir William Cecil that she was ready.

While we waited, I saw de Quadra edging towards me. He paused a moment to ask politely after the health of one of the other ladies, Jane Seymour, who had recently been ill and still looked wan, but then stepped quietly to my side. He was not very tall, and our eyes were almost on a level. We were not friends (one does not search the document cases of one's friends), but we did enjoy a kind of mutual respect. I murmured a greeting.

"Your daughter is well, Mistress Blanchard?" he enquired in French, which we used as a common language. "I heard that you had placed her with friends of Lady Cecil."

"Yes, the Hendersons. They live at Thamesbank, by the river near Hampton. How kind of you to ask. She seems happy there. Her old nurse, Bridget Lemmon, is with her. I'm glad to see her settled in a house where she can be brought up as a young lady, but where people are good natured."

De Quadra nodded. "I know you found it hard to support your daughter on your stipend, but the Cecils have come generously to your rescue. In gratitude for your services to the Queen last year, I imagine?"

"Quite so," I said, stifling a laugh. De Quadra was obviously fishing. The stipend had most certainly been inadequate, since it was never meant for ladies who had no other means of subsistence, and the death of my first husband Gerald had left me with no other means whatsoever. De Quadra had undoubtedly guessed that my services to the Queen were ongoing, and were the solution to my financial problems (not much happened at court without the Spanish ambassador having some inkling of it); this was no time to confirm his suspicions, however. Not just after my discovery in that document case.

"I am not sure if Bridget is quite as happy as Meg," I said lightly. "Mistress Henderson is the soul of gentleness, but all her servants must wash themselves all over once each week, except in the severest winter weather, and Bridget thinks it unhealthy."

"Poor Bridget," said de Quadra, amused, and Robin Dudley glanced round at us and grinned.

"You are much blessed, having a child to remember your husband by," de Quadra said to me. Elizabeth half-turned her head in order to look at him, and a grave smile lit his olive-skinned face. "Is it not so, madam?" he asked.

"I've never seen Ursula's daughter," said Elizabeth, also using French. "Cecil tells me she is a charming child.

She shall come to court when she is older, Ursula. But for now, quiet. Here comes Cecil with my craftsman."

Sir William Cecil entered the room in his usual businesslike fashion, the folds of his formal mulberry velvet gown swinging to his stride. His companion was a short man, whose amber velvet doublet and breeches spoke of prosperity, but whose air was timid. He had an insignificant face, with small features and a blob of a nose and he seemed overwhelmed by his surroundings. He walked two paces in the rear, glancing about him and up at the high, painted ceiling, as though impressed by the size of the room and the costly clothes of the people in it. Another two paces behind him was an oxlike young man, presumably a servant or assistant of some kind, although with those massive shoulders, which were putting his plain dark doublet under strain, he would have made an excellent bodyguard. He was in charge of a cloth-wrapped bundle, which he carried in ceremonious fashion.

Cecil was brisk, as usual. He was a busy man and his days were always overcrowded. The line between his light eyes was clearly marked, probably with impatience, and within his fair beard, his mouth was set in a straight line.

"Your Majesty," he said, as all three of them bowed, "I wish to present to you Barnabas Mew, Master Clockmaker of Windsor, and his assistant Joseph Wylie. Mr. Mew has brought the gift of which I spoke to you some days ago."

The two men straightened up while Cecil moved aside. Wylie came up beside his master, and handed him the bundle. Mr. Mew then stood looking from the sparkling young queen on the dais to the bundle in his hands, apparently wondering what to do next.

Cecil clicked his tongue irritably and took the bundle from him. "This device needs to be demonstrated. May we step on to the dais?"

"By all means," said Elizabeth, and Cecil, pushing Master Mew ahead of him, stepped up beside her.

Cecil unwrapped the cloth and revealed a gilded box, which he placed on the table. The box measured perhaps a foot each way, and was about six inches deep. A delicate pattern was engraved all over it, and the letters E and R were set into the lid in what I thought were moonstones. It was evidently lockable, for it had a little key. After my instruction sessions with Master Bone, I had become observant about such things and noticed that the lock was unusual in that it was placed not at the front of the box, but in the side.

"A pretty toy," said Elizabeth. "A device, you call it? Is it a clock? But how does it tell the time? There is some mystery here. Come, don't be so afraid of us, Master Mew. It requires to be demonstrated, according to Sir William. Well then, demonstrate it."

"May it please Your Majesty . . ." said Mew, his voice was thin and nervous. "It is most gracious of you to allow me to . . . I am only a plain man, although I hope I have some skill in these poor fingers . . ."

"No need for so many words, Master Mew! Show us how the thing works."

Master Mew, accordingly, gave up trying to explain, took hold of the casket and began to turn the key. I realised that he was not operating a lock but winding up a mechanism of some kind. Then, as he finished winding, the box began, in little tinkling notes, to play a tune that we all recognised.

"Why, that is a song my father wrote," Elizabeth exclaimed. "It's 'Greensleeves'!"

"May it please Your Majesty," said Master Mew, in agreement.

"It pleases us well," Elizabeth said.

Oddly enough, this was probably true. I say "oddly" because, as all the court was well aware, the song had been written by King Henry when he was courting Elizabeth's mother, Anne Boleyn. "Alas, my love, you do me wrong to cast me off discourteously," were the first words of the lyric. In the end, however, it was Henry, not Anne, who had done the casting off, and by the most discourteous method imaginable, for he had had her executed, and although Elizabeth scarcely ever mentioned her mother, she was known to grieve for her.

Paradoxically, Elizabeth had admired her father, too. She might justly have loathed the melody of "Greensleeves" because of its bitter associations, but she did not. She had never explained why, but perhaps the song spoke to her of King Henry's cultured, gifted, romantic side. At any rate, "Greensleeves" was played and sung quite freely about the court and even used sometimes in masques.

Now, the Queen said, "We are always interested in fine craftsmanship and new mechanisms. Our master craftsmen are among the glories of our realm. Is it possible to see how this mechanism works, Master Mew?"

"Indeed, Your Majesty." Gaining a little confidence, he lifted the lid, and all who were near enough craned to see. The music was still playing, and we could see that inside the box was a gilded cylinder set with an irregular pattern of tiny pins, which looked like steel. The cylinder was turning slowly, and as it did so, the pins struck the teeth of a steel comb and gave off musical notes. The teeth were hinged in some way, for each, as it made its tinkling sound, lifted against the pressure of the pin and so let the cylinder continue to revolve.

"The teeth are tuned to give the different notes," explained Master Mew, sounding quite self-assured now, as though having his hands on his invention had comforted him. "Each turn of the cylinder goes once through the tune. It goes round three times before it stops. The mechanism which turns it is here, in this compartment." He lifted an inner lid to show the springs and cogwheels within. "But there is more, Your Majesty. You see, the cylinder can be taken out." He lifted another inner lid, this one extending along the back of the casket. "And here within are two more cylinders which will play other melodies. Will Your Majesty hear them?"

Her Majesty would. She beckoned us all to gather round more closely still and we listened with interest while it played "Summer is Icumen In" and then, by way of a change of mood, "Lully Lullay," the sad old Christmas carol about Herod's massacre of the innocents.

When it was over, Master Mew put all the cylinders back in their original places and closed the casket.

Elizabeth, smiling, observed that it was a most ingenious invention. "We applaud it, Master Mew. You must have spent many preoccupied hours in its planning and its making. Your wife is evidently a patient woman."

"Alas, Your Majesty, my wife passed away some years ago, during an outbreak of the sweat, and I have found none to replace her."

"Indeed? We are sorry to learn of it. Have you children, Master Mew?"

"No, Your Majesty. We had not been married long."

"That is sad. My good Cecil and indeed all my council often urge me towards matrimony," Elizabeth remarked, "but it seems as likely to lead to sorrow as to happiness."

"It's commonly thought to be a happy estate," said Dudley, boldly.

Dudley's own young wife had been neglected and unhappy before she finally and mysteriously died. Elizabeth knew, as I did, that whatever gossip might say, he had not actually murdered her, and the whole world could see that the Queen was shaken to the depths by Dudley's swarthy handsomeness and his hot dark eyes. Now, however, the sidelong glance she gave him glinted not only with amusement but with malice.

"Happy?" Her tone was lightly cynical. "Not always. As Master Mew can testify, wives can die. So can husbands. Or, a husband might stray and what can a poor woman do then? She is supposed to be his subject, after all. Perhaps I would be wiser to keep my maiden state and rule my subjects rather than become one."

There was a pause. Mew and Wylie both seemed bewildered, as though the Queen had started to talk in Greek or Turkish. Elizabeth gave a trill of laughter.

"I must wed someone, the council tell me," she

remarked sweetly, "but how shall I choose? I fear to take a foreign prince who may bring foreign swordsmen to English soil, but even if I marry an Englishman, who is to say that he won't do the same?"

The playful cat had put out its needle claws and scratched both Dudley and de Quadra. De Quadra's face remained impassive though his body stiffened, but Dudley's cheekbones visibly turned crimson. They must both be wondering how Elizabeth had learned that if she were to marry Dudley, and the country rebelled because of the gossip about his first wife's death, he was prepared to invite Philip of Spain to bring a Spanish army to support him, in exchange for a promise to restore the Catholic religion. They must also be wondering if she knew that Dudley had even gone to the lengths of asking de Quadra to put the notion to the Spanish king.

Well, if ever Elizabeth had been prepared to consider Dudley as a husband (though I had reason to believe that this was not so, despite appearances), this latest discovery must surely have destroyed his hopes for good. He might remain her favourite, like a household pet, but the title of King Consort could never now be his.

I did not pity him. To me, his offence was too great. My Uncle Herbert and Aunt Tabitha had always followed the old religion, and once, when I was a girl, they had attended one of the first burnings ordered by Queen Mary Tudor. I refused to go with them and they didn't force me (my aunt said afterwards that they feared I would embarrass them by showing sympathy to a miscreant), but on their return, they forced me to listen to a description. When I tried to block my ears,

Aunt Tabitha tore my hands away. I had never forgotten that, and I would never forgive it.

If, to further his ambitions, Robin Dudley was prepared to bring those terrible days back, I would never forgive him, either.

Many of the Queen's ladies sighed over Dudley, but not I, which was not very reasonable of me, for Matthew too had plotted to bring Mary Stuart and the old religion back to England. In what way, I asked myself as I stood there on the dais, was he different from Robin Dudley?

For a moment, I wavered, wondering if I should have written to Matthew, asking myself if it would be wrong to leave Elizabeth's court and travel to France to ally my fortunes to one of Mary Stuart's adherents. In that moment, I wished with all my heart that my first husband, Gerald Blanchard, Meg's father, still lived, but he was gone, and my husband now was Matthew.

To think of Matthew was to conjure him inside my head: tall, bony, wide of shoulder, long of chin, with diamond-shaped dark eyes under dramatic black eyebrows. To think of him was to lean towards him, as though my spirit were trying to leap from my body and vault over land and sea to join him in the Château Blanchepierre in the valley of the Loire.

No. My choice was made. I would give up the court, cease from spying into other people's secrets. I would not be betraying England, or the Queen, as Dudley had been prepared to do; only retiring into private life with my husband and my daughter. That, surely, was not wrong.

The Queen had ceased to speak and seemed to be

waiting for something. Cecil made an impatient movement, then Mew, as if remembering a lesson, went
down on one knee and offered the shining thing to the
Queen. "If Your Majesty would be p-pleased to accept
this, I would be honoured."

Over Mew's bent head, Elizabeth caught Cecil's eye
and he nodded. "With pleasure, Master Mew,"
Elizabeth said, and taking the casket with one hand,
she gave Mew the other to kiss.

The page, who had been hovering in the background, came to escort Mew out of the room. Cecil
also prepared to take his leave. Before doing so, however, he caught my eye, and while Elizabeth, at the
behest of Katherine Knollys and Jane Seymour, played
the musical device again, he came to speak to me.

"My wife sends her good wishes and looks forward
to seeing you at dinner tomorrow, Ursula."

I thanked him. Some of my fellow ladies smiled,
because they knew that the Cecils had found my
daughter her foster home and supposed that there was
some long-established friendship between my family
and the Cecils. There were also a few sour looks,
because some of the Ladies of the Privy and
Bedchambers thought it in poor taste for a mere Lady
of the Presence Chamber to be on dining terms with
the Secretary of State.

Elizabeth, who knew the purpose which lay behind
the invitation, glanced at me and wished me a pleasant
time. I looked from her to Kat Ashley.

"Ma'am—Mistress Ashley—there is a matter,
a . . . a very private matter . . . of some urgency . . . on
which I need to consult Her Majesty. May I have a pri-

vate interview?" I met Elizabeth's eyes and tried to signal the degree of urgency with my own. I wanted that interview before I went to dine with the Cecils. If all went well, I would not dine there at all.

"We will have to see," said Kat Ashley repressively, but Elizabeth recognised my silent signal and gave me a small nod in reply.

"We will send for you," she said.

CHAPTER 3

Jackdaw

Kat Ashley fetched me to the Queen's private rooms later on that day. Elizabeth was in her study, where she often sat to examine correspondence or reports, or read the books on history and philosophy and political theory which interested her so deeply. At the Queen's bidding, Kat left us. I executed my deepest curtsy and made my request. While I stood waiting, there was a long, long silence, and my heart grew heavy.

The weather had turned wet. Rain blew against the tall, diamond-leaded windows behind Elizabeth's carefully coiffured red head, and the afternoon was so overcast that she needed a cluster of candles on her desk in order to read. A fire blazed in the hearth, but even so, the Queen wore a shawl.

"And so," she said at last, "you want to desert us, Mistress Blanchard."

"Not exactly, Your Majesty. I am sorry to leave you, but . . . I want to be with my husband."

Elizabeth said bluntly, "Although he is an enemy of our person, and this realm?"

Matthew didn't think of himself that way, since to

him, bringing Mary Stuart and the old religion to England was the friendliest thing he could possibly do for the land where his mother was born. I did not of course agree with him, nor did I attempt to explain him to Elizabeth. To Elizabeth, I discovered, I could not even speak of love. In her presence it felt for some reason like a confession of weakness. It was hard to know what to say, so in the end I fell back on a simple declaration.

"Ma'am, he is my husband. I took vows."

Elizabeth seemed tired. She had changed out of her formal white and silver; the shawl was draped over a loose gown of ash-grey silk. She had taken off her jewellery, too. The mischief was all gone. Her pointed white face was older than its years, grave and withdrawn.

"And what," she asked me, "if I say no?"

I didn't answer at once, and the Queen's eyes, golden brown under faint, arched brows, grew sharp. Elizabeth could be formidable. One remembered then whose daughter she was. This morning I had thought of her as a playful cat, but that was to underestimate her. She was no house-cat, but a lioness, cub of that Tudor lion King Henry.

"I asked you a question, Ursula," she said presently. "What is your answer?"

"Your Majesty, I have no wish to displease you in any way, but . . . I beg you to release me from your employment and allow me to take my daughter to the Loire valley to join my husband there."

Rain blew against the windows again, harder. The wind was getting up. I had looked at maps of France and knew that the valley of the Loire lay much further south than anywhere in England. The weather might be warmer there, the winters less harsh.

"Your first husband, Gerald Blanchard," said the Queen thoughtfully, "was engaged in—shall we say, secret work?—in the Netherlands, assisting my financier Sir Thomas Gresham. You were there with him and I fancy it was from Gerald that you learned the skills which have proved so valuable to us. Am I right?"

"Yes, ma'am."

"I said valuable and I meant it. Your services have been very useful indeed, Ursula, and I am loth to dispense with them."

"Ma'am . . . I plead with you."

Elizabeth turned away from me, lost in thought. The silence deepened. I waited, hoping desperately, until she sat back in her ornate chair, and gave me her judgement.

"The time of year is bad for sea travel. I would not have you risk yourself on board ship just now. Tomorrow, you are to see Sir William Cecil and receive from him instructions in a task which he and I wish you to perform. You have been having lessons from Master Bone, I believe, to prepare you for this duty."

"Yes, ma'am, but surely I am not the only person . . . ?"

"We need a woman," Elizabeth said, "and you are the only one on Cecil's payroll, as far as this type of work is concerned. Spying isn't popular as a livelihood for young ladies. It doesn't appeal to them and still less does it appeal to their parents."

The golden-brown eyes lit briefly with laughter, but she was sober again almost at once. "I said just now that I would not have you risk yourself on board ship but . . . well, Ursula, Cecil and I do not wish you to take risks, of any kind, but there may be unavoidable danger in what you will, tomorrow, be asked to do. We—Cecil and I, that is—hope that you will still undertake it. Much may depend on it and you will be well paid if you consent. If not . . ."

"Ma'am?" My hands were clasped in front of me, my fingers hidden in the folds of my cream and tawny gown, gripping each other fiercely.

"You may as well undertake it," said Elizabeth. "We give you permission to join your husband and take your daughter, but not until May, when the spring gales have subsided. Until May, you must remain here. And you will of course keep your appointment with the Cecils tomorrow. Hear what Sir William has to say to you. I ask you, Ursula—most earnestly—to consider passing the time between now and May by doing the work he asks of you."

But I've finished with all that! I wanted to cry it aloud. I want to go to Matthew. *Now!*

Elizabeth studied me searchingly, as though she were reading my mind. "Ursula, listen. I can't tell you much about the task that Cecil and I have for you. He has the details. I know only that there is a hint abroad, a rumour—but it could mean that something serious is afoot, something that could endanger me and therefore England. Do you understand? I am just one person," Elizabeth said. "Just one life. I have my councillors, like Cecil, and they are a bulwark to me, but in turn, I am a bulwark to England. Most of the time, I am happy to have it so. I was born for this. Sometimes, however, just now and then, I see myself in the mirror and what do I see? Just a slender, brittle young girl. Not much of a bulwark, when all is said and done. Then I feel afraid. I feel afraid, too, when it is brought home to me that there are those who not only wish me replaced, but are willing to plot to bring it about. Last year, and again in the last few weeks, you have uncovered schemes which could have endangered me greatly. The second one was a greater shock than the first. You know well enough why. I am asking for your help just once more. Go now, and talk with Cecil." She turned away, picking up her pen. I was dismissed.

I wanted to cry out in protest, but for complicated and contradictory reasons, I could do nothing of the kind. I couldn't do it because it meant abandoning this slender, brittle girl who was afraid and needed my help; and I couldn't do it because the same girl was also Her Majesty Queen Elizabeth, and I could not shout, "No, no, I can't. May is a lifetime away—I want to be with Matthew now!" at the Queen of England.

I did pause for a moment, but she did not look at me again. I had to go. I left the chamber, heartsick, silently pitying her, and raging at her, and wondering by what means I could manage to collect my child and get out of England without Her Majesty's consent.

When Sir William Cecil wished to speak to me privately, he sometimes summoned me discreetly to his study at whichever residence the court happened to be using. The Queen continually shifted from one palace to another, back and forth along the river between Greenwich, Whitehall, Richmond, Nonsuch, Hampton Court and Windsor, and to save constant travel up and down the river by barge, often in the rain, Cecil had rooms set aside for his use in each. He found this convenient even at Whitehall, which was so near to his house in Canon Row that when the Queen was at Whitehall, Cecil went home each evening to Lady Mildred.

It was in those Whitehall rooms that I had met Alexander Bone, but Cecil had not then been free to talk to me and I must not make such visits too often. Hence the invitation, issued quite openly, to dine in Canon Row.

Cecil must have had a message from Elizabeth regarding my unwillingness, as he sent an escort to make sure I came.

"Paul Fenn, at your service, Mistress Blanchard," said the young man who had presented himself at the nearest street entrance and enquired for me. He was about eighteen, handsome, with splendid teeth, except that two at the front were slightly crossed, and the beginnings of a moustache. He was smartly dressed, with a dashing blue velvet cap on his thick fair hair, and a matching cloak. I vaguely recognised him as a recent addition to the Cecil household. He was attentive and courteous, with the self-confident deference which you so often find in young men from families of standing. I may be only a boy as yet, his manner seemed to say, but one day I shall be Secretary of State myself.

I therefore set off for Canon Row with Fenn as well as Dale and Brockley. I was mildly amused, for of course I had had no thought of failing to keep my appointment. I was doing so under false pretences, but fifty Paul Fenns could make no difference to that.

After leaving the Queen's presence, I had seethed for an hour and then realised that my decision had taken itself. Somehow or other, I would take Meg and go, without permission or passport, to France. It could be done: the highway of the Thames carried plenty of vessels whose skippers would take anyone anywhere for a suitable consideration. Brockley would find one for me.

Meanwhile, I must appear to accept the Queen's commands, so I took the arm of my unnecessary young escort, and with Dale and Brockley following, we all set off on foot for nearby Canon Row. We were well wrapped against the cold and the continuing rain, the men wearing boots while Dale and I clumped along on pattens to keep our feet clear of the mud. Beneath my cloak, I had donned a fresh cream brocade underskirt, this time worn with a pale green damask, and put on a clean ruff. My heart might not be in this, but I wished to look as though it was.

The Cecils' house was blessedly warm. Fenn took my blanketlike mantle and my clumsy footwear, and waited politely while Dale gave me the fashionable shoes she had been carrying for me. He directed Brockley and Dale to the servants' quarters, then, with a courteous smile which gave me another view of his superb teeth—the slight flaw in the front ones hardly mattered—he observed that Sir William and Lady Mildred were awaiting me, and showed me into the small dining parlour where the Cecils ate when they were alone together or had only one or two guests.

The room was welcoming, with many candles and a bright fire in the hearth, dispelling the January cold. The table was laid, draped in fine white damask. I hadn't been in that room for some time and I noticed that since my last visit, it had acquired new wallhangings: a set of exquisite tapestries and an eastern carpet, in shades of azure and rose. Cecil, coming forward with his wife to greet me, saw me looking at them.

"We have been enjoying a little extravagance lately, in a merchant's warehouse," he said. "I hope you like the result. Welcome, Ursula. Come and sit down."

Cecil in private was easy to talk to, and although Lady Mildred's formidable intellect and preference for austere dark gowns intimidated some people, she had a good heart. They had both been kind to me when first I came to court, and since then, they had been kind to Meg. I liked the Cecils, and it came home to me that the deception I was planning would seem to them like a betrayal. A bleak misery descended on me, so intense that Lady Mildred saw it. In her blunt fashion, she at once spoke of it.

"Ursula, my dear, we know that you are preparing to join your husband and are chafing at the delay, but the Queen is right: it is a bad time of year for travelling, and you are needed here just now. It is only for a while. Spring will be here before you know it. Come by the fire. We're happy to have you, even if this isn't quite a social occasion. We will begin in sociable fashion, at least. No business will be discussed until we've eaten our first course."

I tried to think of a suitable reply and couldn't. Smoothly, Cecil bridged the gap. "My wife is resolved on putting off business until we have eaten our meat. She says it would spoil our appetites, and in this cold weather, that would never do. One must eat well in winter."

"Now, do come over to the warmth," said Lady Mildred, drawing me towards the hearth.

With great skill they then embarked on light conversation about the weather. To this, at least, I could respond. When the meal was served, the small talk continued, drifting from the weather and food to minor court gossip and then to the remarkable musical box which Master Mew had given the Queen. Pulling myself together and attempting to contribute to the conversation, I made some remark about Paul Fenn and what a smart young lad he was, and Lady Mildred said he was a treasure.

"He's from a good family, of course. The Fenns are Sussex people. They're an old family though not especially wealthy. I believe Paul's home isn't far from Faldene, where you were brought up. In fact, I think they know your Uncle Herbert and your Aunt Tabitha slightly—not that that is a recommendation! But young Paul seems none the worse for it."

I agreed that Paul Fenn did not seem to have been contaminated by my uncle and aunt, and then, by way of a further contribution, I made a comment about the new wallhangings. One particular panel had caught my eye. It showed a unicorn trapped in a circle of people with hounds and spears. The spears pointed down at the doomed creature, which occupied the centre of the picture and the heart of a deadly vortex. But its head was high and its single horn proudly defied the spears.

Glistening highlights, made of paler threads, lay along the spearshafts and on the folds of a huntsman's pushed-back sleeve.

"Surely, that's a copy of a Brussels design," I said. "When I lived in Antwerp with Gerald and he worked for Sir Thomas Gresham, we often went to Gresham's house. He had a copy of that. It's called *The Hunt of the Unicorn*. But this is finer. There's silk in those highlights."

"Quite right," Cecil said. "This was made in the Giorgio Vasari workshop in Florence. You can see the workshop's monogram—the G and V intertwined, down in the righthand corner of each panel, with the initials of the weaver as well—HH for Hans van Hoorn—alongside it."

"A Flemish weaver?" I asked.

"Yes. Bernard Paige, the merchant who sold those tapestries to me, knows the background of all his wares and will lecture you on them for hours if you give him the opportunity! According to Paige, this man, van Hoorn, is one of several Flemish craftsmen brought into the Vasari weaving shop a year ago to copy famous designs. Paige is importing the copies and they're selling well. The Queen has commended his enterprise. She wants England to attract wealthy merchants and fine merchandise. Prosperity means solvency and that's one way," Cecil said, "of keeping enemies at bay."

"Such as Mary Stuart," remarked Lady Mildred.

With that, the talk veered for the first time towards matters political, and from that moment, I sensed that it was no longer desultory, and that Cecil had begun to guide it. He spoke, with seeming casualness, of the possible future of young Mary Stuart of Scotland, now that she was no longer Queen Consort of France.

"She may marry again soon. There's been talk of Philip of Spain's son."

"I hardly think so," said Lady Mildred with a sniff. "Don Carlos is said to be deformed and intermittently mad. It's more likely that the wretched girl will come to Scotland and plant herself as a permanent nuisance on our doorstep."

By the time the sweet dishes were brought in and we were choosing between honey and saffron quiche or cheesecakes flavoured with rosewater, the change in the atmosphere was unmistakable.

Cecil, putting a half-eaten cheesecake back on his dish, met my eyes and said, "The servants will not come back into the room unless I call them. It is time we came to the point." The line between his eyes was very noticeable. This time, I guessed the cause was worry. "I wish we need not ask you," he said abruptly. "Tell me, how went your last session with Master Bone?"

"Quite well, I think. I need practice but I hope to become proficient quite soon."

"I don't doubt it," Cecil said. "You have an unusual gift for this type of work, Ursula, although I shall never feel it is suitable for a young woman, least of all a young married woman. Frankly, I'm glad to think that after this you will be on your way to join Matthew de la Roche. Whatever my personal opinion of *his* opinions, you are his wife. You also have a child to rear. However, you have done admirable work for us in the past year. We have disposed of Dudley, I think, at least as a conspirator and probably as a suitor for the Queen . . . well, let us hope so! Though I must say I wish she'd marry somebody, and so do the rest of the council."

The table was still covered in white damask and strewn with dishes, but somehow, in that moment, it became a conference table. I cleared my throat. I knew I must give the impression that I was seriously attending the conference. "What is it that you want me to do?" I asked.

"It's a long story," said Lady Mildred. "Let my husband approach it in his own way."

"The fact is," Cecil said, "that unless and until Her Majesty takes a husband—preferably *not* Dudley—and a lawful prince is born, the Queen is vulnerable: to illness, accident, assassination or scandal. Scandal can be as damaging as death. If anything happens to her, then I don't need to tell you where we shall all be. We shall have a choice between two of her cousins: Lady Catherine Grey, who would support the Protestant faith but is not in anyone's opinion capable of taking the throne and holding it, and Mary Stuart of Scotland, who would bring back the heretic-hunt and the stake. Three hundred died that way in Mary Tudor's reign. If the old religion were restored, there would be more deaths. Probably including my own. Tell me, do you know Señor Borghese, Bishop de Quadra's private secretary?"

"By sight, that's all. Thickset, quiet, well dressed in an unobtrusive way." I was taking pains to sound interested, but despite myself, the interest now began to be genuine.

"That's the fellow. He may well be wise to keep his excellent tailoring unobtrusive, or de Quadra might think he's overpaying him! They are a fine pair," said Cecil. "De Quadra takes backhanders from the French for keeping them informed of events here, and Señor Borghese takes backhanders from me, to keep me informed of his master's doings! Though he doesn't pass on everything. He didn't tell me of Dudley's plans—I owe that to you. By the way, you were watching *Dudley*. What made you think that de Quadra's document case might yield something?"

"I'd noticed that Dudley kept sidling up to de Quadra in anterooms," I explained. "People do that when they want to remind someone of something without an official interview."

"Sharp of you! I said you had a gift. Well, one of the things that Borghese *did* pass on to me was the fact that some prominent former Councillors—men from Queen Mary's administration—have been writing to de Quadra enquiring if he has any ideas about ways and means of restoring the country to Catholicism. I've got them all in the Tower now, as a warning to others."

"I heard about that." Recently, it had been a talking point for the whole court. "But in that case . . ."

"You are thinking that now Dudley and the ex-councillors have been put in check, the danger is over? I wish it were so, but Señor Borghese also handed this to me." Turning, he reached over to a sideboard behind him and picked up a document which lay there in readiness. "This is a copy of the original, but a faithful copy, so Señor Borghese assures me." He handed it to me. "It may not please you to read this," he added, "but I think it spells danger. I am sorry."

It was another dark afternoon. Cecil pushed a candle nearer to me to make reading easier. I took the sheet of paper up and studied it.

"Oh, *no!*" I said, with passion, when I had done.

I felt so strongly, that for several moments I actually forgot about Matthew and my half-formed scheme to travel to France. I had been swept back, beyond my marriage to Matthew, to the previous autumn, when I was travelling in Berkshire and stayed, briefly but memorably, in the household of Leonard and Ann Mason, of Lockhill.

What a bitter misfortune, I thought, that in this unpleasant context, I should come upon the names of people I knew and liked, under whose roof I had slept. I could see them before my mind's eye.

Scholarly, intellectual Leonard had in some ways reminded me of Cecil. They were the same general type, although Cecil had a wife who could match his intellect, and his happy marriage had kept him human. Ann Mason, with not enough servants and too many children; housewifely Ann, who was in awe of her husband without in the least understanding him; poor Ann had a harassing time of it with Leonard, and he in turn had fled to his translations and his books on science as a way of escaping the noise and confusion.

It was a chaotic household, but it was united in its fashion. If Leonard Mason were caught dabbling in treason, Ann and the children would suffer wretchedly, from grief as well as disgrace, and short though my acquaintance with them had been, I now discovered that I minded.

I stared at the letter again. De Quadra hadn't been the tempter, it seemed. De Quadra's correspondent was merely informing the bishop of something that would interest him. This plot, if there was one, did not have its roots in Spain, but in France. Just now, the name of Mary Stuart had undoubtedly been brought into the conversation with intent. Pretty, charming, greedy Mary Stuart believed that she ought to be Queen of England as well as Scotland, and had had herself declared so by the heralds who cleared the way for her when she went to chapel. Cecil was right. This could be dangerous. I could only pray that the writer of this letter, whoever he was, was completely mistaken.

Whoever he was. The name at the foot, which had been copied in a neat and characterless hand, was Jackdaw. It meant nothing to me whatsoever.

"Is Jackdaw a spy's professional name?" I asked Cecil. "Who is he? Do you know?"

CHAPTER 4

King Henry's Groat

Cecil was a spare, well-made man who usually looked younger than his forty or so years, but his light blue eyes were not young. They were tired and experienced. "Oh yes, I know his identity," he said. "His real name is Jack Dawson. Or perhaps I should say it *was* Jack Dawson. He's dead."

"Dead?" I queried.

The knowledgeable eyes became bleak. "He was an agent working for de Quadra. Jackdaw was a codename, yes. We knew all about him, courtesy of Señor Borghese again! His base was in Windsor, and he worked, ostensibly, as a pedlar with a regular round, but he was always willing to go out of his way to carry letters—he provided a messenger service, as it were. Heaven knows how many people have had their confidential letters quietly inspected by Jackdaw!"

"What . . . happened to him?" I asked.

"He lodged with an elderly widow on the outskirts of Windsor, and kept a rowing boat for use on the river. Early in January, he set out one evening, after dark, to visit a young woman on the other side of the river. There was an accident. Next day, the boat was found overturned, floating, and Jackdaw's body was discovered up against a landing stage downstream, near Kingston." He stopped, and there was a silence.

"Drowned?" I ventured.

"It's hard to say. The body had been much bumped about. One side of the skull was dented in." Cecil showed signs of discomfort. I guessed that he did not much like discussing such matters with women. "The landing stage could have done it," he said. "Or perhaps not."

I studied the letter once more. "He says he believes that he has found traces of a scheme to assist the cause and ambitions of Mary Stuart. He then goes on to say, 'I cannot yet be sure whose brain has hatched the scheme or in what it consists, but I shall soon go again to the Masons at Lockhill and will attempt to discover more.' Sir William, I can hardly credit—"

"That this could concern the Masons whom you know?" said Lady Mildred. "But they are Catholic supporters."

"They contributed money," said Cecil levelly, "to train priests for the purpose of undermining our Anglican regime. That's almost treason in itself."

"They wouldn't have thought of it like that," I said. "I've worried about them ever since last year, and others like them. Some of the Catholic supporters I met were such good people, really, so likeable. I never enquired what happened to any of them, but I've thought about them often. I liked Ann Mason especially. She has a difficult life."

"I daresay. In fact, the authorities agreed with you

in the main. Most of the people you visited on your journey were left alone. We didn't even fine them. The only exception was your own uncle, who really had gone too far, and even he hasn't come to much harm. He'll be released from the Tower soon. His gout is causing anxiety and the council are willing to be merciful, now that he has had a good shock. I assure you, neither the Queen nor the council are anxious to interfere in the small activities of ordinary households, even when they're giving money for dubious purposes. However, this suggests something more than a charitable dropping of coins into a begging bowl."

"But . . . you must have made enquiries about the Masons . . . and others . . . ?" I said. "Surely, if anything were wrong . . ." My voice trailed away.

"Yes, we made enquiries," Cecil agreed. "We looked discreetly into the affairs of the Masons and the others who contributed to the cause of training priests. We were merciful, but not careless! The Masons were reported to be loyal and harmless, despite their preference for Catholic forms of worship. This information is a complete surprise. However, for some time, I have thought that *something* was going on somewhere—something quite different from Dudley or the ex-councillors. It's not unexpected. The fact that Mary Stuart is no longer queen of France, but believes herself to be queen of England strikes me as alarming. She's at large on the political landscape like a panther escaped from a menagerie . . ."

My mind was now disturbed for Ann Mason's sake as well as mine, but this made me laugh. Lady Mildred laughed, too. Cecil gave us both a pained look.

"Mary Stuart is a living invitation to intrigue. I was never quite sure how competent the man was whom I sent to investigate the Masons. He's been withdrawn now. My doubts were probably justified! Let us get back to the matter in hand. There have been indications. To begin with, there is a Dr. Ignatius Wilkins. You won't have heard of him, but he was a priest in Queen Mary's day and incidentally denounced two of his parishioners as heretics and got them burned."

"His own parishioners?" I said.

"Yes. Ordinary people, a weaver and his daughter—the daughter was only nineteen." Cecil's eyes were angry. "They couldn't believe that bread and wine could mysteriously turn into flesh and blood, and said so, and they couldn't believe either that anyone would want to hurt them for being, as they saw it, honest. They said it wouldn't be honest to pretend they believed something when they didn't. Rob Henderson, your Meg's guardian, was in their town by chance and he saw them die. Not of his own choice; he was caught up in a crowd. He told me afterwards how he saw their faces through the smoke, full of terror and bewilderment that this could be happening to them . . . he didn't stay until the end.

"Enough of that. It's all over. They can't be brought back." Cecil pushed his emotions down. "Wilkins is no longer a parish priest. He gave up his parish two years ago, because he is Catholic and could not accept the Anglican form of worship. He has been watched, so we know a good deal about him. He now runs a school in High Wycombe. It isn't a very good school. Dr. Wilkins, in fact, is hard up."

I had been reminded of Aunt Tabitha and Uncle Herbert, and that ghastly, gloating description of a man dying in torment. It had left a mark on me. Before then, living as I did in the power of my uncle and aunt, I had feared them, but after that, I began to hate them, for they had filled my mind with images which polluted it and spoiled my joy in innocent things. Never, since then, had I been able to enjoy that characteristic scent of autumn, the woodsmoke of the November garden bonfire. I would breathe it in once—and then Uncle Herbert's face, full of hateful pleasure, and Uncle Herbert's loathsome voice, uttering loathsome words, would force their way into my mind. Even a warm and friendly hearth would disturb me if it smoked, and blew the smell out into the room. I thought of the weaver and his daughter and wished that Dr. Wilkins were not merely hard up, but starving in a ditch. I took a mouthful of quiche and had to struggle to swallow it.

Cecil was continuing. "For a man who is far from well off," he said, "Dr. Wilkins has been splashing money about in a most remarkable way. Ursula—this is not a change of subject—just look once more at our new wallhangings. Not at the tapestries this time, but at the carpet to your left."

I did so. "It's beautiful," I said. "Is it Persian?"

"It is indeed," said Lady Mildred. "We bought that from Bernard Paige, just as we bought the tapestries. It came by way of Turkey and Venice, as all goods from Persia do. It was somewhat expensive, just over . . ."

I was still trying to eat my quiche. The sum she named made me choke again.

"Oh yes," said Cecil. "It's silk, made from thousands on thousands of tiny knots. It would never come cheap, although if we could arrange some direct commerce with the source, which doesn't involve the Venetians *and* the Turks taking a cut, the prices of such goods might come down a little. The council is discussing the possibility, as a matter of fact. We fell in love with that carpet, I fear. We were in an extravagant mood. So, apparently, was Ignatius Wilkins, who was in the same warehouse at the same time. He, too, bought a Persian carpet, but believe me, Dr. Ignatius Wilkins just can't afford that sort of thing."

"Has he been asked where the money came from?" I enquired.

"Yes. I did that myself—a casual question there and then in the warehouse. You must be doing well, to afford a purchase like that, my friend. He said he'd been lucky at cards."

I recalled the cost of Cecil's own carpet and said, "If he was that lucky, he's been cheating."

"Or lying," said Cecil. "And being paid, extremely well, for services unknown. That's one example. There are others. A few words overheard at a dinner party for instance: a cryptic comment to the effect that Mary Stuart might be nearer to the English throne than most people realised."

Elizabeth had called herself slender and brittle. I thought of her, of her pale shield of a face, her glittering dress and slim, jewelled fingers, her intelligence. And her fears. She had said she was a bulwark to England, but she was just one person, she had told me, just one life. Her life, her good name, stood between the realm and . . .

The smell of smoke. I shuddered.

"You don't think Jackdaw died by accident, do you?" I said.

"No," said Cecil. "It was a wonder that he was found, you know. The current in the Thames runs at a deep level. When people fall into the river by accident, they are often swept downstream underwater and straight out to sea. However, found he was, and there was an inquest. The verdict was accidental death, but . . ."

"But?"

"He was an experienced boatman; the evening was calm; and he had claimed to be on the track of a plot against the Queen. How does it sound to you? Incidentally, at the inquest, Dawson's landlady—a very decent woman, sixty years of age—said that she had gone out that evening to call on a neighbour and that when she came back, she had a queer feeling that someone had been in the house—that objects had been moved. Dawson's pedlar's stock, which he kept in boxes in his room, looked stirred up, she said, though Dawson himself was a tidy man. But she also said that nothing had been stolen and the jury dismissed it as all her fancy."

"It would be rather a coincidence," I said, "if someone really had entered that house on the night that Dawson died, but had no connection with his death."

"Exactly," said Cecil, "and I distrust coincidences. The jury, of course, knew nothing of Dawson's secret activities. It seems to me that someone wanted to be rid of him, and that they searched his room for any record he had made—of discoveries at Lockhill, perhaps."

There was another pause, then, from the neck of his gown, Cecil pulled out what seemed to be a pendant of some kind, and lifted it over his head. He handed it across the table to me. "Look at this."

It was a silver chain, from which hung a silver coin, a groat, with a hole drilled through it to take the chain. The date on the coin was 1546, near the end of the reign of King Henry. I turned it over in my hand, puzzled.

"It was given to me in a handful of change years ago," Cecil said. "I kept it to remind me of what needs to be done to make England truly prosperous. You yourself, Ursula, know what it is to be hard up, but your money would have gone further if it had been good money. Look at that groat closely. Can you see that it's discoloured?"

I examined it. He was quite right. I had seen many such coins before though, and there was nothing very strange about this one. I looked at him questioningly.

"It's a genuine coin of the realm," Cecil said, "but it contains less than half the silver that it should. King Henry despoiled both gold and silver coins because he had spent too freely from his treasury. Since then, his son Edward and his daughter Mary have reigned in turn, but although they issued better coins than he did, they left much of the bad money in circulation. Elizabeth, advised by me, intends to have all the bad money removed before the end of this year. We need Elizabeth for more than just holding off a Catholic revival. We need her to make England solvent again. To protect her, Ursula, I am even willing to use you, a young woman who should not be engaged in this kind of work, to help me hunt down anyone who could be a menace to her.

"You know the Masons, and you and Ann Mason apparently liked each other. Like Dr. Ignatius Wilkins, Leonard Mason is hard up. He is not employing any new servants just now, at least, not manservants, but there is a chance of getting a woman in there. Ann is concerned about her daughters. She has a new baby and cannot give the girls the attention they need. Their tutor, Dr. Crichton, is quite unable to instruct them in embroidery or dancing . . ."

"I've seen Dr. Crichton," I said. "I got the impression he was quite unable to instruct anyone in anything!"

"Really?" said Cecil. "No wonder you seem sorry for Ann Mason. Well, my wife will tell you the rest."

"We didn't wish to brief you until we had prepared the ground," Lady Mildred said, "but this has now been done. As it happens, one of the Queen's Maids of Honour is a cousin of Ann Mason's, and they correspond occasionally. As part of William's enquiry into the Masons' affairs, many of those letters have been read. We have learned much about the household. I had a casual talk with Bess, and then wrote to Mistress Mason, saying that I had heard from Bess that she was concerned about her daughters' education, and reminding her of your existence. I didn't claim close acquaintance with you. If something is going on at Lockhill that ought not to be, they will not want close friends of the Cecils on the premises. I pretended that all my knowledge of you came from Bess, and from the Queen.

"For your information, my dear, you have been badly pulled down by a winter illness and need a rest from the court. You have no family to whom you can go—your former guardian, your Uncle Herbert, is unfortunately in the Tower. But I said I understood that you had once visited Lockhill and this had given me an idea! I trust," said Lady Mildred austerely, "that I sounded like an interfering busybody, one of those people who organise the lives of total strangers. I did my best to give that impression. I suggested that you should go to Lockhill and help with the girls."

"There was some correspondence on the matter," Cecil said. "They asked for more details about you— whether you really had a good knowledge of embroidery and dancing, for one thing! As if," he added dryly, "any of the Queen's ladies would not! We gave you a glowing reference . . ."

"We know that you have the skills required," put in Lady Mildred.

"And in the end," said Cecil, "a letter came, saying that you would be very welcome and asking you to write to them yourself, to make final arrangements. Well, Ursula? Will you go to Lockhill?"

Part of me wanted to. I had been appealed to by the Queen, and here in this warm, bright room, I was being honoured—one could say flattered—by the confidence and trust of the Secretary of State and his wife. The memory of Ann Mason and my sympathy for her had been reawakened. Oh, yes. I was almost ready to consent.

However, my mind was made up. I was going to Matthew and I would not be seduced from him. Once

I was away from the court and the Cecils, this spell would break. The sooner I made my escape, the better.

For the moment, I must go on pretending, but the pretence need not go on for very long. It must be convincing, however, so I asked the right question.

"But what am I to do when I get there? Apart from teaching the girls galliards and Spanish blackwork?"

"Let us be clear," said Cecil. "Jackdaw is dead. That amounts to a warning. This may mean danger for you and—perhaps—disaster for Lockhill. Do you understand?"

"Yes. Where does the picking of locks come into it?" I asked.

"I want you," said Cecil, "to get into Leonard Mason's study, and search his correspondence."

CHAPTER 5

Ferry to the Future

One of the tasks which my first husband, Gerald Blanchard, carried out for Sir Thomas Gresham was to find people who could be bought, or blackmailed, into working secretly for Gresham rather than for the Spanish administration in the Netherlands. Gerald always kept a careful eye on them. "Some of them make me extravagant promises," he told me once, "but usually under duress, and that kind of promise doesn't count. I never expect them to be bound by their word."

All the same, the giving of one's word does count for something, whether you want it to, or not. To keep up my pretence of co-operation, I had said to Cecil that I would go to Lockhill and search Leonard Mason's correspondence, and the mere fact that I had said it had a peculiar effect on me. I dithered.

I didn't speak of my secret intentions to Brockley and Dale. They both knew that I intended to join Matthew and that the Queen had said I could go in May. Now, just as if this still held, I found myself explaining my mission to Lockhill to them, and of course impressing secrecy on them. Anyone would think, I said to myself crossly, that I actually *meant* to go to Lockhill.

Cecil had instructed me to write two letters: one to the Masons, accepting their invitation and setting a date for my arrival there, and one to Matthew, telling him that I couldn't come until May.

"I'll find messengers," Cecil said.

I didn't write the letter to Matthew, but I penned the one to Lockhill, setting the date of my arrival there for the following week, Thursday January 20, which left me with time in hand to make my own preparations. Cecil accepted it, because it gave time for my letter to reach Lockhill, and he himself wished to make some arrangements for my escort on the journey.

Now, I said to myself, I must see about getting a passage to France. Yet I still did nothing.

Two main tasks faced me: one was to visit Thamesbank and gather Meg up; the other was to get Brockley to find me a ship. I wanted Brockley and Dale to come with me, and this would mean extra expense. I had more money than I used to have, but I still couldn't afford to charter a ship. Unless Brockley could find a captain who was actually bound for the Loire, we might have to land somewhere else and travel overland on hired horses.

It seemed not only very difficult, but also terrifying, as though I were standing on a cliff edge and trying to summon up the courage to jump. It meant abandoning the shelter of the court and going forth into the world with no official permission. What if I were caught? I was haunted by visions of prison cells, here or in France. Almost equally alarming in a different way was the prospect of being simply brought back and kept at the court, but with my credit gone. I did not know what to do.

Two days passed. I had dined with Cecil on Tuesday, and it was Friday before I found the will to act. I lived through a hard morning with Elizabeth and the other ladies, practising a complex new dance, accompanying the Queen to an audience, trying to sound normal, and worrying, worrying. I was free after dinner, and as Dale and I made our way back to my little cubicle, I decided that I must speak to her and to Brockley at once. I must think about Meg, too. If I told the Hendersons that the Queen had asked me to bring Meg to court, I might be able to remove her from Thamesbank without arousing curiosity . . .

I went into my cubicle, and a letter from Matthew was lying on my bed. Kat Ashley hadn't been needed this time, to work out who the letter was for, because the name on it was Mistress Ursula Blanchard.

Dale saw it at the same moment. "Ma'am! Look!"

"I know!" I snatched the letter up, tearing the paper away from the seal, and sat down on the bed to read it. It seemed to have been written in a hurry. My name, in Matthew's distinctive script, was written clearly, but the seal was faint, as if the wax hadn't been soft enough, and the writing inside was straggly.

My very dear Ursula,

I have seized a chance to come to England. I must keep out of sight, as I am a hunted man in your country, but I am not far away from you. A boat will await you at the river gate of Whitehall Palace, every morning at eight for the next few days. When you can, slip away and board it. The boatman will bring you to me. We will think of a way to fetch your little girl, if you wish. Then we will travel to France together. I have to ask you to leave your servants behind for the time being. Too large a party might attract attention.

In haste, and with love,

Matthew.

I turned to Dale, and knew by her face that my joy showed in my eyes. "Matthew's here. He's in England. He could be maybe not a mile away!"

I leapt up and went to the window, looking out across the Whitehall maze of buildings as though I were a mariner at sea, peering for a sight of land; as though by gazing outwards and concentrating hard, I could detect Matthew, find him with my spirit as a pigeon finds its loft.

It was like a miracle. I had no need, after all, to find my way to my husband through a hostile world. He had come to find me. Moving from the window, I held the letter out to Dale. "Read it if you like."

Dale was literate. She scanned the letter almost as quickly as I had. "Oh, ma'am! How wonderful for you. You're going? Without the Queen's permission?"

"Yes, of course! Matthew's come for me!"

"I'm glad for you, ma'am. Only . . ." She hesitated. "I don't quite like you going without me and Brockley."

"No, nor do I." For a moment I felt dampened.

"But it seems it can't be helped," I said. "I will tell Brockley to find a way to get the two of you to France. Dale, I want you to put a bundle of clothes together for me: linen, some toilet things, something I can carry easily, but it must have all the essentials. Unless the weather is impossible tomorrow morning—as long as it isn't snowing or raining in bucketfuls—I will go then. I'm not on duty first thing, anyway. Oh, Dale!"

I was transformed with excitement. Throughout the rest of the day, I still strove to appear normal, but more than once the other ladies gave me odd looks and I knew that my secret exultation was showing on my face.

It was slightly dampened when I spoke to Brockley, who said that he was surprised that Master de la Roche was not willing for me to bring my servants. "A gentleman of your husband's type and standing, madam, usually expects his wife to be properly attended. I shall come with you to see you safe into his company, at least. I must say, I wish that his letter had said where he actually was."

"He couldn't do that, Brockley. What if the letter went astray and the wrong person read it?"

"Who brought it, madam? Have you enquired?"

"Yes." I had, but the result meant very little. "A young man, moderately tall, that's all the gatekeeper could say. I don't think it was Matthew himself, though. He's *very* tall!"

I was glad to get away to bed that night, although sleep did not come for hours. When I woke next day, the weather was cold and grey but dry, and there was nothing to hinder my departure, except that my inside suddenly clenched up with nerves and I had to go three times to the privy. I began to fear that I wouldn't get myself to the river gate on time at eight, and I didn't know how long Matthew's boat would wait for me. In the event, I was a few minutes late, but the boat was there, a small one, with a solitary oarsman in it, muffled up against the cold, I hurried past the guard and down to the landing stage with Dale behind me, carrying my bundle, and Brockley striding at my side. The boatman saw us and stepped out on to the stage.

"Mistress de la Roche?"

"Yes. And you are . . . ?"

"An acquaintance of your husband." He glanced at Dale and Brockley. "I have orders to bring only you, madam. No one else."

"I must attend Mistress Bl—de la Roche until she is with her husband," Brockley said. "Then I'll take my leave."

"I'm sorry, sir, but my orders are firm." The boatman was unrelenting. "No one is to know where Master de la Roche is. I am to bring his wife to him and no one else. Would you care to step into the boat, madam?"

"Now, listen—" Brockley began, but I stopped him.

"Brockley, it's all right. I'm going to Matthew." I turned to the boatman. "How long will it take us to reach him? Will you at least tell me that?"

"Not long, madam, a matter of a half-hour, maybe, upstream."

"Very well." I turned to my servants. "I just want to get there. You come to France as soon as you can. Let me just vanish." I took my bundle from Dale and kissed her, and clasped Brockley's hand. "We'll be together again soon." I could see Brockley simmering, and longing to restrain me by force, but he didn't, of course. I smiled at them, and let the boatman hand me into his craft.

I sat down, bundle on lap, and stepping in after me, the boatman took his own seat, loosed the painter and picked up his oars. We drew away from the landing stage. I waved merrily to Dale and Brockley. Then we were in midstream and turning upriver, towards Richmond. I looked back at the bank but Brockley and Dale had disappeared.

It was as though, since the moment I found the letter, I had been moving rapidly, surging with eagerness, willing time away. Now, for the first time since then, I sat still, in the midst of the dark, chilly river, alone with the stranger who had forbidden Brockley to come with me, and at that point, when it was just too late, my misgivings began.

In restrospect, I think I already had them, but I hadn't wanted to pay attention. Something had nudged uneasily at my mind when I saw how the handwriting straggled, but I wanted to be with Matthew so much that I had muffled my instinctive doubts as thoroughly as my boatman had muffled his person.

The boatman seemed to have a powerful build, but it was difficult to tell because he was so enswathed in garments: cloak, boots, hat, and even a dark blue scarf across his lower face. Even in this weather, I thought, such clothing must be far too hot for comfortable rowing, and surely it was hindering his movements. I tried to say something of the kind, lightly, but he merely grunted in answer and rowed steadily on.

Time passed. My oarsman was clearly not the talkative type. I looked again at the dark river, rippling under a fretful breeze, and at the banks which here consisted of empty meadows, and thought, *I am travelling into the unknown.* The Thames was like the Styx, the river of Greek legend which the dead must cross to reach the hereafter. There was a ferryman in the legend: Charon. My silent, anonymous companion would do very well for Charon. He was so extremely silent and anonymous that he made me uncomfortable.

"Surely we've been going for more than half an hour?" I said.

"We're almost there." I got a sentence out of him that time. He looked over his shoulder, towards a grassy bluff jutting from the north bank, and changed course. Beyond the bluff there were signs of habitation: a house in the distance, and several boathouses by the water. We were making for them. A moment later, we were alongside another landing stage and my escort was tossing the painter round a bollard. "Here we are, madam. Out you come."

He handed me out. The nearest boathouse, one of the largest, was firmly shut and there was no sign of life. My Charon, however, led me round the side of it on a wooden walkway which brought us to the landward door. I saw with disquiet that although it had probably once had a lock, the lock had been hacked out, and a piece of timber nailed over the place where it had been. Two stout new bolts had been fitted to the door instead, top and bottom. He undid them. "In here, madam."

I looked across the fields, noticing how far away the one house was. The place was very lonely and no one seemed to be about. I didn't want to enter the boathouse, but Charon seized my arm and pushed me, quite roughly. I found myself inside, willy nilly.

"Watch your step now," he said.

The warning was necessary because the interior of the boathouse was very dark, with only a narrow walkway round the sides. The rest was water, on which lay a sizeable barge. I hesitated, still trying to resist, but Charon propelled me onwards for a yard or two and then stopped above a ladder which led down to the barge.

"You go down there. You'll feel safer on the barge. I shan't come with you. Turn round and go down backwards. Go on!"

His manner had unquestionably changed. It was no longer respectful. Badly frightened now, I twisted round to look at him. "Where's Matthew de la Roche?" I demanded.

"You're going to see him, right enough. Down that ladder with you. Go on, now. Nothing to be afraid of."

But there was. There was Charon. I looked at the muffled-up face, with the scarf which covered it from the bridge of the nose downwards, and the overshadowing hat beneath which his eyes too were almost hidden, and all I wanted to do was back away. Suddenly afraid that he might actually pick me up and carry me down, or worse still, pick me up and throw me down, possibly into the water instead of the barge, I accepted the alternative of the ladder. I crept down backwards and stood on the barge, looking up at him.

"But where *is* Matthew? He's not . . . ?"

For an awful, panic-stricken moment, I thought that Matthew might be dead, and that some hideous jest had been played on me, and I had been brought here to see his body, but the flat-bottomed barge was innocent of any such horrors. A quick glance round it showed me that instead, it was provided with a brazier and a tinderbox and some rugs.

"No," said Charon from above me, divining what I hadn't actually said. "He's alive. Don't you worry about that. You're in safe hands. No one's going to hurt you. Personally, I'd be in favour of knocking you out and dumping you in the river, but I'm not the man in charge."

"*What?*"

"You just stop there. There's heat, rugs, and you'll find food and water in that locker under the seat behind you. You just make yourself comfy till you're fetched." He walked away towards the door. Outraged and much alarmed, I shouted incoherent protests after him but he took no notice. He left the boathouse, and I heard the bolts shoot home.

I scrambled up the ladder again, and ran perilously along the narrow walkway to hammer on the door and shout. There was no answer. Pausing, I heard sounds on the landing stage outside, to the right of the big river doors at the other end of the boathouse, where the barge would go out when in use. Someone was getting into a boat. I heard the plash of receding oars, and Charon was gone.

Uselessly, I pounded on the door again and shouted for help on and off for quite a long time before I gave up and went back to the barge.

The barge was big and well appointed, with gilding and paint and smooth, polished seats which were no doubt supplied with cushions when the vessel was taken out. It had probably been laid up for the winter. It had a dinghy, which had been brought on board, complete with oars, and most of the seats on the barge had cupboards beneath them. I started to search the cupboards, and to examine the deck to see if there were any lift-up doors to storage compartments below. A vessel like this might have tools on it somewhere. I might find something—a hammer, a chisel, or by the greatest good luck, even an axe—by which I could hack a way out through that door.

I had no doubt about the need to escape if I could. I did not believe for one moment that I was to be taken to Matthew. Matthew would not have had me treated like this, not even out of anger at last year's betrayal. Oh yes, he had been angry. His first letter had shown me his anger, but it had also shown me his love. Besides, I knew him. This was not Matthew's doing.

I found the food my captor had mentioned. I had been provided with a loaf, some cold bacon, and a sizeable wedge of cheese. There were two big leather bottles of water, too. I had also been left a good pile of charcoal for the brazier. It looked as though I could expect a lengthy stay in the boathouse.

I couldn't find a hammer, or a chisel, or an axe. I had a small knife of my own and I went back to the door to see if I could slide the blade into the crack and somehow shift the bolts. It took only a few moments to show me what a useless idea that was. Treading cautiously, I went right round the walkway, seeking another way out, another door, a weak place in the planking walls or even in the roof, if only I could somehow climb up to it. There was nothing. Disconsolately, I returned to the barge.

I became aware of how cold I was. Well, there was the brazier, and there were the rugs. I lit the one and wrapped myself up in the other. It seemed that I could do nothing but wait. I had no doubt been missed by now but I did not expect rescue. How would anyone know where to look for me?

I ate some food but not too much, for I had no way of knowing how long it would have to last. I was too alarmed to be hungry, anyway—eating was just something to do.

I was swallowing the last crumbs when, once more, I heard oars, and then the sound of someone getting out of a boat on the landing stage. Tensely, I pushed off the rugs and stood up. Whoever it was was now walking round to the landward door. There was only one set of footsteps. Charon? *Matthew?* Could it, after all, be Matthew?

Heart thumping, I turned to face the bolted door. The bolts were being drawn back. The door opened.

Roger Brockley, stepping warily, with a drawn sword in his hand, came through, keeping his back against the door, and peering through the gloom, eyes narrow.

"Brockley!" I gasped, and made for the ladder. "Brockley, I'm here, I'm here! How on earth did you find me?"

His hand, strong and friendly, was there to help me off the top of the ladder. "Madam? You're all right? Unharmed?"

"Yes, yes! Oh, Brockley, I'm so glad to see you! But once again, how did you . . . ?"

"Questions in a moment, madam," said Brockley. "First of all, I think we'd better get away from here!"

"I didn't like it, you going off alone like that," Brockley said as he rowed us back towards Whitehall. The tide had turned and the ebb was draining out of the river, carrying us along. "I just didn't care for it. From the beginning, I didn't think much of the notion that Fran and I shouldn't come with you. What if it did make us a large party? People usually travel in groups. And when your boatman said I couldn't even see you safe to your husband . . . ! Well, there are dinghies the servants in the palace use; I take one now and again and the boatkeepers know me. I had my sword on already, under my cloak. I got myself a boat and rowed after you like a madman. I lost a few minutes and you were a fair way ahead, but I've got good long sight and I had you in view as soon as I was round the first bend.

"I tracked you all the way here. I saw you land and go round to the other side of that boathouse, but while I was still trying to reach it, that walking parcel of winter clothing who was your boatman, got into his craft and came back towards me—leaving you in the boathouse, presumably. With Master de la Roche, I hoped, but it seemed a funny place for a meeting. I was scared for you."

"I was scared for myself," I said.

"I didn't want him to recognise me," Brockley said. "I pulled away over to the bank to let him go past and waited till he was a good long way off. The tide was on the turn then, and it was hard going, the last bit up to the landing stage. I thought I'd never get there. Now, madam, just what happened? There was no sign of your husband, I take it?"

"No. I was to be held there, Brockley, but I don't know why. That man said I was to wait until I was fetched, and that I would be taken to Matthew, but I didn't believe him. That's all I know."

"You've no notion who he was?"

"It seemed to me," I said grimly, "that he'd taken pains to make sure he couldn't possibly be identified!"

"Yes. Likely enough." Brockley frowned, pulling on the oars, then he said, "Whoever he was, he knew of your marriage to Master de la Roche, and—I suppose—of your wish to join him. Tell me, madam—you had a letter purporting to come from your husband. Do you think it was genuine?"

"I've been wondering." I had the letter with me, in a pocket inside my open-fronted overskirt. Reaching under my cloak, I got the letter out and looked at it. "My name on the outside looks convincing enough," I said, "but the letter itself . . . well, it could be Matthew's hand if he were in a great hurry, or it could be an imitation. The seal isn't quite right, either. I think it's a forgery."

"I wonder," said Brockley thoughtfully, "if whoever sent it also knew what you were going to this place, Lockhill, for? The name of your husband would make good bait, I fancy, if someone wanted to make sure that you didn't set out after all."

"But how could that be? Very few people," I said, "know of my marriage, and fewer still that I have asked permission to go to France. It's no secret that I'm to visit the Masons and help with their daughters for a while, of course, but my real purpose has been very carefully guarded. Hardly anyone knows of that."

Brockley rested on his oars, letting us drift on the ebb. "Well, madam, I can tell you one thing for sure, and that is that neither Fran nor I have been indiscreet. When I first heard about that letter and felt doubtful, I asked her if she'd said anything about your affairs—about Master de la Roche or Lockhill—to anyone, and she said no. I believe her because if she'd been careless, I'd have got it out of her. Fran doesn't lie to me."

I nodded, understanding him. Brockley was not the sort of man to whom it would be easy to lie. There was something in that calm, steady gaze of his that always made you feel he knew what you were thinking.

"She wouldn't have been able to look at me," Brockley said. "She'd have admitted it, and cried. But she looked at me straight, and said it was a shameful suggestion. I know my Fran. She hasn't talked and I certainly haven't."

"I accept that. I have never known either of you to be indiscreet," I said.

"Maybe someone else has talked," Brockley said. "Someone from Sir William Cecil's house, could it be?"

"That's ridiculous!" I protested. "Leonard Mason is the master of his own house, presumably! If he heard something about me that made him feel he didn't want me at Lockhill, all he had to do was to write and say it wasn't convenient, or that he was making other arrangements for his girls, or that the children were coming out in spots and there might be infection in his home! It would be easy to keep me away. There was no need for all this nonsense about abducting me and locking me in a boathouse!"

"Then *why* were you abducted, madam? Do you think your husband arranged it after all and that you really were going to be taken to him?"

"God alone knows, Brockley. I certainly don't. I can't believe that Matthew arranged it—unless there's been a muddle. Unless he gave orders that were misunderstood, or some of his people meant to please him by bringing me to him, but went about it stupidly . . . I just don't know."

Brockley took up his oars again and began once more to pull. "Let us get off this chilly river. I take it you'll be reporting what has happened to Sir William Cecil?"

"Not at once," I said. "I want to think."

"And Lockhill? Do you intend to go, or not?"

I considered, while Brockley rowed us steadily on downstream. On the face of it, the notion that my imprisonment in that boathouse had anything to do with Lockhill seemed as unlikely as the idea that Matthew had organised it. Neither theory made sense. And yet . . . if Cecil's suspicions were right, then who knew how far this mysterious conspiracy extended, how many people were involved? Mason might be only one among many. How could I read the minds of these hidden adversaries?

How could I know what was really absurd and what was likely?

I was never one to heed warnings. Last year, I had run into danger largely of my own choice, and my first marriage, to Gerald Blanchard, had been an elopement in the face of outraged objections from both our families. I had taken plenty of chances in my time.

But now, as we moved along the cold river in our small and solitary craft, and I remembered that lonely boathouse and its locked, unyielding door, I felt that all this amounted to a very ominous warning. Dared I ignore it?

I shivered. "I don't know," I said.

But even as I spoke, I knew that I did. The decision had taken itself.

CHAPTER 6

Vision of Wings

"We are going to Lockhill," I said. "Or I am. I have no choice. I've given my word already and unless I go through with it, I risk offending the Queen. And I want to make sure I still have permission to go to France in May. There's no question now of travelling sooner, of course."

I had been badly frightened. Whatever the truth of the matter, Matthew's name had certainly been used to get me to that boathouse. I still loved him and longed for him, and I still believed in his love for me. When we met again, I said to myself, we would put right all misunderstanding, but now, waiting until May seemed not only endurable but inevitable. I was no longer prepared to embark on any illegal journeys to reach my husband. If and when I went, I would do so lawfully, with the Queen's goodwill behind me.

Unfortunately, Elizabeth could be unpredictable. I had better make sure I kept that goodwill. Dale and Brockley knew that too. They listened to me in silence and nodded sagely.

We were all in Brockley's lodgings. As usual when I called there, I had been politely given the best seat in the room, a stool with a cushion in a cover charmingly embroidered by Dale. Dale, I thought, would much rather spend her time doing embroidery than travelling to Berkshire in pursuit of conspirators.

Dale and Brockley sat side by side on the bed, which doubled as a settle. The lodging was very small, though reasonably comfortable, with a little hearth and a sheepskin mat beside the bed.

Dale said, "But after what's happened, ma'am . . ." and stopped.

"I doubt if it had anything to do with Lockhill," I said. "I daresay that if I reported it to Cecil he might have second thoughts about sending me, but I doubt if they would be justified. I can't report it anyway: I can scarcely tell him that I had a clandestine assignation with a wanted man—even if the man in question *is* my husband. Even if I didn't say I was intending to run off with Matthew, Cecil would guess at it."

"You still mean to go to France in May?" Brockley asked.

"Yes, but Lockhill comes first. All this talk of plots may be only a mistake, you know. In that case, I can perhaps put it right, and help Ann Mason thereby. I liked her."

"I agree, madam," Brockley said thoughtfully, "that from what I remember of that household, it didn't seem much like a hotbed for intrigue."

"I damned well hope it isn't," I said, "for Ann's sake."

Brockley studied me. His face was well shaped, with that high, intelligent forehead and the strong bones of nose and jaw, but it was not expressive. I knew him well enough, though, to read his eyes. I saw the expected glint of disapproval at my strong language, and then the dawning of a reluctant acceptance.

"Yes, madam," he said. "In your place, I would feel as you do. But I still wish you'd say no to this."

"I can't," I said.

"So be it," said Brockley. "We will come with you. Someone must look after you!"

"Cecil has given me careful instructions and made provision for my safety," I said. "He's not just sending me off the edge of the known world with no backing at all into the bit marked Here Be Dragons!"

Cecil had also offered me a good rate of pay, simply for going to Lockhill, whether or not I got results. If I were to stay in England until May, I would still have to find the wages for Dale and Brockley, and for Meg's nurse Bridget, whose wages remained my responsibility. Gold is an amazing solvent: doubts and fears dissolve in it in a most remarkable way.

"Don't concern yourself," Cecil had told me, "with the question of who did away with Dawson. Just keep alert and note anything which seems strange or unusual. Take heed of any odd coincidences, and, note who Leonard Mason visits or entertains. Above all, your main task is to get into his study and read his papers. Unlock his document boxes. Do you think you can do that?"

"I hope so, Sir William."

"I've arranged an escort to see you to Lockhill," Cecil said. "Meg's guardian, Rob Henderson, and two of his men will protect you on the road. I believe in secrecy, but Rob knows about your mission. If you need help at any time, you should have someone to call on if I'm not here. I am away on the Queen's business at times. Rob can be trusted."

I had thanked him with genuine gratitude. Now, having persuaded Dale and Brockley to come too, I prepared, in my own words, to go through with it.

I wrote the letter to Matthew after all, thanking him for his forgiveness, sending him my love, and saying that I would come in May; that the Queen would not release me sooner. Cecil duly provided a messenger. Meanwhile, with Dale's help, I stitched pockets inside all my over-gowns, in order to carry my lock-picks, and a little slate and pencil for taking notes. I would also carry a small dagger. The open-fronted gown is an elegant fashion which, I am glad to say, has never gone out. From my point of view, it is thoroughly practical.

The court was in process of moving to Richmond. I was informed that I was officially on leave and moved myself to Thamesbank instead, to say goodbye to Meg, and to join up with Rob Henderson.

The Hendersons were good people. Rob was a cheerful, strapping, tow-haired fellow in his thirties, endearingly fond of his wife Mattie. Mattie was a gracious dumpling of a woman, always trying to behave in a manner befitting a wellbred lady, but given on occasion to uncontrollable gurgles of merriment. I had grown fond of them both. I was glad I would have Rob for company on my journey.

I spent two nights at Thamesbank. I played with my dark-haired Meg, heard of her progress in her lessons, and was delighted to learn that she showed early aptitude on the spinet and lyre.

Early on the second morning I kissed her goodbye and we set off. Rob was debonair, cloaked in green velvet with a matching hat adorned by a kestrel's feather. He also wore a very practical sword, and he and his men all had the kind of broad shoulders which even thick winter cloaks couldn't conceal. In such company, we weren't likely to be attacked by footpads, or anyone else.

It was a pity, I thought, as we mounted, that for some reason, Brockley had chosen to undermine the dignity of the cavalcade by donning some extraordinary garments. His clothes all seemed to be too big for him. His hat was enormous, and when he held my mare, Bay Star, for me to mount, I saw that his doublet was oddly wide across the chest.

He saw me looking at him and gave me his rare smile. Then he raised his hat as if to scratch his head, resettled it when I had had a chance to see beneath it, and opened a button on his doublet to let me see what was under that.

"A helmet and breastplate?" I said quietly.

"And my sword." He lifted his cloak further back to reveal that he too was travelling well armed. "All left over from my soldiering days, madam. Because we may be going into danger, may we not?"

"I sincerely hope," I said, "that it turns out to be all a mare's nest."

"Is that really likely, madam?"

"I want it to be likely!" I told him.

I was whistling in the dark, of course, but I was committed now. A good rate of pay was not, after all, a total antidote to fear, but I had better ignore the shrinking sensation which intermittently attacked my vitals, so I put a good face on things, and tried not to pine for Matthew. The work in hand required concentration.

Rob, who was musical, encouraged us to sing as we rode, and I joined in with the rest. We jogged across the flat, wintry ploughlands and meadows round Maidenhead, singing all the way, and it did make me feel better.

We crossed the bridge into Maidenhead, singing a popular roundelay about the street calls of London. Rob took the chimney sweep's part, and his two men, although they were dragging a lazy packhorse, still found the energy, respectively and hilariously, to vend mutton pies and mousetraps. I sang the strawberry seller, Dale made quite a tuneful attempt at the cry of the milkmaid, and Brockley, whose voice was surprisingly good, was the ballad-monger. In noisy harmony, we arrived at the Sign of the Greyhound in Maidenhead and put up for the night.

Next day we set out again, in weak winter sunshine, reaching Lockhill later in the morning.

The village was as I recalled it: a dozen thatched

hovels and a couple of slightly bigger houses, one of which was a vicarage attached to a church smaller than itself; an alehouse and a well; a blacksmith, working in a cave-like stone building.

We rode through the village and up a lane, with ploughland on either side, cultivated in strips in the old-fashioned way. Leonard Mason, I knew, had little interest in farming and it was no surprise to see that the banks between the strips needed weeding, and that the ditch beside the track was choked with wintry grass and overgrown bushes.

The lane led to a gatehouse. The gate was open and there was no porter, so we rode straight on into the courtyard.

Lockhill manorhouse was attractive, built of a mellow stone, with a wide porch and a small tower at one end. It had a few modern mullioned windows and decorative chimneys, but it had been built over a hundred years ago, when some manor houses still had to withstand seige, and no one would have dreamed of building one without battlements. The walls and tower of Lockhill were crenellated.

We had little chance to stare, though, for just as on my previous visit, we were greeted by the loud baying of a mastiff on a chain, whereupon the same thickset butler as before hurried out to shout at the dog, and just as before, it ignored him. Rob had to shout to explain that he had brought Mistress Blanchard and believed that she was expected.

The butler quietened the dog at last, and as the baying subsided, we heard voices. Out of the main door came Ann Mason, carrying a baby and accompanied by five excited, not to say unruly, children. The Mason family surrounded us, all talking at once.

"So here you are! I'm glad to see you. What a long ride for you, at this time of year . . ."

"Are you Mrs. Blanchard who's going to teach us to dance and sew?"

"Yes, I am. And you are . . . ?"

"I'm Pen and this is Jane and the little one's Cathy. Cathy, you're supposed to curtsy!"

"Do you hear that, Phil? Why, the girls are showing signs of manners!"

"And you boys ought to bow! Where are *your* manners?"

"Will you children hush? Why must you always quarrel? I'm so sorry, they really are dreadful, and *where* is Dr. Crichton?"

"Is this the new baby?"

"Yes, this is my little Ned . . . will you children go inside? George, you're the eldest. Take them indoors and find your tutor! I'm truly happy to see you again, Mrs. Blanchard. And this gentleman is . . . ?"

"Rob Henderson at your service, madam." Rob doffed his hat, though he had to raise his voice above the continuing uproar of the young Masons. "I've escorted Mistress Blanchard here!" boomed Rob. "I will see her indoors and then take my leave. I have two men with me and we wouldn't want to put you to any trouble . . ."

"But you must stay and dine! Of course you must! Oh, here are the grooms. They'll see to the horses."

"Children!" A lanky and unprepossessing figure which I recognised as that of the tutor, Dr. Crichton, swept out of the door. A dusty black gown swished round his ankles and a dusty black cap was set askew on his head. "What do you mean by rushing out of the room in the middle of a lesson like that? Will none of you ever learn how to conduct yourselves? Ah. Mrs. Blanchard. Good day." He swept me a rather ungracious bow.

I answered politely, and he at once turned away to collect up his charges and shoo them indoors. I looked round for Brockley, to give me a hand in dismounting.

Look out, Cecil had said, for anything strange or unusual. What happened next was both, although it could hardly be classed as incriminating. Momentarily, a shadow, as of a big bird, passed over us, and then a thing which was indeed shaped like a bird, except that I never saw one with a blunt snout instead of a beak, or with a fin sticking up from the middle of its tail, drifted down towards the cobbles. It was about three feet long, end to end, but nearer ten feet from wingtip to wingtip. Its tail was a huge fan, tipped with feathers, but the rest seemed to be made of wood and paper. It wavered unsteadily through the air, came down on its nose and cartwheeled in front of our horses.

Bay Star snorted in alarm, and several of the others shied. Brockley's grey cob, Speckle, backed away, and Rob's tall black gelding let out a whinny of fright and reared.

"What in the world . . . ?" gasped Rob indignantly, from an awkward position astride a saddle which was now slanting upwards at an acute angle. One of the grooms, a gangling fellow, clearly the type who believed in delegating tasks to others, pushed a young stableboy forward and the lad caught helpfully at Rob's bridle. The rearing black horse rolled its eyes wildly but responded at last to gentle persuasion and coaxing noises from Rob and the stableboy, and brought its forefeet down again, narrowly missing a trailing wing.

"Careful! Don't let the horses trample it!" cried a voice from above.

We all looked up, and I saw another face I knew, though in an unlikely place. Master Leonard Mason, Ann's husband, stood on the roof of the tower, peering down at us over the ornamental battlements.

"I'm coming down!" he announced. He stooped, presumably to a trapdoor, and then disappeared.

A moment later, Leonard Mason, formally gowned like Dr. Crichton but in tawny velvet with fur trimming, and not looking in the least as though he had just come from a windy rooftop, hurried out to join us and rescue his extraordinary plaything. It was evidently not heavy, since he picked it up easily. He beckoned to the butler.

"Take it back to my workshop, will you, Redman? Watch the wings as you go through the porch."

The butler took the curious device and bore it away, and Mason then turned his attention to his astonished guests.

"Just a little experiment of mine. I am sorry it upset your horses. My apologies. So here you are, Mrs. Blanchard."

He had a long, serious face, with vertical furrows on either side of his mouth, and as he looked at me, I saw to my disquiet that they had deepened with distaste.

"I trust," he said, with unexpected sharpness, "that you will not object if we call you Mrs. in the modern style? It is true that in many respects I am old fashioned. I wish my daughters to grow up modest and virtuous, as young women did in times gone by . . ."

I would have loved to remark that judging from what I had seen of his daughters, his efforts hadn't so far succeeded too well. The thought of Matthew suddenly overwhelmed me. I wanted him with me, so that I could whisper my uncomplimentary opinion of the Mason girls' upbringing to him, and hear him say, "Saltspoon!" The longing was so great that my head swam, but Mason was still talking.

". . . In other ways, however, I am trying to bring up my children to live in the modern world, so here at Lockhill, we have adopted modern forms of address. If you agree?"

I pulled myself together. "I am sure you're wise, Mr. Mason, and I will do my best to help you with your daughters."

"I trust so," said Mason, still sharply. "You seem rather young for the task!"

So that was behind my unfriendly welcome. Or was it? Once more, I experienced that uneasy quivering in my guts. Well, I was here now. If something really was amiss in this house, then my best course would be to seem as innocent and harmless as possible, to keep suspicion from arising, or disarm it if it already existed. I was Ursula Blanchard, who had been unwell and had come to Berkshire for a rest, and to help Ann instruct her daughters in needlework and dancing. I smiled sweetly and said I would try to be of use.

"I'm sure you will be the greatest help to me!" Ann's kind blue eyes were anxious, but I also saw her give her husband a slightly irritated glance, as though wishing he had greeted me more pleasantly. "Please," she said, "all of you, dismount and come indoors. Mrs. Blanchard, would you introduce your companions to my husband?"

Little at Lockhill had altered. The children were as wild as ever, their tutor Dr. Crichton as dowdy and harried, with his ragged, greying beard and his forehead as furrowed as the Lockhill ploughland. Mason himself was as long legged, ascetic and obsessed with abstract ideas as I remembered, and I was sorry to see that Ann Mason, who was wearing an old gown, and had tentrils of brown hair escaping from her cap, still seemed tired and worried. The only item missing was the pack of small yapping dogs which, last autumn, had added to the uproar.

We sorted ourselves out, and the luggage and the horses were taken away. Brockley and the Henderson manservants went with the horses to see that all was well with them.

Ann Mason took the rest of us indoors. We followed her through the big, untidy hall where dust lay unheeded on the antlers which adorned the walls and the vast hearth was cold, and on into the parlour. Here, blessedly, a warm fire burned and the atmosphere was hospitable if not orderly, for there was a cradle in one corner, and almost every surface intended as a seat was occupied by something or other: a workbasket, a pile of mending, a sleeping tabby cat. Ann kept repeating that Rob and his men were not to leave until they had dined.

"Logan can manage, I'm sure. Just a moment." She put the infant Ned down in the cradle and hurried out of the room. An instant later, we heard her exclaiming because someone called Jennet was apparently in the wrong place at the wrong time.

"Jennet, for goodness' sake, what were you doing upstairs?"

"I were just a'dusting the master's study, ma'am," said a slow, slightly aggrieved Berkshire voice.

"Oh, for the love of God! Ann, I *told* you!" Leonard Mason must have followed us indoors, but had got no further than the hall. "Jennet is *not* to dust my things. She disarranges them and then I can't find anything. Only you are to go into my study, Ann. I moved it to an upstairs room just to get it out of the way—of maidservants' dusters as well as the children's noise! Really!"

If anything, I thought bemusedly, dogs or no dogs, the house was even more chaotic than before. I heard Ann sending Jennet to the kitchen to fetch us some wine, and then our hostess reappeared, rubbing her forehead with her fingers as though her head ached. "I'm so sorry about all this to-do—what must you think of us?" She shifted the cat and the other clutter so that we could all sit down. "Ah. Here's Jennet with the wine."

"It's the Rhenish, ma'am. I can't find Redman so I had to guess. Is the Rhenish all right?" Jennet was young, probably about fifteen, though tall and strong. She had slow, heavy movements, large brown eyes in a round face, and sounded as though she took it for granted that the Rhenish wouldn't be all right. Ann, however, merely thanked her, and told her to hand the goblets round. There was one for Dale as well, of which I approved. Jennet took the empty tray away, while Ann smiled gently round at us.

"I feel that I too must apologise for the fright that Leonard's gliding device gave your horses. Leonard," Ann explained, "has become very interested lately in the work of his namesake Leonardo da Vinci. Have you heard of him?"

"He was a Tuscan artist, wasn't he?" Rob said. "I thought he was simply a painter. I didn't know he had experimented with engines of any kind."

"Oh, he did! My husband says he was a great engineer who left drawings and theories concerning many strange devices." Ann's voice was awed. "He had visions, even, of wings that would carry men through the sky. I know little of such things, but Leonard is fascinated by them. He wants to develop some of da Vinci's ideas further."

"But what use is a pretend-bird?" Rob asked reasonably. "What can one do with it?"

"My husband thinks," said Ann, "that bigger versions could be made, strong enough to carry a man."

"Surely it would be too heavy? It would just fall to the ground. No one in their senses would volunteer to try it out, and no wonder!" Rob exclaimed.

"I'd try it out myself. I would hardly ask it of anyone else," said Mason with asperity, as he came into the room. Ann bit her lip and I guessed that he had said this before, and that she had protested in vain. "My theories," he said, "are for the most part my own. I soon realised that da Vinci had not worked his ideas out far enough to help me much."

"I've heard of his theories, I think," I said. "My—" I almost said "my first husband" but stopped myself in time. I must be careful. I must appear ordinary, without any irregularities in my life. "My husband Gerald spoke of them sometimes. He said that da Vinci believed that men could find a way of flying, if they could unlock the secret of how birds fly."

"He was evidently a man of wide interests." Mason spoke courteously enough this time. "He was quite right. Only," he added, with regret, and slight irritation, like a teacher whose favourite pupil has failed to fulfil his potential, "da Vinci never did unlock the secret. He always thought in terms of *flapping* wings, and I have observed falcons and seagulls when they come inland in winter. They rise on the wind with their wings stretched and still. Could the secret lie not in violent flapping, but in the shape of the wing and its size compared to the body?

"Also, there is the matter of speed. When ducks and swans take off from water, they have to get up speed first and a fine to-do they make over it! I am thinking of trying to launch from the tower with a catapult. Heavy stones used to be thrown by siege catapults. Given enough speed for take-off, one might contrive an engine with rigid wings which might hover like a falcon and survey a terrain from above, which could be of use in time of war."

"Ah, now that does sound worthwhile—if it can be done," Rob said.

"And why should it not be done? We live in an age of new ideas," said Mason. "New exploration, new commodities, new inventions; human knowledge expands every day. I have been experimenting with different shapes of wing, placed at various angles in streams of water. My workshop is at the far end of the yew garden, and it's very cold there today, but I have some diagrams of my results in my study. If you would care to examine them . . ."

I would have loved to say yes, because it would have given me a chance to familiarise myself with the study, but he had turned away from me and was only addressing Rob. Rob responded with a well-mannered "Naturally!" and the two men departed, taking their wine with them. The ladies were obviously not invited.

I was left chafing, with Ann, but there was no help for it. Sipping my wine, I asked Ann how her children did, and where their little dogs had gone.

"One of the dogs died of an illness," she said, "and then one ran in front of our coach wheel and was killed. My naughty boys were chasing it. The last remaining dog turned vicious, I think because of their teasing, and bit Cathy. We found it a home with Dr. Forrest, the Anglican vicar in the village. The children were upset, but I told them it was their own fault. That sobered them somewhat."

"I've come to help you with them," I said, "so will you tell me about them?"

"Oh, of course. Well, George is thirteen and Philip is twelve. Then comes Penelope, who is just turned eleven. She has a sharp mind, and lately she has shown interest in her studies. She now shares her brothers' lessons in Latin and Greek—though I fear she is still unruly. They all are! Next comes Jane, who is nine, and Catherine—every family must have its Catherine, mustn't it?—who was seven only last November. My little Henry is not yet one and a half. Well, he is not unruly yet, though no doubt it will come! He is sleeping just now. Of course, your concern will be mainly the girls."

"Seven altogether! You have a big family," I said.

"I suppose I have. They exhaust me sometimes," Ann said, sipping her own wine and looking somehow uneasy about it, as though in the normal way she hardly ever sat down for a little quiet refreshment, "but then, that is a woman's work in the world."

I didn't answer that. Dale had never become pregnant, and had told me she was relieved, while I, deeply as I loved Meg, had had a hard time at her birth. Afterwards, Gerald had taught me how to use a vinegar-soaked sponge to discourage conception. We would wait before we tried to have any more babies, he said. To risk my life would be to risk depriving the infant Meg of her mother. I had been grateful, but I did not think Ann would understand.

Ann noticed the silence, though, and at once filled it with a change of subject. "If you've finished your wine," she said, "would you like me to show you your room?"

It was the same room that Dale and I had shared before, well lit, with plastered walls and a high, beamed ceiling. Its mullioned windows overlooked the topiary yew garden between the two wings of the house. The yews had a sombre air. The bushes were clipped more or less into the shapes of chess pieces, but like so much at Lockhill, they were in need of better maintenance. The timber building just visible beyond the topiary was presumably Mr. Mason's workshop.

The room was in order, however, and while Ann was showing us the empty clothes press and pulling out the truckle bed for Dale, Jennet came in with towels over her arm and a jug of hot water. Soap was on the washstand already.

"There," said Ann. "I hope you'll be comfortable. We shall dine in an hour. Later, I expect you will want to talk to my girls, Mrs. Blanchard—you really don't mind being addressed as Mrs., I hope? Leonard says . . ."

"Yes, that he wants to follow the modern fashion." I did not much care for this particular modern usage but had already realised that it was gaining ground. "That will be quite all right," I said.

"That's good. Leonard is not really unworldly," said Ann, "even if he does often seem to be walking in a fog. His work fills his mind. Sometimes he stays in his study until the small hours and then snatches a little sleep in the room next door so that he can begin again first thing in the morning. At other times he comes to bed, and then gets up in the night and goes to his study because an idea has come to him and he wants to attend to it at once."

Leonard Mason led a busy life, I thought. Between working in his study at night and siring his numerous family, when did he ever find time to sleep at all?

And how was I to examine his correspondence if he

was liable to wander into his study in the small hours? I had been relying on night-time for my search.

Downstairs, someone was calling urgently for Mrs. Mason. Excusing herself, Ann hurried away, to be greeted from somewhere below by a cacophany of raised voices. Tiptoing out of the bedchamber after her, I paused on the little landing at the top of the main stairs, listened, and then traced the sound through an arched doorway to the head of the back stairs. The voices came from the kitchen.

". . . I only wanted a bit of marchpane. It smelt so good and I'm so hungry. Dinner's going to be late again; why can't I just have a bit of marchpane . . . ?"

". . . because I can't have 'ee under my feet," thundered an irritated male voice, another one with a Berkshire accent. "Least of all when I'm a'trying to make dinner for three extra mouths no one told me were coming. The master's always querying the bills so I never make food to spare and now . . ."

"Perhaps, Pen, if you went into the kitchen to help instead of getting in the way and eating food that's meant for the table, it would be different. You should learn to cook. When you have your own home . . ."

"I'll not have any of them learning in my kitchen, madam. We've tried that if you recall, and I'd as soon have imps of Satan under my feet. If I had some extra hands, good, skilled hands in the kitchen, it might be different, but with only Mrs. Logan and Joan and Jennet, and them doing other things half the time and no spitboy . . ."

". . . is there no peace in this house, ever? Why is somebody always shouting?" Leonard Mason had burst upon the scene. "In God's name, what's happened *now?*"

The angry voices receded and a slamming door shut them off from me. I withdrew, to find Dale standing wide-eyed in the doorway of our bedchamber.

"It's just the same as last year, isn't it, ma'am?"

"I'm afraid it is," I said as I led us back into our room and closed our own door, softly. "I feel I've never been away!"

"Ma'am . . ."

"What is it, Dale?"

"Well, ma'am . . . you're here to find something out for Sir William Cecil, isn't that right? That's what you told us. That something might be wrong here at Lockhill."

"Yes, Dale, that's perfectly correct."

"Well, I just wanted to say . . . if you're looking for signs of a plot, ma'am, are you really looking for them *here?*"

I sighed, and sat down on the edge of the bed. "I hardly know. Sir William told me to be alert to anything that seemed odd or unusual. The oddest and most unusual thing I've seen so far is Master Leonard Mason hurling an imitation bird off the tower! Do you think, Dale, that that could possibly qualify as a sign of a plot against the Queen?"

"I can't see how, ma'am! It seems to me that in this house, well, it's all children and uproar and Mr. Mason trying to study all sorts of peculiar things! As for plots—well, I just can't imagine . . ."

For a glorious and comforting moment, I saw my own private vision of Lockhill shared by someone else;

given credence. I saw the Mason household bathed in merriment and innocent muddle, like a dilapidated building in afternoon sunshine. I started to laugh and Dale joined in. "Neither can I, Dale!" I gasped. "Neither can I!"

Then Dale helped me to change my clothes, and we went downstairs to dinner.

CHAPTER 7

Intelligent Conversation

"The children used to eat separately," Ann Mason said across the dinner table, "but Dr. Crichton has lately decided that it would benefit them to join the adults. So now," she commented brightly, "we all eat together, as a family."

I could see that the brightness was an effort. Chronic weariness was evident in her eyes and her voice, but she had put on fresh clothes and was doing her best to uphold her dignity as the mistress of a manor house. Ann Mason had standards. She just lacked the time and energy to impose them in more than one or two places.

She had evidently concentrated her efforts on the dining room. The side table, where Redman was pouring a sauce over a platter of boiled chickens, was protected from the hot dishes by a clean white cloth. There were aromatic strewing herbs among the rushes underfoot, and the dining table was furnished with another white cloth, and with burnished spoons and pewter goblets.

Looking about me, I noticed that, like the Cecils,

the Masons had improved their dining room since I last saw it. Here, too, were new tapestries. The old ones had been very faded, but the walls were now adorned by richly coloured panels telling the story of the Return of the Prodigal.

Rob saw me looking and remarked on them to Mr. Mason. "They're very fine. Florentine, are they not?" he said.

Mason had also dressed for his guests, donning a tailored doublet, faced in fawn silk and embroidered with blue and green leaves. Dr. Crichton, on the other hand, was still in his dusty black gown and didn't even have the presence with which to carry it off. An impressive figure, Dr. Crichton was not. The children, all well washed, padded, brocaded and ruffed, were considerably smarter than their tutor.

Instead of answering Rob's question himself, Mason looked to Crichton for a reply, and it came with some assurance.

"Quite right, Mr. Henderson. The designer came from Florence. The draperies the family in the tapestry are wearing are in the style seen in many Florentine paintings."

I had turned to look closely at the panel nearest to me. "I think—" I began, but Leonard Mason broke in.

"As a matter of fact, although he is too modest to say so, these tapestries actually belong to Nicholas Crichton here. An uncle left them to him as a legacy. Having nowhere of his own to hang them, he is kindly allowing me to decorate my walls with them. They are finer than anything I could afford. Such tapestries as I do own, I inherited from my father and I have lost some of those through moth and mildew. I am grateful to Crichton for his loan."

"Well, I am grateful to have a place to put my legacy," said Crichton. He had a flat, morose voice—no wonder he couldn't command his pupils' attention. "My uncle," he said, "had had them for many years, but fortunately they are still in good condition. On these walls, they continue to give pleasure, and we can look at them and discuss the ins and outs of Italian design. And that, children, is partly why I wished you to share our mealtimes. By doing so, you not only learn how to behave in company, but you have a chance to enhance your education by hearing intelligent conversation. *Penelope!*"

Penelope had let out a shriek and punched Philip, who was sitting next to her. I gazed at them in bemusement.

"He kicked me!" Penelope said. "Philip kicked me!"

"I am thinking," said Leonard Mason coldly, "of finding a school for you two boys. Dr. Crichton can continue to teach your sisters but I think it's time that you boys were taught away from home, where, although I regret it, you may find yourselves subject to a harsher regime than I have ever let Crichton impose on you. Intelligent conversation, indeed! How can one have any conversation at all, if it is to be punctuated by this sort of thing?"

Rob Henderson, however, had a decidedly mischievous streak in his nature. "Did you kick your sister?" he enquired of Philip. "If so, why?"

Philip sulkily applied a spoon-edge to a dumpling and refused to answer.

Penelope did it for him. "He doesn't think there's any point in girls listening to intelligent conversation so as to learn how to do it themselves, because he thinks we aren't capable of it. He kicked me to remind me that he'd said that."

George emitted a snort of mirth, and Jane and Cathy giggled.

Repressively, I said. "The Queen of England would not agree with Philip. Queen Elizabeth has the keenest wit I have ever come across and can follow every twist and turn of a debate between scholars."

"And I'm quite sure," said Ann, "that Queen Elizabeth would not kick or punch anyone. Is that not so, Mrs. Blanchard?"

"Certainly," I said, with doubtful truth. Admittedly, I had never actually seen Elizabeth launch a kick or a punch, but she sometimes slapped her maids of honour, and I had once seen her snatch off a shoe and throw it at Lady Katherine Knollys, for venturing to remark that, considering his clouded reputation, Robert Dudley was being allowed into the Queen's private rooms too often. Elizabeth was less of an example than one could wish, but I didn't propose to say so.

Penelope was impressed by this talk of the Queen. "Have you seen Queen Elizabeth, then, Mrs. Blanchard?" she asked.

"Now, Penelope. You know that I explained to you all that Mrs. Blanchard is one of the Queen's ladies, although she is taking a brief rest from the court and has come to help me meanwhile," said Ann reprovingly. "Tell us something of court life, Mrs. Blanchard.

You must meet many well-known people there. How did you come to join the court?"

Therefore, while Redman served the chickens and we began to eat them, I talked of my past life in Antwerp, and my present post with the Queen, and how Rob Henderson and his wife were fostering my little daughter and educating her so that one day she too might come to court. Rob occasionally put in a remark. I knew I should be effacing myself and listening to the Masons' conversation, in case it contained any of the clues I sought. I also badly wanted a closer look at those tapestries. However, even though neither Mason nor Crichton had addressed a word to me since I came to the table, these people were my hosts and sheer good manners required me to be agreeable. If I were asked to talk, I had better do so.

The Mason children now listened attentively and caused no more disturbance. Indeed, Penelope, possibly bent on refuting Philip's rude dismissal of female intelligence, took to asking searching questions.

"Can ordinary people see the Queen, Mrs. Blanchard—have audiences with her, I mean, not just watch her go by in her coach? Are they allowed?"

"Oh yes, sometimes. Not long before I came here, a quite ordinary clockmaker was granted an audience so that he could present her with a gift. I was there at the time."

"What was it?" George asked with interest. "A golden clock, all set with jewels?"

"Well, it had a gilded case, but it was actually a—"

Penelope's manners hadn't become perfect on the

instant, and she interrupted impatiently. "Of course it was jewelled. It must have been studded with gems! Would you dare to offer a queen anything that wasn't?"

"Yes," said George. "I wouldn't offer her a gem-studded saddle. She wouldn't be able to sit on it!"

"Now, now," said Crichton, but Penelope plunged eagerly on.

"Does the Queen live in great luxury, Mrs. Blanchard? Does she eat off gold dishes every day?"

I looked carefully at Penelope, thinking that although she would never be a beauty, not with that bulging forehead and square jaw, her zest for life conferred its own attractiveness. I liked her. I gave her a smile.

"The Queen lives with proper dignity," I said. "When she holds state banquets, then there are gold dishes and napkins with gold embroidery, and yes, she often wears dresses sewn with jewels—she is particularly fond of pearls. But she is well aware of the need to curb extravagance. She has to strike a balance between impressing dignitaries and avoiding waste. In private, she wears simpler gowns and she dines from gilt dishes, not gold. She is herself abstemious in food and drink."

"One hears rumours," said Crichton, addressing me at last, "of much extravagance at court—in dress and furnishings, and behaviour, too."

I shook my head. "The court is well conducted, and if the furnishings are fine, most of them were there before the Queen came to the throne, or have come to her in the form of gifts. She is careful with the realm's money. She spends much less than Queen Mary did."

"Ah. Poor Queen Mary." Dr. Crichton sighed. "She made many mistakes, but she was a sick and disappointed woman."

"She was also a very extravagant one," I said. If there were people here who wanted to bring back the past, then let them be reminded of the truth about that past. "Queen Elizabeth makes a point of nurturing the economy. One of the first things she did when she came to the throne was to improve the coinage." Cecil had enlarged on this subject before I left the court. "None of her gold money is less than twenty-two carat," I said, "and her sovereigns and angels are above twenty-three."

Mason, interested, also at last embarked on a conversation with me. "It is true that prices aren't rising as fast as they were. I have said it before, at this very table: a realm, like a household, must live within its means. A ruler who forgets that courts disaster, and Queen Mary's reign was indeed flawed in that respect."

"Queen Elizabeth understands the subject very well," I agreed. "She has made a thorough study of such things. I wonder," I added casually, "if young Mary Stuart over in France has used her spare time as wisely."

"Excuse me," said Dr. Crichton, "but is this style of conversation wise? In my experience, political matters are better not discussed too openly. Men have found themselves in the Tower for words said, perhaps not very seriously, at their own dinner tables."

"But no one has spoken against the Queen!" said Ann.

"And who would report it if they did?" asked mischievous Rob. "Redman, are you a spy in the pay of Her Majesty, reporting everything we say to a contact at court?"

Redman, who was arranging syllabubs in a row on the side table, turned round with a horrified expression on his face. "No, sir! Certainly not, sir!"

Everyone laughed, but privately I was annoyed. I did not want Henderson, or anyone else, to put the idea of spies into Leonard Mason's mind. Least of all one minute after I had trailed the name of Mary Stuart across the conversation.

But Mason had already changed the subject, and Ann was asking Redman to bring the syllabubs to the table. I leant aside to get out of Redman's way as he came to serve us, and carelessly knocked an empty goblet to the floor. He made to pick it up for me, but I slid quickly from my seat and retrieved it myself. I rose to my feet again, facing away from the table.

Every tapestry workshop has its own dyemaster; everyone knows that. I had always had a good eye for colour and could design my own embroidery patterns. I had known at once that I had seen *that* tender blue, *that* subtly softened crimson, somewhere before, and recently. The pale highlights on the red robe of the prodigal son's father, and on the blue gown of his mother, were so familiar. Facing the tapestry, even for a moment, gave me a chance to confirm what I had guessed.

I had guessed right.

* * *

Rob Henderson and his men left not long after dinner. I spent most of the afternoon discussing study times with Ann and Dr. Crichton. It was a stilted and tiresome conversation, as Crichton had resumed his unbending manner. Soon after that it was time for supper. Then the winter dusk descended and we all retired to bed. I lay in my bed, hands behind my head, gazing into the darkness.

I had much to think about.

For one thing, I had come across another oddity, something more subtle, and in a way more curious than Mason's unlikely experiments with gliding engines.

For reasons unknown, either Mason or Crichton was lying like a son of Belial about those tapestries on the dining-room wall. When I picked up the fallen goblet and rose to my feet facing the wallhanging behind me, I had not only seen the gleam of silk in the distinctive highlights: I had seen the monogram of the Giorgio Vasari workshop in Florence, where Cecil's copy of *The Unicorn Hunt* had been woven, and the initials HH, for Hans van Hoorn, in the lower right-hand corner.

Crichton's uncle might have left him the tapestries, but he certainly hadn't had them for years. Van Hoorn had only been with that workshop for a year, at most. The uncle might be the one who was lying, of course, though I couldn't think why he should. But then, why should Mason or Crichton want to lie, either?

It was puzzling. Was there a parallel between Cecil's report of a Dr. Wilkins who had bought a carpet with money he couldn't possibly possess, and Leonard Mason whose dining-room walls were adorned with tapestries he couldn't afford? Maybe, but it seemed so thin; it made no sense. Nothing made sense! I thought irritably.

Something in me, though, some instinct, some antenna with which I had been born, had been alerted. Earlier that day, Dale and I had laughed over the idea of plots at Lockhill, but now I no longer believed the place was as innocent as I had hoped. And if it were not, then I had to know why. Cecil's voice spent in my head again, telling me of a weaver and his young daughter, whose terrified and bewildered faces Rob Henderson had seen through the smoke of their pyre. Brockley and Dale thought I was foolish to come to Lockhill, but I was not. I had done right.

I had writing things with me, and before Rob left for home, I had given him a sealed letter for Cecil. In it, I said that my reception at Lockhill had been oddly chilly in some respects and I was wondering if there had been an indiscretion somewhere at court or in Cecil's household. Would it be possible to look into it?

I fell asleep after a while and dreamed of being back in that boathouse, alone and cold and listening to the slop of the river outside. I awoke with my heart pounding. In my dream, the slopping noise had been oddly regular, and now I realised that I could still hear it. Someone in floppy slippers was walking past my door.

I started up, wondering bemusedly if I should follow, until somewhere I heard another door open and shut and then all was silent again. What had I heard? Mr. Mason going to his study? Or a conspirator going to a meeting? My dream had left me shaky and the darkness pressed on me. I couldn't bring myself to get up and give chase.

Lying there, I became deeply aware that Lockhill was a strange place, not my home; that I had no home and that I longed for one. The month of May seemed far distant.

I turned over on to my face. Into my pillow, softly, so that Dale couldn't hear, I whispered, "*Matthew.*"

CHAPTER 8

Taking Steps

"I have agreed to tolerate my offspring at dinner and supper," Leonard Mason said at breakfast the next morning, "but they take their breakfast separately. I insist that we have *one* civilised meal during the day. Crichton is with them. It is a thousand pities he can't regulate their behaviour better."

I had asked where the children were, as much as anything in order to relieve the stiffness in the atmosphere. Ann was chattering brightly of this and that, but Leonard Mason's silence towards me was noticeable. There was no doubt at all, I thought, with a twinge of panic in my guts, that he disliked me, was for some reason suspicious of me. But he had shown no sign of this when I visited Lockhill last year: something had to be wrong in this household.

"Crichton isn't a natural tutor," Ann said. "His real business is that of being a priest." Her husband gave her a sharp glance and she added, "Well, Mrs. Blanchard knows that. When she visited us before, she heard mass with us. Would you wish to do so again, Mrs. Blanchard? You were born a Faldene, and so . . ."

"I am also one of the Queen's ladies," I said politely. "To hear mass on one isolated occasion perhaps didn't matter, but I think it best not to do so habitually. If you don't mind too much."

"Not at all," said Mason, with unmistakable frostiness.

"We mean no harm by hearing mass," Ann said earnestly. "We are a harmless family, God knows, and loyal to the Queen."

"We are a respectable family in all ways," said Mason, regarding me coolly. "Even though it is true that our children are somewhat wild and the girls certainly require more training in feminine skills. My wife was most insistent that you should come, Mrs. Blanchard. You are welcome, whether or not you join us at mass, provided that you conduct yourself at all times as a lady should."

That sounded like a speech he had prepared in advance. Ann looked away and I wondered what Mason thought I was likely to do that was unbecoming to a lady—poke my nose into things he wanted kept private, probably. I would do well to take care.

Mason was enlarging on the religious observances at Lockhill. "Most of my servants and some of the villagers attend mass, but they all go to the Anglican service at their church each Sunday, as well. Our vicar Dr. Forrest presides. The Church authorities know well enough that mass is said here, but they wink at it."

I said I was glad that such a wise accommodation had been reached.

A chorus of youthful shouts and yells suddenly broke out in the distance, and Ann said with a sigh that

Crichton might have less trouble with the children if he looked more impressive. "Why must he dress like a scarecrow? Leonard, can't you persuade him to dress better?"

"Only by paying him more," said Mason gloomily, "which would not be convenient. I'll have a word with him some time and tell him to brush that gown of his, if you wish." He had a restless air, as though he were longing to escape to his private researches into the mystery of flight. He flinched as the uproar crescendoed. "What a noise! I really am considering a school for the boys—which is why I can't even think of raising Crichton's wages. How I am to afford school fees, I can scarcely imagine. For the moment, however, I have work to do. I don't wish to be disturbed." He added, rising to his feet, "If the house catches fire, or some other emergency occurs which means that my presence is *essential*, I shall be in my workshop. I am going to make a new version of my gliding engine."

Ann sighed again. Mason gave her an enigmatic look, favoured me with a brooding one, and strode out. I smile at Ann and said that it was time I set to work as well.

That was the Friday. The weekend passed without incident, but my discomfort did not abate. Mason and Crichton alike remained aloof, rarely speaking to me unless they had to, but I had the feeling all the time that I was being watched. I saw little of Mr. Mason, but when I did encounter him, his unsmiling manner towards me was disconcerting. As for Crichton, when I moved about the house, which I did as much as possible, because I wished to learn its layout, I several times encountered him unexpectedly, as though he were dogging my footsteps.

Leonard Mason: Dr. Crichton. I had set out thinking that Mason, the Catholic master of Lockhill, was the likely conspirator, if anyone was, but Crichton, his priest, was no less probable. That curious lie about the tapestries certainly united them. Both quite plainly distrusted me, and I distrusted them. Now, whenever I saw a door standing ajar, I glanced covertly at it to see if one of them was behind it. I had a continual urge to look over my shoulder.

Monday morning found me sitting in the dormer window of the top-floor room which Ann had given me for sewing lessons. It looked out over rolling countryside, meadow and wood and ploughland, under a windy grey sky. The girls were with me, sewing industriously. I had fitted their lessons into the existing routine quite easily. The children began the day with study, and then the boys were supposed to practise archery and swordsmanship, of which Crichton apparently had some knowledge. "Archery is out of date for warfare," George told me solemnly, "but excellent training for marksmanship and the arm muscles."

Hitherto, the girls had looked on, and I gathered, also cheered, jeered, and during the swordplay, recommended their brothers to slit each others' gizzards. Henceforth, I declared, they should spend this part of the day sewing with me. The new regime had begun on Friday. They were sulky at first but I tried to make the lessons pleasant and this soon wore off. Ann had made spasmodic attempts to teach them to sew and

Penelope had quite a repertoire of stitches. Cathy, though the youngest, wasn't far behind her and even showed signs of talent. Jane was clumsy and apt to stick needles in her fingers but in time I hoped to teach her how not to get blood all over her work.

I had also begun dancing lessons, in which the boys took part, because dancing was a pastime shared by men and women. In fact, by Saturday evening I had been promoted to teach music as well.

"My husband plays the spinet," Ann said, "but he has no time to teach the children. We had an outside music master once but he doesn't come now, at least as an instructor. He visits now and then as a friend." Mason had had to pay him for giving lessons, I supposed. "He takes an interest in my husband's researches and inventions," Ann told me, "so he's always welcome when he calls, but he and Leonard just disappear into the study or the workshop. It's pleasant for Leonard to have someone to talk to, though. He sometimes gets Crichton to help him, but Crichton doesn't like it. He's not that kind of man."

I already knew that. I had once or twice walked through the yew garden to look at the workshop, and on my second visit I had found Mason pounding nails into his new brainchild, which was made of wood and canvas, while Crichton nervously held the nails straight, obviously afraid for his thumbs and just as obviously not enjoying himself.

In the afternoon, the children sometimes rode. Ann said that she also tried at times to instruct the girls in house-wifery, but without must success, because the cook, Stephen Logan, who was large and aggressive, and his wife, the lean angular housekeeper, disliked having them "under our feet."

In the evenings, I had undertaken to see the girls to bed, and then Dale and I would go to the kitchen to talk to the Logans and the maids while we made warm bedtime possets for ourselves. The Logans were civil enough to us. They worked hard and Stephen had reason for his bad temper, since the spitboy had lately died and not been replaced. Logan had to turn his own spit.

The Logans had a son, Edwin, a powerful and unsmiling young man who lived in the village but ran the Lockhill garden with the help of two other village lads. He also acted as the household butcher, slaughtering any animals or poultry needed for the table, and dealing with the carcasses in a gruesome back room off the kitchen, furnished with chopping blocks and an array of knives and cleavers.

I had not really become acquainted with the butler, Redman, but I made a point of chatting with the two maids when I could. Joan was a widow in the middle of years, while Jennet, as I had surmised, was only fifteen. They too worked hard. Lockhill was badly understaffed.

The last member of the household was Ann's maid, Tilly. Tilly was elderly and ailing, and as far as I could make out, Ann looked after her rather than the other way about. Tilly had a little room of her own where she took most of her meals on a tray, and all I had ever seen of her was a wraith-like figure in grey, drifting aimlessly here and there in the house. I had never yet spoken to her.

I had succeeded by now in learning my way about. Lockhill manor house consisted essentially of a frontage with two wings stretching back. The yew garden lay between them. The great hall, which went the height of two storeys and occupied much of the frontage, had once been much wider, but part of it had at some time been walled off and given a lower ceiling so that two extra bedrooms—one of which was mine—could be built above. The cut-off piece of hall was called the Long Room and was used as a passageway between the two wings.

When there was company, Joan had told me, dinner was served in the hall and the dishes were assembled in the Long Room, on top of the arrow chests which held the shafts used by the boys in their archery.

I had also learned, depressingly, that Mason's study was not only apt to be occupied at night, but was inaccessibly placed at the far end of the west wing and could only be reached by first going through Dr. Crichton's schoolroom, then a long, chilly gallery, and then the anteroom where Leonard sometimes slept. To get there from his bedchamber, he would have to pass my door. The footsteps in the night had no doubt been his.

I stitched slowly, repairing snagged embroidery on Mason's fawn doublet. On the Saturday, I had discovered Ann, in an unusually irritable mood, trying to do it in a hurry. "Leonard is fond of this doublet," she had said, "but embroidery takes up time, and poor Tilly can't help, not just now."

I had offered to do it for her, and now I worked at it with a distracted mind, glad that the new project I had found for the girls seemed to be absorbing them. Over the weekend, Mason had worn a cream satin doublet, decorated with the striking geometrical patterns of Spanish blackwork, which was highly fashionable, despite its origins in Spain. I had marked out some similar patterns on pieces of cloth, shown my pupils the basic stitches and set them to work. It was keeping them quiet, and I needed quiet in order to think. I was worried. Three days had passed already and still I had not found a chance to search Mason's study.

The reason was deplorable. Yes, it was true that an opportunity was hard to come by, but as yet I hadn't even tried. The air of unfriendliness and suspicion in Lockhill had affected me, and I had again had a nightmare about being shut in that cold boathouse. Now, I was quite simply afraid of entering that study with my wire lockpicks. What if Mason caught me? What would happen next? I could imagine various answers to that and I didn't care for any of them.

I stitched miserably away and lectured myself. If a plot did exist, then how advanced was it? What if it ripened? What if it succeeded because I had let the chance of foiling it slip through my silly feminine fingers?

Well, Mason's nocturnal habits made a night attempt too risky, but there could be a chance this afternoon. Ann and Leonard had gone out, in their lumbering coach, to dine with friends in Maidenhead. They wouldn't be back until supper. A clear field beckoned. I dared not refuse the invitation.

This afternoon, all the children would be riding, taking turns on the three ponies which the stables boasted. Nearly everyone would be out of the way.

Yes. Brace yourself, Ursula. This afternoon.

* * *

I needed Dale and Brockley to help me by standing guard. After dinner, therefore, Dale and I went to the stableyard, where Brockley was most likely to be found. As a married man, he had been allowed a room of his own which Dale could sometimes share with him. It was next to the grooms' attic over the stables, and Dale said he was putting up some extra hooks for their clothes.

We found him, however, standing with the gangling groom Thomas, at the foot of the outside staircase which led up to the room, and we could tell, even from a distance, that he was taking Thomas to task. We waited, tactfully, until he had finished before going nearer.

When Brockley had had his say, Thomas, not noticeably disturbed, lounged away towards the door of the kitchen, and tried to steal a kiss from Jennet, who had just stepped out with a bucket of leftovers for the pig-barrow, which stood by the kitchen door and was taken, every day, down the hill for the benefit of the pigs, who lived in a noisome sty out of smelling distance of the house. Jennet swiped at him with the emptied bucket and darted back indoors and Thomas, whistling, sauntered off into the harness room.

"Jennet doesn't like him, either," Dale said. "He's sweet on her, Joan says, but she won't have him and no wonder. It's the way he looks at one. As if he was imagining . . . well, I hardly like to say, ma'am."

"I know," I said. Thomas was a bleached individual with disconcertingly light eyes and I too had noticed that appraising stare. He had turned it on me, once or twice.

"Trouble, Brockley?" I said as we joined him.

"That Thomas! I caught him putting fresh straw down in Bay Star's stall without taking the old straw away first. She'll get foot-rot if she stands in old bedding. He's as idle as a broken millwheel. If I were in charge here, he'd be sent off with no character and a sore back. You're looking for me, madam?"

"Yes, Brockley. Have the children gone riding yet?"

"They have. The two younger grooms have gone with them."

"Good. Brockley, it's time."

At this hour of the day, the house was quiet. The Logans and the maids were in the kitchen, clearing up the dinner things and taking their ease before beginning the first preparations for supper. My bedtime gossiping in the kitchen had told me nothing about conspiracies but had yielded a good deal of useful information on the habits of the household members. I knew that Redman usually retired after dinner for an afternoon nap in his attic room, and that when the children went riding, Crichton also liked a snooze. Both of them should be safely out of the way.

I stood with Brockley and Dale just outside the schoolroom. "You know what to do?" I said to them.

"I am to wait here," said Brockley, "and listen for movement downstairs and on this floor. Fran goes up to the top floor to listen for anyone stirring up there. If need arises, we fetch you, as fast as we can. It doesn't matter if you're found in the gallery, but you mustn't be caught in the rooms beyond it."

"That's it."

"Madam, I wish you were not doing this."

"Frankly," I said, "so do I, but it can't be helped. I have written to Cecil asking him to start certain enquiries at his end, but I haven't heard from him yet and I think it's too soon for results, anyway. Meanwhile, I must try to carry out the task I'm here for." I cocked my head. The house was perfectly quiet. "Now," I said.

Dale went softly up the stairs to her post. I nodded to Brockley and went into the schoolroom. It was very untidy, chairs not pushed properly under the two tables, and the tabletops carelessly strewn with books and slates and pens. I longed to restore it to order but I wasn't here for that. I hurried through to the gallery.

This had been created partly as a place for the ladies of the house to walk in during cold or wet weather, and it took some moments to traverse it. During those moments, I was still Ursula Blanchard, gentlewoman, on leave from court, instructress to the Mason girls. If anyone were to come on me unexpectedly, it would not matter; I had done nothing yet that Ursula Blanchard should not do.

The instant I passed through the door at the far end, however, I would step out of character, would become a spy, performing deeds which must be secret because they couldn't be explained away. Since I came to Lockhill, no one had tried to harm me, but if I were discovered at this . . .

Jack Dawson, otherwise Jackdaw, had suspected that something was wrong here at Lockhill. Had he been caught doing something untoward? And who *had* been behind that lying trap that led me to a deserted boathouse?

Jackdaw was dead.

The gallery was cold and draughty. A fire had been laid in its hearth, but not yet lit. The door at the far end was bolted, and I drew back the bolt with chilled fingers. Here was the little room where Leonard Mason sometimes slept. Rugs and a pillow lay ready on a couch. I left the gallery door open behind me, in case Brockley or Dale called me, and crossed to the door of the study. Ann had shown it to me briefly when taking me round the house, although she had not let me do more than glance inside. To Ann, her husband's study was a shrine of learning, to be treated with hushed respect. It had a lock and key, but the door opened when I pushed it. Leonard took it for granted that no one would go uninvited into his sanctum.

Looking at it from the threshold, I decided that this must surely be the gloomiest room in the house. It was about fourteen feet by ten, with ample windows, but they were all half obscured by the books piled up on their deep sills. Where the walls were visible, they were panelled in dark wood, but mostly they were hidden by bookshelves crammed with volumes bound in brown leather and by a ponderous double-fronted oak cupboard. I wondered how the monstrous thing had ever been manoeuvred through the door.

The bare boards of the floor were relieved by a single brown fur rug, and the chair which went with the desk, and was the only seat in the room, had a cushion in a brown velvet cover. The inkstand on the desk and the triple-branched candlestick beside it were pewter. The air smelt of old leather and guttered candles and stuffiness.

The place was icy, as bad as the gallery. The small hearth was empty. Leaving the study door open as well, I tiptoed forward and glanced at the bookshelves.

The books were those which might appear in any gentleman's or scholar's library. Some were in Latin or Italian, one or two in French. Mason, I knew, was a linguist, but he was evidently interested in many subjects. Astronomy was represented here, and so were geography and history.

I recognised Thomas Fabyan's *New Chronicles of England and France*—my cousins' tutor had made us study that. The neighbouring set of shelves held some books on musical theory. Next were works on philosophy and politics: Sir Thomas More's *Utopia;* Niccolò Machiavelli's *The Prince*—the Queen had those, and I had also seen them in Sir Thomas Gresham's library. There followed a good collection of poetry, in several languages, and some books on theology.

There was nothing unexpected there. I turned to the desk. In marked contrast to Crichton's schoolroom, it was very neatly arranged, with papers in tidy piles, more books, some of them with marked places, some lidded boxes with brass hinges, and several wooden trays, which seemed to be Mason's way of keeping documents sorted.

I hesitated, wondering where to begin, then I heard footsteps approaching quickly through the gallery. Brockley's voice, low but urgent, called, "Madam!"

I retreated in haste, closing doors after me, and

met him in the gallery, advancing with a rapid and soldierly step.

"Redman's coming, madam. Seems he's not having a sleep, as you thought he'd be. I heard him downstairs, telling someone he was going up in a moment to light the fire in the gallery."

"A pox on Redman," I said roundly. Brockley raised his eyebrows and I shook my head at him. "It's no good disapproving of my language, Brockley. I'm annoyed. I'll never get another chance like this. The Masons don't go out often, according to the maids."

However, there was no help for it. I dared not be in the study while Redman was nearby. He might easily come in for some reason. With Brockley, I hurried back through the gallery and into the schoolroom. Brockley, however, stopped short at the further door and motioned me to wait. Peering over his shoulder, I saw Ann's maid, the ailing Tilly, wraithlike as ever in one of her grey gowns, appear from the direction of the east wing and drift noiselessly past towards the staircase. We let her go before stepping out of the schoolroom, and instantly found ourselves face to face with Redman, who was already coming up the back stairs, carrying a lit candle.

There was nothing for it but to step aside and let him pass, and try to look as though everything were ordinary, but I knew that my face was burning and could only hope that the dull afternoon would not reveal it.

"There's a good fire in the parlour, Mrs. Blanchard," he said as he went by, "but the master said the family would sit in the gallery when he and mistress got home. Company's expected. If I light the fire there now, it may be warm enough by evening." I saw him glance curiously at my face. The afternoon was evidently not quite dull enough. He went on into the schoolroom and his footsteps retreated through the gallery.

Brockley, stepping quietly back into the schoolroom, looked into the gallery, keeping himself out of sight. Equally quietly, he returned. "He went past the hearth and on into Mr. Mason's anteroom, madam. He left the door open and I watched him. I think he wanted to see if the couch had been disturbed."

"*What?*" I gave Brockley a sharp look. His face was so naturally inexpressive that it was difficult to tell when he was serious and when he was amused. If Brockley made a joke, there was usually an appreciable pause before anyone realised it, but I knew him well, and now I recognised the glint of laughter in the blue-grey depths of his eyes. I frowned, and the glint disappeared.

"I'm extremely sorry, Brockley," I said coolly. "I shall mention this to Dale. I wouldn't like her to be upset by silly tattle. Or you, either!"

Brockley inclined his head politely and said no more, and neither did I. In my strange, unladylike profession, there were, alas, all too many pitfalls.

CHAPTER 9

Chasing Shadows

I had not been caught. Nothing had happened except that in Redman's eyes I probably had a damaged reputation. But I had been frightened of the task to start with and my failure shook me to an absurd degree. How, in this sort of household, could I possibly find a safe patch of time in which to conduct my search? I could not as yet even think of trying again. I told Brockley and Dale that they could go off duty until the following morning.

"I'll unbutton my own sleeves tonight," I said to Dale. "For now, I'm going to sit in the parlour, if it really is warm."

It was. I fetched the doublet I had been repairing and made myself at home by the fire, on a cushioned settle. Threading my needle, I drew Ann's haphazard domestic atmosphere round me like a cosy old mantle. The girls were still out riding, and until they returned I could be quiet.

I worked for some time. My hands trembled at first but presently I grew calmer. When the maid Jennet came in with a woodbasket to see if the fire needed tending, I was stitching industriously, and hoped I looked as though I had never heard of Mary Stuart and wouldn't know a lock-pick from a ladle. Jennet greeted me in amiable fashion.

"Oh, there you are, ma'am. It's been that quiet all afternoon, with the master and mistress away to Maidenhead. Do you want another log on that fire?"

"If you would, Jennet."

"There's a good blaze now up in the gallery, if you want a change, ma'am."

"Even with a fire it's cold up there," I said. "I believe we may be sitting there later but I shall take an extra shawl. A place of that size really needs a good fire every day to keep it anything like comfortable."

I was speaking casually, and Jennet's response flabbergasted me. Turning scarlet, she all but glared at me, and said, "The master's not tightfisted, ma'am, begging your pardon. The Masons just can't afford waste!"

"Jennet, I didn't mean . . ."

If Jennet had a certain resemblance to a bovine, it was now a cow about to charge in defence of its calf. I also noticed with interest that, presumably because I had been teaching the girls more or less as a paid governess would, I didn't have quite the status of a genuine guest of the Masons. Jennet might address me as "ma'am" but she was prepared to take me to task.

"The gallery hearth gobbles fuel, the master says." Jennet knelt and poked the parlour fire quite fiercely. "He wouldn't have fires up there at all, but in winter the place'd get damp without 'em. So the family sit there now and again, just to keep it aired."

"But, Jennet—"

"I've only bin here since November, but at Christmas the master give all us servants lengths of cloth for to make new clothes—linen for underthings and good warm woollen cloth for kirtles and breeches—and I had my linen and piece of cloth same as the rest, though I'd only just come. And Redman says it's the same every Christmas."

"Really, Jennet! You are being quite rude!"

Jennet stopped assaulting the fire, looked round and met my eyes. She stood up hurriedly. "I'm . . . I'm sorry, ma'am. My mam—God rest her, she's been gone since two years now—my mam allus said my tongue'd get me into trouble one day. I didn't mean . . . only I'm that grateful to the master—and the mistress—because this is a good place. Me and Joan even have a feather pillow on our bed instead of a straw one and we get enough to eat, and it just upsets me, thinking that anyone might think . . ."

"Your loyalty is very right and proper, Jennet, but you must not flare up like that. I shall not speak of this to anyone, and we'll say no more about it this time. You're very young and no doubt have much to learn, but your mother was right: you really must control your tongue."

All the same, the financial state of Lockhill could be a fruitful kind of gossip. How was I to strike a balance between quelling Jennet and encouraging her to talk? I did my best.

"I was *not*," I said, "suggesting that your master was mean. I know that isn't true. I know what stinginess is! I was brought up by an uncle who used to give his servants his castoffs every Christmas. Now, he *was* tight-fisted."

"Old clothes at Christmas, ma'am?"

"I'm afraid so. And *very* old ones, at that. I do sometimes pass on a kirtle or bodice to Dale, but they're always in respectable condition and at Christmas I gave her a length of new material."

"My Sunday gown's one the mistress passed on to me, but that was in good order too, ma'am, though I had to let a bit in to make it fit."

"Mrs. Mason is very good hearted," I said. "I am fond of her. She has many worries, I think."

"Well, that's just it." Jennet began to pile wood beside the hearth. "She needs more people in the house. That maid of hers is no more use than a sick headache, if you'll excuse me. Mr. Mason could do with another man about the place, as well. I've heard him say so. But he said, with the children to bring up, they've just got to make do where they can."

"I must tell him to make use of Brockley's services if that would help," I remarked. "Brockley is very reliable."

"He uses Dr. Crichton mostly," Jennet said. "The master's always caught up in something. I hear him talking now and then and I don't understand half what he talks about; I just marvel at it. He's a wonderful man. He's always thinking about deep things and he don't like being disturbed, so Dr. Crichton gets sent on errands. Thomas is allus wanted round the stables."

"Thomas is interested in you, isn't he?" I said.

"*Him!*" Jennet tossed a white-capped head disdain-fully. "I can hardly put my nose outside the kitchen door but he's there, trying it on with me. He's a nuisance. I wish the master *would* send him off on errands sometimes!"

"Is Crichton ever sent to London?" I asked idly, threading a new colour into my needle.

Jennet was too inexperienced to wonder why I had rebuked her one moment and then begun to chat to her in this over-friendly fashion. To her, wanting to talk was as natural as breathing. "Oh yes, twice since I've been here," she said. "I think he likes it. Gives him a rest from those boys. I think they get on his nerves."

"I daresay," I said.

A vague idea had formed in my head although I couldn't quite see how it could help, and it wouldn't be easy to follow up, either. Meanwhile, I dangled another conversational bait, just to see what would happen.

"Jennet," I said, "I have a small daughter, boarded out with friends not far from London—near Hampton, in fact. If I wanted to send a letter and didn't want to spare Brockley, is there any messenger I could use? I believe there was a man called Dawson who used to carry messages for folk in this part of the world. I can't recall who told me, but is it so?"

"Dawson? Oh, him. Yes, ma'am, there was a Jack Dawson used to come round selling knives and needles and ribbon lengths and whatnot. The mistress said he'd deliver letters if you paid him, if he didn't have to go too far out of his way. I wouldn't know, not being able to write. He was a funny sort of fellow with a . . . a kind of shuttered-up face." Jennet was not unobservant, in her way. "I didn't like him. I remember once I asked him to wait in the hall while I told the master he was here, and when I went back to say Mr. Mason was just coming, he'd wandered off into the dining room and I swear I see him listening at the door to the back room. There was someone in there, talking, though I don't know who. He moved away quick when he heard me come in, but not quite quick enough. He was a snooping sort of fellow. He hasn't been round for a while now, though, and I did hear that he'd died."

"Oh, dear. All right, Jennet. I'll think about it and perhaps ask the Masons. That's enough wood, I think."

This time I was dismissing her, and she obediently went. I sat on over my needlework, thinking. So Dawson listened at doors. His discovery at Lockhill was probably something overheard, rather than something seen or read. I longed to know what it was, as a matter of curiosity as well as for the practical reason that I needed the information myself.

I gazed into the fire, frowning. What of the idea I had had while I talked to Jennet? It wasn't much of a notion but it was my only brainwave so far. I must think about it. I admitted to myself that I would rather do that than tackle Mason's desk again. This was craven, but there it was.

I snipped a last bit of frayed embroidery out of the doublet on my lap. If I concentrated, I would finish this task in another half an hour.

When you start probing for information, you never know what you'll learn. While talking to Jennet, I had picked up one further—albeit useless—piece of interesting information.

Unless I were much mistaken, the newest Lockhill maidservant was spurning the advances of Thomas the groom, not so much because she didn't like him (though I could understand it if so), but because she was wildly in love with Leonard Mason, whose mental processes were as far beyond her grasp as the moon in the sky, and to whom she was merely an inefficient menial who muddled up his desk.

Poor Jennet.

The Masons returned at dusk, and I joined them in the gallery, where we were to sit that evening and take supper. It was candlelit and reasonably warm by now, as long as one had plenty of stout clothing, sat within six feet of the hearth and didn't venture into any of the window bays. These were almost little rooms in their own right, and in summer must be pleasant, since they looked outward, not into the yew garden between the wings, but over a knot garden with geometric flowerbeds enclosed by low hedges of box.

That evening, I had my first social encounter with Dr. Forrest, the short, plump vicar of Lockhill and occupant of the vicarage which so overshadowed the tiny church of St. Mark's to which it was attached. He had given a brief, comforting sermon on Sunday, and I had taken to him.

Dr. Forrest was dressed in a formal gown of charcoal-coloured velvet; in fact, we were quite a smart gathering. I was in my pale green damask, and Ann in a becoming shade of rose. She must have used the same roll of material for the girls, for they were dressed to match their mother. The boys wore their black velvet

Sunday breeches and doublets, which made them look older. George was on the verge of manhood, I saw, growing into adult proportions, and with a faint down on his upper lip. He would, I thought, become more of a challenge to his tutor's authority every day, and Philip wasn't far behind. I almost pitied Crichton.

I had finished Mason's fawn doublet in time and he came to supper wearing it. He unbent enough to thank me for what he called my exemplary work. I didn't know whether either of the Masons had spoken to Crichton about his clothes, but he too had made an effort that evening. Instead of his usual ancient black gown, he had put on a dark brown doublet and hose, sombre and quite well worn, but neat. His attitude to me, however, remained acid. Ann remarked on my skill at both dancing and embroidery, and Crichton replied that dancing was of course a required accomplishment at court. His tone implied that this naturally made it questionable.

Forrest was amused. A broad grin appeared on his round face. "Brave of you!" he said to me. "I understand that George and Philip are your pupils for dancing, as well as the girls. I hear that they are a wild lot, apt to rush headlong out of the schoolroom if their studies bore them, and the boys are the ringleaders. I hope they don't serve you in such a way, Mrs. Blanchard."

Crichton looked annoyed and I realised that Forrest had intended this. They represented opposing Churches and therefore they were rivals.

Goblets of wine had been set out for us and I took one, calmly. "Dancing is an amusement. I expect that makes a difference," I said.

"I am tired of hearing about the misdemeanours of my offspring. I long for the day when they are grown up and know how to behave," said Mason. "Now, how about some music before we eat?"

"Mrs. Blanchard," said Ann, "can we persuade you to play the spinet for us?"

There were two spinets in the house, one in the gallery and one in a music room downstairs. According to Ann, the instrument downstairs had been built by Leonard Mason himself, helped by his friend the former music master. I had tried it and found it poor in tone. The gallery spinet, however, was good. I was only a moderate performer, but being anxious to please, I played a piece which I had learned at court, a sparkly tune, but with comparatively simple fingering.

"Oh, I did like that!" Pen exclaimed. "It was merry."

"You could learn it," I said. "It's well within your compass. You've had a good grounding. I believe," I added casually to her parents, "that Pen has talent. Tell me, have you considered arranging for her to visit other households, perhaps places where she might hear really excellent playing, to give her a standard to reach for?"

"We have thought of it," said Ann. Never idle, she was working on some coarse darning, the sort which could be done by candlelight. Her hands moved competently, drawing the wool in and out. "But we do not have a wide acquaintance, you know. We are not fashionable people."

"A visit to France could benefit her," Crichton remarked. "A stay in a convent there, for instance. The best nunneries offer music and needlework to a high standard. There is an abbey near Orléans which has a very good name. The young widowed queen is at Orléans just now. If you were to go there this summer, you might catch a glimpse of her."

"She'll have gone home to Scotland by then," said Forrest coolly. "There are indeed many fine sights to be seen in France, but Mary Stuart won't be one of them for long."

"I don't want to go to France," said Penelope mutinously, "and I don't want to stay in a nunnery. I want to go to court when I'm old enough."

"Mrs. Mason," I said, cutting across this, "I have only just arrived and it is ridiculously soon to talk of going away again, if only for a short time, but it occurs to me that I might do so, with advantage to both myself and to Penelope."

Ann lowered her work to her knee. "Whatever do you mean?"

"You are aware," I said, "that I have a small daughter, boarded at the moment with Master Henderson, who escorted me here, and his wife. They live near Hampton—"

"You have a child, then, Mrs. Blanchard? How charming," Dr. Forrest broke in. "And you are one of the Queen's ladies, so Mrs. Mason has told me. The Queen should marry soon and follow your example. The sooner she has an imp of her own, the better for us all."

He beamed round at Crichton and the Masons, none of whom looked as if they agreed with him. There was definitely more to Dr. Forrest than met the eye, I thought.

I smiled. "Well, my imp—her name is Meg—is in an excellent household. The Hendersons are cultured and kind, and their house, Thamesbank, is beautiful. They often entertain good company."

"Are you asking if you may visit your daughter?" enquired Mason. "But of course. You are free to come and go, just as you wish."

"I did, however, undertake to help instruct your girls," I said. "I have a sense of obligation. I could hardly descend on the Hendersons with three little girls, but I might do so with one not so little one—in this case, Penelope. I could make a visit to Meg part, as it were, of my course of instruction for Pen. If Penelope came with me, she would hear the best music, and see for herself how life is conducted in a house of high social standing."

"The Hendersons," said Mason, "are no doubt Anglican. I beg your pardon, Dr. Forrest, but you are familiar with the beliefs held in this house."

"Oh, quite, but I take it that the visit would be brief. I doubt," said Forrest, "if Pen would come to much harm. It isn't like measles," he added, his voice bland, although his face was creased with laughter. "You can't catch it."

"I should like to go," said Penelope, joining in on my side and gazing at her father with pleading eyes.

"Most decidedly not," said Mr. Mason. "I couldn't think of allowing it. That is my last word."

It cast a blight over the evening, and especially over me. I had hoped that the excuse of furthering Pen's education would get me back to Hampton and then to London, without arousing the interest of anyone at

Lockhill who might be watching me. I might then pursue the curious idea which had occurred to me while I was talking to Jennet. I had failed so far to investigate the study. It was high time that I achieved something!

Admittedly, thinking about it, I couldn't see how any plot could become dangerous very quickly. As long as the Queen did not marry Dudley—which I knew she wouldn't do—then no rising against her was likely to succeed. All the same, I was very aware of Mary Stuart, over there on the other side of the Channel—and if she came to Scotland, she'd be even closer.

When the door at the end of the gallery opened to admit a little procession consisting of Redman, Mrs. Logan and Joan with trayloads of supper, the chill draught which entered with them was like a cold reminder of the outside world.

I looked round at our little gathering near the hearth. We sit here, I thought, in what looks like a cosy domestic world: Ann Mason is darning stockings; Forrest is making little digs at Crichton and his host; Crichton and Mason allude openly to their beliefs— they feel safe here. Anyone would think the wider world, with its perils, its temptations, its hungry ambitions and its ghastly power of bursting into quiet private lives and wrecking them, didn't exist.

I sipped my wine, glad of its warmth, knowing all too well how real that wider world was, and brooding about it until my reverie was broken by Leonard Mason, asking Redman to put a fresh supply of candles in his study.

"I shall be in and out of it a good deal over the next few days, by night as well as by day, I expect."

"You're designing a new version of your gliding engine, I believe," said Dr. Forrest.

"Not only that," said Leonard. "I'm also designing a catapult with which to propel it off the tower roof."

Ann gave one of her sighs. I sighed too, for a different reason. Even if I could find the courage to attempt once more to search Mason's study, my chances of doing so seemed, for the next few days, to be nonexistent.

That night, I was sorry I had sent Dale to spend the night with Brockley. As I was going to bed, I experienced a most terrible surge of jealousy. The maid was going to sleep with her husband while I, her mistress, must lie alone and yearn, uncomforted. I could have hated her for it.

I settled myself in bed and tried to push these thoughts away, but I couldn't sleep, even though I had taken my usual soothing posset. For one thing, I was feeling guilty. I had failed to examine Mason's study properly, and because I had escaped being caught only by a narrow margin, I had let myself be frightened out of even trying to create a new opportunity. I had given way to fear, in a manner most inappropriate for a professional spy.

Last year, I had convinced myself that I was brave. I had ridden boldly into danger then, on a quest of my own, and carried it through. But I had done it in hot blood, angry because a manservant of mine had been killed in my service. Now I was learning that action in hot blood is one thing, and that to walk into danger in cold blood is quite different, especially when one is longing to be somewhere else, anyway.

Suddenly, I sat up. This would not do. I must overcome my fears and do the work I had come here for. Surely, I thought, *surely*, Leonard Mason would not go to his study tonight? He had been out all day and entertained guests in the evening; even Mason must be human enough to need sleep sometimes. I groped for the tinderbox on the table by my bed, lit a candle and put on my slippers and bedgown. I would brave the darkness and investigate that study forthwith.

My hand was on the latch of my door when I heard, once more, the sound which had woken me on my first night here. Somebody in sloppy footwear was approaching from the wing where the Masons slept. Holding my candle well away, so that its light would not show, I opened my door a crack.

Leonard Mason, also carrying a candle, dressed just as I was in a loose bedgown, and with his feet in a pair of ancient, down-at-heel slippers, walked past my door and went into the schoolroom, only a few feet away, shutting the door behind him. I stepped out and listened, and heard the door to the gallery open and close as well. I knew where he was going: straight through the gallery to his anteroom and the study beyond. He had gone to his desk after all. Never was there a man more devoted to his intellectual interests than Leonard Mason. I had once more avoided being caught only by a hair's breadth.

I went back to bed, shaking.

How I was ever going to get into that study now, or

even dare to try, I couldn't imagine. I might as well go back to the court, for all the use I was at Lockhill. The only thing I could possibly do was follow up my idea of the afternoon, even if I couldn't use Pen's education as an excuse for visiting Thamesbank so soon. Could the idea lead anywhere? Was it worth trying?

I tried to think it out, but found my mind drifting waywardly off on another path. I had a weird feeling that events were pulling me in too many different directions and that I was no longer sure who I was. I had been sure enough in the past: I had been the lovechild of my mother, brought up on sufferance in Faldene; later I had been wife to Gerald Blanchard, rising young man in the employ of Sir Thomas Gresham; and in due course, I had added to that the joy of being Meg's mother.

Now, I was . . . who? Well, Meg's mother still, but Gerald was dead and gone. Now, I was a Lady of the Queen's Presence Chamber, a temporary governess to the Mason children and the estranged wife of Matthew de la Roche, an exiled enemy of the realm. I was also an agent paid by Sir William Cecil to hunt out the likes of Matthew here in England—as well as being someone who had been inveigled by a muffled-up and unrecognisable boatman into a deserted boathouse and left there. I was too many different people, some of them quite irreconcilable.

It was time to finish with all this, I said to myself. As soon as I could, I must collect Meg and go to Matthew and become just one person: Ursula de la Roche, lady of the Château Blanchepierre in the Loire Valley. If I did not, my mind would somehow come apart.

I wondered if Queen Elizabeth, torn between her duty as queen and her own longings as a woman— between the urgings of her council, who wanted her to marry, and certain horrors engendered by her terrifying childhood—ever felt like this. To think of Elizabeth, I found, was steadying. My task here in Lockhill was for her, and when I thought about her, it was as if I had been groping my way down a steep staircase in the dark, and had suddenly put my hand on a secure rail. Where Elizabeth was concerned, I knew who and what I was. I was in her service and must not fail her.

With that, my muddled ideas clarified. I could not go to Matthew yet, and it wasn't safe to invade the study just now, either. I would go to Thamesbank. I would take the opportunity of seeing Meg. I would find out whether Cecil had carried out the enquiries I had suggested, and I would follow up this other idea of mine. I might be chasing shadows but I could only separate shadows from reality by making the attempt.

I slept.

CHAPTER 10

Tapestries and Angels

I wasted little time the next morning on making excuses. At breakfast, I simply announced that I had decided to visit my daughter Meg anyway and would be away for a few days.

"Oh dear," said Ann. "Will you be coming back, Mrs. Blanchard? I've been so thankful to have you. Jane showed me some of her embroidery yesterday and you've done wonders with her already."

"But of course Mrs. Blanchard must visit her daughter if she wishes," said Leonard Mason severely. "And she must not be pressed to come back against her will."

"I wouldn't dream of asking her to come back against her will, but I'll certainly be glad to see her if she wants to come," said Ann, quite sharply, making me wonder if she wasn't perhaps a stronger character than she usually seemed.

"I intend to return, and quite soon," I said. "I'll set tasks for the girls before I go and ask Pen to see that they are carried out. Pen is old enough to take responsibility now. It will be good for her."

"I can't understand," remarked Crichton, "why, since I believe you are here in order to rest from your court duties, Mrs. Blanchard, you are not staying with the Hendersons, with your daughter."

I had wondered whether anyone would think of asking that. "One cannot impose," I said. "The Hendersons have shown great kindness in fostering Meg, and there is little I can do in return. Here, at least, I can help teach the children. Call it pride, if you will. Also, it is best for Meg not to grow used to my company for long periods at a time. She will so rarely be able to have it."

"Oh, how sad it is that you have no proper home in which to rear your daughter yourself!" Ann exclaimed.

"No doubt Mrs. Blanchard finds compensations in the interest and freedom of court life," said Mason in a frigid voice. I would be glad to be away from that coldness for a while, I thought.

I took Brockley and Dale, Dale initially riding Mouse, the brown gelding which Rob had lent her and had left at Lockhill for her to use if necessary. We took small amounts of clothing, in saddlebags, and no pack-horse, and we travelled post, changing horses at Maidenhead. We reached Thamesbank easily that same afternoon.

Mattie and Rob were pleased, if surprised, to see me and I found Meg in splendid health, playing with the Henderson children in their big nursery, under the eye of the Henderson nurse and Meg's nurse, Bridget. My daughter ran to me excitedly when I entered the room and then, remembering her manners, stopped short just as she reached me and curtsied. I scooped her up for a hug. "My lovely girl." Never had I wished so much that I could be simply a mother visiting her child.

But I was here on darker business, whether I liked it or not. Mattie Henderson left me in the nursery, saying I should join her in the parlour when I was ready, and for an hour I played with Meg, asked about her lessons and heard her sing a song she had been learning. But at last, perforce, I had to return to my hosts. Promising to return at bedtime and hear her say her prayers, I kissed her and then went to the parlour where the Hendersons awaited me, with Dale. Mulled wine and a filling dish of eels in a herb sauce were brought in for myself and Dale, and Rob Henderson, sitting relaxed on a settle and watching us, asked the question I expected.

"Something to report?"

"No, not that. But I am anxious to find something out," I said. "Two things, in fact. To begin with, I sent word to Cecil a few days ago, saying I thought someone at Lockhill might be suspicious of me and asking if anyone at this end could have been . . . indiscreet."

"Or acting as an informer?" enquired Rob.

"Exactly. Has Cecil made enquiries, do you know?"

"Oh, yes," Rob said. "I would have told you, before many minutes had passed. You've forestalled me. The enquiries have been made and the results were interesting—but not very useful, I'm afraid."

"Really? How do you mean?"

"I mean," said Rob, "that we think there was an informer in Cecil's household. You've met him. I believe he collected you from the court the last time you dined there. Cecil thought of him at once. A well-spoken youth called Paul Fenn. His father is dead now, but he was known to be a Catholic sympathiser."

"Paul Fenn!" I remembered him well: the thick fair hair under the dashing cap; the mixture of respect and complete self-confidence; the handsome young face; the beautiful teeth, and the one front tooth that over-lapped its neighbour.

"We think so," Rob said. "Cecil began by questioning other members of his household about Fenn's movements at certain times. The very first thing to emerge was that Fenn had been seen walking in the street with a Dr. Ignatius Wilkins. Lady Mildred's maid knew Wilkins by sight because she was with her mistress when the Cecils met Wilkins in a merchant's warehouse. It appears that Sir William has certain suspicions about Wilkins."

"Yes, he has. He told me so."

"It also appears," said Rob, "that some of the correspondence between Lady Mildred and the Masons, arranging for you to go there, was left about on various occasions. Of course, it said nothing of your real mission to Lockhill, but if Fenn saw it and was impolite enough to read it, he might have wondered why Lady Mildred was taking great care to imply that the Cecils didn't know you well, when, of course, they do."

"Members of Cecil's household would know that I was on visiting terms in Canon Row," I agreed. I began to think aloud. "If the letters contradicted that, it would certainly look odd. And if Fenn somehow had knowledge of a conspiracy in Lockhill—or was even part of it—and if he spoke of this to Wilkins, and

Wilkins is part of it too . . . What did Fenn himself say? I take it he was questioned?"

"No," said Rob. "That's why I said that the enquiries haven't been very useful. He's disappeared. We assume that he heard that his fellow servants were being asked about him. When Cecil sent for him, he couldn't be found. The quarry has escaped and taken his knowledge with him."

"Which leaves us no further on," I said. "And I've so far failed to examine Mason's papers. Well, well. All mystery and no solution; that's how it seems. But I do have one other idea, though I can't be sure that it will be any use. That's the other reason why I'm here, Rob: I need your help. I believe a certain untruth has been told and I want to know by whom and why. What I need is . . ."

There was a mist on the Thames. From the centre of the river, the banks were mere shadowy outlines, and grey moisture had beaded thickly on our clothes and on the fair hair showing beneath Rob Henderson's hat. The cold was intense. Although we wore thick cloaks and gloves and fleece-lined boots, our noses were mauve and I could hardly feel my feet.

The Hendersons' barge had a tiny cabin amidships, and in sheer mercy to Dale, I had sent her to shelter there, and sent Brockley with her. Rob and I, however, remained outside. The rowers' oars dipped and swung in unison, and Rob glanced round at them, making sure that he couldn't be overheard, before remarking, "I hope I did right to arrange this. Cecil could have had Bernard Paige interrogated."

"I doubt if Paige is guilty of anything," I said "and besides, it's all so vague as yet. In any case, it might get known, if he were questioned. We mustn't scare the game away."

"Is that a pun?" Rob asked, surprising me. "You don't want to scare the game, you say. Do you look on all this as in some measure—a game? An amusement?"

"Of course not!" I said, and then wondered if there wasn't some truth in it. There was a part of me which did enjoy the hunt. Would I, could I, ever, really, be the Ursula I wanted to be, Matthew's wife and Meg's mother?

Kingston lay behind us, and as we passed Richmond Palace we began to feel the silent power of the ebbtide. I could make out the vague outline of the palace on the right bank, and the flicker of candlelight in some of the windows. In such weather, candles were as necessary by day as by night.

"I'm just doing what I have undertaken to do," I said. "I'm doing it for the Queen. I only wish I were doing it more competently. At the moment," I said, "I feel as though I'm sailing into a mist, in more senses than one!"

It is a long journey by river from Hampton to London Bridge. We slid past Whitehall, and there, too, candlelight glinted through the fog. The place wasn't empty just because the Queen wasn't in residence: it was being cleaned. An army of maids and scullions with brooms and buckets was busy in there. There were also supervisors and guards, sanitary engineers emptying out the cesspits, clerks to issue wages to everyone and query the bills of the sanitary engineers, and cooks to cater for them all.

After the palace, came the backs of the big houses along the Strand, with private jetties jutting into the water. We glided on past Westminster Abbey, going more slowly and bearing to port, taking care, for there was traffic on the river now. A lighter carrying livestock was waiting to go upstream when the tide turned, and assorted vessels were moored at the banks. Tall timber buildings appeared.

We came to rest beside a massive landing stage, under the bows of a merchant ship already berthed there. The tide was well down, and the supports of the stage, dripping wet and green with weed, stood skeletally clear of the water. Wooden steps, also wet but clear of weed, led upwards.

Rob put his hands round his mouth and halloo'd, and figures appeared at the top of the steps. "Master Robert Henderson and Mistress Blanchard and party!" Rob shouted.

One of the vague figures on the stage called for the painter to be thrown up, and another, with a more authoritative voice, bade us make our way up the steps, and to take care with our footing. Dale and Brockley came out of the cabin and we all climbed up to the landing stage.

A big, auburn-bearded man announced himself volubly as Bernard Paige, in person: what a cold, abominable day this was; come in, come in, that way, along the landing stage and through the door straight ahead; rowers in at that door to the left, please.

Paige was clad in a thick mulberry velvet gown with three heavy gold chains across his chest, and a mulberry velvet cap with a huge emerald brooch in it. The door through which he whisked us led to a warm reception room in one of the tall riverside houses, and only when we were out of the weather did he allow Henderson to introduce us. He offered us seats and called for wine for everyone. I had beckoned Dale and Brockley to come with us and not go in by the rowers' entrance, and goblets were provided for them, too.

"You must all be cold," Paige declared. "You've come a long way on the river, and in this chill mist! Make yourselves at home!"

The reception room had a coal fire, candles, numerous padded stools and settles, tapestried walls. The tray the manservant brought held chased silver goblets, with wine in a matching flagon and cakes on a matching dish. Our host poured the wine himself and told the manservant to take charge of our out-door cloaks.

Rob sat down beside me and I said into his ear, "I wonder if he gives all his customers this kind of welcome? I know I'm pretending to be rich, but most of his customers are. Anyone would think from this that I was Queen Elizabeth in disguise!"

"If he thought that, the landing stage would be covered in blue carpet! No. The man I sent to make the appointment didn't only say you were wealthy, he also stressed that I am a friend of the Cecils. I expect the name of Cecil worked most of the magic."

Paige, settling himself in a carved armchair, raised

his own goblet. "To your very good health, my friends. And as soon as you're warmed through and refreshed," he added, "we will go through to the warehouse where I have my best merchandise on display. Meanwhile, tell me precisely what you are looking for."

Smoothly, I said, "I have more than one errand. To begin with, I require a few lengths of damask to make gowns for my daughter and myself. These, I hope to choose today. But I am also considering a much bigger purchase. I am shortly to lease a property and will need some new furnishings. I shall not actually buy anything until the lease is signed, but I want to see what is available. I should like, Master Paige, to examine some tapestries."

Cecil had said that Paige virtually lectured people about his wares, and Cecil was right. While we ate and drank, our host held forth with enthusiasm on his merchandise. He had damasks and brocades from Florence, Venice, the Levant. Did we know that not all silk, these days, came from the East? The Sicilians had a silk industry second to none. As to tapestries, did I wish to commission new designs or buy ready-mades? For new designs, he could make arrangements for me with the best workshops in Flanders or Italy, but if I cared to look at his unrivalled stock of readymades . . .

Getting a word in with some difficulty, I said, "Commissioning new work takes up so much time," and tried to look as though time, and not a severe shortage of gold, were the reason why I wasn't ordering custom-made wallhangings by the furlong. "I am quite prepared," I said, "to purchase readymades of good quality. I think—"

Master Paige, aglow at the prospect of a major sale, broke in to assure me that I had come to the right place. Nothing in his warehouse was of any quality but the best. What had I in mind? Narrative designs? Some pleasing verdures, all leaves and greenery, perhaps, for the bedchambers?

"Narrative designs," I said firmly, interrupting in my turn. "I have recently seen a couple of very fine narrative tapestries, copies of—"

"But you must see for yourself. Have you finished your wine? Then come through to my display room," Master Paige exclaimed. "Come!"

The room to which he led us, by way of a creaking wooden passage and a low door, was startling. It was as wide and lofty as a church and as colourful as a rainbow. It had a fireplace and a row of high windows, and a set of wide doors which presumably gave on to the river and were the entrance through which newly arrived goods could be winched up from ships. Otherwise, the walls were largely hidden by shelves packed with fabrics in all the colours God ever invented, and with whole façades of tapestries and carpets, some of them partly furled on rollers, some fully displayed.

A gallery, reached by a slatted spiral staircase, allowed close examination of items hung high up, and there was a counter on one side of the room, with stools ranged beside it, where customers could look at the wares in comfort.

The building was mostly timber, though the floor and the surround of the fireplace were of stone. In the few places where the walls were visible, they were of pale gold wood which added to the glow of colour. The floor was well swept and a grey daylight fell from the windows. Lamps hung on lamp-stands and there was a small fire in the hearth, watched over by a young apprentice.

"My goods must not get damp," said Master Paige. "The river is a blessing in one way since it carries ships, but a curse in another, since it breeds these pestilential mists. *Christopher!* Where are you?" He raised his voice, and a young man who was almost a youthful edition of Bernard himself, except that he was much thinner, appeared as if conjured, hurrying down the spiral stairs from the gallery.

"This is my son," said Paige. "Christopher, here are Mistress Ursula Blanchard and Master Robert Henderson, friends of Sir William Cecil." Christopher bowed courteously, and his father beamed. "Now, shall we begin with the damasks? They are for you and your daughter, you say, Mistress Blanchard. What is your daughter like?"

"Not yet six," I said. "With dark hair."

"She must take after you, Mistress," said Christopher Paige politely.

"Mainly after her father, I think. He, too, was dark haired, and her eyes are brown, like his." My own were hazel. "Her complexion is like mine, though," I said.

Bernard Paige was studying me, not rudely, but with impersonal assessment, as though I were a tapestry which had to be hung in the best light. I realised that behind the endless cascade of words was a rockface of sound knowledge.

"Good clear colours," he said thoughtfully. "Rose or crimson; golden yellow or emerald green, but if green, the shade *must* be jewel-bright. Best avoid green, perhaps. That cream and tawny you are wearing now, mistress, is made of fine material but does not do you justice, in my opinion. Now, I have some excellent materials at only twenty-six shillings a yard." Being accustomed to court standards, Dale and I received this news stoically, but Brockley's eyebrows rose. "Bring out examples of the shades we have mentioned, Christopher, excepting only the green. Master Henderson, can I show you anything? Something for your wife, perhaps?"

Rob asked to see some brocades. Christopher, who clearly did the most active work, set about keeping any inherited obesity at bay by hurrying to fetch out rolls of material and bringing a ladder to reach a row of shelves just below the gallery. While he was thus engaged, I asked if Master Paige would show me the tapestries.

"Master Henderson can choose his brocades meanwhile and Dale can select some damasks for me to look at presently. If that's all right, Master Paige?"

"But of course!" said Paige, beaming anew. "Here, lad!" He called to the boy tending the hearth. "Come along and listen. Learn something about tapestries. That's how they learn," he added to me. "By hearing me talk to customers. Now, let me show you what I have."

He led the way towards some hangings on the far wall of the display chamber, and I followed, feeling like a fraud. The money he thought he was going to make out of me was fairy gold, but I must keep up the pretence.

"I particularly wanted to see *you*," I said, "because lately, in the house of Sir William Cecil, I noticed some copies of the *Unicorn Hunt* series of tapestries. I believe he bought them from you and I wondered if you had any more like them. The weaver was a man named Hans van Hoorn and the workshop was that of Giorgio Vasari, in Florence."

"Ah. Yes, I remember Sir William buying those. Alas, van Hoorn has been making readymades for only a short while, and even he, skilled though he is, cannot produce more than a limited amount of work in such a short time," Paige said. "Though I took all he did make, and those of the other weavers employed at the same time on similar tapestries. In fact, as far as the workshop is concerned, the readymades scheme is as much mine as theirs. When I was in Florence two years ago, I presented the idea to the workshop manager and we made an arrangement under which they would hire weavers and copy some famous works—we agreed on a list—and I would buy up the results. That way, I would carry most of the risk.

"The poor merchant always has to take the risk, Mistress Blanchard. Such is life! A wrong guess about customers' preferences, and we're left with goods that must be sold at a loss. A ship goes down in a storm and we have no goods at all, so our customers go elsewhere and maybe don't come back! I've seen a reverse or two in my time, and my father before me. So will Christopher, when he takes over. And you, very likely, my lad," he added to the apprentice.

"Did you guess right this time, Master Paige?" I asked.

"So it seems! All the van Hoorns have gone and I will have no more until next year. I still have some of the other weavers' work, however. For instance, observe these pretty single wallhangings in the mille-fleurs style." He pointed to a heraldic fantasy, showing a young woman in armour, Joan of Arc fashion, riding a unicorn and escorted by flying gryphons, against a background of little red and yellow flowers. A similar panel beside it had a white stag standing poised against a pattern of tiny pink and azure blooms.

"Those are by a man quite as good as van Hoorn, and if you prefer narratives—you mentioned narratives, did you not?—well, up in the gallery I have a delightful series of five panels by this same weaver, depicting the story of the Wedding at Cana. How many rooms do you want to provide with wallhangings? How much wall is to be covered?"

I hadn't thought this out. Clearly, I had much still to learn about lying and imposture. I murmured something vague about a dining room, anteroom and bed-chamber and hastily invented dimensions which I hoped sounded reasonable.

"And where is your house?" Master Paige enquired as we climbed the spiral stairs, which bounced under his massive tread. "In London? Do I know it? Or would it be in Sussex? The Blanchard family live in Sussex, I believe."

He was knowledgeable all right. He was a successful merchant dealing in domestic fabrics, and probably had a map of England in his head, with little flags marking every big house and the name of the owner inscribed beside it. He was right about the Blanchards: they did live in Sussex. I must produce a good reason for not doing so myself.

"I have been widowed, Master Paige," I said, and it was not difficult to sound sad. "I wish to begin life again amid fresh scenes. My new house, if all goes well with the arrangements for the lease, will be in Oxfordshire."

"My dear Mistress Blanchard, I do apologise if I have said anything tactless!"

"It's quite all right," I said politely, but in a faintly distant tone which would discourage any further awkward questions. "It was some time ago," I added, forgivingly, as we stepped on to the gallery. "Are these the five panels you mentioned?" I had better sound as though I meant business. "Oh yes, I see. Here we have the bride and groom, seated together, and here—yes, this is clever—we have the host spreading his hands in regret because the wine has run out. Very expressive!"

Playing my part industriously, I made a few more comments about *The Wedding in Cana,* and listened while Paige, as much for the benefit of the apprentice as for me, expounded on weaving techniques, and went on to extol the virtues of some Brussels verdures. I was carrying my slate, and I brought it out and made some notes about prices, remarking that the verdures might suit my imaginary bedchamber very well.

As we descended the spiral stairs, I said casually, "If

you are the sole importer of the tapestries made by Hans van Hoorn since he joined his present workshop, I believe one of my future neighbours has been your customer recently, just like Sir William Cecil. His hangings depict the prodigal son's return. Did you supply them to him?"

Down on the ground floor, Christopher Paige had brocades and damasks all over the counter, spilling from their rolls in silken rivers. Brockley was standing politely back, but Rob Henderson and Dale were feeling fabrics with finger and thumb. Paige caught his son's eye, and Christopher, excusing himself, came to meet us.

"*The Prodigal?*" Paige was saying. "Yes, I sold that last November. I can't remember the customer's name offhand, though. Christopher, can you remember who it was that bought van Hoorn's tapestry of the Return of the Prodigal, towards the end of last year?"

"My future neighbour's name is Mason," I said.

Unexpectedly, the apprentice piped up. "I remember! Mr. Leonard Mason! But he didn't come himself: he sent some kind of servant to buy for him. A funny man, like a scarecrow, all in black!"

Christopher instantly shot out a hand and cracked the apprentice across the back of the head, though not unduly hard.

Bernard Paige said in scandalised tones, "That is no way to speak of our customers, young Dickon! Customers are to be respected!"

"Customers," said Christopher, "can come here walking on their hands like tumblers, or dressed in motley. We still don't make fun of them!"

"Get back to watching the fire, boy!" Paige barked. "I'll have more to say about this later! Though he's right, of course," he added to me, as soon as he judged that the chastened Dickon was out of earshot. "Mason did send an intermediary to make the purchase, a dominie, judging from his clothes. He was a trifle odd to look at—well, dusty, if you know what I mean—" I did—"but he recognised quality when he saw it."

"And he paid without haggling," Christopher said. "He had a purse of sovereigns and gold angels with him. He chose what he said his master would want, and paid the bill then and there. No argument about the price and no waiting for the money to be fetched from a bank. If only all customers were as obliging!"

"The man you saw sounds very like the fellow who tutors the Mason children and sometimes conducts business for Leonard Mason," I remarked. "What is his name, now? I'm sure I've heard it, but . . ."

They shook their heads. "I put the purchaser in my ledger as Mason," Bernard Paige said. "I remember now."

Raising my voice, I called to Dickon and he came back. "If you can remember the name of the fellow all in black, whom you thought looked so odd," I said, "maybe you won't get into trouble after all for calling him a scarecrow." I cocked an eye at the Paiges, father and son, and although clearly puzzled, they nodded. I was a customer and therefore must be humoured. I looked enquiringly at Dickon.

"It was Dr. something, madam," he said. "It was a funny . . ." He caught Bernard's disapproving eye.

"I mean a strange name. Sad. Cry something. Cry . . . ton! Yes, madam, that's it! Cry-ton."

"Dr. Crichton! Of course! Thank you, Dickon. You've a very good memory!" I said.

Dickon went back to tending the fire, and the Paiges gazed at me in a puzzled fashion, as if wondering why I was so interested.

"He seems a pleasant lad," I said. "I wanted to give you an excuse to let him off whatever you had in store for him for being so cheeky."

"Ah. You soft-hearted ladies. Well, he will escape with a warning this time," Bernard Paige said good humouredly. My curiosity was explained, and I had learned what I wanted: Crichton had bought those tapestries, and on behalf of Leonard Mason.

"Well," I said, "I'll come back to buy the tapestries when my lease is signed, but could I see the damasks now?"

Bernard Paige would be disappointed of a tapestry sale, but we bought several costly lengths of brocades and damasks. I had been paid rather well for my prying into de Quadra's document case, and could afford it, but if I could persuade Cecil to count it as expenses, I would.

The transactions over, we parted from the Paiges with many bows and expressions of thanks on both sides. We dined at an inn and caught the tide for home, rowing upstream through the cold, sharp-smelling fog.

This time, I went into the little cabin with Dale. There were rugs there and we sat together, muffled under them. Dale dozed, but I was trying to think.

My question had been answered, but where did it lead?

I tried to work it out. I had suspected that Mason, or Crichton, or both, had been lying about the origins of the tapestries in the Lockhill dining room, and while talking to Jennet in the parlour and hearing how Crichton ran his employer's errands, I had begun to wonder if the tutor had been sent to London to buy them for Mason. I had been right.

Yet Leonard Mason was a man who worried about the expense of lighting fires in the long gallery and hesitated to replace a spitboy. Good God!

But what did it mean? Did it necessarily mean anything sinister? And where did Crichton come in? Was he involved or was he only Mason's cat's-paw? No, he had to be involved. He evidently disliked my presence at Lockhill as much as Mason did, and he was a Catholic priest who regularly held illegal masses.

I had hoped that finding out the truth about one mystery—in this case the provenance of the prodigal son wallhangings—would somehow lead to fresh discoveries; that it would be like a pulled thread which, if tugged, unravels a knot. However, it had done nothing of the sort.

I was still fretting uselessly when I heard sharp exclamations from Henderson and Brockley, who were outside, standing in the bows. Dale did not stir, but I went out to see what was happening.

The weather was clearing. There was a wind now and the fog was lifting away, swirling like smoke past the face of a pallid sun. The exclamations I had heard were nothing to do with the weather, however.

Brockley was leaning over the bow to the port side, and as I emerged from the cabin, Henderson was picking up a boathook and ordering the barge to change course.

"What is it?" I asked.

Brockley pointed, and leaning over the bow beside him, I saw something rolling in the wash from our vessel. I glimpsed pale fabric, like soaked linen, and strands of something like weed, or hair; and then, most horribly, a face, greenish white. It was a body, still partly clad in a shirt and breeches. The breeches had held some air and kept the corpse afloat.

The barge turned, and Henderson reached with the boathook, which caught in the thing's clothing. Brockley had found another boathook and was leaning beside Rob. He recommended me brusquely to go back into the cabin but I stayed where I was, doing no more than move out of the way as the rowmaster came to their assistance. The barge did not ride high in the water and the rowmaster had long arms. He bent double, leaning over the gunwale, and the boathooks held the body firm while he got a grip on it and heaved. The dreadful object was hauled, flopping and sodden, over the side and on to the deck.

It lay on its back, staring sightlessly up at the vapours and the faint sun. I wanted to gag as I looked at it, but I wouldn't let myself. There was a dent in one side of its head but the face was still recognisable.

"But that's . . . that's . . ." Rob seemed lost for words.

I had glimpsed the face while the body was still in the water, which was why I had not gone into the cabin, but had waited, however sickened, for a closer look. I had recognised its teeth, those excellent teeth, perfect except that two of the front ones were slightly crossed. They were now bared and feral between drawn-back lips, but I had last seen them exposed in a charming smile. Their owner had had thick, fair hair and I could see that when it was dry, this poor thing's hair would be the same.

"It's the young man who was in Sir William Cecil's employ," I said. "Isn't it? The one who vanished?"

"Yes," said Rob Henderson grimly. "It's Paul Fenn."

CHAPTER 11

Council of War

On the following day, Her Majesty Queen Elizabeth took it into her head to enswathe herself in furs, travel by barge from Richmond to Hampton, and pay a visit, accompanied by her good friend the Secretary of State Sir William Cecil, to her loyal subjects, Rob and Mattie Henderson of Thamesbank.

The visit had been arranged in advance, of course, albeit very hastily. After an hour or so of carefully organised informality, the Queen and Sir William, together with Rob Henderson, repaired to Rob's study for a comfortable chat. I was invited too.

"My dear Ursula," Elizabeth exclaimed. "How delightful that one of our ladies is actually staying here just now. You shall attend on us!"

The study, unlike Leonard Mason's den, was friendly and full of colour, with crimson velvet curtains to keep out draughts, and brilliant rugs on the floor.

It was a tall room, graciously proportioned, which was to be expected, for Thamesbank was a gracious house altogether. It was not very old, and had been built in the modern style, with brick lower walls, and upper walls of white plaster and black timbering. The garden was a delight, with grassy spaces and cherry trees, a pleached lime walk, formal flowerbeds and topiary, all in a casual jumble like a tossed salad. The topiary yews, clipped into sprightly bird shapes, were dotted about, well apart. The result was ornamental without being oppressive; it was not sombre, unlike the yew garden at Lockhill, with its dark, unrelieved foliage and deep shade.

On the river side of the house was a broad sweep of grass, regularly cut (what with that and the patches of grass in the garden, the Henderson gardeners had to be as handy with the scythe as Old Father Time). The lawn extended to the river and had a path across it, leading to the jetty. From the study window we could see that the Henderson children, with Meg and the nurses, were playing on the grass, enjoying a gleam of winter sunshine. We could hear their laughter.

There was no laughter inside the study, however, where a council of war was in progress.

"I have to say, boldly," declared Rob, "that in my opinion, Mistress Blanchard should not go back to Lockhill. It's too dangerous. She is obviously under suspicion, and Paul Fenn was murdered!"

"It could have been an accident," I said.

"Jackdaw's death could have been an accident," Cecil said, "but that both of them were—no, hardly."

"There," Elizabeth said, "I must agree. At least we would be foolish to assume otherwise." She had been established in a dignified armchair, with a fur rug over her lap. Her golden-brown eyes were grave.

Elizabeth and I had a curious bond. I served her as a lady in waiting, and once, long ago, my mother had similarly served Elizabeth's—until the day came when my poor mother was sent home in disgrace, pregnant by a court gallant whom she would not name, to take shelter with her parents and produce me, the embarrassing family byblow. When her parents died, my mother stayed on with her brother Herbert Faldene and his wife Tabitha, and I was brought up with my cousins, educated—I had to admit that—but portionless, and taught to believe that my future would be as unmarried household dogsbody.

I had put an end to that notion by falling in love with Gerald Blanchard, who was due to marry my cousin Mary, and causing him to fall in love with me. We had fled together and taken refuge with some friends of Gerald's, in the town of Guildford, and there we had been married.

Our families were furious, but we were happy, and I knew that my mother, had she been still alive, would have been glad for me. She had always done her best for me, and I knew, from one or two things let fall by the Cecils, and from Elizabeth's liking for me, that she must have served Queen Anne well and with kindness.

There was a tradition of royal service in the Faldene family, so deep rooted that it amounted to an instinct. I had it, too. I was like the rope in a tug of war, with Elizabeth on one end and Matthew on the other.

Cecil was speaking. "I am quite sure that Fenn was killed, and that he was somehow involved in the mystery we are trying to solve. I would guess that when my enquiries began, he fled to his principals for advice and they decided for some reason that he was a liability. Perhaps he was threatening to throw himself on my mercy! At any rate, they disposed of him."

"Have we no idea where he went?" I asked. "It wasn't to Lockhill."

"No, and he didn't go to his old home in Sussex, where his brother has now inherited the property," said Cecil, "or to High Wycombe, where Dr. Wilkins usually lives. Rob has told you that he was seen with Dr. Wilkins? We sent men to both places very quickly: one was a travelling dentist who lost his way and called at the Sussex house for shelter, and the other was the father of a prospective pupil for Wilkins' school, wanting to inspect it. They both returned saying they were as sure as they could be that Fenn wasn't in either place. On the other hand, we did find a ferryman who took a young man answering to Fenn's description upstream on the morning he disappeared. He put him ashore, to my surprise, at a boathouse which happens to be mine—at least, I rent it and keep a barge and a dinghy in it which I'd laid up for the winter. Fenn knew of the boathouse."

"Indeed?" I said.

"I went there myself," Cecil said. "The boathouse had been tampered with, although whether by Fenn, planning an escape if he needed one, or by somebody else, for some purpose unknown, I can't say. It was very puzzling. The lock had been cut out of the land-ward door and a piece of wood nailed over the gap, and two new bolts had been fitted on the outside. None of my boatmasters could explain it, and they certainly hadn't ordered it. The dinghy had gone, and Fenn could well have taken it."

"How extraordinary!" I said. Meg's voice, calling to the others, came through the window, and I looked round Rob's study, thinking how safe and friendly it was, and how thankful I was to be there.

"It seems to me," Cecil said, "that we have enough information now to justify a swoop in Lockhill. Leonard Mason can be brought in and questioned, and if there is any written evidence in the house, we'll find it."

Oh no, I said to myself. No, I don't want this. No, please no. I heard myself say, painfully, because I didn't want to say it, and one half of Ursula was silently screaming at the other half to stop it at once, "But *have* we got enough? After all, what does it amount to?"

They all looked at me.

"We can't prove a link with Lockhill," I said. I much regretted it. I was sure in my own mind that my unpleasant experience in that boathouse was linked with this business, but the hard evidence was still lacking. I remained determined not to speak of that boathouse, since it would be very difficult to do so without admitting that I had hoped to meet Matthew. Even if I didn't say I meant to run off with him, the inference would be made. "What if you pounce," I said, "and find no evidence after all?"

"Once we have Leonard Mason in our hands," said Cecil, chillingly, "he will tell us all we need to know."

"But will he?" I asked. "He lied about those tapestries, but that isn't against the law. What if he just explains the lies away? It looks as though he has more money than he's admitting, but he could say he wanted to conceal it from creditors, or even, for some reason, from his wife! Perhaps he won it while gambling and she would object! Or she wants him to spend it on one thing and he wants to spend it on another. There could be any amount of explanations. The tapestries prove nothing."

"Ursula," said Cecil, "you have an ingenious mind. Do you yourself believe that there is a conspiracy at Lockhill?"

"There's *something*," I said. "I do think that. But this web of treason obviously extends beyond Lockhill. Fenn wasn't murdered there! Nor was Dawson. Don't we want to bring them all in? Arrest Leonard Mason before we know who the others are, and they'll be warned. If their names are written down in any compromising documents, then we might have time to seize them, but if we have to wait until we can wring them out of Mason . . ."

"They won't be warned if we move quickly and quietly," said Rob.

"And if we arrest the entire household at Lockhill and the village too?" I asked.

"What do you mean?"

"She means," said Elizabeth, following my mind with uncanny accuracy, "that this unseen organisation no doubt has its own methods of communication.

The various parties must be able to get in touch with each other. It is reasonable to suppose that someone has been given the task of passing on the news, if there is any kind of swoop on Lockhill. It could be anyone: a butler, a groom, a village youth. And, yes, the conspirators would be warned and could slip through our fingers."

"Ma'am," said Cecil reprovingly, "one of the purposes of this meeting is to decide on a course of action which will not further endanger Mistress Blanchard." Which, being translated, meant: Elizabeth, Your Majesty, beloved and wayward lady of England, whose side are you on?

"I went to Lockhill to look for written evidence," I said, "and I haven't yet managed to read Mr. Mason's papers, but what if there is nothing there to read? It may be more a matter of watching to see who comes to the house; finding out whom Leonard Mason meets. He could have gone to a conspirators' meeting under my nose, come to think of it! He and his wife went off to Maidenhead one day in the coach, to visit friends. I don't know who they were. Perhaps the ladies were left talking of children and recipes while the gentlemen talked to Mary Stuart in another room. On other occasions, though, the conspirators may come to Lockhill. I believe it's too soon for a swoop. We should have someone there, watching."

"Perhaps we should," said Rob, "but not you, Ursula. Not now. Not now that Fenn has been killed."

"Quite. This is no task for a woman," Cecil agreed.

"My father," Elizabeth observed, using the informal first person which meant that she was speaking as

Elizabeth Tudor rather than the Queen, "believed that ruling a country was no task for a woman. He suffered greatly, for lack of a son. Others suffered too." Elizabeth never spoke publicly of the mother whom my mother had served: Anne Boleyn, who had been executed by King Henry. I had once heard Elizabeth mention her mother in private, but only once. She did, however, make very occasional oblique references. This was one of them.

Cecil uttered an exasperated snort, and I said, "Sir William, let me make sure of one thing. In your house, was there anything at all in writing that Fenn could have seen, which definitely revealed that I was going to Lockhill as an agent?"

"Certainly not!" said Cecil. "That was never put in writing. I would not do such a thing."

"Nor I," said Elizabeth.

"I did discuss you with my wife on occasion," said Cecil. "I doubt if anything we said would have meant much to someone who knew nothing of the subject in hand, but to someone who had been planted there . . . I do remember that Fenn came into the room once when I was saying to my wife that although I hoped Ursula would learn something at Lockhill, I was not sanguine. That, added to the curious fact that Ursula Blanchard, described in my wife's letters to the Masons as the merest acquaintance, is known to my household as a regular visitor, could have been enough to alert him."

"More than enough," said Rob. "The guilty flee even where no man pursueth," he added sententiously. "This would seem like very obvious pursuit!"

"But as long as I am not caught prying, they can't be sure," I said. "I behaved very quietly while I was there. By now they may have decided that I am harmless after all."

"Are you saying, Ursula, that you *want* to go back there?" Cecil demanded.

"No," I said. "I'm saying that I ought to, and that perhaps the danger's not so great after all: my coming to harm at Lockhill itself would attract just the kind of attention they don't want. As long as I'm careful, I think I shall be safe enough."

"What I can't understand," said Rob, "is why Mason ever let you into Lockhill at all, if Fenn thought that there was something suspicious about you. Surely Fenn—or Wilkins—could have got word there in time for the invitation to be stopped!"

"I've wondered the same," I said, "but I think the reason is Ann Mason. She really does need help. Before I came away, she told me how thankful she had been to have me there. If she is quite innocent, and I believe she is, then Mason could have found it hard to refuse her. He wouldn't be able to explain to her, you see."

Cecil looked at Elizabeth as if imploring her to say something. She responded, but not with the words that Cecil and Rob obviously wished to hear. "It's for Ursula to say. There is no compulsion, Ursula. You have already done well. You will have your reward."

"I know of your plans to go to France," said Rob, "and I wouldn't blame you for asking leave to go at once!"

"And we would grant it, now," said Elizabeth. "If, on the other hand, Ursula, you are prepared to try again at Lockhill, I will not order against it." Her eyes were asking me to go back to Lockhill.

Both of the men burst out in protest, but I was silent. As their indignant expostulations died away, I said, "When you talked to me at your home, Sir William, you spoke of Dr. Wilkins. You told me that in the days of Queen Mary, he had two of his parishioners burned, a father and daughter. And Rob, you witnessed it. You saw their faces through the smoke."

Rob's cheerful face became drawn, startlingly so, as if a cloud from nowhere had vanquished a midsummer sun. "You know about that?"

"I told her," said Cecil.

"I'd sooner not be reminded. I never witnessed such a thing before and I hope I never will again. I got away as fast as I could but the screams followed me. I thought I'd never get out of earshot . . ." His voice faded away.

"If it isn't to happen again," I said, "if those days, when such things could happen to honest, innocent people, are not to return, then we *must* find out what is going on at Lockhill. I have to go back. Don't you see?"

I took certain steps before I returned to Berkshire, however. Later that day, when the Queen and Cecil had gone, I made a will naming the Hendersons as Meg's guardians, if for any reason I were to die. One of Rob's clerks drew it up and Dale and Brockley were witnesses. It was something I should have done long ago.

"But it won't be needed," I said, "or not on account of Lockhill. I can't promise not to catch small-pox or plague, of course. Gerald died of smallpox. It can happen to anyone."

Brave words. Inside myself, I was very much afraid of returning to Lockhill, and the desire to abandon this dangerous and unnatural way of life and simply go to Matthew, was almost unbearably strong.

I had said I would go because of a private phenomenon which, to myself, I called the small cold voice. Last year, I had taken bitter decisions because that little voice in my mind had said that the safety of a realm must come before warmer, more human, more private considerations. During our council of war, it had spoken again, telling me that my fears for myself and my longing for Matthew must give way to greater matters. And perhaps Elizabeth let me do it because she too was acquainted with a small cold voice.

It was a hard decision, for me, anyway. Since girlhood, I had in times of trouble been afflicted by violent, incapacitating headaches which would not clear until I had been sick. The day after I made my will, I woke in the morning to find myself in agony, a steel ring round my head and a hammer pounding above my left eye.

I lay in a darkened room all day, and towards evening I vomited, not once but several times. The pain eased a little and I slept that night, but I woke the following morning to find that the ghastly cycle had begun again.

At three o'clock that afternoon, I vomited again, painfully, because my stomach muscles were aching and I had nothing to bring up now except my own watery juices. After that, I recovered. During the long hours of anguish, deep within me, a battle had been fought and won.

Next day, I kissed my darling Meg farewell and set out once more for Lockhill.

CHAPTER 12

Variations on a Spinet

I returned to Lockhill on Wednesday, March 5. The weather had turned mild and sunny, with a light breeze, and this at least did something to put heart into me. I needed it, for I was having trouble with Brockley and Dale. I had never told them about Dawson, but they had been on the barge when Fenn was found and exclaimed over. They knew he had probably been murdered and that this was somehow linked with Lockhill. That, on top of the boathouse incident, made them very reluctant to return there. They obeyed orders, but under protest.

We arrived to find that strange things had happened during our absence. The top of the tower was now adorned with an extraordinary structure like a huge capital H, at least three times the height of a man, with a plank leaning against its crosspiece and lengths of rope trailing from it. George and Philip, meeting us in the courtyard, announced that this was the catapult with which their father hoped to give his new gliding engine the impetus to stay airborne. The engine was nearly finished, they said.

"Mother is upset about it," Philip told us.

"Father's thrilled, though," George said. "He didn't think he could assemble it so fast, but our old music master has paid us a visit and lent a hand. He's interested in such things. Here he is!"

"George! Philip!" A small, busy man in an amber velvet doublet and breeches came through the porch, calling their names. "Dr. Crichton is asking where you are!" He had a thin voice, and as he came towards us, I saw that he had small crumpled features, and an insignificant blob of a nose.

"Mrs. Blanchard," said George, "this is Mr. Mew who used to teach us music and still comes to see us at times. Mr. Mew, this is Mrs. Blanchard who is staying with us, and helping my sisters with their needlework. She has been visiting her own daughter briefly. Did you find your daughter well, Mrs. Blanchard? You were anxious about her, were you not?"

"I become anxious for no good reason on occasion," I said. We had all dismounted, and I nodded to Brockley to take the horses away. "Parents often do! Meg is perfectly well, I am glad to say. I had a pleasant few days with her. Good day, Mr. Mew. Mr. Barnabas Mew, is it not?"

I had half-recognised Mew before George began his introductions. I gave him my hand, and a smile, hiding my surprise. I did not know what to make of this. Was it one of the coincidences which Cecil so rightly distrusted? Or pure chance? Dr. Crichton had now also emerged from the porch. He gave me a cursory greeting, collected up the boys and marshalled them indoors.

"Dr. Crichton," said Mr. Mew, "has been helping Mr. Mason to find a school for those boys. The fees are a hindrance but Mr. Mason says he must find them somehow. I understand that the school's proprietor may actually have an errand this way soon, and if so, will call and see the boys for himself, in their own home. School is probably what those lads need. I found them very difficult, myself."

"I'm sure you're right," I said. Dismissing Brockley, I walked indoors beside Barnabas Mew, and Dale followed.

We strolled into the parlour, which was no tidier than usual, with the baby's cradle in the middle of the floor and Ann's workbox, alongside a pile of mending, occupying most of one settle. However, the fire was lit and it was warm. Dale took my cloak and disappeared, and Jennet arrived with ale for myself and Mr. Mew.

"Surely," I said to Mr. Mew, as we sipped, "we have met before. You come from Windsor, do you not?"

"Yes, indeed. I am a clockmaker there. Have you been in my shop, Mrs. Blanchard? Are you a customer?"

"No, but I saw you at court a short time ago. Did you not come to present a musical gadget to the Queen?"

"*You* have been at court?" said Mew, scanning my face intently and apparently with dismay.

"Yes, indeed! Wasn't the gadget," I said, "a little box which could be wound up and made to play a tune?"

"Oh my goodness. Oh, Mrs. Blanchard!" Barnabas

Mew, who had taken a comfortable stool, twisted about on it as though it were upholstered with nails instead of padded with a plump cushion in an embroidered cover.

"What is it?" I asked. "Mr. Mew, is something wrong?"

"My dear Mrs. Blanchard. Since you've been here, have you mentioned my visit to court, or spoken of my little musical plaything at all?"

"Well, no." I had begun to speak of it once, I recalled, but Pen had interrupted me. "No, I haven't."

"I am relieved, I must say. Oh dear, how awkward!"

"I don't understand. Of course I won't mention it if you would rather I didn't, but why not?"

"It's Mr. Mason," said Barnabas. "Oh my goodness, this is so *difficult*. He is a fine scholar—I believe his translation work, especially between English and Italian or Latin, is second to none—but he also likes to try his hand at gadgets of this kind or that. He often has good ideas, but he isn't skilled enough with his hands to make things well. He made a spinet once, with my assistance, but it was a poor effort, and then he tried to invent a new kind of spinet altogether and—oh dear. He actually built the instrument and showed it to me, but alas, it had no volume to speak of and a very flat tone. He was most disappointed, and in the end he broke it up in, well, in a temper. The design was quite good, in my opinion, but the construction was faulty, you see . . ."

Here, Mr. Mew ran out of breath and appeared to lose his thread. I made encouraging noises.

"Well, now," said Mew, "he is trying to make an

engine to fly on the wind. In fact, during the last two or three days I've been helping him as best I can. But I fear that this won't prosper either. I have the advantage of being a trained craftsman: I was apprentice to a clockmaker and goldsmith and studied both crafts for years. I had the best of masters—a hard man, mind you, heavy handed, and many a time he made me weep for my own shortcomings—but he knew his work. Now, looking back, I value every hard, weary day of my apprenticeship. I am a very simple man, Mrs. Blanchard, but I understand my craft, and my little music box is the flower of it. Leonard Mason, I fear, is no true craftsman. If he knew that I had made something that I could present to the Queen, at court, well, he might be upset."

"You mean he would be jealous?"

"Oh dear. It's a hard thing to say of anyone, but yes, jealous, that's the word. Please, Mrs. Blanchard, don't mention that you saw me at court, or say anything about my music box."

"Of course I won't, if you don't want me to," I said.

Ann came into the parlour with the baby, greeted me with much more pleasure than Crichton had done, and observed that Mew and I had introduced ourselves. She then deposited the infant Ned in the cradle, picked up her workbox and sat down on the settle beside the pile of mending.

Mr. Mew, evidently feeling uneasy amidst these feminine concerns, excused himself and went off in search of Crichton and the boys. "I still take an interest in my former pupils," he said.

Ann delved into the mending, picked up what I now

saw was her husband's blackwork doublet and began to repair a split. "I spoke to George just now and he tells me you found your daughter well. I'm so glad," she said.

I watched her worriedly. While she worked, she was rocking Ned's cradle with her foot, but Ned had started to whimper with annoyance because the motion was erratic. Then I saw that despite her efforts to stitch and rock and make ordinary conversation, Ann Mason was near to tears. I went to her and put my arms round her and she dropped her work on her lap and began to sob helplessly.

"Mrs. Mason?" I said. "Ann? Is this to do with that silly gliding engine?"

"Yes, it is! That hateful thing! Leonard's running mad over it. He's changed the shape of the wings, he says. And now he's building a catapult to shoot it off the tower . . ."

"I saw it."

". . . but he says it needs to be guided. It needs to be turned this way and that to catch the air currents. And he says . . . he says . . ."

I knew what was coming next. I remembered what Leonard Mason had told us on the day I arrived at Lockhill.

"He says," declared Ann in a desperate voice, "that the thing he ought to do is launch *himself* off the roof, sitting in it! He'll kill himself! I keep trying to reason with him but he won't listen! Oh, why couldn't he have gone on translating things and studying and . . . making musical instruments? Even bad ones that won't play!"

"Like his spinet?" I tried to introduce a lighter note.

Ann responded by hiccuping indignantly. "Yes! Did Mew tell you about that? Leonard's built one poor spinet, and one that finished on the scrapheap. His flying machine will be no better. I know it. So does Mew: he's more or less warned me. Why he's let Leonard persuade him to help with it, I just can't think. He's weak and Leonard talks him round, that's what it is. Leonard will break his neck and then what will happen to me and the children? I sometimes think we're not real to him!"

"Please don't cry," I said. "Ann . . . I mean, Mrs. Mason . . ."

"I don't mind if you call me Ann. If Leonard kills himself, there'll be hardly anyone left to call me by my name. Even Cousin Bess just addresses me as Cousin when she writes. Please do call me Ann. Can I call you Ursula?"

"Yes, of course. Ann, listen, I'm sure you have more influence over Leonard than you think. It will be all right. These ideas are all very well in theory but when it comes to the point, he won't want to launch himself off the roof any more than you want him to."

"I hope not," said Ann. "I just hope not!"

"I'm sure of it," I said, wondering unhappily whether death from a crash off the roof into the courtyard might not be the best thing that could happen to Leonard Mason. I picked up Ann's sewing, which had slipped to the floor, and observed that her efforts to pull the split seam together looked decidedly wild. "Shall I see to this for you?" I asked.

The baby was wailing. Ann got up and went to the

cradle. "I think he's hungry." She gave me a shaky smile. "You're very kind, Ursula. You've made me feel better. If you could take that doublet off my hands, I'd be very grateful. You can use my work-box."

Ann began to feed Ned and I set about unpicking the haphazard seam, thinking hard as I did so, not about Leonard Mason or his glider, but about Barnabas Mew. I had said that I should not only try to read Mason's papers, but that I must also try to observe the people he met, notice who came to the house. Was Mew's appearance significant?

The word *Windsor* kept pounding in my brain. Jackdaw had come from Windsor, and been killed there. Paul Fenn, it now occurred to me, had been found floating downstream, below Hampton. He had been last heard of near the boathouse. He had probably stolen the dinghy, and if so, he could have gone upstream. Windsor was above Hampton. Had he gone there? The word *coincidence* joined *Windsor*, chiming with it in my head.

It was a double coincidence, in fact. Here was not only a link between Lockhill and Windsor, where Jackdaw had died, but also with someone who had been at court, at just about the time I had received my briefing from Cecil. Someone with whom Fenn and Wilkins might have conferred; a regular visitor to Lockhill, who might have carried the news that I was, from their point of view, a doubtful character.

It fitted. Too well.

Presently, there were interruptions. Jennet came

and deposited the toddler, Henry, on the floor along with a handful of wooden bricks. She said that she'd been trying to keep an eye on him but that she'd tripped over him and his wooden bricks twice while she was sweeping the floors upstairs and please could he play with his toys in here?

Jennet returned to her broom, but almost at once, Ann's wraithlike maid Tilly appeared, to announce that she had sponged and pressed her mistress's brown dress as instructed and might join us at supper that evening. She gave me a word of greeting, but the tone was not friendly.

On the morning I had set out for Thamesbank, Tilly had shown signs of recovering from her indisposition and I had exchanged a word or two with her at last. These were few, because Tilly, too, seemed to disapprove of me, just like Mason and Crichton, though I couldn't believe it was for the same reasons. I couldn't see her as a conspirator.

I felt no enthusiasm for eating my supper with Tilly eyeing me across the table as though I were a black-beetle. Ann noticed her tone, and when the maid had gone, commented apologetically that Tilly could be difficult sometimes.

"She is becoming a worry. She isn't very much use to me now, I'm afraid. Her eyesight isn't what it was. She can see things in the distance but she can't do much sewing. I need another maid, but we just can't afford another set of wages, not if we're to pay school fees for the boys. They really are going to school—did you know?"

"Mr. Mew said something about it when I arrived."

"I think it will be good for them, but we have to find the money somehow, and without throwing Tilly out. She has no family. Besides, well, she's one of us. Catholic, I mean."

I wasn't sure what to say in answer, but Henry, who was down on the floor with his bricks, saved me the trouble by choosing that moment to try to stand upright, and bumping his head on the corner of a table in the process. He sat down again, roaring.

"He's tired," Ann said. "I'll see to them." She gathered up both children and departed upstairs, leaving me to stitch and think in solitude.

Theading a fresh needle, I shook out the blackwork doublet and took the split seam between finger and thumb to get it straight. It was a well-worn but useful garment, warmly quilted for winter, and it had a couple of practical inside pockets. Something, paper or parchment, crackled in one of them.

I pulled it out at once and looked at it, hoping, improbably, that I had found a letter to Mason from Mary Stuart, which would answer all my questions.

I hadn't, of course. It was a very ordinary piece of paper, folded in quarters, and I saw at once that it wasn't a letter, just a bill, much creased and written in a florid hand, all loops and swirls, which wasn't easy to read. The words "To Master Barnabas Mew" were, however, written quite clearly across the top, and this seemed odd. Why should a bill to be paid by Barnabas Mew turn up in Mason's pockets? It wasn't in Mason's writing, which I had seen during my unsuccessful visit to his study. Mason's hand was neat and sparse and nothing at all like this.

I moved to a seat nearer the window and examined my find more closely. I made out at length that the bill was for the unusual commodities of copper and tin in bars, as raw materials. The supplier's name meant nothing to me and there was no address, but the amounts supplied were astounding.

Sir Thomas Gresham, the financier for whom Gerald had worked, had been sent to Antwerp ostensibly to raise loans for Queen Elizabeth from Netherlands bankers, and to improve her credit standing by any means he could. He had also, under the counter as it were, robbed the Netherlands treasuries by whatever means came to hand, justifying this on the grounds that as a result of various bygone dynastic marriages, the Netherlands were under Spanish and therefore enemy control. They were fair game.

Gerald had not only served Gresham by finding individuals who could be bribed or blackmailed into forging requisitions to get valuables out of vaults, or divert them before they ever reached the vaults in the first place. He had also, on occasion, handled the stolen goods. More than once, we had had them hidden in our lodgings. Not all of them were in the form of precious metal: we had once hidden a consignment of twenty copper and fifteen tin ingots under our bed for three nights. I knew what such ingots looked like.

Barnabas Mew was a clockmaker and no doubt used all kinds of metal in his work. He would need these two to create bronze. Normally, however, he would make his clocks on commission and the customer would supply the materials. Mew might keep a modest supply of his own, but not twenty bars of copper and another twenty of tin! Even small-sized bars would be excessive.

Look out for oddities and coincidences, Cecil had said. I had certainly found them. I had found Leonard Mason frightening his wife with a gliding engine and sending Crichton to buy tapestries which Lockhill couldn't afford, and both of them lying about it. And Barnabas Mew, clockmaker, of Windsor, where Jackdaw had died, was regularly visiting Lockhill, apparently engaged in large-scale dealings in copper and tin, and his supplier's bills were turning up in Mason's pockets.

There were so many puzzles and they seemed so absurd that I felt a strong impulse to go to the stables for a handful of straw, thread it through my hair and sing "hey nonny no" while dancing dementedly through the topiary garden. Well, why not? It would be no more ridiculous than Mason's gliders.

As usual, I was wearing a gown with a hidden pocket and carrying my lock-picks, slate and dagger. I took out the slate and noted the salient points of Mew's extraordinary bill. I put the letter back where I had found it and went on with my sewing. I would finish it and hand it to Ann before supper. Then I must put my mind to other matters. Tomorrow, no matter how much the prospect scared me, I would search Mason's study.

Even if I had to lock half the household in cupboards to keep them out of my way.

* * *

Occasionally, just occasionally, the angels smile, even on those who augment their incomes by inspecting other people's belongings. Barnabas Mew left the following morning, directly after breakfast. Over breakfast, he said that he had urgent work awaiting him, although he hoped to make another visit to coincide with that of the boys' prospective schoolmaster. "I can't help but take an interest, Mr. Mason. I hope I'll be a welcome guest."

"Any time, any time. I may be ready to launch my glider by then. I know you'd like to see that," Mason assured him. He then announced that he intended to spend the morning in his workshop. "Mew won't be here, so Crichton will have to help me. Send for him, will you, Ann? The boys can spend the morning riding round the fields and inspecting them for me, and the girls can have an extra sewing lesson, perhaps."

Ann's face became bleak at the mention of the glider, but I secretly rejoiced, and rejoiced even more when she said, "Very well, if Ursula agrees. I shall be much occupied. Tilly had a relapse this morning and cannot leave her bed. She can hardly get her breath, and she has such pains in her bones. She did too much yesterday."

"Indeed?" I said. Tilly had duly taken supper with us, and spent the meal glowering at me across the table. I wondered if intense glowering qualified as doing too much.

"I must take her some food and sit with her," Ann said. "And then I really must spend some time in my stillroom. Ursula, I depend on you to look after the girls."

They would all be out of the way, the girls included. I would find something to occupy them. Mason's study would be empty. The maids wouldn't go there to dust because only Ann was allowed to do that, and Ann would be busy. I assured Ann that she could depend on me.

The children had breakfasted early and gone to await their tutor in the schoolroom. Straight after breakfast I went to tell them of the new arrangements, and then went to find Brockley.

Dale was engaged in shaking out the clothes which had become creased in the saddlebags during our journey back to Lockhill, so I was on my own. Capricious fate at this point decided not to make my life *too* easy. I found the stableyard empty and made for the stable to see if Brockley were there. Thomas, the lanky groom, emerged from it just as I got there.

"Good day to you, Mistress Blanchard," said Thomas. "You're looking truly bonny this morning." Then, outrageously, he put an arm round me and attempted to kiss me. I resisted indignantly, keeping my mouth tight shut against his attempts to push his tongue into it, and trying to pull myself out of his grasp. He held on, so I stamped hard on his instep. He was wearing boots, but they were made of some kind of soft hide, and when I ground my heel into his left foot at the point where the toes joined on to it, he hastily let go.

"Now, now. There's no need for that."

"There's every need for it. How dare you? If I report you to Mr. Mason, you'll lose your position."

"Oh no, I don't think so," said Thomas easily,

although I was happy to see that his left foot clearly pained him. "It's not a crime to steal a kiss, not from a woman who's free with them. We've all heard the gossip."

"The what?"

"Not that I'm blaming you, mind, don't you go thinking that. You're a lovely wench and all alone in the world, I hear, and you've your longings, like we all have. And you can do better than make do with a stiff-faced middle-aged manservant."

"Make do with a . . . ? *What* gossip?"

"It was all round the house before you got here. Mr. Mason didn't want you to come, but his good lady needed a hand with the girls and she said she didn't believe the talk. You'd been here before, hadn't you? She met you then."

"*What* talk? Who's been saying these things about me?"

"That I wouldn't know, but said they certainly were." Thomas grinned. "And since you've been here, well, we've all noticed how thick you are with Brockley. Redman saw you coming out of an upstairs room together, with that kind of look on your faces, or so he said. A bit hard on your maid, perhaps, having to share her husband, but then you're a temptation for him and no mistake."

So Mason *had* tried to stop me from coming to Lockhill, and that had been his excuse for Ann's bene-fit. He had pretended to have heard gossip that I was a woman of poor morals. Ann, evidently, had used her own judgement and resisted, but the beastly innuen-does had gone all through the household.

"See here, Thomas, you shouldn't pay heed to idle talk. Brockley is my manservant and nothing more. Redman should be ashamed of himself, making up such scandalous tales. Don't you dare ever lay a hand on me again. Be good enough to spread the news round the household that I'm not quite the lightskirt they think. Where *is* Brockley, may I ask?"

"Fetching the ponies from the meadow for the lads to ride."

"Good," I snapped. "I thought," I added as I stepped away from him, "that you were after Jennet. It seems to me that you're the one who's too free with your favours! Those who try to snatch too much sometimes end up with nothing."

On this virtuous note, I made for the side gate to the meadows, hoping to meet Brockley. To my relief, he was just coming, perched astride one pony and leading the other two. I didn't mention Thomas's behaviour to him. It would have made him angry and I didn't want him distracted from the business in hand, still less getting into a fight. I would be on my guard in future, and I would not go to the stableyard unaccompanied again.

I told Brockley what I wanted while I helped him put the ponies in their stalls. Then I went back to the house, making sure I didn't catch Thomas's eye on the way.

Presently, when the boys had gone to saddle up, I settled the girls in our attic room. I set each of them a task and told them that I had an important letter to write.

"Pen, once again, I leave you in charge of your sisters. Set them a good example, now. I'll be back within the hour."

So much for the girls. I went down to my own chamber and looked out through the window, across the yew garden towards the workshop. It had double doors which I could see were wide open. I glimpsed two figures moving about inside. Good. Mason and Crichton were definitely out of the way. I noted with disapproval that Mason was wearing his newly repaired black and white doublet. Hardly the right garment for manual toil, I thought, hoping he wouldn't burst my painstaking stitches.

A further stealthy reconnaissance revealed that Ann had gone to her stillroom, Tilly was in bed, and most of the other servants were in the kitchen, preparing dinner. Redman was in the wine-buttery, rearranging casks, and young Edwin Logan was working in the knot garden.

I went to Crichton's empty schoolroom, where I found Brockley waiting with Dale. "All right," I said. "The arrangement as before. I'll be as quick as I can."

This time, as I hurried through the gallery and anteroom, I did not think about being frightened. The task must be performed, and besides, I was so furious with Leonard Mason for telling lies about me, that for the time being rage had drowned fear.

In moments, I was back in his gloomy study. Once more leaving the door open in case my sentries called, I surveyed the terrain afresh.

Bookshelves. Map. Gargantuan cupboard. I stepped across the room and took a quick look in the cupboard, which had no lock, just a simple handle on each door. The right-hand side had shelves, packed with more books. I pulled back the other half of the double door and found that the left-hand side was almost empty, except for a couple of cloaks, presumably an insurance against getting chilled in winter, hanging on hooks at the back alongside a nightshirt and tasselled cap, no doubt for the times when Leonard sat late and slept in the anteroom. A pair of fleecy slippers was ranged neatly on the floor beneath.

Closing the cupboard doors quietly, I went to the desk. It was as tidy as before. The books Leonard was currently studying were mostly either about music or natural history, with a bias towards birds. The boxes, four of them, were still there, and so were the wooden trays. It didn't seem as if my lock-picks would be needed after all, for of the many things in the study, only the boxes had locks, and their keys were all obligingly in place.

Trying to be methodical, I picked up the nearest tray. It held a number of papers. The top sheet was headed "Remarks on the Limitations of the Spinet" and consisted of an essay comparing spinets and virginals with stringed instruments such as the violin— "the which, newly introduced in living memory, is remarkable in that a note, once created, can be raised to a crescendo or be changed between loud and soft, whereas those instruments played by keyboard lack this and therefore lack expression."

According to Ann and Barnabas, Mason had tried to design a new kind of spinet. The essay went on to discuss ways by which the drawbacks of keyboard instruments might be amended in very technical language with many abbreviations but there was nothing suspicious.

Leafing through the papers below, I found another essay, this one on the principles behind chiming clocks, and some diagrams of various keyboard instruments, some quite detailed, some very vague, as though Mason had been playing with ideas.

One showed what seemed to be a keyboard, but the rest of the mechanism was missing except for some arrows. It could represent a spinet, I supposed, with the arrows showing the ways the squills moved to strike the strings. If so, however, the squills moved very oddly. If this were Mason's attempt at a new design—well, it was certainly new! Nothing here could concern Mary Stuart, anyway.

I reached the bottom of the pile and found the name Dawson burnt into the wood of the tray. I already knew that Jack Dawson, the drowned "Jackdaw," had visited Lockhill. Leonard must have begged or bought a few trays from him to use as a filing system. Had Jackdaw overheard Leonard engaged in some kind of compromising conversation? But . . .

Something scratched at the back of my mind, and then slipped elusively out of reach as I tried to grasp for it. I puzzled over it for a moment, but then gave up and hurried on. I was becoming nervous again. Another tray held drawings of wings, and notes on the flight of birds and the properties of water when poured over curved surfaces; a third held a copy of a lengthy poem in Italian and a half-completed English translation of it. The translation was smooth and poetic; here, Mason was in his natural element. The fourth and last tray contained sheets covered with figures, rough and ready accounts by the look of them.

I tried the four boxes. One held correspondence, but of the most mundane kind, to do with sales of wool and corn, exchanges of very ordinary family news with a brother in Devon, and a letter from Mildred Cecil, the one which first suggested that I should come to Lockhill. Another box proved to be where the official account ledgers were kept. One held blank paper and one was empty.

I took a last look round to make sure I had missed nothing. There were no drawers under the desktop, no hidden cupboards. I even ran my fingers over the wall panelling and the map to make sure.

Once more, something scratched at my mind, something new. Something—surely—to do with that peculiar drawing of the keyboard. Looking at it again, I was reminded of something, but I couldn't think what it was. I was still staring at it when footsteps in the anteroom snatched me from my concentration. I spun round, just as Brockley appeared, looking alarmed.

"Mason's coming," he whispered. "I glimpsed him starting up the stairs and now I can hear him coming through the gallery behind me!"

There was no time to position ourselves innocently in the gallery, so I pulled open the left-hand door of the cupboard and hustled us both inside, drawing the door to after us.

We were taking a fearful risk. We would have done better to walk out and face Mr. Mason, with some tale or other about searching for something Ann had dropped. A convincing story to account for our presence in the study would have been easier to invent than a convincing story to explain why Mrs. Ursula Blanchard and her manservant Roger Brockley had been found squashed into Leonard Mason's carved oak press along with his cloaks, slippers and night-rail.

Yesterday, I had made a private joke about locking the household into cupboards, but if we were caught now, our presence in this one would be no joke at all. I realised this too late, and so did Brockley.

"We've made a mistake. We should have brazened it out," he whispered.

"I know, but he's here," I breathed.

Peering through the crack that I had left open, I caught the flash of blackwork on cream satin as Mason came into the study. Then, afraid that the gleam of an eye, a fold of skirt, might be seen, I shrank away to the further corner of the cupboard, pulling one of the cloaks across me.

"What's he doing?" Brockley's words were a thread of speech, close to my ear.

By the sound of it, Mason was at the desk, rustling papers, and clicking his tongue in an irritated fashion. Tidy though his habits were, it seemed that he couldn't find what he wanted. Had I left any trace of my search? Disarranged something?

We listened, motionless in the dark. I was acutely aware of Brockley's warm, breathing presence beside me. He moved, probably also trying to draw a cloak over him, and momentarily pressed against me. I remained still, very frightened, and was grateful for the presence of another person. I had a terrible impulse to lean against him and press my face into his shoulder.

Suddenly I went rigid, appalled at myself, and hit suddenly by a new fear.

I knew very well that if we were caught like this, we were more likely to be suspected of wanting to make use of the couch in Mason's anteroom, than suspected of spying. Redman would report what he had seen earlier. My reputation would be ruined. Mason would start believing his own lies!

That wouldn't be all. After our encounter with Redman, I had had a few reassuring words with Dale, explaining the circumstances. Later, I had warned her of the lies circulating in the household. If we were found like this, though, she might well begin to wonder about her husband and me. Worse! If I had any more impulses like this, I would begin to wonder, too!

I clenched my teeth, horrified. What was happening to me? What would Gerald say if he could see me now? Perhaps he could! What if the dead watched over the living? But if they did, then he had seen me with Matthew, my current husband, lawful though now absent. He would have seen us . . . I wondered if it were possible to go insane while standing rock-still and completely silent in a dark cupboard with one's manservant.

I came back to reality with an unpleasant jerk as purposeful footsteps approached the cupboard. The right-hand door was pulled open. Daylight streamed in. The two halves of the cupboard were divided by a partition which extended from the back to within a few inches of the doors. From where we were cowering, half hidden behind the cloaks, we could see one of Mason's padded shoulders as he rummaged in the shelves. I had a depressingly good view of his left ear and a patch of my own stitchwork, where I had repaired the embroidery. If he glanced to the left, he would see us. The concealment of the cloaks was inadequate, and our feet would show below them, anyway.

He did not glance to the left. After pulling impatiently at the books on the right-hand shelves, as if to look behind them, he backed out and shut the door. He also closed the door on our side, leaving us undiscovered but imprisoned in an impenetrable darkness. I doubted if I could pick the lock from this side of the door, and began to tremble.

"Don't be afraid," Brockley's minute whisper came again. "My knife will open that door catch."

Outside, papers were rustling again and wooden trays were apparently being picked up and slammed bad-temperedly down on the desk. Then came a triumphant "Ah!", and at last, *at last*, Mason's footsteps retreated. We heard the study door shut.

"Wait," whispered Brockley. "In case he thinks of something else and comes back."

We stood still. Nothing happened. My eyes were adjusting to the blackness and I saw that there was indeed a thread of light where the leaves of the door met. Brockley edged past me and steel glinted as he applied the tip of his belt-knife to the join. The catch yielded, sliding back into its socket. Catching hold of the door edge to keep it from opening too much, Brockley peered cautiously out.

"The study's empty. Wait."

He went out ahead of me and stepped to the door of the anteroom, where he repeated the process of cautiously opening it a quarter of an inch. He came back, looking relieved.

"All's clear. I can see right through to the gallery and it's empty."

Emerging from the cupboard, I examined the desk. "I think he wanted his drawings of wings," I said. "They were in this tray here, though not on top. They're gone now."

"And so should we be," said Brockley in heartfelt tones. "Did you find anything useful, madam?"

I shook my head. "No. We've taken all these chances and we've nothing to show for it. Let's get away, but not together, in case we meet Redman again, or anyone else." I felt hot with embarrassment as I said it. "You go first. I'll wait in the gallery until you're well away. If necessary, I'll pretend I'm looking for something I've dropped."

We escaped this time without being noticed.

Afterwards I badly wanted time to think, but people seemed to be constantly clustering round me. Ann called me to look at something in the stillroom, and then it was dinnertime. I had to help Ann keep the children in order, for Crichton was having his meal out in the workshop with Mr. Mason. During the afternoon, I felt that I must attend to the girls, and suppertime came before I knew it.

The men did appear for supper. Mason had changed into his fawn doublet, having no doubt dirtied the other one in the workshop. Crichton wore his dusty, unimpressive old gown, which caused Ann to look at him and sigh, although she said nothing.

What with one thing and another, all that day I could not settle down to think until at last night came, and I was in my curtained bed.

Once more, I lay long awake, turning things over in my mind, and once more I was quite immune to my soothing evening draught. I kept the habit up, because I still harboured a vague hope that the gossip in the kitchen while I was making it would one day yield something useful, and the valerian and camomile mixture recommended by Mrs. Logan was sometimes genuinely sleep-inducing. In fact, although Dale had given up taking it with me, because she didn't really like herbal brews, my bedtime posset was by now an institution. Ann gently teased me about it, and the Logans had given me a special goblet for it, a pewter affair with a small dent in the side.

That night, as on the night before I went to Thamesbank, when I had lain aching for Matthew and feeling as though my mind were disintegrating, the goblet might as well have held cold water. I stared into the darkness, and went over everything I had done and learned since I came to Lockhill.

Twice, during my search of Mason's desk, something had niggled at me. There were things—two of them at least—that I should have noticed, or recognised or understood, but I could not bring them to the surface.

I turned over restlessly, brooding on tapestries, coincidences, bills for tin and copper, and people who spent money they didn't possess. I felt haunted by this curious financial theme. Again I asked myself: *what* were the two fugitive recollections which had stirred in the depths of my mind in Mason's study? What had I missed?

I did not sleep until nearly dawn, and woke on the Friday weary and low in spirits. I was late arriving in the attic schoolroom, but when I got there, I found that Pen had taken competent charge, although she and her sisters weren't sewing. Pen had produced a lute and was strumming a melody, not very smoothly but with plenty of verve, while Cathy and Jane sang.

"Oh, Mrs. Blanchard! This is a song that Mr. Mew taught us, when he used to teach us music. It's such a pretty song."

I had struggled half the night to drag unidentified recollections to the top of my mind, and now that I wasn't thinking about them at all, one of them emerged, in response to the name of Mew.

"Begin the song from the beginning and let me hear it all," I said, and then I sat down and listened with half my mind, while the other half went back to the court, to the day when Barnabas Mew presented his musical box to the queen. Again, I watched while he showed her how it worked, and then, once more, I visualised the mysterious drawing in Mason's study, the diagram I had taken to represent his new idea of a spinet. It wasn't a spinet at all. What I had taken for a sketch of a keyboard was the comblike device in Mew's musical box, with the teeth which tapped musically against the little knobs on the revolving cylinder. The arrows which had seemed so meaningless showed the direction in which the cylinder turned and the way the comb teeth were pushed upwards.

It still made no sense, but one thing had emerged from the fog of absurdity: there was a link between Barnabas Mew and Lockhill which was not to do with teaching music. A bill addressed to Mew had turned up in Leonard Mason's doublet; a drawing of Mew's musical box—which Mason was supposed to know nothing about—was lying among Mason's papers. And Dawson, who had suspected trouble at Lockhill, had been murdered in Windsor, where Barnabas Mew lived.

I was looking in the wrong place. I ought to be in Windsor. Cecil had told me not to investigate Dawson's death, but what if that death were so closely entangled with Lockhill's secret that they couldn't be separated? What if the same applied to Fenn's death? He could certainly have been mur dered at Windsor.

The thought of going there myself was frightening, but I wanted to know much more about Master Barnabas Mew. I wasn't sure how to go about it, but I could begin by looking at Mew in his own territory. Ann had told me that the boys' prospective school-master was definitely coming to Lockhill next week, and that Mew would return at the same time. She hadn't mentioned the exact day. I had best make haste, to be sure of catching Mew while he was still at his shop. I would take Brockley and Dale, on an apparently innocent errand and in broad daylight. Surely that wouldn't be too dangerous?

Beyond this seemingly harmless step there were others, much less harmless. I knew they were there, but I wouldn't look at them directly, not yet.

For the moment, I said to myself, I would simply go to Windsor, to Barnabas Mew's shop, and order a musical box for Meg.

CHAPTER 13

A Gift for Meg

I had barely returned from Thamesbank, but it couldn't be helped. I worked the girls hard that Friday and Saturday and wouldn't let them take their ease even on the Sunday, but made them do a further two hours of embroidery, as soon as mass and breakfast were over.

I had hoped to see both the Masons at the breakfast table on Monday, but only Ann was there. To her, I said that the girls had earned a short holiday, and that I wished once more to make a short journey on a private matter. "I shall only be gone overnight," I said.

"We had better tell my husband," Ann said. "He broke his fast early and went out again to his workshop. He doesn't like to be disturbed, you know."

"I'm afraid the matter is urgent," I said. "If you think I shouldn't go without telling him, then I must see him."

"Well, he would expect to be informed," Ann said, pushing her platter away. "We'll go together."

Though I had been out to the workshop several times, I had only paused to watch for a few moments, never to interrupt, and I had not been out there since

I came back from Thamesbank. Now, it gave me a surprise.

Leonard Mason's working shed was large, with wide double doors and a roof steeply pitched to give plenty of height inside. Even so, it was hardly big enough for the vast wood and canvas bird which was taking shape within. Ann and I hesitated, wondering how to get ourselves and our farthingales past the wings which blocked our entrance. Ann called, and after a moment, Leonard appeared from the dim inner regions, ducking under a wing and regarding us testily.

"What is it? I am really very occupied just now. I asked Crichton to help me again before he started work with the boys this morning, but he put his thumb in the way of my hammer in the first few minutes and now he's gone off in a fit of temper."

"Oh dear. Poor man," said Ann anxiously.

Her husband merely looked annoyed. "What about poor me? Some tasks are very difficult when one is on one's own. Now, what is it you want? I can see from here that the house isn't burning down."

Ann explained. The furrows deepened between Leonard's nostrils and the corners of his mouth. "Another jaunt, Mrs. Blanchard? Well, as I have said before, you are free to come and go. I have to admit that Pen acquitted herself well while you were away. You are evidently training her to take responsibility. For that, I suppose I must commend you. What is the purpose of your journey this time?"

Clearly, I ought to produce some sort of reason for my sudden departure. I couldn't pretend to an urgent message, as they knew quite well that no messenger had arrived for me. I fell back on the useful excuse of discretion.

"It is a matter which arose when I was at Thamesbank. I have been worrying about it and I have come to the conclusion that I need to attend to it personally. Please forgive me for not saying any more. It concerns . . . an errand for Her Majesty." Well, it did, more or less. "We—her ladies, that is—are taught never to discuss the Queen's business, even the most trivial matters."

"The Queen's business, is it? It sounds very grand." Mason shrugged. "Well, travel safely! What more can I say?

I thanked him, and then, noticing that the huge wood and canvas wing beside me was a curious shape, curved on one side and flat on the other, I made an attempt at politeness and asked its creator why.

For once, Mason smiled at me, the furrows on his face bending into sharp outward angles. Mason's work was the way to his heart.

"Ah! Now, that is to do with a theory of mine. Come into the workshop—just press back your skirts and you'll find that you can edge through. You too, Ann . . . that's it."

"Oh, *Leonard*," said Ann protestingly. "I'm sure Mrs. Blanchard doesn't want to—"

"Over here, both of you," said Leonard, unheeding.

The interior of the workshop was furnished with a workbench along the back, a small brick furnace, and a brazier. To one side lay a pile of timbers and wooden slats, and on the floor stood a pail of water, fairly clean, and a rusty old bucket full of what smelt like glue. An earthenware jug and basin were on the workbench, along with a set of drawings, assorted tools and a couple of large spoons. A sizeable leaded window at the rear of the shed meant that the light was good.

Mason dipped a jugful of water from the pail and then pushed back his right sleeve, picked up a spoon and held it pointing downwards into the basin.

"Now, Mrs. Blanchard. Just take up the jug and pour water very slowly and carefully, down over the spoon, from above, where I am holding the handle. Never mind about getting my arm wet. Observe how the water behaves."

I couldn't imagine what I was likely to observe, but I did as I was told, while Ann watched with an air of patience.

"There! Do you see?"

"Er . . . no," I said. "The water just flows down over the spoon. Doesn't it?"

Mason sighed. "Dip another jugful and try again. Very slowly, now. Watch carefully. Does the water flow over the spoon in a thin stream, or does it spread out over the curve at the back of the spoon?"

I peered at the spoon as I poured. "It spreads out. But it spreads over the inside of the spoon, as well."

"Yes, but what if I filled in the inside of the spoon so that it was flat? Then, the water would have to spread over more metal at the back than at the front. A curved surface is bigger than a flat one. When I saw that, I realised that if the wing were curved on top, then the air passing over it in flight would be thinned out, because it would have to flow over a bigger surface than the air flowing below, across the flat underside of the wing. And perhaps that would help the wing to be buoyant. Do you see?"

"I think so, but would it make so much difference?"

"Can you really understand it?" Ann asked me. "It all seems so extraordinary to me."

I understood it well enough, but I still didn't think it would work. However, to say so would have been tactless, so I merely repeated to Mr. Mason that I had grasped the point. Almost beaming now, he picked up his drawings and began to show me exactly how he intended to use the structure on the tower roof as a catapult.

In the end, it was another half an hour before I could get away, but by the time I did, his manner towards me was more friendly than at any time since I arrived at Lockhill.

What a good thing, I thought, that when he searched his study cupboard for drawings of glider wings, he hadn't glanced to his left. Thinking of that incident would bring me out in a sweat for the rest of my life.

We set off an hour later. It was a bright, fresh day, with sunshine and racing clouds and sounds of birdsong, but I soon noticed that Dale and Brockley were very quiet, and before long, I had grasped that they were scarcely on speaking terms. Clearly, they had had a tiff. Well, that was between husband and wife and there was nothing I could do about it. All couples have their quarrels.

Attempting to distract them I suggested that we sing. My two obedient servants tried, but their efforts were so unenthusiastic that I gave up.

I was provoked into saying, "Do cheer up, you two. Look what a lovely day it is!"

All they said was, "Yes, indeed, ma'am," in flat voices. I stopped trying.

At heart, I wasn't too cheerful myself, if truth be told. I was anxious about the task ahead. I had come to the conclusion that I would need Dale and Brockley's help, and I just hoped that they were willing to give it.

I wanted to speak to Brockley first, out of Dale's hearing. Choosing a place where the road was wide enough for two to ride abreast, but not for three, I edged Bay Star alongside Brockley's cob and began to talk.

". . . I need to look at Barnabas Mew on his own premises, and to see the premises themselves. I'm not sure exactly what I'm looking for, but I'll tell you how far I've got." I described the bill for the remarkable quantities of copper and tin, the discovery on Mason's desk of a diagram for Barnabas Mew's music box, and the strange matter of the dining room tapestries.

"Mason and Crichton say they were left to Crichton by an uncle, but they weren't. Crichton bought them on Mason's behalf. Only, Mason can't possibly afford them. I think someone is paying him secretly for something, and perhaps he is looking for ways to enjoy the money without being too conspicuous. It's very mysterious," I said, "but it does look as if Barnabas Mew and Mr. Mason are somehow entangled, and Barnabas lives in Windsor."

"And so, madam?" Brockley gazed at me from under the large hat, which I knew, without asking, once more concealed his helmet.

"Barnabas Mew," I said, "may have been concerned in a murder."

"Paul Fenn?"

"Possibly, but not just Fenn. If I've been too reticent, it's because I don't want to frighten Dale. Fenn's death has frightened her already, which is why I'm talking to you alone at this moment. There was another man, a Jack Dawson . . ."

I explained all I knew of Dawson's mysterious demise on the river, and the fact that his landlady believed someone had searched the house that same evening. "I'm not going to investigate his death in any obvious way," I said, "but he claimed to have discovered traces, at Lockhill, of a scheme to aid the cause of Mary Stuart. He then met his death, probably at Windsor. Barnabas Mew links the two places."

"It all sounds," said Brockley disapprovingly, "most confused, madam, and I can't see that any of it really points a finger at Mew—or adds up to a reason for prying into Mr. Mew's affairs, either."

I said slowly, "I think . . . it's like a midden."

Brockley looked astounded, as well he might. "A *midden*? Madam, I don't understand you."

"A mass of bits and pieces," I said. "All in a pile, breaking down at the edges, melting and oozing into each other, creating a bad smell, but . . . fertile. Something might sprout from this heap of dubious oddments; I really think so. At least, I must try to find out."

"But, madam, how *can* you can find out? You can hardly question Mew openly!"

"I know, but I can do what I did in Mason's study and search his papers. He must have a room for writing letters and adding up accounts. I must get into it if possible. I'm interested in the extraordinary amounts of metal that he's been buying. Sir William Cecil told me to look for oddities, and that's an oddity if ever there was one."

"I don't like the sound of this, madam."

"Neither do I," I said frankly, "but if there is a scheme and it's allowed to mature—what then?"

"The English aren't fools," said Brockley. "How many people would really want to exchange our Elizabeth for a French-reared chit nearly ten years younger?"

"Quite a few," I said. "Those who are so in love with the old religion that they would put anyone on the throne who would restore it, whether it be a prattling baby or a convicted murderer, let alone a pretty princess. And then there are those who are in love with gold and can be bought. What if such people caused something to . . . to happen to Elizabeth. The door would be open for Mary. And what if she came through it with a foreign army? I don't *think* Spain is in any position to put an invading force in the field for Mary, but if the prize were sufficiently tempting, who knows what Philip might do? If any action I can take will help to prevent such things, then take it I must."

"I follow you, yes." Brockley nodded. "You may well be right, but . . . I know I've said this before, but I'll say it again: it's not a lady's business!"

"The Queen is a lady, Brockley." It had been Elizabeth's own justification for letting me return to Lockhill. "It's her business, is it not?"

Brockley made a noise which I could only call a growl, but then he said, "Just tell me what to do."

I described the plan which I had formed, through much brooding, over the weekend. Brockley listened and raised no more objections beyond saying, "Well, you're right to keep Fran in the dark over this. She needn't know what Mew might have anything to do with Fenn's dying—and she'd better not know about Dawson at all."

We dropped back to ride one on either side of Dale and explain to her what was wanted. Even without any suspicions that we were riding into the lair of a possible killer, her response was to look both unhappy and sullen.

"I'll do my best, but I'm not sure about it. I can't abide lies and deception and—"

"You'll do as the mistress says!" snapped Brockley.

"I said, I'll do my best!" Dale's tone was anything but enthusiastic and she wouldn't look at either of us.

"Thank you," I said, blankly.

Towns are smelly. After riding through fields and woods, one always notices it. Windsor is a small, compact community which has grown up around the castle it serves, but its few streets are as fetid as any street near London Bridge. They assaulted our nostrils with the usual reek of horse-dung, rotting litter from spilt nose-bags and carelessly swung shopping baskets, and the half-invigorating, half-repulsive smell of the river, which bore rubbish as well as fresh water downstream to the sea.

Which had been known, I thought grimly, to convey corpses.

I knew the town already, and I believed I knew where Barnabas Mew's shop might be. I led us over the bridge and on into Bishop Street, skirting the castle walls. We passed the public meeting place, which is a roofed shelter with a cross on top, and at the crossroads in front of the castle, I guided us to the right, into Peascod Street. This was lined with houses and shops, and there before us was the clockmaker's sign I had half-remembered. And, yes, it was Mew's. We drew rein and dismounted.

The shop was modern, its white plaster walls patterned with timbers, its roof neatly thatched. Its second storey overhung the street, supported on black timber pillars. Instead of an open shopfront, it had an ordinary door, and a window alongside, with examples of its owner's handiwork displayed behind the leaded panes. Tethering posts had been invitingly placed at the edge of the roadway. We tied our horses to them and went up the steps to the door.

It was opened for us before we got there, by a beefy young man who looked faintly familiar. Oh yes, I thought, of course. He was the assistant who had come with Mew to court, and carried the musical box for him. He must have been on the lookout for potential customers. As we followed him inside, I heard Brockley mutter something to him, and I sensed that Brockley had stiffened. I turned to him to ask why, but read a warning in his eyes. I had better wait until we could be private. However, if something had alerted Brockley, then I too must be alert. I looked keenly about me as we stepped into the shop.

It was in good order, strewn with fresh rushes.

There was a counter, with stools for customers, and the wall behind the counter had shelves, displaying various timepieces.

On our left, a staircase led upwards, and beside it hung a big, ornate clock, set in a gilt surround featuring heraldic creatures and extraordinary curlicues. It had a pale blue enamelled face with gold hands and golden Roman figures, and its works—its weights and wheels and pendulum, also gilded—hung glittering below, complex and beautiful, like a celebration of machinery.

I noticed that the windows and doors of the shop were well provided with bolts and shutters. Under the window, a chubby apprentice, fair and blue eyed as a cherub although marred by acne, sat at a table, concentrating on an arrangement of tiny cogwheels.

Wylie stepped behind the counter, and stood resting proprietory hands on it. "How can I help you, ladies, sir?"

Brockley took command. "Is Mr. Barnabas Mew here?"

"Mr. Mew is at his ledgers, but I am his journeyman assistant: Joseph Wylie, at your service." He was an odd sort of clockmaker, I thought. It was a trade which seemed to call for neatness, patience and the deft handling of small mechanisms, but, as before, Wylie's doublet was strained over his broad shoulders, and the fingers now spread on the counter were as thick as farmhouse sausages. His black hair fell into his protuberant brown eyes, and his face displayed the high flush of short temper.

This temper flickered in his voice as he barked, "Timothy, set a stool for the lady!" at the cherubic apprentice, who sprang to obey with a speed which suggested nervousness. "Did you wish to commission a clock?" enquired Mr. Wylie.

"No. We wish to see Mr. Mew." Brockley was firm. "Mistress Ursula Blanchard, lady-in-waiting to the Queen, desires to see him personally."

"Mistress Blanchard!" There were doors in the walls behind the counter and Mew now came scurrying through one of them, eager and smiling. He must have heard Brockley asking for him. "I am most honoured! But what brings you all the way here when we were bound to meet so soon at Lockhill? I am returning there tomorrow. Did you not know?"

"Tomorrow? No, I didn't know," I said, more or less truthfully, relieved that I had moved so fast. "But it makes no odds. I . . ."

"Set the stool there, Timothy. Do be seated, mistress."

"I am anxious for a private word with you, Mr. Mew," I said clearly. "Do you have a room for confidential business?" I let my eyes go to the door through which he had come. "Meanwhile, perhaps my waiting-woman might sit down. Take the stool, Dale. Dale," I explained to Mr. Mew, "felt unwell on the way here. Brockley can stay with her."

Mr. Mew eyed Dale with some alarm. "Er . . . what is the malady? Has she a fever?"

"No, just a headache," I said. "Horse travel doesn't suit her. But headaches can be unpleasant. I have them myself sometimes. Could she sit here while we . . . er . . . talk?"

"Oh, of course, of course. As long as you are sure

that there is nothing, well, nothing contagious. Of course, it isn't the plague season yet but—"

"I've not got plague!" said Dale indignantly. She caught my eye and put a hand to her brow. "It's just a bad headache. I can't abide horse-riding for any distance, that's all."

"Perhaps a tisane of camomile or marjoram?" I suggested. "Surely there's an apothecary nearby?" I know there was: I'd seen one in Peascod Street.

"Maybe the lad could run out to him, if so," Brockley said helpfully. "I'd sooner stay with Fran. She's my wife, as it happens."

"Oh, by all means. Timothy, make haste to Master Humfrye's shop and tell him a preparation is needed for a lady with a bad head due to travelling. What was it you said, Mrs. Blanchard? Camomile or . . ."

"Marjoram," I said. "Or both. Here's some money." I pressed a few coins into the hand of the spotty cherub and watched with satisfaction as he departed. That had got rid of the apprentice, anyway. "Now, Master Mew . . . ?"

"Oh, yes. Would it be on the Queen's business?" His voice fell to an eager whisper. "Wylie, mind the shop! Through here!" said Mr. Mew, beckoning me round the end of the counter to the door which I had guessed led to his office.

Once there, I continued to glance sharply about me while Mr. Mew dusted another stool for me to sit on, and begged me to tell him how he could be of service.

He evidently took trouble to make his shop welcoming for customers, but out of their sight, paid little attention to comfort. The back room was a dismal place. Its plain brick walls were adorned only by a dull hanging of painted cloth, over part of the wall on the right-hand side. The hearth was lit, but only with a small fire which did little to relieve the cold, and the window overlooked a regrettably untidy garden.

I was interested, though, in a long shelf which held ledgers and a box with a brass lock. Also of interest to me was the table in the middle of the room, where lay an open ledger and various other documents. A casual tilt of my head told me that they were bills and invoices.

"I'm not here directly on the Queen's business," I said, "but it springs from that presentation you made to the Queen—the musical box, I mean. You yourself wish that to remain confidential, I believe? That is why I wanted to see you here, and not at Lockhill. I want to give my little daughter a music box as a present. I can't afford gold, but perhaps you could suggest something less costly which would still look pleasing? If it were satisfactory, and were shown about at court . . . well, who knows who else might want one? Perhaps Her Majesty might!"

"Oh yes, of course." Mew was plainly disappointed that Her Majesty wasn't ordering one forthwith, but he rallied. Business was business. "The casing could be polished wood, or silver or bronze. Personally, I think that wood, with a pleasant grain, is as charming as anything. I could make a musical box in polished walnut, with gold hinges, perhaps."

There was a pause. Mr. Mew presumably supposed me to be visualising a walnut box with gold hinges. I pursed my lips and looked doubtful. "Could you give me a quote for walnut, and also for a silver casing?"

Mr. Mew picked up a slate from his desk and did some calculations, while I strained my ears for sounds from the shop, wondering what on earth Dale was doing, or rather, why she wasn't doing it. Get on with it, Dale! Mr. Mew came up with some figures. "Well, I could just afford the silver," I said doubtfully, "but it is rather costly. Perhaps I could see an example of a walnut casing . . . whatever's that?"

Outside in the shop, someone was moaning. There came a thud, and then Brockley called me, his voice urgent. I rushed to the door and flung it wide. Dale was lying on the floor in a most artistic faint with Brockley crouched beside her and Wylie gazing down at them in alarm. Brockley shook Dale, whose head lolled unresponsively, and looked up at me with a convincing air of fright.

"Madam, she's collapsed! My wife's collapsed! She just slid off the stool and—"

"Oh, my goodness. Carry her into the office. What if a customer comes in and sees her lying on the floor like that?" Mew could hardly have been more obliging. "Wylie, take her feet . . ."

"Brockley and I will manage," I said. "Mr. Mew, would you or Mr. Wylie go after your boy and tell the apothecary what has happened? If we wait for Timothy to come back, there'll be delay. Ask the apothecary what he advises!"

"But, surely, madam, if you were to send your man . . ."

"I can't leave Fran while she's like this!" said Brockley, sounding convincingly like a panic-stricken husband, if not altogether like a respectful manservant.

."No, no, of course you mustn't! Help me into the office with her. He's her *husband*, Mr. Mew, and we've never seen her like this before! *Please* go to the apothecary or send Mr. Wylie. One of you can still guard the shop," I added, ruthlessly organising Mew's business for him.

"And you know where the apothecary is. I don't!" Brockley said, as he and I bore the sagging Dale through the door of the office. "Hurry, man! Fran, Fran, wake up! Oh, madam, what can be the matter with her?"

"Lay her here." We set Dale on the floor and I took off my mantle and folded it tenderly under her head. "Oh, Mr. Mew, please do *something* about asking the apothecary what to do! Or fetch a doctor!"

Between us, we gave Mew little chance to argue. He found himself, willy-nilly, leaving the shop to Wylie and rushing off in the wake of his spotty-faced apprentice. I shut the door between us and the shop, and there we were, with the back room to ourselves. Dale sat up and Brockley helped her to her feet.

"Well done!" I said.

"Thank you, ma'am," said Dale rather stiffly, but she did look quite pleased with herself.

In a low voice, Brockley said, "Madam, there's something you should know. It's about that Joseph Wylie."

"Yes. Something caught your attention as we came into the shop," I said. "What is it?"

"I've seen him before. Madam, he was your muffled-up boatman, the day you were told you were going to meet Mr. de la Roche and you were taken to that boathouse."

"What?" I stared at him and Dale's mouth opened. "How can you tell?" I said. "He was wrapped up like Cleopatra in a carpet!"

"When he got up and handed you into his boat, I saw his back view. I recognised the set of his shoulders. I recognised his voice, too. It's him all right."

"Oh, my God!" said Dale, and turned white.

Brockley looked as though he would like to seize my arm in one hand and Dale's in the other and run us straight out of the building. I felt just as horrified as they obviously did, although I had been suspecting Mew of worse than mere abduction, as had Brockley. But we were here now.

"So we know we're in the right place," I said. "Don't let's waste any more time. Quickly. Search!"

They looked at me, but I stood my ground and they obeyed me. Both were reasonably literate and I set them to looking through the bills and invoices for any-thing that didn't seem quite right for a clockmaker, such as huge quantities of metal, or payments for mys-terious services rendered. "Or to messengers to or from France—or for any mention of France at all," I said.

I turned my own attention to the shelves. Here, the most inviting target was the box. It was locked. Now, for the very first time, I needed the skills acquired from Alexander Bone.

I at once discovered that theory and reality are two quite different things. No matter how carefully you practise a skill, the first time the real world asks you to do it, you find yourself dealing with the unexpected. Master Bone had left me six lockable boxes to practise on, with locks of varying sizes and designs, but this one seemed to be nothing like any of them. My hands shook with nerves as I probed and nothing either moved or gave way. I tried first one pick and then another, in vain, cursing silently at the waste of time.

I was about to give in and give up when I felt something yield, fractionally. Holding my breath, I pressed harder and slid a second wire in. I forced myself to be calm. The lock clicked softly and surrendered.

The result was hardly worth the trouble. All the box contained was a copy of the lease under which Barnabas held his premises. I noted that extensive cellars were listed in the description of the property and wondered where the entrance to them was.

Disappointed, I closed the box. I tried but failed to lock it again, and stopped trying, for fear of doing damage. I stepped to the table and picked up the ledger. "Anything?" I asked the others, in a low voice.

"I fear not," said Brockley. "What about you, Fran?"

Dale, who was peering at a pile of invoices, shook her head, then she stiffened, listening. "That's the street door!"

Brockley pushed his wife down on to the stool, and rapidly arranged her with her elbow on the table and her head in her palm. Outside in the shop, we could hear Mr. Mew's voice, giving orders to someone.

Brockley took up an anxious stance behind his wife. "Madam!" he said to me in a fierce undertone. "Put that ledger down!"

It was too late. The ledger was still in my hands when Barnabas Mew scurried back into his office, carrying a glass phial and a spoon. He looked at me in amazement.

I retrieved the situation as best I could, with a bright smile and an anxious apology. "I'm so sorry!" I said. "I am incurably inquisitive. How neatly you keep your ledgers, Mr. Mew! You write a pretty hand, I must say." I could feel Brockley boiling but I ignored him. "Do forgive me! I used to help an uncle of mine with his ledgers and I can see that your records are in perfect order. Could the apothecary help? Dale has come round, as you see, but she is still very out of sorts."

Barnabas held out the phial. "The apothecary says it's best taken in a little warmed wine. My maidservant's heating some in the kitchen. The draught won't do any harm, even if the lady is with child," he added.

Dale blushed and Brockley said, "Well, I never thought of that."

"What a happy thing, if so!" I said brightly.

There was a tap at the door, and in came a young maidservant, stirring a filled goblet and hoping that the wine would be warm enough. We all fussed and exclaimed while Mew added the medicine to the drink and gave it to Dale, who choked and spluttered and said she didn't like the taste.

"It seems to be bringing you back to life," I said consolingly. "Now, you sit there while I talk to Mr. Mew and settle what I'm ordering; then we'll go to an inn and you can rest. We won't start home until after dinner tomorrow, Dale. That will give you plenty of time to recover. Mr. Mew, I think I'll face the expense and buy my daughter a music box in silver. Goodness me," I said, smiling sweetly at him, "what a worry it must be, having to keep supplies of precious metals to hand. Do you keep them here? And do you also keep copper and tin ingots on the premises, to make bronze?"

There was an astonished silence, during which Brockley drew a sharp breath in through his teeth, and Mew stared at me anew. Mew's tongue-tip appeared and licked his lips. "What an extraordinary question, Mistress Blanchard."

"Is it?" I asked innocently, and noticed with satisfaction that although the room was not over-warm, there was a gleam of sweat on Mew's pale forehead.

"I keep modest supplies of raw materials, but really very little. I buy them as requested by my customers, in the usual way. I am a clockmaker, not a metal dealer." Mr. Mew attempted a patronising air.

"I'm afraid I know very little about these things," I said, with a self-deprecating laugh. "I know little about anything, except dancing and embroidery. How are you now, Dale? Ah, you look much better. You'll be quite well again by tomorrow, but I won't hurry you. You'll be at Lockhill before us, Master Mew, if you're going there tomorrow."

"Alas, I may not be able to do so after all." Mew tried to sound important. "I have so much work on hand, and this very moment, when I went to the apothecary, I met a customer in the street who wishes me to attend on him in his home this afternoon. I shall gain a commission, I trust! But it will take up a good deal of time. There is never enough time. I fear I will have to defer the pleasure of seeing the Masons for a while. I was expected, however, and I must send word. If you are not returning immediately, Mrs. Blanchard, I'll send Wylie with a message. And now, Mrs. Blanchard," said Mew, "shall I show you some silver casings?"

"If you would be so kind," I said.

CHAPTER 14

Mousetrap Cheese

There was an inn in Peascod Street called the Antelope. We had stayed there briefly the previous autumn, and there, I knew, we would find good food and a comfortable parlour in which to eat it. Brockley, however, was quietly simmering, and over the meal, choosing his words with care but eyeing me grimly, he gave voice to his feelings.

"Madam, whatever possessed you to let Mew catch you with his ledger in your hands? And was that enquiry about tin and copper ingots really wise?"

"Roger . . ." said Dale, wanly protesting.

"It's all right, Dale. I apologise, Brockley. I asked about the ingots because we hadn't found an explanation and it might all have been quite innocent. If so, I hoped to draw an explanation out. As it was—well, did you see him sweating? It's *not* innocent: there's something out of order there, I'm sure of it, though God alone knows what it is."

"But we know something is out of order, madam. That was obvious the moment I recognised Wylie."

"We need all the confirmation we can find," I said.

"I'm really very sorry about the ledger. It was the purchase ledger and there was no mention in it of copper or tin, but I was looking to see if they were there in disguise, as it were. I heard Mew come in, but I thought he'd paused to give orders to someone. I just wasn't quick enough."

"And did you see any disguised items, madam?" enquired Brockley, managing to convey icy reproof without for one moment ceasing to be the deferential manservant.

"No, I didn't, but I'm sure no harm was done," I said soothingly. "He just thinks that I'm a silly, nosy woman, who knows nothing about anything except dancing and embroidery, to repeat my own words."

Brockley and Dale greeted this with a silence which was more effective than any amount of polite contradiction.

"Well," said Brockley, at length, "what now? We are to stay away overnight, are we not, madam? You intended that from the beginning. Have we other business to conduct?"

"I had thought of taking a trip down the river to Thamesbank," I said, "to see Meg. We can hire a craft from here and leave the horses in the inn stables. We'll come back for them tomorrow."

"I think you miss your little girl," said Brockley, in a kindlier tone.

I nodded. He was quite right. I was glad of an extra opportunity to be with her.

I would not let myself repine, because in making that opportunity, I had an ulterior motive. I lived now in a world where nothing, ever, was wholly unsullied.

Everything, even affection, even goodness, had another face.

Even a visit to a child not yet six.

It was a happy visit, although the Hendersons and all their household gazed in some astonishment at Brockley in his outsize hat and doublet. On our earlier visit, he had worn more ordinary garments. No one was rude enough to comment, however, and Meg's joy at my unheralded reappearance moved me deeply. She was undoubtedly happy with the Hendersons and her nurse Bridget, but she always ran to me when I came to see her. She must wonder sometimes why her mother, who so obviously loved her, could not be with her for longer, or more often. Well, one day, when she was older, I might be able to explain to her that without my long absences, she might not have had the shelter of Thamesbank, or even clothes for her back.

Perhaps I would even be able to explain that because of those absences, the world she lived in, the world of Queen Elizabeth, was that much safer.

It was a pleasant idea, said a cynical little voice in my head, although if the Queen's world were truly in danger, my efforts so far had done precious little to preserve it.

We spent the night at Thamesbank and travelled back up river in the morning. Rob lent us his barge and we returned in style. We ate, once again, at the inn, rested for an hour and then took horse for home, through breezy weather with sunlight and occasional showers. The road was good, and although Brockley and Dale were still subdued with each other, the atmosphere wasn't so marked as before.

I didn't this time suggest that we sang. In any case, I had too much on my mind. I did, however, make trivial conversation: about the weather; an overloaded ox-wagon which we overtook and which was surely going to become bogged before long; the promising buds on the apple trees in an orchard; the deplorable slackness of some parish councils, which were no longer keeping the bushes cut back for a bowshot on either side of the road.

My companions responded amiably enough: Dale agreed that the ox-cart was heading for trouble; Brockley said that a few words in the Queen's ear about casual parish councils wouldn't come amiss. Dale said that he was quite right and she for one couldn't abide laziness in any form, and she hoped we wouldn't meet any footpads. Whereupon, Brockley smiled at her quite kindly and patted the hilt of his sword in reassuring fashion.

If I kept at it, I thought, if I went on for long enough, anointing their sores with soothing commonplaces, they might recover altogether.

Three miles or so from home, my efforts were rewarded. We had reached a stretch of road where the trees and scrub had in fact been properly cut back, and there were broad grass verges between the track and the edge of tangled woodlands. Here, we could ride three abreast with ease. As we settled into this companionable formation, Brockley for the first time raised a topic of his own accord.

"I wonder how far Mr. Mason's got with making a

gliding engine big enough to put himself in? Mrs. Mason's frightened, and no wonder. If she's wise, she'll creep out at night and do a bit of stealthy damage so that the wings fall off as soon as he tries to hoist the thing up the tower."

"Brockley!" I said. "That's outrageous!"

"Not at all. Just good sense, madam."

"He'd never forgive her!"

"If she were clever enough, he needn't know anyone had deliberately done anything," Brockley pointed out.

"But she isn't clever," I said. "I believe she's stronger of mind than she seems, but she's not a woman of intellect and she's terrified of that glider."

"And no wonder," said Dale. "It's not right, a man risking his life like that when he has a wife and such a big family."

"That's not always so," Brockley said slowly. "It depends on how important the thing is that you risk your life for. Men have to go to war and fight at times, and they'd be shamed if they refused. Even the wives and families agree. And then there are matters of principle. I was fifteen when Sir Thomas More was beheaded—it would be before your time, madam, but you'll have heard of him?"

"Yes." Sir Thomas More had died when I was a year old, but Uncle Herbert and Aunt Tabitha had held him up to me as a martyr for their faith, and in Gresham's house in Antwerp I had not only seen but had read More's *Utopia*. "He was executed," I said, "because he wouldn't agree that old King Henry had the right to declare himself supreme head of the

Church in England and divorce himself from his first queen, Catherine of Aragon."

"That's right, madam. Well, I mind what my father said about it: that it was hard on More's family, but that he was defending a principle. More didn't think even a king could override the laws of God, and he felt he'd lose his integrity if he'd pretended otherwise. Integrity matters, my father said. But making a machine that glides, and gambling with your life in it—that's hardly a principle. Integrity doesn't seem to come into it."

"Well, how could it?" said Dale with energy.

"I think Mr. Mason would call it a scientific principle," I said, pleased to note that they were now both so interested, that they had forgotten to be stiff with each other.

Bay Star, sensing that her stable was not far distant, tossed her head and lengthened her stride. I patted her. The breeze had turned colder and the woods were drawing closer to the track again. The light was fading. We would all be glad to reach Lockhill.

"At supper this evening," I remarked, "I've half a mind to raise the question—are scientific principles as important, as much worth risking your life for, as moral ones? It might intrigue Mr. Mason, although I hope his wife won't guess what's behind it. Perhaps—"

Something swished past my head, so close that I saw the flicker of its passing and felt the wind of it. It struck Brockley's hat and clanged on the helmet beneath. I saw it bounce on the ground—a three-foot longbow shaft. A second shaft came after it, missed us, and stuck in the ground just ahead.

"Crouch! Spurs!" yelled Brockley. *"Madam!"*

I had done so already, hunching down and driving my spurred left heel into Bay Star's side. Ears flattened, the mare shot forward. Out of the corner of my eye, I saw Brockley grab Dale's reins and follow, dragging his wife's horse with him. Another arrow hit Brockley's hat, and this time stuck there, and one skimmed Bay Star's haunch and sent her squealing into redoubled efforts at flight. The three of us, all bent low to offer the poorest possible targets, hurtled together along the track.

If there were any more arrows, we didn't see them. We went like a cavalry charge for nearly a mile, until we were clear of the woods and out among open pastures. Snorting, eyes rolling, foam flying from their bits, the horses slowed down and stopped. My breath came in jolts. Dale's face was all huge blue eyes and Brockley's mouth was set in a hard line. He put up a hand to remove his hat, with the shaft still sticking in it.

"Whoever was shooting had a very poor eye," he said, "and they weren't quite in range. Thank God there was still some sort of gap between the woods and the path. A longbow shaft from a skilled archer can go clean through a breastplate. Or a helmet."

"Dear God," I said in a low voice. Twisting in the saddle, I looked at the thin line of blood across Bay Star's haunch, just above her tail. I fraction of an inch lower and the arrow would have shattered her spine, leaving a good horse crippled and dying and bewildered, and her rider thrown to the ground and exposed to the enemy.

Brockley was pursuing his own line of thought.

"They were keeping out of sight, and bare trees are poor cover—that would have kept them well back, too. It may have saved all our lives." He jerked the shaft free of the hat, and held it out to me. "If that had stuck itself in any of us . . ."

I looked at it and shuddered. The arrowhead was no smooth V-shaped point, but had sharp barbs pointing backwards from the flanges. If such a shaft went into you, it could not be pulled out without tearing the wound wider.

"R-robbers!" whispered Dale, looking back towards the woods. "Can't we get away? They might come after us."

"They can't cross the meadows without us seeing them," said Brockley soothingly. "Don't be afraid, Fran. But you're right: we should get on to Lockhill."

We all gathered up our reins and moved off, but I kept us to a walk. I had something to say. "It may not have been robbers," I told them.

I must speak now. I knew it. After this, it would be unforgivable not to do so, and it would be better to tell them out here. Whatever words had to be said, could be spoken away from other people, and we could have time to don our normal faces again before we rode into Lockhill.

"I thought I would be the only one in danger," I said, "I never intended . . ."

"Madam," said Brockley. "What do you mean?"

"That I intended Mew to catch me looking at his ledger. I did it deliberately, Brockley. My question about the ingots of copper and tin was also deliberate. And I made sure he knew I wasn't starting home until the next day. We visited Meg so as to give him time to think . . . and plan."

"You mean—Mr. Mew?" said Dale blankly. "Roger, you thought his man Wylie was the boatman, the one that kidnapped Mrs. Blanchard. But this . . . this is . . . different! *Worse!*"

"The fact is," I said, "that my enquiries are getting nowhere, but if there really is a plot, then I cannot go on wasting day after day, beating the covert for a quarry that won't run. In Barnabas Mew's shop yesterday, I did my best to flush him out, and it looks as though I may have succeeded."

"You mean," said Brockley, evidently intent on getting things quite clear, "that since Wylie quite certainly abducted you in London, and you suspect that he and Mew had something to do with the deaths of Dawson and Paul Fenn, you hoped they might attack again? with a full-scale attempt at murder?"

"M-murder?" Dale was grappling with the implications of this. "Fenn? But who's Dawson? Ma'am, what is this all about?" She was so pale that her pockmarks stood out like the stippling of raindrops on snow.

"Hoped is the wrong word!" I said. "But otherwise, well, yes. Dale, I asked you to counterfeit illness in the shop, but for your own peace of mind, some things have been kept from you. I'll tell you now. Listen."

I filled the gaps in for Dale. She sat quite still, seeming to shrink inside her cloak. She did not speak.

Brockley said, ominously. "You took it upon yourself, madam, to trail a lure for him. You have exposed not only yourself, but me and my wife to a terrible danger, without asking our consent."

"I know," I said bleakly, "but I felt that I had to do something."

"Was it really necessary, madam," said Brockley, "to do something quite as mad as this? Just what have you proved? And how could you bring yourself to take such a risk?"

"It wasn't so very easy," I informed him dryly.

Nor had it been. I wouldn't have done it, but for one thing. As we slowly rode on, I told them of the weaver and his daughter, and what I had been forced to hear from Uncle Herbert. I made myself repeat some of what he had told me. I watched their faces as I spoke, and saw them trying to understand.

"Queen Mary's times were terrible," Brockley said, "but even so . . ."

"They were so terrible that they must never happen again!" I almost blazed it at him. "I meant only to drawn danger on myself! I was forewarned: I hoped that would protect me. I didn't expect him to risk attacking all three of us!"

We jogged on for a little way in silence. "What I did," I said at length, "I did as a matter of principle, if you like, but I didn't mean to harm my companions. As for what I've proved—well, if, as you put it, I trail a lure for the enemy, and footpads promptly attack us with arrows, it's too much of coincidence, don't you think? I feel that I've proved Mew is up to something discreditable. We need that proof. We need real evidence, so that Cecil can act."

"We've got evidence: I recognised Wylie," said Brockley.

"The back view of a man all bundled up in clothing?

He has only to roar with laughter and deny it. *Now,* however, all we lack are the details of what this discreditable business actually is. I'd like to know. I'd like," I said, "to hunt down my quarry and bring it to bay. If you can understand that."

There was a further silence. Steadily, I said, "You are both, of course, at liberty to leave my service at any time. I would in that case give you the best possible references and enough money to see you through for some time. Do you wish to leave me?"

That took them by surprise. I awaited their answer, forcing myself to be cool and remote, to maintain my authority, despite my few years and female sex. If they decided to abandon me, I could hardly blame them. In the eyes of most servants, I had become a quite impossible employer.

However, they were good metal, those two. At last, in a trembling voice, Dale said, "We only want to keep you safe, ma'am. I'm frightened, and that's the truth, but I won't leave you unless Brockley bids me to."

"Brockley?" I said.

"I have no wish to leave you, madam, and I understand why you felt obliged to take this dangerous step. I think it was a mistake, though: he may try again and succeed, and what use will that be to the Queen or anyone else? You should have consulted me, madam."

"What would you have suggested, Brockley? I wish," I said thoughtfully, "that I could have seen Mew's cellar."

"Did the shop have a cellar?" Brockley asked. "There was a staircase, but it only went up, not down, as far as I could tell."

"I saw the deeds of the place, in the box I opened. It mentioned cellars, and I think there was a door to behind that wallhanging in his office. That could be the way to them."

"If you believe," said Brockley, "that there is something worth seeing in Mew's cellar, then searching it is a much better idea than turning yourself into the cheese in a mousetrap, madam. When we get to Lockhill, I'll take a fresh horse and start back to Windsor." He looked up at the sky. "The weather's clearing and there should be a moon. I can ride by night well enough. If I can get into the house, I'll search that basement. What am I looking for?"

I had hunting instincts. I knew I had them, and Rob Henderson had recognised them too. Now, Brockley seemed to be developing them. Dale, however, was not, and gasped, "Oh, Roger! Please, no!"

"Brockley, I don't expect you to do this alone. I will come with you. It's my duty. I—"

"You most certainly will not come with me, madam. I'll make sure of that even if I have to knock you unconscious," said Brockley, emerging briefly from his disguise of the perfect servant and sounding for once like the soldier he had once been. "I'll search that basement on my own, and that, believe me, is that."

"I don't see how you could get in," I said. "Mew probably lies over the shop, and I saw for myself that all his doors have bolts on the inside. The place would be secure at night."

Brockley produced his rare grin. "I didn't notice the door behind the wallhanging, madam—there you were the one with the sharp eyes—but I noticed one or two other things: for instance, that that back room had a window on a kind of garden and that the garden was a disgrace."

"I know," I said. "He seems to be cultivating dandelions and thistles, but I don't see—"

"It wasn't only the garden. The fence at the back was ramshackle. If I can't get through or over it, my name isn't Roger Brockley. I also noticed that although the front windows of the building have shutters, the back room window has not, and the window frame is warped. A sharp knife blade pushed in there would lift the catch very neatly, I should think."

Just as it had lifted the latch of Leonard Mason's cupboard. I felt myself grow hot.

Brockley, however, went smoothly on. "He's a silly, careless man, is Mew. He puts shutters on the front windows, because they open on to the street, but thinks the garden and its fence are protection enough at the back. Foolish! Oh yes, I fancy I can get into that house, but on my own, madam."

"Roger, please! Please don't go!" Dale implored him.

"I must," Brockley said. "Madam is right. It's Sir Thomas More's principles all over again, Fran. The purpose behind this is worth taking risks for. Now, once more, madam—what am I looking for?"

I had gone on thinking: all the way down the river to Thamesbank and all the way back, and during the night in between. I still didn't see where the musical box came in, and I still couldn't call to mind that second fugitive memory which had worried me as I searched Leonard Mason's study. However, Mew's curious dealings in metal and Mason's secretive purchase of tapestries he couldn't afford, had made a pattern in my mind. It wasn't the kind of pattern I expected, for I couldn't see what Mary Stuart could have to do with it. This looked like plain straightforward crime, yet the idea kept on coming back to me. At least it would do no harm to share it with Brockley.

"You'd better do your searching with an open mind," I said. "The idea that I have doesn't fit in at all with what I'm looking for, but for what it's worth . . ."

CHAPTER 15

A Man Called Lenoir

We went on walking the horses while we talked the details over, even going aside into a field to finish our discussion while still out of sight of Lockhill. We made sure that there was open ground between us and any prowling bowmen, but we saw no sight of any. The afternoon was all but gone when we finally rode under the gate-arch.

"I'll slip off quietly," Brockley said. "I'll say goodbye here, madam." I half drew breath to speak, but he shook his head at me. "The job needs doing and it needs a man to do it. Is there anything further that I should know?"

"No, Brockley. I can only say good luck, and take care. Take great care."

"I'll be home by morning, madam," Brockley said.

I left Dale with him, to make her own farewells, and went into the house alone.

As so often at Lockhill, I was at once enveloped in chaos. The first sight to greet my eyes was Edwin Logan, the gardener-cum-butcher, wrapped in a bloodstained white apron, grasping a meat cleaver and informing Ann Mason that he was that sorry, ma'am, and no offence, he hoped, but he had enough to do, carving up that pig carcass, and he couldn't put up with that there Dr. Crichton walking in on him and complaining that the topy-airy, or what you may call it, needed attention.

"And what's it got to do with him, I'd like to know?" Edwin demanded. "They b'ain't his yew trees!"

"Oh dear," said Ann worriedly. "I do apologise. Of course you must get on with cutting up the pig. The boys' future schoolmaster is here as a guest, with a friend, and they must have a good supper. I shall speak to Dr. Crichton. The children have upset him today. I saw him striding round the yew garden. Perhaps he took out his annoyance by criticising the topiary. I'll see he doesn't disturb you again."

"Thank you, ma'am. I'm sorry!" At the moment, Edwin looked like nothing so much as an assassin with an exceptionally blatant *modus operandi*, but he was normally a polite enough, though solemnly young man. "But things being as they are . . ."

"Yes, well, all right. Please go back to your work. You won't be worried again, I promise."

Edwin and his cleaver retreated into the back regions, and Ann, turning, saw me on the threshold.

"Ursula! Oh, I *am* so glad you're back. Everything is topsy-turvy. Not the girls—they've been angels—but Dr. Crichton says that the boys have been *fiends*. And when their father took them to task, all they would say was that Crichton provoked them by finding fault over nothing—I can hardly believe *that*! Dr. Crichton flung out of the house in a rage, and when I saw him in the yew garden, he wasn't just striding round it, he was *stamping* round it! And earlier, we had a message to say that Mr. Mew won't be joining us after all, and Leonard's annoyed about it because he particularly wanted to show Mr. Mew his progress in the workshop. What with Leonard in a bad temper, and then Crichton, and now Edwin Logan being difficult, I hardly know whether I'm coming or going. Was everything all right? Have you concluded your . . . business or whatever it was?"

"Thank you, yes. I had better change my dress. I must look well for supper, since you have guests."

"We'll sit in the gallery beforehand. I must get the fire lit! Leonard is in his workshop showing that horrible gliding thing to our guests instead of to Mr. Mew. Oh dear. I'm sure Leonard and Crichton wouldn't be so cross now if they hadn't been in bad humours even before we heard about Mr. Mew, and before the boys started misbehaving. You were there, weren't you, when Leonard said he'd hammered Crichton's thumb by accident? Well, the nail turned black, and Crichton was angry about *that*, and this morning he said he wouldn't help Leonard any more, which made *Leonard* angry. And now the little ones are crying. Oh, if it isn't one thing, it's another!" Poor harassed Ann rushed away to cope with an outbreak of infant wails, and I went to my room.

I was shivery. We had all come close to death in that ambush. Was some emissary from Mr. Mew still lurking in the neighbourhood, waiting for a second chance?

What if they were lurking here in the house? I could assume that I had enemies under this roof, but they would be foolish to attack me actually in Lockhill. I hoped that this wasn't wishful thinking, but I'd better believe it, or I would flee from the place in fright.

My room felt safe enough. Candles were set ready and a fire laid. I called Jennet to light them. Presently, Dale joined me, and we set about preparing me to sup with company. I asked if Brockley had gone yet, and she said yes, and told me how he had picked a good horse and pretended that he had permission to take it. However, her voice faltered, and as she combed my hair, I felt her fumble. I met her eyes in the mirror and saw that she was crying. She looked away, but I reached up gently to take the comb from her.

"Dale?"

Her reply was a gulp and a quick brush of the hand across her eyes.

"Are you anxious about Brockley?" I asked.

"Yes, ma'am. I know it's not my place to say so, but what he's doing might be dangerous—that's true, isn't it?"

"Never mind about your place." I swung round on my stool and looked her in the eye, woman to woman. "Yes, it's dangerous, and yes, the peril should be mine and not his. If that's what you're thinking, Dale, then I agree with you. But he wouldn't let me take the risk myself."

"No, I know, but why," wailed Dale, "does there have to be any risk at all? A lady like you shouldn't be tangled up in such things—it's not right!"

She buried her face in her hands. I had taken the

comb but she still held the hairbrush, and the bristles caught the edge of her headdress, pushing it back to release a straggle of greying brown hair, pathetic and absurd.

"Dale," I said gently, "it's for the Queen, you know. We are all the servants of Elizabeth."

"Is it for the Queen?" Dale sobbed. "Is it really? Has he gone into danger for her sake, ma'am, or for yours?"

"For both, I suppose," I said. "Dale, I'm worried about him, too, but Brockley is a capable man. He'll be back by dawn, you'll see. I think you need some supper. You'll feel better when you've eaten."

"I had something, ma'am. With Brockley, before he left," Dale hiccuped, between a sob and a laugh.

"I'm glad he was wise enough to eat before setting out. Well, you've supped," I said, rising and making for the door, "but you are to have some wine with me now. We both need it." I put my head out of the door. *"Jennet!"*

The merchant Bernard Paige had criticised my cream and tawny, and implied that green was a difficult colour for me. Up to then I had liked my tawny and my pale green ensembles, but his remarks had dampened my enthusiasm. However, I had let him sell me some golden yellow damask, and while sewing with the girls before I left for Windsor, I had made it up into a bodice and overskirt which looked much better over the cream kirtle than either of the others did. This evening, I would wear the golden yellow for the first time.

To go with it, I chose a clean ruff, gold-embroidered slippers, and a pearl pendant with matching earrings. Once, I had had to sell my jewellery to maintain Meg, but since then, the money earned from watching Robin Dudley had enabled me to replace it with new pieces. Dale, who had cheered up a little after taking the wine, packed my hair into a gilt net. I touched my wrists with rosewater, and sallied forth.

The door to the empty schoolroom stood open, and from the gallery beyond the further door came a flicker of candlelight and the sound of conversation. Someone laughed, and there was a snatch of music from the spinet. Walking through to join the company, I saw that all the Mason family were there. Pen was wearing a very grown-up gown with a lace-edged ruff. I noticed with amusement that she was still being responsible and looking after her sisters. Now that the weather was not so bitter, the heat of the fire could reach the nearer window bays, and Pen had marshalled Jane and Cathy into a bay where they were all stitching away, with Pen overseeing the work, for all the world like a conscientious governess.

George and Philip, stiffly dressed in their best, were seated near the hearth. They had a chastened air. Crichton, in one of his gloomy black gowns, although this one did seem to have been brushed, stood by the fire, talking to a stranger, a heavily built man with grey hair. He too wore clerical black, and this, I supposed, was the boys' prospective schoolmaster. The other man, presumably his friend, was seated at the spinet and idly picking out a melody. He had his back to me as I came in, but I could see that he was tall, a rather splendid figure in a crimson doublet veined with silver thread. Hearing the Masons greet me, he turned, rising courteously to his feet.

"Ursula," said Ann Mason, "this is Mr. Mark Lenoir. Mr. Lenoir, may I present Mrs. Blanchard, who is staying with us? And this," said Ann, turning to the grey-haired stranger, "is Dr. Ignatius Wilkins, who keeps a school in High Wycombe, which we hope George and Philip will shortly join."

Ignatius Wilkins, schoolmaster, of High Wycombe. There could hardly be two of him. So this was the man, and here he was at Lockhill. He bowed to me. "Delighted, Mrs. Blanchard." He didn't sound delighted and didn't seem the kind of man to experience delight very often. He had a powerful voice, thick with phlegm, and brown eyes which were curiously watchful, looking out from a fleshy face scored with the harsh lines of pride and authority. Even if I had known nothing about him, I wouldn't have taken to him.

"And I too am delighted," said Mr. Lenoir, coming forward and offering me a strong right hand. It was over-strong: the grip of it almost crushed my bones. His voice, unlike Dr. Wilkins' voice, was warm. He had a trace of French accent, and the dark eyes which looked so intently into mine were hot and hard. "You are charming to behold, if I may say so, Mrs. Blanchard. The court is sadly deprived while you hide yourself in the country. It is hardly kind to deny yourself to those who have a right to gaze on you."

"Er . . . th-thank you," I said.

Many ladies, especially those who pull their stays

too tight, are capable of swooning almost to order, and just then, a swoon would have been a pleasure, but although my knees felt so weak that it was mostly Mr. Lenoir's powerful grip which held me upright, I did not actually faint. I was obliged to remain one of the gathering.

Dr. Wilkins' too-watchful eyes were studying me, and inwardly, I recoiled. I was glad it was not *his* hand that I was grasping.

However, in the circumstances, Mr. Lenoir could hardly be described as a comfort. Mr. Lenoir was an even bigger shock than Dr. Wilkins.

I knew him, and his name wasn't Mark Lenoir at all. His name was Matthew de la Roche, and since last October he had been my lawful wedded husband.

I don't know how I got through the evening. I remember being invited to play the spinet, and having to decline because my hands were so unsteady. Whenever I spoke, I stammered. Matthew managed much better than I did, probably because he would have known in advance that I was here. He played the spinet instead of me, very competently, and the music prevented too much talk, but supper was another matter.

Leonard Mason obviously wanted to impress his sons' future schoolmaster, and the meal was served in style in the big hall, where the hearth was lit. The antlers had been dusted, and the dishes—far more of them than usual—were assembled in the adjacent long room and borne to the dinner table in formal triumph by Logan and Redman, for all the world as though we were at a court banquet. And, of course, there was conversation.

In a daze, I partook of roast pork, and beans in a piquant sauce, and fresh manchet bread, and listened to Dr. Wilkins describing the studies that George and Philip would undertake at his school. I entered into a polite conversation with Matthew and Mr. Mason, about spinet music.

I received the odd impression that although the two of them were travelling together as friends, Wilkins and Matthew were not in charity with each other. They virtually ignored each other, and I did not think this was just because Matthew, who was opposite me, hardly ever took his eyes off my face.

Dale was present, although, having supped with Brockley, she did not sit at the table, but waited to one side, ready to attend on me if I needed her. Her eyes had widened at the sight of Matthew. I knew I could trust her not to speak out of turn, but I was aware of her, watching us, all through the meal.

Last year, I had married Matthew and then run away from him. Had he not fled the country almost at once, he would have died a traitor's death.

The marriage was forced on me. I had chosen to abandon it, and with reason, yet the parting had grieved me so deeply that I had written, asking if we could begin again. He had replied and said yes, but his anger, his sense of betrayal, had been there in his answer, all the same. Now that we were face to face, that betrayal hung between us, uncompleted business which must be resolved before we could hope to come together.

Nor was it the only uncompleted business. There

was also the matter of a lying message in Matthew's name, and the incarceration in that boathouse. No doubt Matthew had much to say to me, but I in turn had questions to ask of him.

The tautness in the air grew like a gathering thunderstorm, until I felt that at any moment, lightning would fizzle down from the ceiling of the hall. Ann, sensing the atmosphere and puzzled by it, tried to set things right with ordinary conversation and remarked on Mr. Lenoir's excellent command of English.

"You are a Frenchman, but you speak our tongue so well that I wonder if you were brought up in England. You must have spent time here, surely?"

"My father was French and my mother English," said Matthew. His eyes were still on my face. "I was brought up in France but I learned English from my mother. After my father's death, I brought her back to England, but she did not live long and I returned to the Loire valley. I do still have . . . business interests in England and occasionally visit, but not often. I am a supporter of the same religion as yourselves, and perhaps my views are somewhat stronger."

"Oh, but surely!" Ann exclaimed. "Is that really a difficulty? We live very happily, in accordance with our own beliefs. No one has persecuted us."

"I still feel that England is not the right place for me. I would prefer not to be faced with a direct clash between loyalty to the Queen and loyalty to my faith. A traitor's death is a very horrible one."

That was meant for me, but I had thought about that horror many times, in dread and grief, until I knew for sure that Matthew was safe out of the country. I knew that in coming back to England, he had put himself once more in that danger. Tender pork and fresh bread turned in my mouth to a mass of woolly fleece. I had to force myself to swallow.

"I saw a man hanged and drawn once," said Dr. Wilkins conversationally. "The sounds he made . . ."

I wanted to stop my ears, but as a guest at someone else's table, I was constrained by good manners. Dr. Wilkins on this subject was as hateful as Aunt Tabitha and Uncle Herbert on the subject of death by fire. It came home to me then, more powerfully than ever before, that not only had I endangered Matthew, but the work I now did for Cecil and the Queen might send many others to the terrible fate which Dr. Wilkins was describing.

And them, the expected flash of lightning came, but not from the hall ceiling. It sprang from me in a crackle of anger. I interrupted Wilkins. "Would you say that a traitor's death is worse than a heretic's?"

I threw it out as a challenge, but he was unmoved. "It is not the same. Heretics are damned to an eternity of flame unless we see that they pay their debt here on earth. It is for their own sake that they must burn."

He spoke with complete assurance, as though he had just had a personal interview with the Almighty, and a guided tour of Hades. It silenced everyone, with the exception of Philip, who exclaimed, "It must be quite a sight to see!"

"I wouldn't want to see it. You're horrible, Philip," Pen declared.

"Please!" said Ann. "This is not suitable talk for a mealtime. Both of you will be good enough to be quiet." On the rare occasions when Ann was decisive, she was very decisive indeed. Philip and Pen subsided at once.

Leonard Mason changed the subject. "Yes, let us speak of pleasanter matters. I must tell you, Ann, that our friends were most interested in the new gliding engine. I am making good progress, even though Crichton here says his injured thumb won't let him help me any more!"

"It's too painful," said Crichton. He displayed his right thumb, with its empurpled flesh and blackened nail.

"I got Thomas to lend a hand instead," Leonard said. "Now, don't look like that, my dear." He shook a reproving head at Ann. "I know that you worry, but believe me, so do I! I'm not sure how to achieve a soft landing. I have decided to make the first attempt at flight with a dummy man in the machine, so you needn't fear I shall break my neck!"

"Oh, thank God," said Ann, and crossed herself in an excess of relief.

"I shall use a sack of meal, about the same weight as myself. Of course, the sack won't be able to use the controls, but if there is a steady wind I may be able to get some idea of whether or not the device will work, and how to overcome the problem of the landing. The catapult is finished now, too. Mr. Lenoir, Dr. Wilkins, how long can you stay? If you can remain with us for a few days, you may actually witness the experiment."

"Alas, we have business elsewhere," Wilkins said, "and cannot put it off. I would have been delighted to stay, otherwise, and so would Mark, no doubt."

"Yes, that is so," Matthew agreed, "but we must both ride on tomorrow. Some of the affairs I had in hand in England have not speeded as I wished. They need my attention."

And what, I wondered, might those affairs be? Just what was Matthew doing here, in Dr. Wilkins' company? I finished my supper in a bleak mood.

Afterwards, we returned to the gallery where Pen and George, who could both play the spinet reasonably well, provided music. The Masons rose to dance, and Matthew came to me, holding out his hand to me, to lead me on to the floor.

At court, when we first met, I had been in mourning for Gerald and I had not been taking part in dancing. It was Matthew who had persuaded me to begin again and Matthew who was my first partner since Gerald. I had been glad to dance again for I was tired of sitting still: the rhythms of the music constantly got into my feet. With Matthew, I surrendered to them once again, joyously.

Now, as I paraded down the gallery with my hand in his, my feet moving in time to the melody, those happy days came back to me. I could almost pretend that the intervening months hadn't happened; that we were still courting, with all our hopes ahead. Memories flooded back, not only of dancing, but of riding with Matthew in Richmond Park, on a hot summer's day, with the dust blowing up round our horses' feet; of cheering him proudly on at tennis or tilting; of walking with him in a July garden full of the scent of roses and lavender, and the sleepy sound of bumble bee and dove.

But this was the first chance we had had to exchange any private words, and those words had to be said.

"Matthew, what are you doing here?"

"I've come to collect my wife, what else?" He made an arch of his arm and I twirled under it, turning at the end of the twirl to face him. "You wrote that you wanted to come to me," he said, "but when I answered yes, what do I receive but a letter saying you cannot come until May! As it chanced, business with Dr. Wilkins brought me across the Channel, and the next I hear is that he is to visit Lockhill, and that Ursula Blanchard is staying there! I invited myself to Lockhill too. I wanted to see you."

We separated, drew apart, came together again, and once more took hands. "What a coincidence!" I said.

"You haven't changed a bit, Saltspoon. Yes, it is a coincidence, but a useful one. We must talk properly. Wilkins and I are in the tower suite. Where is your room? I'll come to you tonight."

I was afraid of what lay between us; afraid of waking the past and very afraid indeed of the present. I had longed for him so much, and now I feared to be alone with him.

Yet I wished for it, too. At my first sight of him, every bone in my body had leaned towards him. I told him where he could fine me.

"Until tonight," he said.

CHAPTER 16

Love and Danger

My soothing evening posset quite often failed to encourage sleep, but I didn't want it that night, all the same. As luck would have it, of course, Dale remembered for me and went to fetch it. Jennet came up with her, carrying my warming pan.

"I had your drink mixed ready," Jennet assured me proudly. "I remembered how much cinnamon you like. I've a good memory—even Mr. Mason once said so." As she spoke his name, she went pink and her calf-brown eyes glowed. She was as transparent as air.

"And I was glad of a chance to come upstairs," she added confidentially. "That Thomas is on the prowl. He keeps putting his head into the kitchen. He wants to marry me, but I won't have him, and that's that. He's idle and he's not kind. I've seen him get really rough with the horse sometimes."

"It might be as well," I said to Dale, after Jennet, having taken her time while warming my sheets with the pan, had reluctantly departed, "if Thomas did get married, though obviously not to Jennet. Dale, you can go and sleep in Brockley's lodging tonight. I . . . shan't need you here."

"Oh, ma'am! I did wonder . . ." Dale's eyes were warmer than they had been for some time. "I mean, he's your husband, isn't he?"

"You attended the wedding," I said dryly. "Yes, he is. God knows in what frame of mind he will come here tonight, but I expect him, yes. You go and sleep in your husband's bed. I expect you'll find him slipping in with you at daybreak." As an afterthought I handed her my posset. She was sure to be worrying, and even though she didn't care for herbal drinks, I said, it just might help her to sleep.

As the house sank into stillness, I waited for Matthew alone, fully dressed, sitting on my window seat, with a single candle, placed so that it would light the room. He was a long time in coming, so that I wondered if he had really meant to come, or whether he meant to leave me sleepless and disappointed. Yes, disappointed. Desire was stronger than fear. Well, if necessary, I would wait the whole night through and then appear in the morning looking as though I had slept well, and cared nothing. I had my pride. If he thought he could hurt me by withholding himself, well, I would disappoint *him*.

And then my heart began to hammer, for somewhere a door had opened and closed softly. I strained my ears but I never heard his footsteps and only knew for sure that he was there when the doorlatch lifted and he stepped noiselessly in.

He, too, was still fully dressed. He closed the door

after him and stood with his back to it. The candlelight showed his strong, dark features, his long chin and dramatically slanting eyebrows. His nostrils and eyes were pools of blackness.

"I'm here," I said. "On the window seat.".

He picked up the candle, holding it so that the light could fall on me. "Ursula! I thought for a long time that I'd never see you again, or ever want to. Are you well?"

"Very well. As you see. Tell me," I said in social tones, "how do you happen to know Dr. Wilkins?"

"He used to be a parish priest in Sussex, not far from my house at Withysham. He still visits old acquaintances in that district. I met him at a dinner party last year."

"I didn't know where his parish was," I said.

"Does it matter? Why the devil are we talking about Wilkins? When your first letter reached me, Ursula, I did not know what to think or feel. Even now, I'm not sure whether I want to make love to you or throttle you."

I sat with my back quite straight. "You wrote to say I could come to you."

"And *you* wrote, saying that the Queen would not release you until May. Do you need her permission to join your own husband? Ursula, why in heaven's name didn't you set out for France at once? The weather's been passable for sailing—I managed it! Our letters crossed the Channel! Why couldn't you? *Why?*" As though he had suddenly lost control of his feelings, he strode across the room to stand over me.

I shrank away. "Matthew, don't . . ."

"Why not? Give me one good reason why I shouldn't strike you or strangle you. Do you take me for a plaything?"

"No, I do not! Never that!"

"All right. Don't be afraid of me. I shall do you no harm. Ursula, when I leave for France again, are you coming with me?"

"I don't know! I never thought to find you here. Does Wilkins know you are my husband?" I asked.

"Why do you keep talking about Wilkins? Yes, of course. You are the reason why I wanted to come to Lockhill with him. I ask you again: will you come back with me to France?"

"That depends," I said.

"Depends on what, may I ask?"

I was rigid with the effort of remaining aloof, of not flinging myself into his arms, crying his name, and swearing to forget the past if he would forget it too, but there was a question which had to be asked.

"Matthew, there is something I must know. A few weeks ago, did you try to arrange for me to be brought to you from England?"

"Did I . . . ? What are you talking about?"

I had the letter with me, the letter which might be a forgery, which had led me to get into that boat with its Charon-like boatman. I took it out and gave it to him. "Did you send me this?"

He read it, holding the candle so as to see the writing clearly, then he turned to me again. "I did not write this. Someone has imitated my hand. I would not have dreamed of saying that your servants should not come with you. As my wife, you are the lady of the Château Blanchepierre. I would never ask you to travel unescorted. Did you do what this says?" He handed the letter back to me. "What happened?"

"I got into a boat with a man I didn't know, who said he was going to take me to you, but wouldn't even let Brockley come with me to see me safe into your hands. He took me," I said shortly, "to a lonely boathouse and left me there. He said I would be fetched to you in due course and then he left me there. I had rugs and a few days' supply of food and water. Fortunately, Brockley had followed us and got me out."

"It had nothing to do with me. That I swear."

Relief flooded through me. He could not know that Brockley had recognised Wylie. If Matthew had been involved, there was no real reason why he should not say, yes, I did try to have you brought to me, but my wishes were misunderstood, my arrangements went wrong.

And then I would have known, for sure, that he and Wylie were linked, and therefore, assuredly, that he was involved in this business, whatever it was, that I was trying to investigate. As it was, I could still hope that he was not, that his acquaintanceship with Wilkins was no more than the coincidence it seemed.

Oh God, I said inside my head. Let it be so!

"And now?" Matthew said. "I asked you a question. You replied with another, which is hardly an answer. Will you come with me to France? Or," he added, with bitterness suddenly invading his voice, "does your excessive obedience to the Queen mean that you have had second thoughts about me? Did you come here at her bidding, for some reason?"

"No! I had been ill." I held on to the story that the Cecils and I had prepared. "I came here for a rest. The Queen allowed that. She wouldn't let me sail to France because she thought the seas too dangerous at this time of year."

"How am I to trust you? I am a wanted man in this country. I have to travel under an assumed name. Will you send Brockley for the parish constable in the morning? So that I can be committed to the Tower and the scaffold?"

"No, Matthew, no! When I fled from you last year, I waited a day in London before I reported what I knew, to give you time to realise your danger and make your escape. I gave you a chance, and no one was more thankful than I when I knew you had taken it!"

"Oh God, Ursula." Setting the candle down on the window seat, he turned away and leant his forehead on the wall. "Why did you do it? How could you betray me like that?"

"I had to betray someone; I had no choice. You were part of a plot which would have endangered the Queen and the whole English nation! What else could I do?"

He straightened and took the candle up again, once more holding it so that he could see my face clearly. "You are so beautiful," he said wonderingly. "To behold, you are so sweet, so womanly. You wrote so tenderly. But if you loved me, you couldn't have left me as you did."

"Wrong."

"Wrong?"

"Yes. I do love you. I did then, too."

So much so, that from the first day I met Matthew, Gerald had begun to recede over the horizon of the past. After I fled from Matthew, Gerald's memory had revived for a time, for what had been between Gerald and me had never been sullied, and thoughts of my first marriage were therefore balm and comfort. To recall Matthew, on the other hand, meant pain and bitterness. But from the moment that I heard from Matthew, Gerald was once more one of the regretted but buried dead.

Matthew said nothing, and I spoke again. "What do you imagine I really felt, when I decided that I must leave your side in the name of—in the name of integrity, I suppose? Do you think it wasn't a struggle? I tell you, I tore my heart out of my body and stamped on it! Do you think I didn't want—long—yearn—to stay with you?"

"Then why didn't you?"

"Haven't I just told you that?"

"Because you had to put the Queen first? Why? You are a woman. For all that salty tongue of yours—which I loved you for, if you remember, and have missed—you are a woman. Women—wives—follow the lead their men give them. Women are not asked to put the outside world, matters of rulers and realms, before their husbands. No one expects that of them."

"It's expected of them every time their men march away to war!" Brockley had said that, more or less. "Women are more than you think."

"You can't justify what you did and still claim that you loved me."

"I can. I do. In memory, I have treasured those few

days and nights of our marriage. They are my Eden, from which I was driven by—"

"Elizabeth with a flaming sword?" said Matthew sardonically. Matthew was essentially kind. That he could sound like that, was a cruel indication of how badly I had hurt him.

"I suppose you could put it like that," I said, "but she needs loyalty in her servants."

"Does she? She's an unnatural woman, Ursula. Why does she refuse to marry? When I was at court last year, there were whispers that she wanted to marry Dudley, but there was another set of whispers, too. There were those who said she would never wed anyone: some said she was a faery creature who was too ethereal for the marriage bed, and some said she loved only power and was too cold of heart to love any man. I think that may be true. I also fear that your heart resembles hers; that you have a point of ice at the centre of it."

"The Queen isn't cold of heart," I told him, and then, wishing to defend Elizabeth, I repeated to him what she had once hinted to me. "She fears marriage. When she was two, her father had her mother beheaded. She was too young then to understand what it meant, but when she was eight he had her young step-mother Catherine Howard beheaded as well. The one illuminated the other. Anne Boleyn and Catherine Howard both saw an adoring husband turn into the monster who sighed their death warrants. Elizabeth will not forget."

"What nonsense. She is a queen in her own right. Who would sign her death warrant?"

"Mary Stuart," I suggested. "Or her advisers."

"Oh, for Christ's sake, Ursula! That salty tongue of yours again! Are we back again to the plots and politics that made you abandon me? Why can you not leave them alone?"

"I want to, but . . . tell me something, Matthew. You say you came to England to complete some business, and you are riding on somewhere with Wilkins tomorrow. What is the business you have in hand?"

"Oh really, Ursula. Does it matter?"

"Yes, it does. You said yourself: I am your wife. There are things I have a right to know."

"For the love of God! Last year, I had to get out of England in rather a hurry, if you remember! Various matters I had in hand had to be left unfinished. Practical matters! I had left money in the hands of various people—one of them was Wilkins—to buy seed, farm animals, stone and timber, for Withysham. I was repairing it and stocking it. I had to leave transactions half-settled and in a state of confusion. I have come over in exasperation to sort out the muddle, and—I hope—to take some of my own money back with me. Is that enough for you?"

"After last year," I said quietly, "can you blame me for fearing that you are once again caught up in some political plot?"

"To hell with plots! To hell with this passion you have for nosing out intrigue! There is no intrigue! I've got a herd of cows grazing in another man's pastures, and a dispute to settle over whether I did or did not actually buy a pair of draught horses!" Even in the flickering light of the single candle, I saw his eyes blaze. "Satisfied? I am tired of this kind of talk. We're man and wife, joined by a priest in the presence of witnesses! *Ursula!* Ursula . . ."

The first time he spoke my name, it was a cry of exasperation. The second time, it was a groan.

"Ursula . . ."

The third time, it was a prayer.

Setting the candle down once more, he came and sat on the window seat next to me. I could feel the warmth of him. The night, the pool of candlelight, encircled us, closing us in.

"I'm as weary of plots as you are," I said fiercely. "Why can't we just live together and be happy?"

"We can still be happy," said Matthew. "Now, this minute, we can still be happy."

He pulled me into his arms and his mouth came down on mine. I yielded without resistance, and let him pick me up and carry me across the pool of light to the dark cavern of the curtained bed.

He laid me down and moved away briefly to blow the candle out, then he came back to me, jerking the curtains closed, shutting us into a deeper blackness than ever. In it, we fumbled with each other's clothing, undoing ties and buttons, pulling and pushing until at last we were free and our two bodies were together without barriers or hindrances.

We held each other gently at first, exchanging caresses, but my betrayal and desertion still lay between us, and when the gentle caresses suddenly turned savage, I knew I had half-expected it. I did not care, though, for my spirit was as wounded as his. I, too, had a core of savagery in me. Let him grip and bruise; let him bite; let him thrust. I could give it all back and with interest. My fingers dug deep into his shoulders; my nails tore his back. My teeth scored his smooth skin and padded muscle, and when he drove, my loins rose in reply; until the cleansing flame kindled at last, and cauterised the suppurating rage and pain in us; and rose like a fiery wind and hurled us out of the world, back into our lost Eden.

We fell apart at last, aching, gasping, exhausted. And then we were turning to each other, this time for comfort, holding one another, giving way helplessly to what, through it all, was still love.

Some time later, we were united again, and this time gently, in kindness, in pleasure which rose smoothly to its height and then melted easily into the sighs and kisses of completion. Afterwards, we lay curled together, as in the past, as in the memories I treasured. My back was curved into his chest, his arms around me. In my ear, he whispered his old endearment. "Saltspoon!"

We were fast asleep when the uproar began, when the kitchen door crashed open and we heard Thomas the groom shouting frantically for help.

The house was full of babble and slamming doors and running feet. Sitting up, fuddled with sleep, we heard someone hammering on my own door and shouting to me to wake up. Calling that I was coming, I was coming, just a moment, I scrambled out of bed. Matthew was up already and struggling with candle and flint. As always happens when one is in a hurry, he couldn't at first get a spark to strike. He did it at last, and somehow or other he and I got ourselves into some kind of clothing: Matthew into shirt and hose; me into shift and wrapper.

I whispered, "Wait till all's clear before you come out!" and ran out to find a crowd on the landing, including a dishevelled Thomas with his shirt hanging out of his breeches, Redman in the act of shoving a flaring torch into a wall-bracket, Mrs. Logan behind him with a triple candlestick, and Jennet, who rushed at me, crying that Mrs. Mason had gone over to Brockley's lodgings to help Dale.

"She's ill, ma'am, and Mr. Brockley's not there!"

Thomas pushed forward. "I sleep with the other grooms in the loft next to Brockley's rooms, ma'am! We all woke up, all of a sudden, because there was a noise from there. A sort of choking, like, and someone trying to call for help and throwing themselves about. So we ran in and Dale was there, alone, in some sort of fit, struggling and heaving and half off the bed . . ."

Without more ado, I pushed past them all, rushed down the back stairs and through the kitchen regions to the back door into the stableyard. Pelting across, I went up the outside staircase to the loft rooms as though it were a rope ladder, reaching for the steps above with my hands to pull myself up faster. I burst through the door at the top to find a lantern on the table in the outer room and candlelight wavering beyond the door to the bedroom beyond. There were horrible noises in the bedroom.

Ann, dressed in a wrapper just as I was, was administering something to Dale from a pewter mug, while Dale gagged and choked. As I came in, Dale pulled away and lunged for a basin which was on the bed beside her. Ann caught hold of her to steady her, glanced at me over her head and said calmly, "I'm giving her salt water. I think it's going to work. She'll need strong wine afterwards, as a stimulant."

What looked like most of the household had followed me and now crowded up the staircase after me. Ann caught sight of the butler in their midst. "Redman, go and fetch some wine. Hurry! It's all right, Dale. We're all here. That's it, bring it all up. Where's Brockley got to, Ursula? I know he came back with you today."

"I . . . er . . . I had another errand. I had to send him back to . . . to Maidenhead," I said, inventing rapidly. "I told him to lodge there overnight. Oh, Dale, however did this happen? Let me help her, Ann!"

Ann surrendered her place to me. "There's more salt here—Brockley eats here sometimes and keeps it handy, I suppose. There's water in the pitcher on that chest. Ah, Jennet, there you are. Mix some more brine. We've got to get all the venom out of her, whatever it is."

"Ugh. No more . . . no more salt water . . . !" moaned Dale, between retches and gasps.

"I know you can't abide it, but you must," I said.

It went on for a long time. Jennet kept on stirring salt into water, and I worked on Dale as passionately as though she were my sister. She was more than a servant to me: she was a dear friend. I forced the solution down her throat, and held her when she threw up, until at last her system was empty, though her greenish pallor and gasping breath still terrified me. Redman had brought the wine, and when we felt that Dale had no more to bring up, Ann and I poured her a draught and I helped her to drink.

The room had been cleared. Mason, who hadn't

been in the first wave of people to come crowding into the room, had now appeared, decided that there were too many people there and chivvied everyone out, except for Ann and myself. Even Jennet was shooed away. Matthew, tactfully, hadn't put in an appearance and neither had Dr. Wilkins.

"At least," Mason said, surveying the three of us as we sat on the edge of Dale's bed, Dale in the middle, with Ann and myself on either side, "the rest of us are well, so there can't have been anything wrong with the food at dinner."

"I should nope not!" said Ann indignantly.

"But what caused it?" I asked in bewilderment. I held the winecup to help Dale drink again.

"I don't know," said Dale wanly. "Perhaps something while we were out. We ate at inns, and you never know with inns." I was still holding the cup to her lips, my face turned towards her. Her icy fingers had closed on my wrist and her eyes were on me. Her lips moved, framing words which were only for me. "Let me speak to you alone."

I turned to the Masons with a reassuring smile. "Do please go back to bed. I'm sorry your sleep has been so disturbed. I will stay with her. Take some more wine, Dale."

They withdrew, though Ann insisted that she would stay up and return if needed. "Just send a groom for me."

As the door closed behind them, Dale whispered urgently, "It was that posset, ma'am. That posset you passed on to me."

"*What?*"

"There it is," said Dale, and pointed to where my dented goblet still stood, on a shelf beside the bed. "You were kind enough to give it to me and I didn't like to say no, but I just don't care for these mixtures. I brought it over here but I didn't drink it, or not at first. Only, I couldn't sleep, Roger not being here, and I thought, well, it's got cold and it's bound to taste funny, but still, I'll try it and maybe it'll get me to sleep. But when I sipped it, I didn't like it, not one bit, so I didn't take any more. And then I started to feel ill, oh, so ill! I couldn't breathe! I was so frightened!"

"Oh my God!" I said.

Blessedly, Dale's breathing was now more or less normal and a trace of colour had reappeared in her face. "I think I shall be all right now, ma'am," she said presently. "Thank you for what you've done for me."

"Ann Mason got to you first," I said. "I shall thank *her*, for both of us. If anything had happened to you . . ."

It was too much. I had gambled on Lockhill being safe, on the grounds that our enemies would not, as it were, foul their own doorstep and cause the smell to attract unwanted attention. I had been wrong, completely wrong. I put my face in my hands and found myself being held by Dale and soothed as though I were the patient and she the nurse. The sleeve of my wrapper fell back and she saw the marks of Matthew's fingers on my arms.

"Oh, ma'am, look at that! Was it . . . did Mr. Matthew . . . ?"

"He came to me. We've been together. Don't ask any more, Dale. I don't know what will happen next."

After that, I cried for a long time on Dale's shoulder and Dale, too, grew tearful, apparently with remorse.

"Oh, ma'am, I should have known. It's always been Mr. Matthew for you. And I've been thinking such things. That Redman has a forked tongue. I'm sorry. I'm so sorry!"

"What sort of things?" I asked, sitting up and wiping my eyes with the backs of my knuckles. And then I understood. "Oh no! Has he been making nasty remarks about me and Brockley?"

"Yes, ma'am," said Dale forlornly.

"Dale, I did warn you that there might be gossip. I told you that Redman saw me and Brockley come out of the gallery, that first time I tried to get into Mr. Mason's study, and that he was obviously thinking things. Is this why you and Brockley quarrelled?"

"How did you know we'd quarrelled, ma'am?"

"It was plain enough!" I said.

"There's been talk from more than Redman, ma'am," Dale said wretchedly.

"I know, and it isn't true."

"But it gets into one's mind, like poison. Like *that!*" Dale pointed at that posset. "We made it up before he went off last night," she said. "We did that, at least, but if only he'd come back. I want him!"

I knew that feeling all too well. I had felt like that when Gerald, covered with festering pocks, lay motionless on his bed with coins on his swollen eyelids. And nowadays I felt it all the time, for Matthew. I put my arm round Dale.

"He'll come soon, I'm sure. It must be nearly dawn. I'll wait with you. Listen, Dale, there's something I want to know. It's about that posset. I recall Jennet saying that she'd remembered to get it ready. Had it been standing somewhere? Could anyone have got at it? Did people know it was for me?"

"I found it on one of the tables in the long room next to the hall, ma'am—well, on one of those narrow chests they use as tables. All the things to eat and drink were set out there yesterday evening. I recognised your goblet." She pointed to it. "Jennet said she put it there because the kitchen was in a muddle, with that big supper. It might have been thrown away by mistake if it was in the kitchen while they were clearing up. It must have been standing for some while, because when I felt it, the goblet was nearly cold. I had to take it to Jennet in the kitchen and say, is this Mrs. Blanchard's posset, and if so, will you warm it up. She said yes, it was for you, and put it in a pan straight away."

"So there it was, standing, and people were coming and going, all over the place." I thought back. "At the end of the evening, we didn't all just go straight from the gallery to our bedchambers, did we? I went downstairs myself for a moment—I'd left a shawl in the hall. While I was there, I saw Mr. Mason come down with his guests. They went out into the courtyard for a breath of air. Redman was looking to see if the dining table had been properly cleared and I think Tilly got curious about what was going on. She never joined us during the evening but—yes, she drifted through the long room, come to think of it."

"The boys went out, too, last thing," Dale said.

"When I went down for the posset, Crichton was just calling them in. Everyone in the house could have gone through that long room, ma'am, and everyone knows about your posset and your dented pewter goblet. Mrs. Mason jokes about it sometimes."

There were no answers here. Anyone could have put poison into my bedtime posset. Anyone at all, including Mr. Mason.

We fell asleep in the end, Dale and I, side by side on Brockley's bed. When we woke, well after dawn, he had still not returned.

"Wait awhile," I said. "He could have decided to sleep somewhere. He could have gone to an inn and be resting there now. He'd be tired."

"Oh, ma'am, where *is* he? I must get up! I can't just lie here."

"Yes, you can. You need to rest."

Somehow, I persuaded her to stay in bed, and fetched her some bread and milk from the kitchen, feeling that this would be kind to her abused stomach. To my relief, she ate some of it. "Just stay there. I'll come back soon," I said. Then, once more, I returned to the house, this time to dress myself properly and go to my own breakfast.

On the way, I found Thomas talking to a flushed and irritated Jennet, who was banging a mat outside the kitchen door. As I came past, Jennet turned away from him, evidently glad of an excuse, and asked how Dale was.

"Much better," I said. "My thanks for all your help, Jennet." Jennet looked as though she wished I would linger and talk and thereby protect her from Thomas, so I added, "Leave that mat now and come inside. It's chilly out here." Gratefully, she followed me in, and Thomas, with a shrug, took himself off.

At breakfast, everyone asked after Dale, including Dr. Wilkins, who had apparently slept through it all and had only just heard of the night's events. I reported that Dale was recovering and, as she herself had done, put her illness down to something she must have eaten while we were travelling.

I did not want to mention the posset until I had had time to work out whether this would be a good idea or not. Would it warn the enemy off, or make the poisoner feel that my suspicions made me more dangerous than ever? I was careful to take only food which others were sharing, and I scanned the faces at table, seeking for disappointment, or eyes that would not meet mine.

But all I saw was Matthew, once more watching me across the table, which had been laid this time in the dining room. The moment he entered the room, I felt the lightning zigzag between us and it amazed me that no one else sensed it. When we rose from the table, I found him beside me. I went with him, and we found our way into the stableyard.

"Wilkins and I must leave today," Matthew said. "It is a matter of urgency. After that, he will go home and I will set out for France. But first, I will return for you—if you are willing to come with me, that is. I warn you, Ursula, I will have no more shilly-shallying. You will come to France with me when I leave—or never. You can bring your servants and we will collect your daughter, too. Do you understand?"

I was silent, thinking. I stood there, twisting my wedding ring. Matthew looked at it.

"That is not the ring I gave you."

"No. It's Gerald's. Yours is different, heavier, and someone might have noticed, so I keep it in my jewel box. Few people know of our marriage."

"And you don't want them to," said Matthew bitterly.

"It makes my life easier if they don't," I said. "Matthew, you can't have entered the country legally. How would we travel? Have you made arrangements?"

"Yes. I used a helpful fisherman, a Catholic, last year when I escaped, and that's how I'm travelling this time. I landed secretly and I intend to leave the same way. We can make a detour to fetch Meg—her mother can take her for an outing, surely? Once she leaves wherever she is staying, in your company, then we can be off."

"Are you sure you want me?" I asked. "*Can* you ever trust me again, after last year?"

"You didn't give me time enough, last year, to win you over," Matthew said. "A little longer and I think you would not have been able to tear yourself away. Am I right?"

Again, I was silent. He was perfectly right. Even those few short days of marriage had almost undermined me. I had come so near to yielding myself and staying with him.

When I didn't speak, Matthew said, "I felt it last night. Was I mistaken?"

"No. You were not mistaken. Matthew . . ."

It was as though I were standing in a river, in a

strong torrent which roared with a loud voice and pressed against me and in a moment would carry me off my feet. I fought to keep them. I put aside a momentary, unwise urge to confide in Matthew. He had not conspired with Wylie or Mew to abduct me, but nevertheless, he had come here with Wilkins, *Wilkins*. What if this unfinished business of his *was* something to do with the unknown plot at Lockhill?

And where—*where*—was Roger Brockley?

I had said to Dale that he might have stopped somewhere to sleep. Or his horse might have gone lame, or he might have missed his way. Arrows flying out of a wood, and a poisoned posset said otherwise, but the thunder of the river drowned their voices.

He'd be back soon, quite safe. At the last moment before I left England with Matthew and Meg, I would send word to Cecil, telling him all that I knew or guessed. When Brockley returned, he might have information which I could add. I would then have discharged my duty to Cecil and the Queen. The plotters, whatever the nature of their plot, would be apprehended, but not Matthew. If he were one of them, he would escape. And I would go with him.

I said, "Go and deal with your unfinished business about cows and draught horses, then return for me. I will come with you."

"You mean it?"

"I mean it."

We sealed it in the time-honoured way, with a long kiss. Then Matthew went back into the house and I went to sit with Dale in Brockley's lodging. Presently, I saw two saddled horses being led to the front of the house, and slipping downstairs again, I ran to the arch which gave on to the courtyard, to watch Matthew and Wilkins ride away. Then I returned to keep Dale company and wait for Brockley.

Two hours later, there was still no sign of him.

Dale, though still obviously weak, was too worried to stay in bed. She insisted on getting up and dressing. "Something's gone wrong with him, ma'am. I've got to be up and doing."

That was when I realised that in agreeing to go with Matthew, while my own business was still incomplete, I had behaved like a lunatic. I had been optimistic past the bounds of reason.

Brockley had gone off to search the premises of Barnabas Mew, and Mew might well be a very dangerous man. How could I blandly have assumed that Brockley would be back any moment? I had behaved like a reckless innkeeper in a bad comedy, who says "yes, sir, of course, sir" to a guest who wants gryphon steak for supper, and a unicorn saddled ready at six o'clock tomorrow morning. While Brockley was still missing, I could not possibly set out for France, and that was that.

Well, if love had made me mad, then I must stay mad. I must hold on to my insanity and attempt the impossible. Brockley was missing, so I must find him. Once before, a man had gone on an errand for me and died for it. I would not stand idle while history repeated itself. I would be back by the time Matthew returned, I told myself, or else I would not be back at all.

"Dale," I said, "I'm going to Windsor. I'm going to find out what's happened."

"But you can't go alone, ma'am!"

"I can and I must. I owe it to Brockley. There's no time to ask advice or send for help," I said. "Although . . . Dale, if I saddle Bay Star, could you ride behind me as far as the village and then deliver a note for me? To Dr. Forrest at the vicarage? I think he'd let you rest there until you felt well enough to make your way back."

"You think he'd help me, ma'am?"

"Well, he's an Anglican vicar. It's a reasonable hope."

"Why don't you just go to him yourself and ask him to do . . . whatever needs to be done?"

"Because then he might try to stop me from going, and I can't tolerate delay. Can you do it, Dale?"

"Yes, ma'am. For you and for Brockley, yes I can."

"Then," I said, "I'll get my cloak and put a few things together for the saddlebag, and we're off. Wait for me here. I'll find your husband and bring him back to you, Dale. If it's possible at all, I'll do it."

On which note of valiant optimism, I hastened down the wooden steps to the stableyard, called to a stableboy to saddle Bay Star for me and have her standing ready, and then hurried back to the house and headfirst into unforeseen disaster.

CHAPTER 17

Saddling a Unicorn

I went straight to my room. I changed my clothes, selecting my sturdiest pair of shoes and donning an old kirtle and open-fronted gown with a very small ruff. Once dressed, I sat down to pen a rapid note to Dr. Forrest. Folding it, I pushed it into my hidden pocket, added a purse of money, my lock-picks and my small dagger in its sheath, caught up a cloak and sped down the main stairs.

At the foot, I was accosted by Mr. and Mrs. Mason together.

"Ah, Mrs. Blanchard." Leonard Mason's long face was cold and his voice unfriendly. "I have been looking for you." He noticed my cloak. "Were you going out?"

"I am going across to sit with Dale. The stableyard is chilly."

"Dale must wait, I'm afraid. I wish to speak to you in the study. Ann, will you fetch Tilly and Redman?"

I looked at Ann in astonishment. We had after all met at breakfast, and I had seen no sign of this extreme hostility then.

Ann looked back at me with anguish in her eyes. "I

can't believe it. I'm sure there is some explanation . . ."

"Explanation of what?"

"Ann," said her husband on a warning note.

"Oh *dear!*" Ann, muttering in a desperate fashion, hurried away.

"What is all this?" I asked Leonard. "Must it be now? I really should get back to Dale. I must apologise that I can't teach the girls this morning but—"

"I think it extremely unlikely," said Leonard Mason "that you will ever even speak to my girls again, let alone teach them. I should never have let you come here. I did so only to please my wife, who was so certain . . . well, never mind. Come, Mrs. Blanchard. At once!"

He motioned me to go back up the stairs ahead of him. I went, perforce, furious at being interrupted now, and bewildered too. In the study, Leonard sat down at his desk, leaving me to stand. Taking care not to look towards the cupboard which held such embarrassing memories, I took up a position facing the desk, hands clasped before me.

"Mr. Mason, will you please explain what this is about?"

"Wait."

And wait we did, in a simmering silence, until footsteps came through the gallery and the anteroom, and Ann arrived with the butler and Tilly. Redman, stocky and muscular as ever, wore the apron he used when scouring silver; Tilly was all in black, relieved only by the little white ruff at her neck, although even that had black edging.

Tilly did not go in for farthingales, and her dark

skirts hung limply round her bony form. Her face was gaunt and white, the skin about the faded blue eyes almost transparent, and a violet vein pulsed on one temple as though a parasitic worm were embedded there. She was a sick woman, by the look of her. She came to stand a few feet away from me, and her washed-out eyes regarded me with that incomprehensible loathing of hers.

Ann, her sweet face unhappy, went to perch on the window seat, taking the few spare inches not already occupied by books.

"Very well," said Mason. "Let us take all this in order. This morning, Tilly, you came to me and told me of things you had recently observed. You also said that there was talk in the household because of something Redman had seen. I have since spoken to Redman, and since his part of the story comes first, in terms of time, I'll begin with him. Redman?"

Redman hadn't looked at me at all. Solidly, he said, "It wasn't long after Mrs. Blanchard came here—not as much as a week after, if I remember aright. I came upstairs one afternoon to light the gallery fire, and I saw her and her groom Brockley come out of the schoolroom door. It seemed a bit odd to me that she should have her groom in the house at all. And there had been talk, sir, before she came. Talk that in London she had a certain reputation . . ."

"I have *not!*" I burst out.

"I did not ask you to speak," said Leonard. "Redman, continue."

"Well, sir, when she saw me, Mrs. Blanchard went scarlet. It looked funny to me."

"I have been aware for some time," I said, breaking in again, "that before I came here, someone had slandered me. May I know precisely who it was?"

"Slander? Your behaviour bears out what was said! Mr. Mew gave us warning. He had been in London and heard you talked about."

So it had been Mew's idea. Clever! I thought in fury.

"My wife," said Mason, "did not believe it. She had a good impression of you on your first visit, as indeed had I. I agreed to give you the benefit of the doubt and now regret it. We have heard Redman—"

"We have heard Redman talk nonsense! Brockley undertakes many tasks for me."

"That I can believe," said Redman, and grinned.

"Be silent," said Mason, to me, not to Redman. He turned to Tilly. "Now, Tilly, will you repeat your part of the tale?"

"I don't feel well enough to get about much these days," Tilly said, "but now and then I take a turn in the house, and if I go through the gallery, I mostly rest awhile in one of the window bays. From the bay nearest the schoolroom, you can see down into the stableyard." She had a thin, quivery voice, but part of the quiver at least was banked-up outrage. "One morning, I saw her and Thomas, your own groom, sir, kissing. And that's not all, not by a long way."

She paused for effect and my stomach turned over. Oh no, it couldn't be, she couldn't have. How on earth . . . ?

It was. She had. Matthew had been careless.

"It was last night, when this person's maid took ill."

This person was me. In Tilly's eyes, I had lost the right to the courtesy of my own name. "I got up to see what the uproar was, same as everyone else, but I was slow. Everyone else was off down the stairs by the time I got near them and near where her room is." She pointed at me. "But there was a cresset in a wall-bracket, so I could see well enough. I saw Mr. Lenoir, him that's gone now, and good riddance."

"Tilly," said Ann from the window, "that is not the way to speak of the master's guests."

"Isn't it, ma'am? When this guest was seen coming out of a young woman's bedchamber at dead of night? Because that's what I saw: Mr. Lenoir putting his head out of *her* door—" again she pointed at me—"and looking round furtive like, and then coming out and going away, back towards his guest room. They'd been together, and he'd kept hidden till he thought he could come out and no one would see him, that's what."

"What was he wearing? Was he dressed?" Ann asked suddenly.

"Shirt and breeches, ma'am, but they looked as if they'd been pulled on fast."

"Well," said Leonard. "There you have it. What have you to say, Mrs. Blanchard? You may speak now."

"Thank you," I said ironically.

I was so angry that I was lightheaded. I should by now be mounting Bay Star, getting Dale down to Dr. Forrest and myself on the way to Windsor. My time was being wasted, my energies diverted, and for what? Because of a snooping butler and a prurient lady's maid, and because the whole world laboured under the delusion that if a man and a woman were alone together it had to have something to do with sex, and if a man kissed a woman it was always with her approval, and even if it wasn't, it was still her fault somehow.

"I speak to my manservant Brockley where and when I choose," I said furiously. "He is the husband of my maid, Dale. I regard them both as my friends. *Friends*. That and nothing else." I glared at Redman. "Yes, I saw you putting the wrong construction on it. If I looked embarrassed, it was because I hated what you thought, not because you were right. And because of the lying gossip that someone put about before I set foot in Lockhill, Thomas thought I would be easy meat, so one day, in the stableyard, yes, he pounced on me. If you were looking as avidly as you seem to have been," I added, turning on Tilly, "you would also have seen me stamp on his foot and break away!"

"And last night?" said Leonard cynically. "Did you stamp on Mr. Lenoir's foot?"

"I had no need to. Mr. Lenoir did not come to my room for purposes of illicit lovemaking." This was literally true. Lovemaking between a married couple is not illicit. What I said next was less truthful, however. "I saw him this morning," I said. "He spoke to me. He was asleep when the alarm was raised about Dale, and he, too, was slow to reach the stairs. Tilly wasn't the only one! He had heard people shouting and heard my name and he thought I must be still in my room, asleep." I didn't sound very convincing and their expressions proved it, but I ploughed on. I hadn't much alternative, after all.

"He knew where my room was, as it chanced. He

banged on the door, and when there was no answer, went in to wake me, if I were there. I was not, so he left the room again. He left cautiously in case he were seen and someone thought ill of him and me. As has apparently happened!"

I didn't invent all that on the spur of the moment. It had worried me all along, that someone might have seen Matthew come out of my room. During the ghastly night hours, while I dosed Dale and held her head and kept her awake, I had worked out what to say if I were challenged. However, although it was the best story I could think of, I knew how feeble it was.

Ann was crying, but more in sorrow at my perfidy than grief for a victim of injustice, and Leonard Mason was staring at me, his lip curling scornfully. "Do you expect anyone to believe this . . . this tarradiddle?"

"Of course she doesn't. How could she?" Tilly's scorn was searing. "And tarradiddle's the right word! I saw them again this morning. They were kissing in the stableyard!"

I opened my mouth, couldn't think of anything to say, and shut it again. I couldn't look at Ann.

Tilly stared at me with hatred. "You can see what sort she is! She's had a husband and a child, so I hear. If I'd been that blessed, I'd be grateful all my life and down on my knees giving thanks to God. Not grabbing at every man that came my way like a greedy baby that's never satisfied."

"Tilly!" Ann burst out, and even Leonard and Redman looked slightly bemused.

"I see," I said. "Jealousy plays a part in this, too. I ought to be sorry for you, Tilly, but you make it too difficult." I turned back to Leonard Mason. "I don't expect you to believe me, as a matter of fact, but nevertheless, I am innocent. I suppose you will want me to leave Lockhill, and I shall be only too happy to go, I assure you!" Matthew would be coming back for me and I must make sure he could find me, but all that lay on the other side of Windsor and my quest for Brockley.

"I trust," I said, "that I may have time to pack and to move Dale to the village? She is not yet well enough for a long ride, but I will leave her at the vicarage. My man Brockley is away on an errand for me. When—" I must not say *if*—"he returns, perhaps someone would direct him there. I would like to say goodbye to the girls."

"You will not set eyes on my daughters again. I will not allow you to contaminate them," said Mason. "However, I shall not," he added, "send you off unescorted. I know my duty. One of the under-grooms will accompany you wherever you choose to go—to the court or Thamesbank, I suppose. I will permit you to make your own explanations when you get there."

This was too much. First I was hindered from setting out after Brockley, and now I was to be encumbered with a Lockhill groom. I had had proof enough last night that danger lurked in Lockhill itself, and not merely outside, in ambush along the road.

"I can do without an escort, thank you," I said. "I will remove myself and Dale at once. Ann, I really am innocent, you know. I think you know it by instinct, and your instincts are right. Good day to you all."

I turned on my heel to leave the room, but Leonard

said, "Redman!" in a sharp voice and the butler barred my way.

"I said," said Leonard Mason, "that I wouldn't send you off alone. A gentlewoman, even one as benighted as yourself, must not be galloping about the countryside on her own. While I arrange for a groom to escort you, I can't have you wandering about at your own will. You might yet encounter one of my girls, and that I will not allow. Redman, show Mrs. Blanchard to her room and lock her in. You can have half an hour to put your things together, Mrs. Blanchard, while the groom who is to go with you prepares his own. Then I will fetch you myself and take you to the courtyard, where your horse and escort will be waiting."

Rage is quite an interesting physical sensation. I examined it with clinical care while Redman, with a painful grip on my left elbow, marched me to my room. It was as though a fire were ablaze in the pit of my stomach and sending waves of rippling air up into my brain. Redman pushed me through my door. As he did so, he whispered that he'd dearly love to come in with me, but the master might object.

"I'd object still more, believe me," I said as he shut the door on me.

I heard him turn the key and remove it. I smiled grimly. A lock without a key, I could deal with. A bolt would have been a serious problem. I waited until his footsteps had retreated downstairs, then I fished out my lock-picks and set to work. Five minutes later, I was out on the landing, heart thudding and ears stretched. Which way? Main stairs? Back stairs? I reconnoitred, listening at both stairwells. From the top of the main staircase, I could hear Ann's voice, speaking on a note of protest, and Leonard answering her, irritably. They were in the hall, but moving away from me. I tiptoed to the back stairs, but someone was talking near the foot of it—the Logans and Joan, by the sound of it. I tried the main stairs again, cocking my head. I could still hear Ann's voice but it was further off now. I took a deep breath, and started noiselessly down.

The staircase descended into a space where the partition between the hall and the long room stopped short and the two rooms opened into each other through a wide archway. Creeping forward, I peered into the hall. It was empty. The Masons' voices came from the parlour, which opened off the other end. The parlour door was open, but only a little and with luck, the Masons wouldn't see me cross the hall. The door to the porch was halfway along the opposite wall. On tiptoe, I ran.

I was out on the porch, down the steps, out in the courtyard. The mastiff stood up, but recognising me, lay down again without barking. I noted that, as usual, the outer gate stood wide. I turned left and sped past the kitchens, stooping to avoid notice through the windows, and darted through the archway to the stables. No one was about, but Bay Star was there, ready saddled and tied by the mounting block. Thanking providence that I had thought of ordering her to be saddled before I went indoors, I ran towards her. Dale appeared, hovering doubtfully at the top of the stairs from Brockley's rooms. I signalled to her to come down, which she did, all in an anxious flurry.

"Ma'am, what's happening? You've been so long and you're all put about!"

"Explanations later," I said breathlessly, tightening Bar Star's girth. "Quick!" I whisked off the halter which was on over the mare's bridle, bunched my skirts and scrambling up the steps of the mounting block to put myself into the saddle. "Come on, Dale!"

Obediently, Dale also clambered on to the block and on to Bay Star's back behind me, hitching her own skirts up and sitting down astride.

"Oooh, it's awful without a pillion saddle! It's all slippery!"

"Don't you dare fall off! Hold on to me! Oh *God!*"

I had been lucky so far, but good fortune rarely lasts. There were shouts from the kitchen and Redman burst out of the door, loudly demanding that I should stop. Mason, Crichton and a distressed-looking Pen ran out after him, followed by Ann, who snatched Pen back. Meanwhile, Thomas had erupted from the stable, and another groom from the harness room. I wrenched Bay Star's head round, pointed her at the gate, and drove my heel into her. She went like a loosed arrow. Redman actually tried to block the way, arms outstretched, but I swore at Bay Star and threw her forward, straight at him, and he jumped aside.

We hurtled through the arch into the courtyard. Edwin Logan was crossing it, and Redman, running after me, bellowed at him to shut the outer gate. He tried to obey, but Bay Star was past him before he came within yards of it, and we were through the gatehouse and out in the lane. The shouts faded behind us as we thundered down the lane, with Dale's arms wrapped round me like ivy round an oak.

"Dale, please!" I gasped. "I can hardly breathe."

It was only a quarter of a mile to the village, and at the speed we were going, it took us hardly any time to get there. I slowed down as we reached the houses, for there were children playing in the road, not to mention fowls pecking and a dog nosing at the gutter. The place was busy, the day's work well under way. The cottage chimneys gave off hearthsmoke and a darker smoke came from the forge. Women were chatting by the well or sweeping dust out of open cottage doors. We attracted stares, even when we slowed to a trot: possibly because Dale looked odd, bumping behind me; possibly because Bay Star was champing with excitement and foam was flying from her bit; possibly because we gave off urgency and desperation like a smell.

"There's the vicarage!" said Dale. "And the church."

She mentioned the vicarage first because it was so much the bigger of the two, standing beside its church like a mare beside a foal. I pulled up outside. "All right, Dale. Slip down now." I felt in my pocket for the note and also for my purse. I counted out some coins, and as Dale descended to the ground, I handed them to her. "Two weeks' wages. You may need some money and—well, it's just in case I don't get a chance to pay you later."

"But, ma'am!"

"And here's the note. Here comes Dr. Forrest. Give it to him. I hope he'll do as it asks. Plead with him if necessary! I'm off! I've got to do my best. The innkeeper could disguise a bit of beefsteak with a sharp sauce and maybe glue a piece of straight oxhorn on a white pony's forehead and get away with it, but I can't cheat. I've got to serve up genuine gryphon and saddle that bloody unicorn."

Dale, understandably, gaped.

"Never mind, Dale. I haven't lost my wits, don't worry. Goodbye."

I applied my heel to Bay Star again and was away, leaving Dale in the road outside the vicarage, with the job of convincing Dr. Forrest that I was not demented or drunk and that my note must be taken seriously.

I could only hope that she was equal to it.

I was still aflame with rage and excitement, but after a mile or two I slowed the pace, because it was over half a day's ride from Lockhill to Windsor and I must take thought for my horse. I must also, I said to myself, think carefully about Brockley. His failure to return *might* be just a matter of a lame horse or the need for a rest. In that case, he would surely have gone to an inn. A lone female making enquiries at inns after a missing manservant would have an odd appearance, but I would have to do it.

I had an odd appearance anyway. The weather was mild and clear and the main track to Henley was busy, with people driving carts or riding on horseback, or trudging along on foot. Many of them glanced at me with puzzled interest. A young woman riding alone, and with an air of purpose such as mine, was an unusual sight. People, in the main, are civil, however, and mind their own business. No one troubled me.

If I found no trace of Brockley along the road, then I would in due course arrive at Windsor. What then? Did I ride straight to Mew's door and demand news of Brockley?

If Mew was a conspirator, or even simply a criminal, I would be walking into a trap. What could I hope to achieve, alone?

The grim truth was that, far from stopping to rest or meeting with any accidental mishap, Brockley had probably walked into the trap ahead of me. He had known the risk beforehand, but forewarned wasn't always forearmed, as I had discovered for myself. Brockley's body might already be rolling along in the depths of the Thames, on its way to the sea. He might never be seen or heard of again. Dawson and Fenn had been found only by chance.

In that case, all my haste was a pointless response to panic with no common sense behind it.

As I left Henley after a fruitless enquiry or two, I decided that I might as well let Bay Star go at her ease. It would be no use at all to enter Barnabas Mew's premises until darkness had fallen.

Enter Mew's premises? At night? The thought had taken shape in my mind without warning, and I came up against it as though it were a wall. Was I considering *that*? But Brockley had been going to search Mew's basement for evidence of conspiracy, and it was in the basement that I must look for him. If he were not to be found, then I should myself seek the evidence we needed. To do that, I must get in after dark and go down into the cellar myself. It was the only way. It was a horrible prospect, but obvious. If

Brockley had come to harm there, then it was because he constituted a threat. If the only thing I could do for him now was to find the secret which had killed him, then I must try.

I had summoned help, but I dared not wait for it, because I did not know for sure if it would come. Unless and until I knew for sure that Brockley was dead, I could not give up hope that he was alive, perhaps a prisoner, and if I could rescue him in time, I must.

I rode on, grimly thinking this over. At Maidenhead, I stopped at the Sign of the Greyhound, where the landlord recognised me. He was obviously surprised to see me travelling alone, but I forestalled any questions by asking my own. Did he remember my man Brockley, and had Brockley lately passed that way? "He went on an errand for me and hasn't come back. I'm worried about him."

Brockley, it seemed, had indeed called at the Greyhound late the previous evening. He had stopped for half an hour, taken a meat pie and a beaker of ale, and given his horse a nosebag. "I don't know which way he was bound, but he was all right then," the landlord said.

I bought some food to take with me, and set off again, going briskly once again, because it had occurred to me that perhaps I would be wise after all to make the best speed I could, in case I were pursued from Lockhill.

I was still thinking. I had deliberately given Barnabas Mew a chance to send a man to kill me, or else to contact Lockhill and get someone there to do it. He had taken the chance. In the last twenty-four hours, my life had been attempted, albeit unsuccessfully, twice over.

Was Mason responsible for these attempts? It would be a bitter thing for his family if so, but it was all too likely. Crichton was probably in it too. He had certainly consented to the lie about the tapestries. But Crichton took Mason's orders. When Dawson listened at a door in Lockhill, had he been listening to Mason giving the tutor instructions oddly unrelated to education? What orders had Mason given about me, I wondered, and to whom?

Redman and Tilly, with their silly accusations, I thought, must have come in very useful, the triumphant fruit of the seed which had been planted so carefully before my arrival. I wondered if Mason had really believed Mew's lies on the subject of my reputation or if *I heard it from Mew* was merely an excuse, a façade of innocence. Mason and Mew could well have concocted the slander together. Not that it mattered. Mason was certainly making use of it now. He was in a position to order me out of his house with every appearance of righteousness. I could then be disposed of somewhere else, where suspicion wouldn't point to him.

How had he meant to do it? He had tried to send an undergroom with me. The two Lockhill under-grooms were young lads, open-faced and friendly, not at all like potential assassins. But I could be wrong about that. Mason might have meant to send me off with my killer. Or else to send me into another ambush. He could have other accomplices—men in the village, perhaps.

Having thought things out that far, I turned off the

road and covered quite a segment of my journey by
riding across country. It was a nuisance, but it felt like
a wise precaution. I got lost once, but I hailed a farmer
who was taking muck to his fields in a donkey cart, and
he put me right. I ate my packet of food, which consisted of ryebread, cheese and a wrinkled last year's
apple, as I went along, and both Bay Star and I drank
from a stream. By late afternoon, I was in Windsor.

I rose right past Barnabas Mew's shop, and had to
quell a ridiculous impulse to dismount, tether my
horse, walk into the shop and ask if Brockley had been
there. It was difficult to believe that nervous, humble
Mr. Mew could really be dangerous, that it wasn't safe
to walk into a perfectly ordinary shop and say, "Have
you seen Mr. Brockley?" but I had had warnings
enough that the danger was real.

I did, in fact, dismount and go into a shop, but it
wasn't Mew's. It was well away from the clockmakers,
and sold lanterns. I was going to need one.

I bought a candle-lantern, stowed it in my saddlebag and betook myself to the Antelope Inn. Here I did
enquire after Brockley.

"He was here with me, only yesterday," I said to the
landlord. "He was on a speckled grey cob then, but he
came back to Windsor yesterday evening, riding a
chestnut."

"Did he now?" The landlord was a large, self-
assured man with an aggressive manner. "I've not
seen your man, mistress, no, but the horse—would it
be a gelding, sixteen hands, maybe eight years old,
with a narrow white blaze and one white sock on
the off fore?"

"Well—yes, that sounds right. You've seen it?"

According to Dale, the horse which Brockley had purloined from Lockhill so that he could ride back to Windsor without overtaxing Speckle, was Mason's second mount, a very good animal. Brockley had got away with it by simply declaring that he had permission, and Lockhill being Lockhill, which meant disorganised, no one had questioned it. When Dale described the horse to me, I knew which one she meant. It was called Blade, because it had a dagger-shaped white streak down its nose. It certainly stood about sixteen hands, and it had a white sock, too, though I couldn't recall on which foot and I hadn't the slightest idea how old it was.

"Seen it?" said the landlord. "I've got it! There's a horse like that running about loose in my paddock. The paddock was empty last night, but this morning there was this horse in there, grazing. My ostler called it in with a sieve of oats and fetched me to see it. I took a look at its teeth and I'd say eight years old or thereabouts. I told Martin to give it some water and leave it in the paddock for the time being. And I'll tell you something else: I had a look round, wondering if it was a stray that had got in through a break in the hedge. I couldn't find any breaks, but under the hedge I found a saddle and bridle. Someone came in the night and turned that there horse out in my paddock a'purpose. The tack's in my harness room now."

I went to inspect both horse and tackle. It was impossible to be perfectly sure—chestnut horses with white markings are as common as dandelions in spring, and the saddle and bridle were plain and anonymous—

but it was highly likely that both steed and tack were Brockley's.

If so, he had reached Windsor. He had put his horse in the inn's pasture, hoping no doubt to return for it before long, and then he had gone in the darkness to Mew's shop. And vanished.

"Stable the horse," I said to the landlord, "at my expense. I'll talk to you further tomorrow. I shall need a room for the night and a meal of some sort as well."

"And Mr. Brockley?"

"I hope," I said, "that he'll be here by morning, but if not, as I said, I'll pay the bill for the horse."

"I'm not that worried about the horse," said the landlord, frankly. "What I'm worrying about is you. Were you meeting this fellow here? You're not running away with him, are you?"

Another of them! Redman, Tilly, and now this.

"No," I said, "I am not. He is my manservant and is at the moment carrying out a commission for me. I expected to meet him here."

Once more, I was overwhelmed without warning by a longing for Matthew. If only, if *only*, Matthew could be here to help me now. When I bade him farewell at Lockhill, I had had a mad urge to confide in him, but I knew I had been right to resist. Even if he were not entangled in this business, he might still sympathise with it. Even for Brockley's sake, I dared not tell him the truth.

How I wanted to investigate Mew's shop in the company of someone large and tough, though! Matthew would be my preference, but the landlord of the Antelope would do! What if I told him everything and asked for his help?

But he probably wouldn't believe me, and if he did, he wouldn't let me come with him. He would go alone into danger, as Brockley had, and it is a heavy burden, to know that you have sent men into peril.

So I stood there steadily and looked him in the eye until he shrugged and gave over questioning me. Then I asked to see my room and ordered my supper. There was no parlour to spare this time and I'd have to eat at the same time as everyone else, the landlord said, but when I said I would take the meal in my room and not join the rest of the guests at the long table in the main dining parlour, this seemed to allay his suspicions about me.

"Quite right. A lady travelling alone should keep her privacy," he said.

I was now so nervous that I felt sick rather than hungry, but I knew I must eat if I could. Also, I was thinking ahead. I asked, therefore, for half a cold chicken as well as a wedge of hot veal pie and a dish of preserved plums. Some of it might prove useful during the night to come.

CHAPTER 18

After Dark

Before eating, I went out again, to reconnoitre on foot while there was still some daylight left. I put up the hood of my cloak, in case Mew should be about.

I was becoming very frightened of the danger and difficulty which lay ahead. I must go out after dark, find my way to Mew's house—which would be occupied—break in and enter the cellar. Only for Brockley's sake could I have contemplated it at all.

My only chance of getting in would be from the rear, as Brockley himself had said. All the doors, back or front, would certainly be bolted, and the lockpicks would therefore be useless. But according to Brockley, in that back room where I had seen what could be the cellar entrance, the window might be vulnerable.

Walking through Peascod Street, I looked keenly at the shops and cottages to either side. Most of them adjoined each other, but there were a few alleyways giving access to the rear. Such an alley ran between Humfrye's, the apothecary, and the next shop along, a bakery. I counted the shop doors between Mew's and the apothecary—I would look very foolish if I burgled the wrong house—then I made for the alley.

At the far end, I found myself on a path which ran past the back gardens of the shops and houses. On the other side were sheds and paddocks. I saw animals grazing: horses, a cow or two, a few goats. Beyond the paddocks lay ploughland, turning grey in the gathering twilight. I turned left along the path, meaning to inspect Mew's fence, and was abruptly accosted by a loud voice from the direction of the bakery.

"Here, who are you? What are you a'doing of, prowling about along here when it's nearly night? What are you after?"

A gate creaked and the owner of the voice appeared, male, bulky, clad in workaday clothes with twine holding his baggy breeches in at the knee. He was inquisitive and frowning. To judge from the flour dust on the breeches, this was the baker in person.

"Well, I'm damned! It's a lady! Are you looking for someone, mistress? What brings you here?"

"My dog ran away!" I said. As a spur-of-the-moment liar, I thought, I was undoubtedly improving. "I'm looking for it. It's a little white lapdog. I didn't mean to disturb anyone. I'm so sorry."

"What do you mean, disturb anyone? No one's asleep yetawhile. If you're looking for a dog, what's its name?"

I tried frantically to think of a name in a hurry, and saw a thistle near my feet. "Thistle!" I said.

"*Thistle!* Of all the funny names. What you want to go calling a dog Thistle for?"

"He's got a rough coat. Thistle!" I called. *"Thistle! Thistle!"*

We pursued the absurd hunt for a nonexistent dog for some time, all along the path. The baker insisted on coming with me. I thanked him graciously and seethed beneath the surface. At last I gave up, said that I must have been mistaken in thinking that Thistle had run into the alley. I would return to my lodgings, I said, and see if the dog had run back there ahead of me. As I set off for the inn, the baker stood in the mouth of the alley, staring after me.

I had done my reconnoitring, all the same. I had identified Mew's back garden, and I had observed that he didn't seem to possess a dog, although one of his neighbours did—it had barked as we passed. I had seen, too, that the path was lamentably neglected and that quite a few people used it as a convenient dump for rubbish. Several heaps of old fabric and various items of thrown-out furniture lay along the verge. There was a cracked stool and a battered truckle bed and some old wooden boxes of various sizes. If I needed an impromptu ladder, the means were to hand.

I had also ascertained that to reach the path I need not go through this alley. Two others came out on to the same path, so that I could keep well away from the bakery.

Once back in the Antelope, I did a little prowling on the ground floor to familiarise myself with it and then went to my room. My meal arrived and I forced the pie and the plums down my gullet, but I cut the half-chicken in two and secreted it in my hidden pocket. I had other uses for that. Then I rested until the darkness had fallen completely, and I even dozed a little. The night before had been disturbed, and the one to come would be worse.

When the time came to set out, I had to shake myself into action. I was unwilling to leave the safety of the inn, and there was no doubt that I was tired, but I overcame these weaknesses and made myself set about leaving the Antelope.

The front door, of course, was heavily barred at nightfall and couldn't be unbarred without making a noise, while the spitboy and a couple of other servants slept in a room off the kitchen, which made it difficult to leave by way of the kitchen door. But my prowlings had taken in the parlour where I had dined with Brockley and Dale. Memory had told me that it was promising, and memory hadn't lied. The parlour was at the front of the house and had a low window. This had a bolt, but it was small and the room was well out of earshot of anyone sleeping in the house.

Having lit my lantern from the candles in my room and then blown the candles out, I crept downstairs. The parlour was quiet and empty. Kneeling on the window seat, I slid back the bolt and peered into the dark street; then I hitched up my skirts, and climbed quietly out. Reaching in to retrieve my lantern from the seat, I pushed the window almost shut behind me and hoped that no lurking robbers would notice the weakness in the inn's defences.

In the darkness, the world was hushed. A few houses showed a gleam of candlelight but no one was about. Most people fear the dark to some extent: night is when ghosts and murderers walk. Even indoors, in rooms with lamps and candles, the corners have shadows, and sometimes the shadows have curious shapes. The doorways of Peascod Street were like black mouths, and the sound of an owl made me jump. My breath was uneven with nerves as I made my way along the road, and I trod with care, for my lantern was not bright and at first I could hardly see where I was going.

Presently, the moon, which was only just past the full, came out from behind a patch of cloud. Aided by this, I found an alley, not the one I had used the first time, and went round into the path at the rear. However, the blanched moonlight cast such dense black shadows that it was of little use for seeing fine detail. Holding the lantern up, I moved warily along the back fences. I found Mew's fence, but the neighbour's dog began at once to bark. I threw one of the chicken pieces over the fence, and to my relief it wasn't one of those overtrained guard dogs which won't take food from strangers. It fell on the chicken with a growl of pleasure and I set about a close examination of the fence.

The baker's presence had stopped me from doing this the first time, and what I found now was discouraging. Brockley had said that the fence looked ramshackle, and so it was, but at close quarters it wasn't quite ramshackle enough. The gate was solid, and although the fence was breaking away from the post at one end, I still couldn't squeeze through.

Well, I had supposed from the start that I would probably have to go over the fence rather than through it, and I had seen how it might be done. My teeth expressed an inconvenient wish to chatter, but I quelled them and began gathering useful items from the thrown-out objects beside the path. One box was rotten and fell apart when I touched it, but I found one which was sound, and put the cracked stool on top. Despite the crack, I hoped it would bear my weight.

As I stepped on to it, however the dog next door, his chicken finished, barked again and threw himself against the fence. I fumbled hurriedly for the rest of the meat, and tossed it to him. Once more, he pounced on it, and the barking subsided into low, muffled growls. I hitched myself side-saddle on to the top of the fence. It shook ominously but I swung both feet over together, and let myself down with an awkward slither because I needed a hand for the lantern and could only spare one to hold on to the fence.

I crouched in the overgrown garden, wondering if anyone had heard me or the dog. Nothing stirred. No sudden candlelight showed; no one opened a window to stare out into the night.

The moonlight now seemed too bright and so did my lantern. As I rose to my feet, they threw my shadow across the straggling grass, and the lantern danced, sparkling, in my shaking hand. If anyone did peer out, I would be horribly obvious. Lifting my hem, I ran forward, feet brushing through the weeds and thistles scratching at my legs, until I could shelter in the darkness close against the house.

Here I leant against the wall, trembling, until I was sure that I had still not been discovered. Next door, the dog whined a little, but had evidently decided that I was a friend, for it didn't bark loudly again. I turned to look for the window to the back room.

At once I encountered a new puzzle. Mew's premises were quite large. The back wall boasted a kitchen door, and three other windows as well. I had no idea which window was the right one, and when I tried the door, it was bolted on the inside, as I had expected.

I shut my eyes, trying to visualise the interior of the shop. The door to the office had been . . . where? Behind the counter, yes, but there had been another door as well, further to the left, leading to some other room. Standing as I was now, facing the back wall of the house, those rooms would be to my right. The office window wouldn't be the last on the right, then, but might be next to it.

Crouching low, I edged along the wall. A gleam of red light from the furthest window alarmed me, but peering cautiously round the edge of the frame, I saw that it was only the glow of embers from a dying fire. I made out a cushioned settle and a backgammon table. Some of Mew's living quarters were evidently on the ground floor. I had gone past the window I wanted, so I edged back. This window was utterly dark and I had to risk shining a light into it. I did so, with caution.

Yes.

This was the office. Now to see if I could get into it. I put the lantern on the ground, took out my little dagger and inserted the tip of it between window and frame, below the latch. The dagger's silver hilt was embossed with a spiral pattern which gave a firm grip, and the fine steel blade was razor edged, no less lethal for being small, but thin enough to slide easily into the crack and then to move upwards until it pressed against the latch. I pushed, hard. With a small scraping noise, the latch began to rise. Up . . . up . . .

I felt the window yield. Keeping the blade in place with my right hand, I used the fingernails of my left to pull the window open. Then I was climbing over the sill, lantern once more held awkwardly in one hand, and skirts getting in the way. If I had to do much more of this sort of thing, I said to myself, half hysterically, I would go in for wearing breeches.

I closed the window after me but didn't latch it, so as to leave myself a quick way out. I stood still to listen. All was silent. I directed my light to the wall-hanging. The door was there, mostly concealed behind the fabric, but with one edge just showing. Lifting the hanging aside, I found that this door too was bolted, but on my side. The bolt slid back as smoothly as if it had been lately oiled, and I opened the door.

I had read the deeds correctly: this was the way into the basement. I was standing at the top of a flight of steps which led steeply down between stone walls, stained with damp. The lantern light glinted dully on the iron hinges of a door at the foot.

To say that I didn't want to go down would be an understatement. The mere thought of descending into the depths of the earth like that, alone, at night, filled me with cold terror. It was not simply the fear of being caught by Mew—at that moment, I would almost have welcomed the arrival of an outraged but human Barnabas Mew. What I felt was a deeper level of my fear of the dark. It was the ancestral dread of demon and ghoul, of things that crawl from ancient graves, and clutch from the darkness beyond the light of lamp or candle.

If only dawn were near, I thought timorously. The

faintest glimmer of light in the eastern sky would drive away the demons. If only there were just a little, tiny trace of greyness visible through the window, then I could dare the steps into the depths. I had only to wait for dawn . . .

A tradesman's household woke early, however. People would be astir before daybreak.

I had to do this, for Brockley.

I made sure that although the window was not latched, it would still look as though it were, if someone glanced at it across the room, by candlelight. I could not bear to shut the basement door behind me, but I set it just ajar, and the wallhanging hid the open edge. I put my lantern in my left hand and took my dagger in my right. If anything did grab at me from the darkness, I would stab first and ask questions afterwards.

Down and down. The air was cold and dank. The door at the bottom was bolted, as the one above had been, but this bolt, too, slid easily back. I opened the door slowly and peered in, holding the lantern ahead of me.

I saw nothing more alarming than a table with two branched candlesticks on it, furnished with candles. I crept forward, and put my dagger on the table. I picked up a candle, lit it from the lantern and then lit all the others. Light filled the room.

The basement was large, maybe twelve feet square, lined with brick. It had a stone floor and a vaulted stone ceiling, quite high. The air was fresher here, and as I looked up, I saw a grating in the ceiling, and beyond it, even as I watched, an edge of cloud, faintly silvered by moonlight, glided away and revealed a single star.

The grating was probably in the garden. The star, serene evidence of the open sky in the world outside, was immensely comforting. Feeling braver, I looked around me. The room was a workshop of some kind, with a small furnace set in one wall and a workbench along another. Various tools were arranged on it, very much as in Leonard Mason's shed. Some hooped chests and two crates lay beside the opposite wall. A stack of something—logs, perhaps—occupied one corner.

Putting my lantern down beside my dagger, so as to leave my hands free, I investigated the furnace. It was out, and had been raked clear, but it was faintly warm, and had been recently used. Straightening up, I noticed that what I had thought might be logs, was actually metal ingots, probably copper. They were smallish, only brick sized, but there were a lot of them. Then the candlelight picked up a brighter gleam behind them and I saw that at the back lay several bars of silver, and half a dozen or so of gold.

This was evidence, hard, physical reality. An ordinary clockmaker might well need a small furnace, but he wouldn't need all this metal, and Mew had specifically said he didn't keep much in the way of raw material on the premises. I went to look at the crates. The word "tin" was painted on them both. Either Mew was making clocks for the entire nation, or else . . .

Excitement made my pulses thud and I almost forgot to be afraid. I tackled the hooped chests. They were locked, but I was more confident with my lock-picks now. I had one open in less than a minute, and threw back the lid.

Inside were leather bags, closed by drawstrings. I undid one. The bag was full of sovereigns, shining and new. I lifted a couple out and examined them, wondering. I had two sovereigns of my own on me, and I got one out and made a careful comparison before putting everything away again and turning to the workbench.

Among the tools there were several hammers and a set of small steel cylinders, each with a pattern engraved on the circular face at one end. The patterns included, among other things, the profile of Queen Elizabeth. They were meticulously done. It occurred to me that I could guess now who had forged Matthew's writing on that false letter.

I had found what I expected to find, although I could still see no connection with Mary Stuart. Were there two sets of miscreants in or around Lockhill? A gang of coiners and a set of conspirators on Mary's behalf? Just what—just *which*—had Jackdaw discovered?

I went to look at the chest of sovereigns again. They seemed fractionally lighter in colour than my own coins, but they were most convincing. It had taken great skill to judge the mix of metals so well, and to prepare such perfect dies. I assaulted the locks of the other chests and found that all were filled with bulging bags of sovereigns.

Somewhere in the house above me, there was a sound.

I froze, straining my ears. It had been a very small sound, perhaps no more than a piece of furniture creaking. I waited. Nothing happened. Someone had got up to relieve himself, perhaps. All the same, I looked affrightedly about me for a hiding place, an equivalent of Leonard Mason's cupboard. That was when I saw what I had not noticed before: that opposite the door by which I had entered, shadowed by a recess, was another door.

I blew out the candles, seized lantern and dagger and made for it. This door, too, was equipped with smoothly running bolts. Opening it quickly, I peered through the aperture, lantern raised and blade at the ready.

This second room was very small, also with a grating—I saw the glint of moonlight at once. The lantern showed me the room's interior: there was a table with a glass beaker and a jug on it, and then, as I moved the light, I saw a couple of brackets in the wall, where some kind of fitting—shelves or an oven, perhaps—had once been. A chain ran through one of them. My lantern followed the double chain down, past a padlock, to a truckle bed, where a man lay under a rug. The chain vanished under it and must in some way be secured to him.

The man was awake and sitting up, peering narrowly at the lantern. His chin was covered in an unfamiliar stubble, and even by lantern-light, I could see that the rest of his face was grey tinged with strain. Gold freckles stood out on his skin. I could see, too, the reddened bump on his high sloping forehead. I shifted the lantern so that its light fell on my face.

"It's me," I said. "It's Ursula Blanchard."

"*Madam!*" said Roger Brockley.

CHAPTER 19

Ill-Assorted Conspirators

"How did you get here?" Brockley demanded. "Are you alone? Madam, you shouldn't have . . ."

"Yes, I should. Help will follow, with luck. I left Fran with Dr. Forrest, the vicar, and gave her a note for him. If he does as he's asked, we'll soon have reinforcements. How did you get caught?"

"Mew and Wylie heard next door's dog. Wylie's here—he did take a message to Lockhill, but he came back straight away."

"Yes, I know. He told them that Mew wasn't coming. I think," I added grimly, "that he delivered another message as well, but that was certainly the pretext for going."

"No doubt. I'd spent an hour," said Brockley in an aggrieved voice, "hiding in the garden until the brute stopped barking, and much good it did me. You were mad to venture here! If you've sent for help you should have waited for it to come, and kept away yourself! How on earth did you get in?"

"The way I suppose you did: over the back fence, through the window and down the stairs."

"Alone? In the dark?"

"Yes."

Brockley had always treated me with respect, even when he was criticising me, but always, there had been in it a tinge of patronage: age to youth, worldly-wisdom to innocence; man to that natural inferior, woman. Now, in the lantern-light, I saw in his eyes another kind of respect: that of comrade to equal comrade. It was warming.

"And I saw what was going on in the room next to this," I said. "Did you?"

"Coining, just as you suspected. I was running my fingers through imitation sovereigns when Mew and Wylie burst in on me. I fought, but Wylie hit me on the head with something. It knocked me right out for a while, and when I started to come round, with a splitting headache, the two of them were standing over me and arguing about whether or not to finish me off and drop me in the Thames." Unexpectedly, at this point, Brockley stopped short. As if embarrassed, he turned his head away.

"What is it?" I asked. "Is your head badly hurt?"

"No. It's better now." He met my eyes again, his own curiously sad. "Have you got your lock-picks with you?" He pushed back his rug and I saw that the chain was run through another, which encircled his midriff and was fastened with a second padlock. "We have to get out of here," he said. "Just set me free. I'll talk while you work. Madam, I have something terrible to tell you."

"Brockley, what's wrong?" I set down lantern and dagger once more, got out my lock-picks and tackled the padlock. "What's the matter?"

"I'll take it in order, madam. Go through it calmly." Brockley took a deep breath. "When I heard them talking about finishing me off, I was only half conscious. They thought I was still knocked out and they just talked across me. Mew said, 'Who sent him here?' and Wylie said, 'It's got to be that Mrs. Blanchard. He's her servant.' Then he said, 'I told you I should have seen to her myself instead of just leaving word at Lockhill,' and Mew said, 'And I told *you* I don't want us tangled up personally with any more murders.' "

"Well, we assumed that they'd killed Dawson and Fenn," I said. I tried to speak offhandedly, but the very word murder turns you cold, believe me, especially when you're an intended victim yourself. It makes you feel hunted. You can hear hounds baying in your mind. My hands were unsteady and the padlock resisted my efforts.

"Yes, madam. Dawson and Fenn." Brockley nodded. "That was made clear later on. Let me finish. I was wide awake by then and I wanted to keep my eyes shut and stay quiet in case they said any more, but I couldn't. My head was that bad and I knew I was going to be sick. I sat up, groaning a lot, so they'd think I'd only just woken, and they broke off talking and I started to retch. Mew cursed me but he did bring me a basin. Wylie kept on saying they ought to put an end to me but Mew wouldn't have it. He said he'd meant to go to Lockhill to meet someone, and as he hadn't gone, the man in question would turn up here, as like as not, and he could take the responsibility. Till then, I'd better stay alive. I gathered that he'd been going to meet a Dr. Wilkins at Lockhill, but . . ."

My hands froze on the lock-picks. "And did Wilkins come?" I said. "And was he alone, or . . . ?"

Brockley was not given to swearing in my presence except in moments of stress. This was one of them. "Madam, will you bloody well get on with opening that lock? We've got to *get out of here!*"

"I'm trying. I'm trying! For God's sake tell me about Wilkins! *Did he come alone?*"

"No, madam. I'm sorry. This is the thing you will find terrible. He had a companion. He . . ."

"It's all right, Brockley. I already know. It's my husband, isn't it? Matthew de la Roche? Are they still here?"

The padlock clicked open at last and with a sigh of relief, Brockley shook off his chains and swung his feet off the bed. "Not very comfortable," he said dryly. "Although I did have enough play to get at the water jug and the chamber pot. Yes, madam. They're both here. They only arrived after dark last night. Didn't want to arrive openly, in daylight, it seems."

I said nothing. There was nothing to say. Matthew was here, close to me, but he was with Mew and Wilkins. He was one of the enemy.

"Mew and Wylie brought them down here," Brockley explained. "You know, I could have liked your husband if we'd met in some other way. He saved my life. Wilkins wanted me put down. He used those words—as if I were a rabid dog. But Mr. de la Roche wouldn't have it. He said that I was your servant and that you were his wife and you were coming to France with him and that I was to come too, and he wouldn't have me touched, for your sake. Then Wylie let out that you were probably dead, and your husband got hold of him and slammed him up against the wall and asked him what the devil he was talking about. I spoke up then, and shouted that we'd been ambushed by an archer yesterday and nearly killed . . ."

Heartsick, I sank on to the end of the bed. Brockley regarded me with sympathy, but pressed on with his tale.

"Mew tumbled it all out then, about you peering at his files and asking strange questions. He said he hadn't known what to do—how was he to know you and Mr. de la Roche were married? He just about knew that Mr. de la Roche existed, and he never expected to meet him. You'd alarmed him and he'd tried to get rid of you. And with that," said Brockley, with some enjoyment, "your husband let go of Wylie, caught Mew by the throat and shoved *him* up against the wall instead. Mew had your husband's fingers on his windpipe and I never saw a man so terrified.

"He kept on choking out that he was frightened and he'd been doing his best. He'd had enough of killing, with Dawson and Fenn . . . it all came out about them, too. It seems that your husband knew nothing about them. He demanded details. Wylie had done most of the dirty work, it seems, like knocking them on the head, though I don't think he's any too competent, even at murder." Brockley sniffed disdainfully. "If he was trying to kill me when he hit me, he didn't succeed, and he said he'd tied weights to Fenn's feet before he dumped him in the river. If so, they came off! Your husband was furious about it all, if that's any comfort to you."

"What happened then?"

"Well, I think he would have choked Mew outright, but Wylie and Wilkins pulled him off. Then he started striding up and down, being frantic about you. He wanted to rush off back to Lockhill then and there, except that he couldn't, because he didn't have a horse. His own horse and Wilkins' mare were both tired and so was Mew's roan, because Wylie was out on it, delivering commissions to customers today, and stables don't like hiring horses out overnight unless you've got orders with an official seal on. Mr. de la Roche cursed and swore and then tore his hair. He really did, madam. I never saw anyone do that before."

I had never seen it, either. For a moment I even felt a glow, remembering the passion which had exploded between us at Lockhill, proud that this man was so much in love with me that he would tear his hair to think I was in danger.

The glow didn't last. Danger surrounded us all and there was no time for self-satisfaction. "What then?" I asked shakily.

"Mr. de la Roche said he'd wait until dawn and then take his own horse and go. He said he'd try to get a little sleep, but I doubt if he's slept much."

"Matthew was at Lockhill when we got back there," I said. "You went off without seeing him. Dr. Wilkins was with him. According to Cecil, Wilkins may be involved in this mysterious plot we're investigating. I knew that Matthew might be in it too, but I hoped . . . I hoped . . ."

"Did you promise to go to France with him?" Brockley asked. "At once, I mean, instead of in May?"

"Yes, I did, but now . . . I've been mad, blind! I

didn't want Matthew to be involved and I made myself believe he wasn't! I've done everything wrong! I've sent for help! I've betrayed Matthew again! If he's caught here . . . Brockley, I've got to speak to Matthew, get him away somehow. Even if the others escape too, I *must* save Matthew. I . . ."

Brockley's hand closed on my arm. "We've got to save ourselves first. We get out of here first, then we think of how to warn Mr. de la Roche. We're wasting time. Come on, now. If we—"

"Shhh!" I said urgently. "I came in here in the first place because I thought I heard something. I've just heard it again. Someone's moving upstairs."

We stood there, waiting. "I fed the dog," I whispered, "on cold chicken, but it barked once or twice, just the same. And if Matthew's been lying awake, which is highly likely . . ."

We heard feet and voices descending the cellar stairs.

One of the voices belonged to Matthew.

Brockley picked up a length of chain and swung it to and fro, but I shook my head at him, and he put it down. I took up my dagger, but only to put it away in my inner pocket. There was no point in fighting. Matthew and whoever was with him had reached the adjacent room. We heard Mew's voice, shrill with alarm (and also slightly hoarse—Matthew had strong fingers, as I well knew), exclaiming that he could smell the candles: they must have been used. A familiar and beloved voice told him to light them again. For Brockley and me, that voice was our chance of survival, but I had not wished to hear it in this place.

Then the door was flung open and in came Mew, with a lantern in one hand and a dagger in the other, and an air of having dressed in a rush. His feet were slippered and he was in shirtsleeves, with half his lacings undone. A scarf, however, was knotted round his neck, no doubt as a comforter after my husband's ministrations. Behind him came Joseph Wylie, similarly attired, except that he hadn't needed a scarf, and was equipped with a three-branched candlestick and a cudgel. Next came Wilkins, bearing neither light nor weapon. Wilkins had dressed himself in gown and shoes, but he still had a nightcap on his head. The effect would have been ridiculous, except for the cold anger in his eyes.

Matthew, the tidiest of the four, feet shod, shirt more or less fastened and a doublet tossed on top though not done up, brought up the rear, a drawn sword in his hand. He stopped short at the sight of me, and I saw that he could hardly believe what his own eyes were telling him.

This time he spoke my name twice. The first time was a question. "Ursula?" The second was an exclamation of horror. "Ursula!"

"Matthew," I said, and then, feebly, "It must be well past midnight by now, so . . . good morning."

I couldn't think of anything else to say. I wanted to shout to Matthew to get away quickly because I'd sent for help and he risked being taken, but Mew and Wylie were there, and above all, so was the odious Wilkins. They chained my tongue.

I needed to speak to Matthew alone, but for the moment, I couldn't see how. "I should have known you'd come here," I said tiredly. "It was so obvious."

"It wasn't obvious at all." Matthew sounded exasperated. "You don't know as much as you think. But what are *you* doing here? How did you get in here? And why?"

"Because Brockley came here on my behalf, of course! He didn't come back, so I came to find him. I was afraid for him. I got in over the back fence and through the window."

Matthew's three companions all stared at me as though I were myself a gryphon or a unicorn. "Well," said Wilkins grimly. "What now?"

"We go upstairs," said Matthew decisively. "I'm not going to conduct this conversation in a cellar. Come along."

He was very much the one in charge. I was simultaneously proud of his powers of leadership, and in despair because, once more, what he was leading was something utterly repellent to me. With Brockley, I followed Matthew out of the basement and up the stairs. The others came behind us, and I was uneasily aware of Wylie's cudgel and Mew's dagger. Only Matthew, I knew, stood between us and death at their hands.

Upstairs, Matthew led us out of the little back office and into the parlour which I had seen through the window. Wylie was still carrying his candlestick, and used it to light those in the parlour. It was cold there, but a faint glow still came from the hearth, where a half-burnt log lay on a pile of ash.

"I don't see why we all have to freeze," Matthew said briskly. "Someone do something about that fire!"

Wylie obliged, stirring the ash roughly with a poker

and tossing in twigs from a woodbasket. A small flame sprang up. I sat down wearily on a settle and Brockley sat next to me.

Matthew stood facing us. He looked at me with a sadness and a bewilderment which I found grievous to see. It was as though I were no longer the Ursula he had known; no longer his Saltspoon, but a puzzling stranger.

"I didn't believe it, you know," he said. "Wilkins warned me. He said that you were at Lockhill and that Cecil had sent you there, and he thought Cecil was using you as an agent. He had a man in Cecil's house—Paul Fenn, who has I gather come to a sorry end—and Fenn said he had heard Cecil say you might learn something at Lockhill and that the Cecils were pretending they didn't know you well, when they did. I said it was nonsense: who would employ a young woman as a spy? It *still* seems impossible, but it seems that believe it, I must."

"After what she did to you last year, I wonder you found it so hard to credit," Wilkins said. He, too, had remained standing. "She is a heretic spy. Well, I did my best to save her, since you care for her. As you know."

"Dr. Wilkins has now told me that he tried to have you brought to me, when he first became aware of Cecil's plans," Matthew said. "After you told me of that attempted abduction, I challenged him. It appears," he said wryly, "that I must apologise to you for that unhappy experience. You wouldn't have been left long in the boathouse, but there was some difficulty over finding a ship to carry you to France."

I remembered fretting over that very problem. It

was faintly amusing that the self-assured Dr. Wilkins had run up against it too, but my sense of humour wasn't working too well just then. "If you didn't believe that I could be employed by Cecil," I said, "then I didn't want to believe that you were Dr. Wilkins' partner. I wish you were not."

"I'm not," said Matthew. "I told you, you know less than you think."

He did not enlarge and I felt too weary and too disbelieving to ask questions. Wilkins, growing tired of standing, now seated himself coolly in a massive carved armchair which looked as though it belonged rightly to the master of the house. Mew, as if feeling himself at a disadvantage even in his own home, had sunk meekly on to a stool. There was a pause, while Wylie got the fire going properly and Matthew went to pull curtains across the window. Wilkins watched him coldly, and once more I sensed bad feeling between them.

I was glad of Brockley at my side. I knew him better, in many ways, than I knew Matthew. Brockley was part of everyday life. I was gradually realising how deeply exhausted I was. I wondered how long it would be until dawn.

How could I get Matthew alone, to warn him? He might well warn the others anyway, but that would be his choice. The idea of alerting them myself stuck in my gullet. Well, there was time in hand yet; help could surely not arrive before morning. Even if Dr. Forrest had acted at once, his messenger would have a long ride before the rescue proper could hope to set out.

If only, I thought feverishly, I could think of a way

not just to speak to my husband privately, but to detach him from these others, turn him against them, so that he would see what they truly were, and abandon them . . .

The small-hours parlour, growing warmer now as the fire burned up, had a dreamlike air. In the candle-light our shadows were huge and distorted. They fled or glided over the panelled walls and the one wall-hanging (another cheap affair of painted cloth) and across the ceiling when anyone moved.

I was aware of the tangled relationships among us, as complex as a maze: man and wife; lady and manser-vant; prisoners and captors; and this odd collection of conspirators. Wilkins was a priest and must have a degree in theology—what was a doctor of theology doing hand in glove with a clockmaker? What was the term for conspirators such as these? A sort of trai-tors . . . an assortment of traitors . . . such an ill-assorted set of traitors . . .

I jerked myself awake. It was hardly the moment for falling asleep, but nature had almost outwitted me. Brockley was speaking, his voice comfortingly normal. "I suppose," he said, "that it was next door's dog that gave the alarm."

"Yes. I heard it," Matthew said. His eyes were on my face. "I couldn't sleep," he said, "for my anxiety over you."

"I wasted some good chicken on that dog," I remarked.

That made Matthew smile, only briefly, but just for a moment, his diamond-shaped eyes sparkled and the tiny laughter-lines at their corners deepened. That smile had haunted my dreams.

Desperately, I opened my mouth to say, "Matthew, we *must* speak privately!" but Wilkins spoke first.

"Like it or not, Matthew, your wife and her manservant are not of our faith, and they have learned too much of our plans. They have seen the cellar. You won't deny that, I take it?"

"Your plans, not mine," said Matthew. "And what does it matter what they've seen, or learned? They have had no chance to tell anyone what they saw."

He turned to me. "I can still hardly believe what I now know of you, Ursula. Last night, I was half mad with fear for you—I couldn't help myself. But all the time I keep asking myself, what *are* you? What kind of woman? What kind of wife? But perhaps it isn't too late to turn you back towards me and towards God. You remain my wife, and I still care for you." His voice was harsh with pain and conflict. I could hardly bear to hear it. "You must come to France now," he said. "You have no choice any longer. Perhaps we can still do something about fetching your daughter. Where is your woman, Dale?"

"At Lockhill. She knows nothing," I added firmly, "except that I've seen you and intend going to France with you. She thinks Brockley is merely on an ordinary errand. I felt it would be safer for her."

"Quite right. Dale and I are married. I protect her," Brockley put in, backing me up.

"Good. You will write to Dale, Ursula, and enclose a note for whoever is caring for Meg, saying that you want Dale to bring her to you. Tell Dale to bring Meg to the coast, to my friend, the Sussex fisherman who will take us over the Channel," Matthew said. "I'll dictate the direction. Fetch pen and ink, will you, Mew?"

Without warning, a hammer blow of sheer agony hit me over the left eyebrow. I was starting a headache, out of nowhere. "Oh *God!*" The words burst out of me. "Oh Matthew, why did you have to be involved in this? Why?"

Mew, who had half risen in response to Matthew's order, was so startled by my impassioned tone that he sat down again, staring. Matthew, engrossed with me, ignored him.

"Did you not hear me say that the plans were Ignatius's plans, not mine?"

"But you're here! And you said yourself that you had some mysterious business or other with Dr. Wilkins. You said something about draught horses. That wasn't true, was it?" Bitterness came into my voice. "The real business in hand is coining!"

"The draught horses were a lie. I'm sorry. But the truth isn't what you suppose. I have nothing to do with what you presumably saw in the cellar. Am I the sort of man to dabble in coining? What do you take me for?"

"Then what are you doing *here?*"

"I came to England," said Matthew, "to deal with unfinished business, as I said. Specifically, to find out just what use was being made of a large quantity of money and treasure which I collected last year on behalf of Mary Stuart, and left here in the charge of Ignatius Wilkins! I had it at Withysham and I couldn't take it all with me when I fled. I had to travel light and I couldn't transport a pile of chests and coffers. I had four sets of gold plate and ten of silver, and a lot of coinage and jewellery. Ignatius was in the district—that part was true—and I handed it over to him. And now . . ."

"I have put the treasure," said Wilkins in that thick, authoritative voice of his, "to the purpose for which it was intended: to further the cause of the rightful queen of England, Her Catholic Majesty, Mary Stuart. Skilfully used, counterfeit coin could so disrupt the finances of this realm that the people will begin to murmur against Elizabeth, and meanwhile, if further monies can be collected and an army raised for Mary . . ."

"Good God!" I said involuntarily.

"And you set about your scheme," said Matthew to Wilkins, "as I keep repeating, although you are obviously not prepared to admit that it was wrong, without either permission nor consultation. You merely wrote to me to announce what you had done." Matthew turned to me. "I am responsible to Mary Stuart for that treasure! To learn that it was being squandered on this silly plan . . ."

"It is not silly," said Wilkins. "You will not speak to me, a priest of the Catholic Church, as if I were a child or a fool. The plan would take time to mature, yes. It would start with a quantity of false coin, the first wave of a rising tide, good enough to pass cursory examination, released into the hands of merchants who would take it to the Florentine and Genoese banks. The banks would soon discover it was false and their confidence in English money would be damaged. Later on, we would send in another wave of counterfeit. And then another. Little by little, Elizabeth's credit would be undermined. She would find loans harder to raise and her merchants would find it hard to trade. Prices would rise. Meanwhile, Mary would be making preparations and her priests would be going about in England, building support for her. The English would suffer hardship and their hearts would turn towards Mary, and God. I saw the hand of God himself in this idea!"

"It might work," said Matthew, "if the scheme were big enough, but it isn't. The treasure was valuable, but not this valuable. Wishful thinking, Ignatius."

Wilkins glowered.

"And venal thinking!" said Matthew. "I haven't said this to you before. I wanted to see first just how much you had achieved. Well, now I have! And while I lay awake tonight, I took my mind off my fears for Ursula by thinking over what I'd seen. You've been deceiving yourself. Oh, I don't suspect *you* of being in this for profit, Wilkins—I know you for a true believer and a loyal adherent of Mary Stuart—but I suspect that your fellow conspirators are clear enough about the other purpose behind this.

"The money will be released into the economy by buying tapestries and carpets and other valuables, or duping acquaintances into buying them for you. The various purchases will then belong to you and your friends. No doubt you'll sell yours and give the money to the cause, but I wonder if all your associates will do the same? Or will they just pocket the proceeds?"

The silence that ensued was best described as shattering. It was as though the conspirators had until that moment been one cohesive whole, like a pane of glass, and Matthew had thrown a stone at it, sending cracks across it in all directions. One good push, and it would fall apart.

Brockley grasped the situation at once and did his best to administer the push. "Maybe," he remarked to Wilkins, "a scheme like that was the only way your fellow conspirators could think of to get that treasure out of you, my friend!"

There was a further staggered silence, during which Wilkins stared at Mew and Wylie as though seeing them for the first time, then Wylie laughed. "How did you know?" he said to Matthew.

"It's called using one's brains," said my husband coldly.

Wylie laughed again. "Well, we've got our hands on a fair amount of that treasure, and as long as these two pretty pigeons here don't go cooing into Cecil's ears, we'll all end up rich."

"You . . . !" The venom in Wilkins' voice was terrifying and Mew quivered on his stool.

Wylie, however, remained unmoved. "You can't trump up a heresy charge against us and send us to the stake," he said. "Nor can you inform on us, not without dropping yourself in the mud at the same time. You've still got your scheme. Be content with that and leave us our profits. We've earned them."

"You have earned a modest commission. That, yes," Matthew said. "This is a dismal plot, but it's now so far advanced that we may as well try it. It could achieve something. Elizabeth has been very outspoken about improving the currency. This will make her look a fool, if nothing else."

I said nothing. My head throbbed. I knew that it was useless to point out to him the horrors—the civil war, the heresy-hunting—which would be unleashed if Mary Stuart were ever to take the throne. I had said it all to him before, last October, and I knew that he didn't understand and never would. He couldn't believe that the English, at heart, were not longing for a Catholic monarch. His mind was full of an exalted vision of an England restored to what, to him, was a true and simple faith. Through his otherwise keen intelligence, that vision ran like a flaw in a gemstone.

Matthew was kind and Wilkins cruel, but Wilkins had the same flaw, the same singlemindedness which was also simplemindedness. Any attempt to reason with either of them would be in vain.

Matthew was speaking again. "We'll make the best of what has been done already. And, yes, a rate of commission will be worked out and you will be paid. That I accept. But any valuables bought in the process must be sold again and the money directed back to Mary Stuart's service. I gathered that money: I will not see one penny diverted illicitly into any man's private purse. I must return to France, and when I go, I will leave matters in your hands, but you had better be careful. When Mary is on her throne again—and one day she will be: God will see to it—then you could all find yourselves called to account instead of rewarded. So beware."

Not two plots, I thought, just one, all the time. I wondered how Mew, at once prosperous and timid, had been drawn in. I wondered, too, whether Crinchton was in it or not, and what precisely Dawson had heard at Lockhill which had brought him to his death. The fugitive thought I had had when I saw the name Dawson burned into the tray on Mason's desk still would not surface.

However, I had guessed at the coining, which was the central plot, and at the way the coins were to be used. The bill for metals and the strange purchases of such things as tapestries and carpets, with their accompanying lies, had formed a true pattern in my mind.

Now I saw how Mary Stuart had been brought in: as bait for Wilkins. I had missed the clues which linked the scheme to her: Sir William Cecil showing me King Henry's rotten groat had been one; and so, oddly enough, had Leonard Mason's comment over dinner, the day I came to Lockhill. He had virtually spelt it out: "A realm, like a household, must live within its means. A ruler who forgets that courts disaster." By such logical, business-like persuasions, the fanatical Wilkins had been cozened into surrendering the treasure. A pretty plot!

My head went on pounding and nausea now began to grip my stomach. Matthew's anger with the conspirators, though, was hopeful. If I could put a wedge into that split and widen it . . . if only, through this pain and nausea, I could *think!*

Mew was spluttering. Matthew looked at him, and Mew burst into speech. "I don't want the money! They said I'd have my share, but I don't want it. Conspiracy and murder! I hate it all! I was forced into it!"

From nowhere, the words to make the wedge I needed came into my head. "Did you need so very much forcing?" I asked. "Dawson and Fenn are dead, and an archer shot at me only the other day. You had something to do with all of it. And what of the attempt to poison me yesterday night?"

"*What?*" said Matthew.

"Oh yes," I told him. "When Dale was taken ill, it was because she had sipped a posset made for me." Beside me, I felt Brockley jerk and I added swiftly, "Fran is all right, Brockley! She only swallowed a little. She was unwell that night but better in the morning." I stuck my elbow into his ribs, and remembering what I had said about Dale and Forrest, he held his tongue.

Matthew had always been against murder—I knew that from the past. This might, just might, be enough to tip the balance. My head still hammered and the candles hurt my eyes, but, painfully, I went on. "They have no pity on anyone, your associates, Matthew. Fenn was little more than a boy. Did you know?"

"He was eighteen," Wilkins said. "A boy? Children as young as seven have been martyrs for the faith, and a grown lad with a beard coming can die for failing it. The Fenns were my neighbours and parishioners in Sussex. Paul Fenn was a younger son of the house. I recruited him when I learned he was to take up a post with the Cecils. I thought it might be useful to have someone in there. As our scheme was put into effect, we would want to know what result it was having, how alarmed the council was, and whether we were in danger of discovery. Regrettably, young Fenn lost his nerve."

Ignatius Wilkins, I thought, was like the opposite of a talisman: he was bad luck, walking about on feet. To be either his friend or his parishioner put one in peril.

"Fenn said Cecil was enquiring about him, and he

didn't know what to do." Mew was huskier than ever, through fear. "I *told* you," he said to Matthew. "It was obvious that he'd crack under questioning. He even said that perhaps the best thing he could do was confess! He was dangerous."

"You should have offered to get him away to France," Matthew said.

"We did, but he didn't want to go. He was scared of exile as well. He was just a child, under all those fine airs of his."

"You see? They are ready to kill children, or as near as makes no difference!" Trying to ignore my physical anguish, I drove the wedge deeper and saw Matthew's face darken. "These are the people with whom you are entangled!" I said to him fiercely. "What do you think of them all now?"

Surely, surely, this would do it. In a moment, I would have to speak. The night must be passing by now.

Wilkins was staring round, from one face to another, his own full of contempt—but then, contempt for others was his nature. In some stone prison, not unlike Mew's cellar, his two hapless parishioners, the weaver and his daughter, had been interrogated about their beliefs. They had been too honest to lie, but he had had no respect for that.

"In this," he said to Mew and Wylie, "despicable as you are in other ways, you were not at fault. It is a sad thing that the faith must at times be defended by force, and that even women and youths must suffer, but so renegade is human nature, that such is the case. You guarded us from discovery. I will grant you absolution whenever you wish."

"You will not," Matthew said grimly. "Let them live with their guilt. I am opposed to the murder even of those who are not women or boys. I—"

"But we had to save ourselves!" Mew cried.

"That Dawson was a damned nosy-parker of a pedlar," Wylie said pugnaciously. "He listened at doors. He found out too much!"

"And we didn't *want* to harm your good lady, sir," Mew, bursting into a new fit of husky self-defence, was nearly in tears. "We didn't know who she was then, of course, but still we didn't want to hurt her. Fenn said she was a spy, though, and then when I found her poking about in this office . . . What'll happen if we're caught! There's all that in the cellar, and I've turned in endless reports to Cecil that there's no disloyalty at Lockhill! I'll be called a traitor twice over! What would happen to me?" I gaped at the unlikely reference to Cecil, but no one noticed.

Matthew was glowering at Mew. I saw that he had no fear of his homicidal partners. On the face of it, they could have killed Brockley and myself despite his objections, and killed him, too, if he tried to threaten them. I don't think it even occurred to them, however, and not just because they were too much at odds among themselves to act together: they just accepted him as their leader.

"Well, Ursula," he said, turning to me, "it seems that you have run into peril of your own choice, and brought your manservant into peril with you. You and Brockley are safe now, however. We shall soon be on our way to France. Wilkins, I shall leave you with full power to make sure that my orders are carried out."

I saw with despair that although he now detested the others, he still regarded them as his men. He, too, accepted his place as their leader. The wedge hadn't gone in far enough. I glanced again at the window. Its blackness was no longer absolute but tinged with blue. Time was running out.

My ploy had failed, yet it had dne something: Matthew's distaste, his wish to be away from his fellow conspirators, was evident. A new way of exploiting it sprang into my mind.

"Matthew!" I said. "I hate being in this house, in this room, with these men. I'd like to leave for France at once, within the hour, for preference. I'll write the letters for Dale while the horses are being saddled. Are there horses for me and Brockley? Ours are at the Antelope." If I were once in the saddle and we were on our way, I hoped my head would get better. It would have to!

"Horses are the least of our problems," Matthew said. "We've got all the horseflesh we need in a paddock at the back, and it's had a night's rest. I agree that this place and this company are not for you. We'll be off at daybreak. We'll take my bay gelding, Ignatius's mare for you, Urusla—sorry, Ignatius, but it can't be helped—and your roan cob, Mr. Mew, will do for Brockley. By the way, Mew, I asked for pen and ink about a hundred years ago. Where are they? Wylie, go and saddle up. Now! I've friends between here and the coast, Ursula—they will supply a messenger to take the letters to your tirewoman."

Wilkins began to argue, not about his mare but because he said Brockley couldn't be trusted not to break away and raise a hue and cry.

"Brockley will do as I bid him!" I snapped, and applied another warning elbow to Brockley's ribs as I spoke.

Wylie disappeared and Mew brought the writing materials. Matthew gave me details of where Dale was to bring my daughter. I moved to a table and sat down to write.

I was going to win, I thought. God willing, I would flee with Matthew. The others would be taken; Matthew would not. And I would be off to a new life with my husband.

I hoped that Cecil and the Queen would understand and forgive me, and that they would let Meg come to me. I hoped, too, that Dale would not be blamed for remaining faithful to me, and that she, too, would join us soon. Maybe Brockley would forgive me for dragging her into all this.

My pen pressed on across the paper, writing the words Matthew expected me to write, preparing the two useless letters, which were only for show. I was signing my name to the first when Wylie came back.

"The horses are ready. They're in a shed across the alley."

"Good," said Matthew. "Are you done, Ursula?"

"Yes." I signed the second letter, picked up the sander and shook it over the wet ink.

"You'll want sealing wax," Mew said. His insignificant features still had that crumpled look of misery, and his voice, though less hoarse by now, was subdued. "I've got some in a cupboard here. You—"

He stopped short, staring at me, his face disgusted, as though he had just found a caterpillar in his salad. I was that caterpillar. "She's lying!" he said. "About her woman not knowing anything! That woman was in my office with her, when I caught Mrs. Blanchard looking through my ledgers. They were only in there because the woman—Dale, is it?—was conveniently ill! Rather too conveniently! She knows all about it, mark my words."

"What? Ursula?" said Matthew.

I licked my lips. My headache crescendoed, a nightmare drumbeat. I was about to embark on a back-to-the-wall denial, however unconvincing it might sound, when we heard the hoofbeats thundering through the main street. They were coming fast, and there were so many horses that even here at the back of the house they were clearly audible. They clattered to a halt outside. Feet descended to the ground and someone pounded at the door.

Pretence was at an end. I looked sadly at Matthew. "Did you really suppose I would not take precautions? I sent Dale for help, but I didn't think it would come so soon. I hoped you and I could get away."

"Leaving these others to their fate?" Matthew demanded.

"They tried to kill me," I said. "They nearly did kill Dale."

Mew ran to the window and peered round the curtain. He let out a squeal. "There're men in the garden!"

In lifting the curtain, he had let a glimpse of candlelight escape. A series of whistles echoed and a familiar voice outside bellowed, "Open up, Mew! Open up or we'll make you!" Someone started attacking the front door and the shuttered shop window with axes.

We could hear neighbours, no doubt enraged at such a rough awakening, shouting in protest.

My note to Dr. Forrest had been brief, and I could remember the wording as though the sheet of paper were before me:

> Dr. Forrest, I am short of time, but please, I beg you, do what I now ask you. I have the right to ask: I was in Lockhill on the orders of Sir William Cecil. Please send urgently to Mr. Rob Henderson of Thamesbank, near Hampton, and ask him to bring armed men to Barnabas Mew's shop in Windsor. Brockley has gone there and may be in danger. I am going to see if I can help him. Please do this, Dr. Forrest. Dale will answer any questions.
>
> Yours in haste, Ursula Blanchard.

It had worked. Dr. Forrest had moved swiftly, and at Thamesbank, so had Rob Henderson. He and his men must have ridden throught the night to reach us.

CHAPTER 20

A Candle in the Dawn

I was by now feeling very ill. Nothing seemed real, and my mind was skidding as though it had lost its footing on ice. I remember that as Matthew sprang to the parlour door and opened it to see what was happening, I tried, for no good reason, to invent a stupid pun about lock-picks and pick axes. Then the street window fell inwards and my rescuers started clambering through.

"*Fight!*" roared Wilkins, and rising massively to his feet, snatched up a stool and dashed past Matthew, out into the shop. Through the open door, by the faint light of dawn as it came through the smashed window, I saw him drive the legs of the stool at the first man over the sill. He had guts in a way, I thought hazily.

Wilkins, however, was thrust back, and a split second later, the parlour emptied as Wylie, Mew and Matthew also rushed out to fight. Brockley went after them, unhindered, shouting to Rob Henderson. I stumbled to the door. Beside it hung a heavy curtain, used, I suppose, to keep out draughts. Clinging to this, I watched the shop disintegrate in a storm of violence.

It was noisy: shouts, gasps, cries; Wylie cursing obscenely as he laid about him with his cudgel; the clash of swordblades; the scuffling of feet; the tinkle and crash of destruction. A clock which had been taken apart and laid out in pieces on the counter, was swept to the floor in a shower of glass splinters and little metal wheels and rods, which were instantly crunched to shards beneath furious booted feet. A careless sword-slash glanced off the pale blue face of the big ornate clock by the staircase, giving it a dent like a silly grin. Another blade caught the machinery below, setting it a-jangle and starting the clock chimes off to add to the uproar.

I couldn't tell how many men Rob had, but there seemed to be hordes of them, all helmeted, all wielding swords. The conspirators were outnumbered, but they fought with a rage which was astounding. Wilkins, who despite weight and age was remarkably agile, tried to escape through what seemed to be the door to the kitchen. He came out again almost at once, backwards, with two men after him, presumably the ones who had been in the garden and had now forced an entry through the back door. Wilkins had made good use of his few seconds in the kitchen, however: he had dropped his stool and now held a knife in one hand and a broken glass tumbler in the other, its jagged edges as lethal as a handful of daggers.

Brockley had got hold of a sword, and was trying to get at Wylie with it. I saw Wylie's cudgel smash the jaw of one of Rob's men, laying him flat on the littered floor. Splashes of blood joined the bits of broken clock underfoot.

Mew, whose name now seemed weirdly appropriate, since he was uttering strange, shrill noises like the cries of a distressed cat, had got behind the counter and was attempting to keep the enemy off with his dagger. He seemed as upset about the danger to his stock as to himself, and when one of Rob's retainers bounded over the counter, swiped at Mew with his sword, missed and swept a row of clocks off a shelf instead, Barnabas yowled as loudly as though the sword had bitten into his own body. He also closed with his adversary, stabbing with the dagger, and it was the retainer who suddenly dropped his weapon and doubled up and then slid to the floor.

Wilkins attacked someone, horribly, in the face with the jagged glass. I heard the scream and saw the blood spurt and then saw Wilkins' knife go home. The scream crescendoed and then faded as the victim slumped. Wilkins stooped and grabbed the man's sword. Brockley appeared from the mêlée, and attacked Wilkins, but was driven back. The detestable Ignatius had obviously been trained in the arts of war.

Then, from the midst of the confusion, Rob and Matthew appeared, engaged in a one-to-one duel. I cried out in fear for them both and they heard me.

"Get back! Out of harm's way!" Rob shouted, and in a weird moment of agreement with his enemy, Matthew echoed him. A sword hissed frighteningly close to me, proving their point, and I jumped back, just as someone barged into Rob and knocked him aside, away from Matthew. Matthew seized the brief respite to swing round and slam the parlour door, leaving me inside.

My head was red hot. Suddenly, my stomach heaved. I staggered across the room, wrenched back the window curtains and opened the window, and was sick over the sill. I leant there for a few seconds, and then, forcing my leaden legs to work, I reeled back to the door and opened it again.

The scene had changed: Mew had been seized and two of Rob's men were binding his hands, and Wylie was dead, lying on his back on the floor, eyes glassily fixed. Wilkins, backed against a nearby wall, was still holding off attack, using his sword like a veteran, and Matthew and Rob were still locked into their duel. Matthew shouted at me once again to get out of the way, back into the parlour.

"Come in here, Matthew!" I shouted back. "Come this way! Quickly!" I opened the door wider and flattened myself against it. "It's your only chance! Hurry, *hurry!*"

He understood what I meant, shifted ground, and jumped through into the parlour, but Rob was too hot after him, and when I tried to shut the door between them, Rob's foot struck out and knocked it wide again. They were both in there, swords striking this way and that in a space much too confined for them, points scraping the low ceiling and scoring the panelling, feet tripping on rugs.

I snatched a triple candlestick off the table just before they overturned it, and blew out the candles. It made no difference to the light, for now the dawn was growing strongly. There were other candles in wall sconces, and a second triple candlestick on a shelf, all alight but with their flames growing faint in the daybreak. So far, the swords had missed them. They had also, so far, missed me, and as I ducked away from them, I could only hope my luck would last. I tried to reach the doorway, but was pushed back as Wilkins, scarlet faced, gasping and streaming with sweat, came in crabwise, holding off a swordsman. He crashed the door shut in his enemy's face. It had a bolt on the inside and he shot it. He leant against the door, gulping for air and rubbing a sleeve across his soaked forehead. His knife and broken glass were both gone, but his sword was smeared with blood.

Crouched by the wall, I shouted to Rob and Matthew to stop, but they couldn't hear me, or if they did they ignored me. Black spots danced before my aching eyes and I knew that I was crying. Matthew was my husband and Rob was my friend and rescuer; I didn't want either of them killed, but there was nothing I could do.

At least, there was, but I didn't think of it. Ignatius Wilkins, however, did. Though still gasping for breath, he caught hold of the heavy curtain beside the door and used his sword to hack it free. Then he stepped forward, threw the curtain over Rob's head and neatly tripped him up.

"*No!*" I screamed, as Rob crashed to the ground and Wilkins raised his sword. I threw myself forward and landed on top of Rob. "Leave him alone!"

"Ursula, get up!" Matthew caught my arm and tried to drag me to my feet.

I resisted, holding on to Rob with all my strength. "You'll kill him and I won't let you!"

"I don't kill helpless men wrapped up in curtains!" barked Matthew. "Get up and let him up as well."

"No! I don't want either of you hurt!" I shrieked into Matthew's face, and jerked my arm away.

"I'm your husband! Do as I say!"

"This man came to save me! Don't you understand?"

"Drag her off," said Wilkins angrily. "I'll finish him if you won't, Matthew! I've no time for chivalrous airs."

"You had no right to interfere in my fight!" Matthew snapped. "You interfere too much! Stand back!"

Someone was beating on the door. Brockley's voice demanded to know what was happening in there.

"I'm safe, Brockley, I'm safe!" I shouted. "Leave me be! Don't try to come in!" I heard an argument break out on the other side of the door as I got shakily to my feet, trying to fight off another wave of nausea. "Matthew," I said urgently, "the window's open and I don't see anyone in the garden. Can't we get away? If we go now, quickly . . ."

"Help me tie him!" Matthew said brusquely to Wilkins. "*Tie* him, not kill him. Do as I say!" Rob, cursing in muffled tones, had almost struggled free of the curtain. They knelt on him together, turning him on to his face, while Matthew, producing a belt knife, slashed at the curtain and then used his teeth to tear a couple of strips from it.

Rob, resisting furiously but vainly as they secured his hands and feet, saw me and demanded, "Is this your husband—is this de la Roche?"

"Yes, Rob." They weren't going to kill him. It would be all right. In a moment, I would be away with Matthew. I'd have to put up with Wilkins as well, but go to France with Matthew I *would*. "Rob, thank you for coming—God bless you for coming—but I must go with Matthew. He *is* my husband. My place is with him. I'm going to France. I'm sorry. You've got the others. Make sure you look in the basement. The door to it is in the office . . ."

"You can't do this, Ursula!" Rob shouted. "Are you out of your wits? You can't go with him! These men are traitors!"

"Quiet, you!" said Wilkins, jerking a knot tight.

"Open this door!" Someone outside, not Brockley, was demanding entry. "Open, I say!"

"In here, hurry, hurry!" Rob yelled.

"I said, be quiet!" Wilkins snarled, and gave Rob an open-handed blow on the side of the head. I caught at Wilkins' wrist, shouting at him again to leave Rob alone, but he shook me off. "Mind your own business! Must she come with us, Matthew? If ever this were proof that women are a snare and a temptation to men . . ."

"*Ursula!*" Rob raged. "You can't go with them! *Think!*"

"I already have," I said, wondering how, feeling as I did, I would even get out of the window and reach the horses in their shed across the alley, let alone climb into a saddle and ride for my life. I wanted to lie down and die.

Outside the door, Brockley was shouting my name again and somebody else was threatening to break the door down. I shouted once more that I was safe, let me be!

Matthew said, "There's no time to lose. Come on, Ursula. Come on, Ignatius!"

"What about your daughter?" Rob demanded from the floor. "What about Meg? I won't let her go, Ursula! Nor will the Queen! You can't take her to live with enemies of the realm!"

"We'll see about that," said Matthew to me. "We'll find a way. I promise. I *promise!* Come *on!*"

Something crashed into the door. Wilkins had tightened the last knot on Rob's bonds and was already at the window, with a knee on the sill. Matthew caught my hand and pulled me towards the window too.

I meant to go with him, I swear it. What happened next is a mystery. Did God command me, or something deep in my own mind? I do not know. Most people believe in God—after all, who or what made the world?—but sometimes I have wondered. We are taught to pray and told that our prayers are heard, but are they?

When Gerald fell ill with smallpox, I prayed for his life, and so did he, but what did it avail us? Afterwards, when Sir Thomas Gresham's chaplain came to offer me spiritual comfort, I asked what sort of deity had let my husband die like that, while he was still young and Meg and I needed him? The chaplain had said that there must be a purpose and I must have faith. I would have preferred an explanation. We are given no reasons for our suffering, but still we suffer. So, when later on I described what happened next to a vicar—Dr. Forrest, as a matter of fact—and he said that God must have moved me, I had my doubts. I have them still, but the mystery remains.

As Matthew pulled me across the room, I stumbled on a rucked-up rug, and with my free hand I caught for support at the shelf which held the second triple candlestick, knocking the candlestick to the floor. As it fell, the flame caught the edge of the one cheap wall-hanging, and a line of red licked up. Snatching my hand away from Matthew, I clapped the smouldering edge between my palms.

Why did I do such a thing? At my feet lay the rug which had tripped me. I could have caught that up to muffle the fire. I did not need to use my bare hands. They put out the little flame at once, but my palms were seared as they did so, and I jumped back, crying out in fright and pain.

For a few seconds, everything stopped. In those seconds, the door was attacked once more with some kind of ram, and once more I shouted to the men out there to stop. In those seconds, too, I looked at Ignatius Wilkins, half in and half out of the window, struggling with his gown, which had caught on something, and I thought of the weaver and his daughter: their faces, which Rob had seen through the smoke, and their screams, which had pursued him as he tried to get away. I remembered, yet again, the ghastly description of a burning, to which Uncle Herbert and Aunt Tabitha had made me listen.

Such thoughts, such memories, reduced even my feelings for Matthew to the trivial. If he were prepared to bring *that* back, to consign not traitors or murderers, but honest men and women to death by flame, simply because they would not believe what he believed, then . . .

"I can't go!" I gasped to Matthew. "I can't, I can't. Don't ask me! Go on your own! Save yourself! Quickly, quickly! I can't come to France, I'm sorry but I can't."

"What? Ursula? But . . . ?"

"You're *her* man!" I wailed. "That damned Stuart woman! If she ever comes here as queen, people would die at the stake again and you know it." I pointed at Wilkins. "And *he'd* send them there! Go, Matthew, go!"

Outside the door, there had been one brief pause, but now the battering ram had begun again. There was no more time.

"God damn you," said Matthew. He spoke quietly, but his voice shook with anger. "You've betrayed me twice!"

"No, I haven't." The tears were pouring down my face. "I want to save you. You know that. You *know* that. Go! *Go!*"

He turned away, heaved Wilkins unceremoniously over the sill into the garden, and scrambled out after him. The garden, misty and silvered with ground frost, was mercifully still empty. No one had thought to go round again and guard the way out through the parlour window. Few people are completely efficient in moments of great excitement, and Rob and his men, thank goodness, were among the majority.

I watched Matthew and Wilkins run down the garden; saw them struggle briefly with the bolts of the gate and then disappear through it. He was gone. My husband was gone. I would not see him again—of that I could be sure. I had made my choice.

I gave him what chance I could. Once more I cried out to my would be rescuers that I was all right and they were not to break down the door. I prevented Rob from contradicting me by putting my hand over his mouth. But my voice was full of tears, from grief and the pain of my hands, and Brockley, hearing it, demanded to know what was the matter. Somebody else shouted, "For God's sake, let's get in and find out!" and with that, the ramming grew heavier.

The parlour door was stout, but no door could have withstood such an attack for long. When it gave way under the onslaught from what turned out to be a kitchen bench, I was kneeling at Rob's side, pulling his bonds loose, not very skilfully because I was weeping too much to see what I was doing.

I remember thinking, absurdly, that it was frosty outside and hoping that Matthew's doublet would keep him warm enough. He had no cloak.

Not until Brockley took hold of me and lifted me to my feet did I realise that my headache had suddenly, miraculously gone.

CHAPTER 21

Engaging a Craftsman

After that, came all the explanations and the business of coping with the aftermath of violence. Two of Rob's men had been killed, as well as Wylie, and others were hurt. A neighbour had called the parish constable, who arrived in haste to find out what the affray was about. He was astounded to find himself in a clockmaker's shop which looked as though it had been sacked by Attila the Hun in person, and had a basement full of counterfeit coinage.

The constable and Rob knew each other, however, for as a friend of the Cecils, Rob had been to civic functions at Windsor Castle and the two of them had met before. They co-operated well. Too well for my peace of mind, in fact, for despite my pleas, Rob told him to start a hue and cry after Matthew and Wilkins.

"I shouldn't worry," said Brockley comfortingly. He had held me against his shoulder while I cried myself out, and he was now dressing my seared palms with butter and bandages made of torn-up sheeting from one of the bedchambers. "Your husband'll be well away by now, and that mist out there is turning into a proper thick river fog. I doubt they'll even be sighted, let alone caught."

Meanwhile, the spotty apprentice Timothy and the maidservant, who both apparently lived out, had presented themselves for work, bewildered to find a crowd in the street outside. They were nearly arrested, except that Rob could see that they were scarcely out of childhood and quite innocent. He wouldn't allow it, though he said they must hold themselves ready for questioning.

The house was put under guard, the bodies removed, the injured men taken to the castle to be doctored. Ale and food were found in the kitchen so that we could have breakfast of a sort. Someone had discovered a silver music box under the shop counter, and brought it into the kitchen for us to see. It was in good working order.

"I want to speak to Mew," I said.

Mew had been bound and dumped on the floor of the shop. He was able to use his bound hands to hold food and a beaker, and someone had given him something to eat and drink, but he hadn't taken much of it. His small, compressed features were dirty and very pale, and there were tears in his eyes as he looked up at me.

"That silver musical box?" he said, resentfully. "I was making that for myself. Well, I shan't want it now. Take it! Why not? It's about the only thing in the shop that hasn't been broken. All my lovely clocks, all my handiwork. It's not right."

My palms still hurt badly and this did my temper no good. "I didn't think an arrow out of the undergrowth was altogether right, either," I said. "Nor a poisoned bedtime drink. I'll take the musical box, but as I'm honest, I'll pay for it. I'll leave the money in your office. It will be good coin and the shop will be under guard. Your heirs will get the money in the end, or else the crown treasury."

It was a savage thing to say, but I felt savage. I had lost Matthew now, for ever. I was like someone who has had a poisoned limb amputated. The pain, the loss, the sense of being crippled, must still be endured. Mew turned his head away and I saw his tears seeping down on to the floor, but my heart remained hard.

I went to the counter and found the musical box. I took it, and left the money as I had said. Meg should have her plaything.

Brockley's helmet and breastplate and the sword he had started out with had been taken away and his clothes were dirty and bloodstained, but in a room upstairs he found some garments, probably Wylie's, which fitted him. He made himself look respectable and went off to fetch Bay Star and the chestnut—which was indeed the Lockhill horse Blade—from the Antelope. I gave him money with which to pay the bill at the inn. He was back very quickly, and we were ready to set off at last.

Our destination was Lockhill and we were taking Mew with us. He was to be brought face to face with his probable fellow conspirators Mason and Crichton. "And we'll see if anything interesting transpires," Rob said grimly.

The mist was dispersing. We rode briskly, but it was an uneasy journey. For one thing, I had followed an interrupted night by another night with no sleep at all, and I was so tired that my eyes felt as though they were full of grit. Riding with bandaged hands was awkward, and light-hearted, gallant Rob, who had his ruthless side, was angry with me because I had wanted to go with Matthew, and attempted to delay the hue and cry. I found his company uncomfortable and edged Bay Star away from him, only to find myself close to Mew.

I discovered that, after all, I pitied Mew. His horse was being led by one of Rob's retainers, because Mew's hands were bound to his pommel and his feet to the stirrups. His eyes seemed to be staring at some dreadful private vision. Once, in a voice still slightly hoarse, he asked what was going to happen to him, and one of Rob's men obliged him with an answer.

"You'll be tried for treason, fellow. And after that . . ." Graphically, the retainer made a glugging noise, let his head flop to one side and his tongue loll out, and then, grinning, drew a forefinger slowly and evily down the length of his own stomach from ribcage to crotch. Another of the retainers laughed. Mew whimpered like a hurt child.

I shivered, turning my head away, imagining the horrors which lay ahead for this terrified man riding so near to me. It was being borne in on me that we were riding to Lockhill not only to confront Mason and Crichton with Mew, but also, whatever happened, to bring them in for questioning. We were on our way to arrest Ann Mason's husband.

In Maidenhead, the retainers bought bread and cheese and ale, and we pulled up to make a meal, but made it quick. We clattered into Lockhill village that afternoon, and Dr. Forrest rushed out to meet us, puffing with exertion. "Mrs. Blanchard! Mr. Brockley! And would this be Mr. Henderson?"

"It would," said Rob. "And you, sir?"

"Dr. Forrest, sir, at your service. I did right, then, to send for you? I was in two minds what to do. Your pardon, Mistress Blanchard, but yours was a strange note to receive from a young gentlewoman."

"You did quite right," said Rob. "And now there is more to do, up at Lockhill. You should know . . ."

He explained, while Dr. Forrest listened, his round face growing more and more shocked. While Rob was talking, Dale came running from the vicarage, and Brockley trotted to meet her and lift her up behind Blade's saddle.

"Dale!" I said, as Brockley brought her back to us. "How are you?"

"Oh, ma'am! I'm well enough now, but I've been that worried. It took me a good while to persuade Dr. Forrest! And then he only had his servant to send, on a pony. The man had to go to Maidenhead to get a fast horse from the Greyhound. I've fretted myself to a shadow."

While I was assuring Dale that she had done well and I would not forget it, Dr. Forrest begged our indulgence while he saddled his mount. He scurried off, and five minutes later he reappeared astride a placid brown mare with the bulging sides of age and idleness. We rode on, up the lane between the fields of Lockhill, towards the manor house.

As usual, we received a noisy greeting from the

mastiff, but with no immediate result. No one was about.

"Now what?" said Rob exasperatedly, sitting in his saddle, hand on hip. "Where in the world is everyone? And what, for heaven's sake, is that contraption up on the tower?"

"That's Mr. Mason's gliding engine," I said, awed.

The assembly on the tower had been spectacular enough when it consisted merely of the H-shaped structure, but now a long plank, long enough to reach beyond the edges of the tower, had been laid across the central bar of the H, using it as a fulcrum. Attached to one end was a rough and ready cradle, which held Mason's flying engine. The nose of the machine pointed into the air, and one of its vast wings extended perilously close to the sloped roof of the house. The great fantail of wood and canvas, with its fin sticking up from the centre, slanted down over the side of the tower.

The whole cradle was fastened down with a stout rope so that the other end of the plank was high in the air, but this, too, had attachments, for two bulging sacks hung from it. They were apparently full of rocks: the sharp edges had torn holes in a couple of places and jutted through. Another sack, possibly containing meal, sat in the body of the flying engine.

If the rope were released, I supposed, the sacks of rocks would crash down, the cradle would shoot up, and the device, swinging from upright to level at the top of the arc, would be flung into the air above the gatehouse.

We were all still marvelling when Redman, at last, came out. He quietened the dog and Rob Henderson rode forward. Before either he or Redman could speak, however, Leonard Mason and Dr. Crichton came through the porch together, talking. They could not have heard our arrival, for at the sight of the crowd of riders, they stopped short.

Mason saw me and strode forward, with the butler and Crichton on his heels. "What is this? Do you dare to return here, Mrs. Blanchard? With armed men? Who do you imagine you are?"

"That's right. The master ordered her out of Lockhill! She's no business here!" Redman made a gesture at me as though he were trying to shoo me away. Crichton said nothing, but eyed me with dislike.

"Mrs. Blanchard is with us!" Rob snapped. "And we have come on serious business which we can hardly discuss out here. If we could dismount and come inside . . ."

I had said nothing, because the moment Mason and Crichton appeared, I had been dumbstruck, first with astonishment, then with hope, and then with fear that the hope might be misplaced. Had a light been shone into a dark place, or had it not? I found my voice again. "Just a moment!"

Surprised, Rob paused. "Dr. Crichton," I said. "Did Mr. Mason give you that blackwork doublet you're wearing?"

Everyone was silent, presumably amazed by the irrelevant and frivolous nature of the question, but I persisted. "Well, did he?" I demanded. "And if so, when?"

Crichton had come quite close to me. I pointed at the doublet. "I repaired it myself. I can see my own stitchwork there. But I thought it belonged to Mr. Mason."

"Mrs. Blanchard," said Rob, "what is all this about?"

"It's important, believe me!" I said. "I'm not out of my mind. Brockley!"

"Madam?"

"Last Thursday, when—er—when you said to me that you had seen Mr. Mason approaching . . . you recall the occasion?"

"Yes, madam," said Brockley without expression.

"Well, did you actually recognise his face, or were you going by the doublet?"

"By the doublet, madam. I glimpsed the cream and black. But no, I did not see Mr. Mason's face. Mr. Mason and Dr. Crichton are alike in build, and yes, it could easily have been Dr. Crichton I saw. I realise that now." Brockley had followed my line of thought at once. "Mr. Mason, if Dr. Crichton won't answer the question, I suggest that you do. It could be worth your while."

Mason looked at him in outrage, but Rob barked, "Well, someone give us the answer and be quick about it!"

Mason said, "I gave it to Crichton quite lately. He badly needed some smarter clothing. Black and white are suitable for a priest. He did ask my wife to repair it—my wife, not Mrs. Blanchard. He wore it once before that, I think."

"And also afterwards? Last Thursday," I said, "he had a gown on later in the day, but was he wearing that doublet during the morning? And did you, that morning, send him to your study to find something for you?"

"Mrs. Blanchard, I dismissed you from my house. I will not be questioned by you!"

"I assume Mrs. Blanchard has her reasons for asking. If you won't be questioned by her, then answer me instead!" said Henderson.

"Then the answer is yes, possibly! I often send Crichton to my study for this or that. And yes, I think he did have that doublet on last Thursday. That was the only other time he used it before today, I believe. Yes, he tore it on a nail in my workshop on Thursday and had to change, and Ann had to mend it again."

"Crichton!" I said to Rob Henderson. "It's been plain enough that Crichton is probably in this, but what if, as far as Lockhill is concerned, it's *only* Crichton? I did the first repair to that doublet, to help Ann. In it I found an invoice for tin and copper, made out to Mr. Mew. That's why I went to Mew's shop. But if Crichton had already worn the doublet—I'd been at Thamesbank: I wouldn't have known—then he could have put the invoice there, not Mr. Mason at all."

Recollections were tumbling through my tired mind, and weirdly, my very exhaustion seemed somehow to have opened the way for them. We had heard Mason, as we thought, searching irritably in his study for a mislaid paper, but Mason was methodical, not given to mislaying things. Crichton was the untidy one.

Yes, Crichton, priest by profession, employed here to say illegal masses; Crichton whose clothes were all so dusty and worn; Crichton who was underpaid by the Masons. The clues pointed to him far more than to Mason.

And then, at last, the answer to that second puzzle which had nagged at me when I searched Mason's study swam upwards into view. Jennet had seen

Dawson listening at a door, to people talking on the other side of it. She said she didn't know who was in there, but she had just spoken to Mr. Mason herself, to tell him that the pedlar had come. She knew, therefore, where Mr. Mason was. Whoever was on the other side of that door, it couldn't have been Leonard.

And it was Crichton who had bought tapestries from Bernard Paige, saying they were for his master! Both Mason and Crichton had said that they were a legacy, but what if only Crichton were the liar? What if Crichton had bought them and told the lie to Mason?

"They know everything!" said a frightened voice from behind me. "They know it all! They broke into my basement and saw my work there!"

Surrounded as he was by Henderson's men, Barnabas Mew had until now been out of sight of those who had come out of the house. Now Henderson, smiling grimly, had him brought forward. Rob's notion that confronting the inhabitants of Lockhill with Mew might bring results, was now gratifyingly justified. Leonard Mason simply stared, and Redman's mouth dropped open, but Crichton turned the colour of tallow and began to shake.

"Dr. Wilkins got away. So did Mr. de la Roche. And they killed Wylie," Mew said miserably.

"Who the devil is Mr. de la Roche?" demanded Leonard.

"That's the real name of Mark Lenoir," I told him. I looked at the quaking Crichton. "The tapestries you lent to Mr. Mason to put on his dining-room walls," I said. "Costly purchases, paid for in cash. A way of feeding counterfeit money into the economy and making a profit for yourself at the same time. That's what you bought those tapestries for, isn't it, Dr. Crichton?"

"What *is* all this?" demanded Mason.

Rob supplied the details. Mason listened, his brow furrowed.

"Barnabas Mew? Making counterfeit coin in his cellar?" His astonishment was almost comical. I rejoiced, for it pointed to his innocence. Ann and the children might yet escape heartbreak. His reaction when Rob had finished was, interestingly, the same as Matthew's.

"It's a ridiculous scheme! It couldn't work unless it was on a gigantic scale! I know I've often said, here at my own table, that no country can survive unless its economy is sound, but between a healthy economy and one so sick that its ruler is endangered, there is a huge gap. I never heard of anything so unlikely as this! Was I—am I—under suspicion of being part of such a demented notion?" Mason asked with loathing.

"You will be required," Rob told him, "to accompany us to London for questioning, but if you are not guilty, you have little to fear."

"Not *guilty?*" Mason was scandalised. "I should think not! I am a good Catholic and I wish the Queen would have a change of heart and return to the true religion, but do you think I would touch a scheme like this? Good God! My wife wouldn't let me, anyway!" Some of the retainers laughed and Mason glared at them. "And if your wives are half as honest as my Ann, you're fortunate men! Money I always need, but I would scorn to make it in a way such as this! I trust to make money from my inventions one day. Coining, indeed!"

"Tell me something, Mr. Mason," I said. "Barnabas Mew originally taught music to your children, did he not? When the idea of that was first mooted, did he approach you first, or the other way about?"

"Crichton introduced him as a friend. I think they met in a tavern in Henley. And—yes, it was Mew himself who suggested he should teach my children." Mason was so overturned that he actually answered me without protest.

"Well," I said, "I believe he was originally meant to keep an eye on your household on behalf of Sir William Cecil." Out of my memory, I dredged Cecil's words when he first told me that something might be wrong at Lockhill: "I was never quite sure of how competent the man was whom I sent to investigate the Masons. He's been withdrawn now." However, the agent had not let himself be withdrawn. He had gone on visiting, and plotting with Crichton.

"You drew suspicion on yourself last year," I said to Mason, "when you gave some money to a charity for financing young priests. Mew was here to investigate your loyalty. I have it right, haven't I, Mew? For reasons which I don't understand—the chance of making money, perhaps?—you have joined in this scheme which is at least partly designed to help Mary Stuart."

"I didn't do it for money. I can earn that. I'm a good craftsman." Mew, sitting miserably on his horse with his bound hands clutching the pommel, nevertheless spoke with a weak kind of pride.

"Then *why?*" said Mason. "You're not even a Catholic!"

"They made me do it," said Mew, addressing Rob. "Oh, not Mr. Mason. He's got nothing to do with any of this . . ."

"Thank you!" said Mason.

". . . It was the others. They made me change sides and help them work against the Queen."

"They? Who?" Mason snapped.

"Crichton," said Mew wretchedly. "And Wilkins."

Rob gave a quiet order and four of this men dismounted. Their horses, well trained, stood without being held.

"Made you?" said Rob. "Well, we haven't questioned you yet. You may as well tell us your tale now."

In a near whisper, Mew answered him. "I stole an idea. It was Mr. Mason's notion for a clockwork box that would play a tune. But Crichton found out. Mr. Mason had shown him the design. I should have foreseen it! I knew Mr. Mason used to discuss his ideas with Dr. Crichton! I found the design and I took it and I started making it, in my shop, and . . . and . . . I wasn't well one week and didn't come to Lockhill when I was expected—to teach music to the children. Crichton came to Windsor to find out why, and he saw what I was making. I had it in the shop, under the window, for the sake of the light."

"So that was it!" I said.

"You . . . stole . . . my . . . design?" Mason enquired.

"It was a beautiful thing!" Suddenly Mew's voice was clear and passionate. "You couldn't have made it. You're not good at making things. You could draw it but you couldn't *make* it. I could! I did! I made it with gold and moonstones and took it to court once when I was taking a report to Sir William Cecil, and presented it to Her Majesty!"

"You did *what?*" shouted Leonard Mason.

"He did, I'm afraid," I said. "I was there at the time."

"Crichton asked you if you'd arranged for anyone to make the music box and you said no," Mew said to him. "Then, the next time I came to Lockhill, he told me that unless I did as he wanted, he would tell you that I'd stolen your idea. They needed me to *make* the coins, you see. They had to engage a craftsman, so to speak. Crichton said I'd be held up to ridicule, or perhaps taken up for some kind of theft . . ."

"You are all mad!" Crichton tried to sound lofty. "I don't know what anyone is talking about! I'm not involved in any plot!"

"Forgive me if I seem slow witted," said Leonard Mason. "I am trying to take all this in. Am I to understand that I have had *four* traitorous knaves at various times sleeping under my roof and dining at my table? Mew, Wilkins, Lenoir—or whatever his name is—and my children's tutor—my God, *my children's tutor!*— Dr. Crichton?"

"It would seem so," said Henderson dryly.

"But I tell you, this is all a tarradiddle!" Crichton's attempt at dignity had failed and his voice was almost a squawk. "You can't . . . you can't believe that pitiful creature!" He pointed at Mew. "Can't you see that he is merely trying to pass the blame on to others, to save his own skin?"

Dr. Forrest had been sitting on his portly brown mare, listening to all this in an amazed silence. Now, however, he spoke.

"Disentangling truth from fiction will be a jury's task. It really can't be completed here in this courtyard. Should we not all get down and go inside, as Mr. Henderson has suggested? You'll hardly set out for London today, Mr. Henderson. Most of you have been up all night and the horses must be worn out too. Mrs. Blanchard also seems to have injuries to her hands. Clearly, Mr. Mason must answer questions about the people who have frequented his house, though perhaps we need not place him under arrest . . ."

I heard this with relief. A further enlightenment had come to me, like cool water on a fevered wound. I turned to Mew. "Mr. Mew, did you tell Mr. Mason that I was a . . . a woman of dubious reputation?"

"Yes. I did. Fenn reported that you were coming to Lockhill, and it looked suspicious. So I got here ahead of you and tried to persuade Mr. Mason to say you couldn't come."

Mason had said that the slander came from Mew. If Mason were innocent, then perhaps he had just, quite simply, believed it.

"He wouldn't listen, or his wife wouldn't!" said Mew in aggrieved tones. "Fenn and Dr. Wilkins were in London, and I had to send Wylie back there to tell them and—"

"I seem to have created a flattering amount of furore," I said, cutting in before the incident of the boathouse could cease to be a secret. I had an amusing mental picture, though, of Mew and Wylie scurrying to Lockhill, and Wylie scurrying away again to consult with Wilkins and work out how to export me. They had done a lot of hard work for nothing.

"Never mind all that." Forrest kept us to the point. "Mr. Henderson, surely you should arrest Dr. Crichton forthwith? No doubt there is somewhere in this house where he can be kept close until tomorrow morning? You have authority?"

"Any citizen has authority to arrest a miscreant," said Rob, "but in this case, I have Sir William Cecil's written mandate too." He nodded to the four dismounted men and they moved forward. "Dr. Crichton, in the name of our sovereign lady Queen Elizabeth, I place you under arrest. You will be taken to London and . . ."

Crichton's eyes had been going from side to side, looking for a way of escape. Before Rob's formal speech could finish, he ran for it, apparently hoping to dash round the crowd of horses and make for the gatehouse. The men on foot at once stepped into his path. They were grinning, half crouching, and holding their arms out wide, as though in parody of a children's game. Crichton made a high-pitched sound like a hare in the jaws of the hounds, spun round and fled back into the house. All four sprinted after him.

"They'll bring him back in a moment," Rob said, after a pause. "Meanwhile, I suggest that we all go inside and that something can be found for us all to eat. We had very little on the way and—"

"I think," said Dr. Forrest, "that panic has driven Crichton out of his senses. What in the world is he doing, Mason, up on top of your tower?"

CHAPTER 22

Tragedy and Farce

Startled, we followed Forrest's gaze upwards to the tower. Crichton was indeed up there, apparently trying to shut the trapdoor behind him. Someone below, however, was resisting him, and as we stared, Crichton backed away, bumping into one of the catapult supports. One of Rob's men hoisted himself up through the trap and called to Crichton to come along quietly now—he'd have to in the end. "Nowhere you can go from here, fellow, unless you jump into thin air!"

He did not at once lay hands on Crichton. Instead, he paused to wait for a second man to emerge from the trapdoor behind him. Up on the tower, we heard Crichton give his hare-squeal again; then he turned to the engine in its cradle, yanked the meal-sack out of it and scrambled into its place. Producing a belt knife, he leant over the side to slash at the rope which held the cradle down. The weight on the other end of the cat-apult came down with a rush and the engine shot upwards and then hurtled out of its cradle, over the gatehouse and into the air beyond.

Down in the courtyard, everyone cried out simultaneously. The giant assembly on the tower was visible from the stableyard, and Thomas, together with one of the young undergrooms, ran out to us, pointing and shouting. After them, with a pail of pigfeed in her hand, came Jennet. Rob Henderson barked a sharp order to two of his men to stay where they were and guard Mew; then he wheeled his horse and rode for the gate. Everyone followed except Mew and his guards, horsemen and people on foot together pouring out through the gatehouse to see what had become of Crichton.

Spurring Bay Star, I arrived in time to see the huge imitation bird's last moment of wavering flight before it plunged headfirst towards the Lockhill ploughland. Brockley was at my side, with Dale on his crupper. Leonard Mason appeared, running. Rob reached a hand to him and Mason scrambled up on to the horse behind Rob's saddle. Thomas dashed forward to open a gate, and all those on horseback thundered through, leaving those on foot to follow.

We galloped across the furrows to pull up beside the heap of wreckage in the midst of them. The horses snorted and shied, and when I dismounted, pulling Bay Star's reins over her head, she tried to sidle away. I gentled her with one hand but dragged her forward with the other until I could see.

Crichton lay trapped in the ruin, his whole body horridly twisted. A long splinter of wood was driven deep into his chest. Blood bubbled out round it and poured from his mouth and nose, but he was still alive and his eyes rolled, looking at us as we clustered round him.

He was still coherent, too, despite his wheezing breath and the oozing blood. When Dr. Forrest, sliding off his mare and leaving the placid creature to stand, hurried forward, speaking the words of the last rites as he came, Crichton exclaimed thickly that he would let no Protestant pray over him, and raised a feeble hand to swat Forrest away, as though the vicar were a gnat.

"Hoped to fly away. Cheated the disembowelling knife, anyway," he said, spitting. His eyes rested on me. "Hate interfering women. Should stick to your embroidery."

Leonard had also dismounted. Impatiently pushing bits of shattered wing out of the way, he came to Crichton's side. "*Nicholas!* I took you for a friend. How could you so misuse the shelter of my house? Oh, for God's sake let's get you out of this tangle!" Mason attacked the wreckage and some of Henderson's men came to help.

Brockley joined them, leaving Dale to look after Blade. Crichton squalled as the splinter in his ribs was knocked, and the blood bubbled faster from the wound, spreading in a wide red stain across the beautiful blackwork doublet.

"Careful!" said Henderson. "Stop!" Crichton's shuddering agony passed its peak and though his mouth was still twisted in pain, he spoke again.

"Idea was mine!" he said. "About the coinage. Told my friend Wilkins. Thought he might like it. Knew it wouldn't do much harm. But it might do some, to that redhaired heretic you all call a queen and I'd get some money out of it. Sick of being hard up. Wanted good clothes of my own—not castoffs—and my own house . . . *my* tapestries in *my* dining room. Wilkins . . . no financier. Easy to talk round. You gave me the idea, Mason and . . . didn't know it."

"What are you talking about, man?" Leonard demanded.

"Said . . . over dinner, so often . . . a country . . ." His eyes were going out of focus and his voice was losing strength. His consciousness was fading, but he got his final words out.

"A country . . . needs a sound coinage to survive . . ."

"Oh my God," said Leonard Mason, and watched without pity as Crichton, his body arching, choked on his own blood. "It was my fault. I gave him the idea."

The people on foot were only just catching up. Thomas, indolence for once abandoned, was in the lead. Ann Mason had appeared, adding a note of inappropriate domesticity because she was holding a pan and a hearthbrush. Jennet, who was a big girl and not fast on her feet, arrived last, stumbling on the muddy furrows.

And then, without warning, tragedy turned to black farce. The breathless Jennet, seeing the bloodstained blackwork doublet on the slack and motionless figure in the wreckage, thrust a muddle of wood and canvas out of the way, threw herself on her knees by the body, and burst into tears.

"Oh, Mr. Mason, poor Mr. Mason, oh, how horrible!" wailed Jennet, and with that, she caught Crichton's shoulders, lifted him against her and planted her lips on his forehead.

"Jennet!" shouted Thomas, wrenching her away. "Let go! Don't make such a fool of yourself!"

"Leave me be! Leave me be! Poor Mr. Mason! He's dead and I can't bear it . . ."

"*Jennet!*" roared Leonard Mason from barely four feet away. He realised that he was hidden from her by the remains of the wing, and rose on tiptoe to shout at her over the top. "What's the matter with you? That's Nicholas Crichton!"

Jennet twisted in Thomas's grasp and saw him. Her mouth opened. Leonard, who looked and no doubt felt somewhat absurd, standing on his toes to peer over the wreckage like a gossiping housewife over a fence, marched round the wing instead and confronted her. She turned scarlet.

"B-b-but I saw the thing fly off the roof with you in it! I've never seen nobody but you in that black and white, sir, and I hadn't seen you today at all," said Jennet lamely, taking in that this morning Mason was wearing brown. "I thought you was dead, sir," she said blankly.

"What is the matter with this girl?" Leonard Mason demanded. "Anyone would think she was—"

"And so she is! It's perfectly obvious! I've been harbouring a hussy in my house and I never knew it. Shame on you, girl! Shame on you!" Ann, still clutching her pan and brush, marched forward and shouted her indignation into Jennet's face.

Meanwhile, Leonard, too, had turned scarlet. "I have never," he said to all of us impartially, "by word or deed encouraged this girl to regard me with affection beyond that of everyday respect. Never!"

Thomas, who had a restraining arm still wrapped round the sniffing Jennet, said, "Don't be too hard on her, sir. Or you, Mrs. Mason. These wenches get greensick and fancy themselves in love, but it means nothing. She ought to be married. I'd marry her today if she'd have me. I wish she'd listen to me. I wonder, would she listen to you?"

"You'd still marry her?" enquired Leonard Mason, in tones of unflattering if understandable disbelief. Her damaged reputation apart, Jennet was not a prepossessing sight just then, with her red, tear-stained face, and her fustian skirt all stained with Crichton's blood and what was probably spilt pigfeed. There was no sign of the bucket, which she had presumably dropped in her rush to reach the wreck.

"Willingly, sir," said Thomas.

"Then marry her you shall!" Ann took control. I saw clearly now what I had only glimpsed before: just how strong a character Ann actually was. She had turned Leonard from his scheme of flying off the roof along with his invention, and she had never been in any danger of having a traitor for a husband, because she would never have let Leonard become entangled in a plot even if he'd tried.

"You have it right, Thomas," Ann declared. "Single, she's a menace, and even married, we can't have her at Lockhill. If you wed her, she'll have to live with your mother in the village and not come up to the house. In fact, Thomas, if you look about you for another position, I'll give you the best of references."

"Ann . . ." said Leonard complainingly, but his wife was relentless.

"I don't want this girl anywhere near Lockhill. I want Thomas to take her in marriage and take her to another county as well! Jennet, be quiet! You can marry Thomas and leave Lockhill with him, or leave Lockhill without him and without a character, either. You could go back to your own mother, I suppose."

"She's dead and so's my father! I ain't got anywhere to go!"

"Then you'll wed Thomas. Dr. Forrest, come here!"

On the long ride from Windsor, I had wondered what awaited me at Lockhill, what grim or dramatic or extraordinary scenes would there be enacted.

But I hadn't for one moment expected to be a witness at a spur-of-the-moment wedding engendered by the absurd and trivial fact that Jennet had never chanced to see Crichton in the blackwork doublet. Nor, in my whole life, had I never expected to witness a marriage ceremony in the middle of a ploughed field, beside a dead body trapped in the shards of an insane machine which had been intended to fly but couldn't. A wedding, furthermore, with a priest who stumbled over the vows because he had no prayer book with him, while the weeping bride was given away by one of Henderson's retainers and bullied into her responses by Ann Mason.

I stood there obediently, dizzy from lack of sleep, joining in the prayers, and silently shaping a prayer of my own, that my husband would escape the hue and cry and flee unharmed from England. While Jennet was being saddled with a marriage she didn't want, my husband was going out of my life for ever. If Sir

Thomas Gresham's chaplain had appeared at that moment and told me to have faith in the deity's plan for mankind, I think I would have hit him.

When it was all over, Thomas led the still-sobbing Jennet away, the horses were taken aside, and the work of freeing the body was resumed. Rob Henderson exchanged a few rapid words with the Masons and then beckoned me to join them.

"We all know the truth about you and Mr. de la Roche now," Ann said. "I knew you were a decent woman, and I am sorry that you are parted from your husband. How can you bear it?"

Mason's face was less friendly. "I suppose I should commend you, Mrs. Blanchard—that is the name you prefer, I understand, though it is not your legal one. You serve your queen well, but you seem to have harboured appalling suspicions of me without my knowledge, and through you, I have lost a priest and a tutor and a maid-servant, and will shortly have to find another groom. You have also brought about the destruction of my gliding invention. You will forgive me for saying that I hope you will not wish to stay long under my roof."

"Only until tomorrow, I think." I looked at Rob. "We are leaving in the morning?"

"Yes. You are still required to come with us. So is Mr. Mason."

"Quite," I said. "Well, tomorrow, with your permission, Mr. Mason, I will this time say goodbye to the children before I go. At least you need not now fear that I will contaminate them. *Have* I your permission?"

Mason, though annoyed, was a fair man. "Very well. I regret my accusations, Mrs. Blanchard."

"The children are out riding on their own," Ann said. "I am only thankful that they saw nothing of all this. They will be back very soon. I must decide how much they should know." She looked at the pan and brush in her hand. "Oh, how absurd. I heard the shouting and saw a shadow as that gliding thing went off the roof and I just ran. I didn't even stop to put this down. Look, Ursula, isn't this odd? I'd been going round the house to see that Jennet had done her work properly this morning. She can be so careless. I went into Crichton's room because she was supposed to clean it before dinner. She hadn't done it very well. And look what I found on the floor!"

She held out the pan. She must have been carrying it instinctively so that it would not spill its contents, and the sweepings from Crichton's floor were still there: dust, what looked like marchpane crumbs, and several little twigs, bearing small, green, needle-like leaves.

"I think it's from a yew tree," said Ann. "Crichton was making a fuss about the topiary the other day. I suppose he tried clipping it himself and brought this in with him, caught in his clothes, perhaps. I don't like finding it in the house, I must say. It's poisonous. One of the home farm cows got into our garden last year, and died in convulsions after browsing on a yew tree. Cattle have no sense."

"Yew twigs?" I said. "Ann, that day when Crichton made a fuss about the topiary and upset Edwin Logan . . . Crichton was angry with the boys, wasn't he? He went out in a temper?"

"Yes. Why?" Ann was puzzled.

"I came back from a journey late that afternoon," I

said. "You said—I believe—that you had just seen Dr. Crichton in the yew garden. Had he only just left the house?"

"Oh, no," said Ann. "He stormed out much earlier. I don't know where he was in between. Does it matter?"

"Crichton taught archery to the boys," I said slowly, "but I don't think I ever watched him. Did he shoot well?"

"Certainly, though not so well with the bad thumb that Leonard's hammer gave him. Ursula, what is all this about?"

It was about Crichton, alerted by Wylie's message, deliberately provoking the boys into rudeness which would give him an excuse to abandon them. It was about Crichton, making his stealthy way, bow in hand, using the cover of bank and spinney and boundary hedge, to lie in wait for me on my return. And, fortunately, being unable to shoot straight because Leonard Mason had such a poor aim with a hammer. We had lingered on the way, discussing what Brockley should do when he got back to Windsor. The angry and frustrated Crichton had had time to return to Lockhill and make a show of his presence there, striding round the yew garden and annoying young Logan.

That wasn't all he'd done, either.

"Ann," I said. "All this is very dreadful, but take heart. Leonard is coming to London, but he will return to you safely. I am already sure that your husband is innocent—and I think you have just found one more piece of evidence in his favour." I knew now who had tried to poison me.

* * *

Before I left Lockhill, I enquired into just one more thing. I went to the arrow chests in the long room and examined their contents. In one, I found the simple shafts with plain points which the boys used in their archery practice, but in the other, I found a bundle of very different shafts, a reminder of the days, not so long ago, before army commanders began to prefer firearms to longbows. These deadly-looking arrows had the ugly, barbed heads which had so nearly killed me and Brockley and Dale as we returned to Lockhill from Windsor.

Odd to think that all three of us probably owed our lives to Mason's mad theories of gliding on the wind, and Crichton's blackened thumbnail.

And poignant to realise that I also owed mine to Matthew. It was because I was expecting him that night that I had not drunk that posset with its poisonous dose of yew extract.

CHAPTER 23

The Broken Toy

"An excellent outcome," Cecil said. "The mischief never even began. It seems that the purchases made by Crichton and Wilkins—the carpet and the tapestries—were experiments, using genuine money, to see which merchants examine high-value coins carefully, and which just check the amount and then send them straight to the bank. Paige was among the careless ones. His Genoese bankers have politely requested him to be more thorough in future."

"We are grateful to you, Ursula," Elizabeth said.

We were in the furthest bay of a gallery in Elizabeth's private rooms at Hampton Court. Other people were nearby but not within earshot. The Queen had placed herself in a window seat, hands folded in her elegant lap. Her dress was dove-coloured satin embroidered with black. In fact, it was a form of mourning, for one of her favourite ladies, Jane Seymour, had died not long ago. Elizabeth had given her a state funeral. I had missed it and was very sorry, for I too had liked Jane. But if today there was no sign of the mischievous feline being who had subtly gibed at Dudley and to whom Barnabas Mew had presented his music box, it was not on Jane's account. This grave, withdrawn air was because Elizabeth had once more been the target of conspiracy. All her defences were in place.

"We have been shocked by Mew's revelations," she said, "but also mightily thankful because the danger has gone by and not touched us. Our reward will be generous, Ursula."

I said, "Did Mew have to be . . . forced to speak?"

"Dear, tender-hearted Ursula," said Elizabeth. "No. It wasn't necessary."

"He was only too anxious to tell us all he knew." Cecil, dignified in a formal blue gown, showed a grim amusement. "And how much he despised Dr. Wilkins. Wilkins was the only one who really believed in the plan. Mew says that Wilkins was sure that any scheme carried out on Mary Stuart's behalf was a plot in accordance with the will of God and therefore bound to succeed. Mew thinks he's a fool, though Wilkins was quite careful, in his way: when the plan went into action, he said that they must all make their purchases under fake names. He also meant to arrange for some of the buying to be done through intermediaries, and he intended to use a false name for dealing with them, too. He financed Mew and told him to buy the base metals, but Mew had to present all his invoices for inspection. He did it through Crichton—hence the one that was found in Crichton's doublet."

"Crichton was an untidy man," I said. "I expect he left it there by mistake."

"No doubt," said Cecil. "To make their false coins they needed both base and precious metals. The treasure your husband had collected included money enough to buy the base metal, and also plate and the like, which they melted down to get the gold and silver. But when they tried to use the precious metals in some of the coins and melted those down too . . ."

Cecil's smile startled me. It so closely resembled a leer. "It didn't give a good yield," he said. "Most of it was bad money from the fifteen-forties. Except that it was struck in an official mint, it was practically counterfeit coin anyway!"

"King Henry's groat," said Elizabeth. "Cecil has shown his keepsake at the council table, Ursula. One should not speak ill of one's parents, but my father was . . . not always wise."

"The plan would have done little harm, but it might have done some." Cecil was grave again. "Well, Mew will suffer the rigours of the knife. Perhaps that will discourage other would-be plotters. It may also discourage people from changing sides as he did. The word for such a man, Ursula, is a doublet. Quite a coincidence, seeing that a blackwork doublet had a part in all this too."

"He was blackmailed into it," I said. "I almost feel sorry for him."

"He wouldn't have been blackmailed if he hadn't stolen that design from Mason," Cecil said relentlessly. "He's a poor, shabby little man, I'm afraid. Good quality agents are as rare as pigs with wings."

"Now, Cecil," said Elizabeth solemnly, "that is not

courteous to Mistress Blanchard!" Her eyes, just for a moment, danced.

Cecil said, "Mistress Blanchard is an admirable exception. Nor does she resemble any kind of pig. Your pardon, Ursula."

"Granted," I said, with gravity to match his. "You told me never to trust coincidences," I said, "and I didn't. When Mew turned up at Lockhill, it made me suspicious at once. There was one real coincidence, though, was there not? When you happened to be in Bernard Paige's warehouse while Dr. Wilkins was buying that carpet?"

"Yes. They do happen sometimes," Cecil said. "If I had known that Mew was still calling at Lockhill," he added, "we wouldn't have sent you there. Would we, ma'am?"

"We might." The Queen's eyes were serious again. "We needed someone there, and it had to be a woman. Ursula was an obvious choice."

There was a pause, then Elizabeth said, "The musical box that Mr. Mew gave us," she added, "has been broken up. The gold and the moonstones have gone into our treasury and the mechanism has been smashed. The sight and sound of it alike offend us."

I inclined my head. I had given Meg her box—why deprive the child of her toy?—but I thought it better not to tell Elizabeth that.

"I believe," said Cecil, "that Leonard Mason has given up any idea of trying to construct an engine that flies. We live in a splendid age for new ideas, but some of them turn out to be unworkable. Besides, he has been heavily fined for hearing illegal masses. He will have to pay more attention to his land, if he is to keep out of debt."

"It will be hard on Ann," I said with regret.

"At least," said Elizabeth dryly, "her husband didn't break his neck in his wretched airborne engine. And he isn't in the Tower awaiting execution for treason, as Mew is. It is a pity that two of his fellow conspirators got away, even though one of them is dear to you, Ursula. You have decided against going to France now?"

"Mr. de la Roche was not actually a conspirator, ma'am," said Cecil. "Though Wilkins was."

"That's true," I said, "but no, I shall not now go to France. I . . . might no longer be welcome."

"No, perhaps not." Elizabeth considered me with, I thought, compassion. "But you have a home here at court. Remember that. In time, the thought may heal you."

I looked away, out of the windows to where early summer had turned the grass and trees to vivid green and birds were flying here and there, gathering food for their nestlings. Matthew would live. I had that at least to hold on to. He would live: he would breathe the air and see the sky. Sun, moon, stars: when they shone on me, I could think; well, he can see them too. For his sake I could even accept the thought that the hateful Wilkins would also live. Only pathetic, cringing little Barnabas Mew would die.

Brisk, masculine footsteps approached. Robin Dudley, splendid in dark red with peacock slashings and gold embroidery, was making his way along the gallery, bold and disrespectful as usual, calling to someone over his shoulder, telling a page to run ahead and announce him to the Queen, and throwing a compliment to a maid of honour.

Elizabeth, hearing his voice, lifted her own. "We are here, Robin! Come and join us!"

Dudley stroke into the window bay, saw that the Queen had company, and halted. He bowed to her and then stood up straight and searched her face intently.

"My dear Robin," said Queen Elizabeth, dismissing the fate of traitors from her mind without noticeable effort. "How very good to see you."

"And good to see you, Your Majesty. I half feared you might have run off to Austria already, to marry the Archduke," said Dudley.

Early that morning, in the presence of Robin Dudley, Elizabeth had granted an audience to de Quadra, and hinted that a marriage alliance with the Austrian Archduke, a relative of King Philip, was something that she might be brought to consider. De Quadra clearly didn't know whether to take her seriously or not, and we had all gazed fascinated at Dudley's dark and handsome face, because to smile broadly and scowl ferociously at one and the same time is a remarkable feat and we were wondering how he did it.

"Not at all," said Elizabeth calmly, giving nothing away. "Such matters can hardly be decided so quickly. Here, as you see, are Mistress Blanchard and my good Sir William. Let us send for our musicians, and have some dancing."

I obtained permission next day to visit my daughter. I walked with her in the garden at Thamesbank, amid the roses and the topiary and the flowering trees, and thought, hard.

When I returned to the court, I sent a note to Cecil.

"It can be arranged," Cecil said, "if I think it appropriate." I was standing before his desk while he remained seated. His light blue eyes regarded me penetratingly. "But I would like to know why you want to see Barnabas Mew. You never asked to see your Uncle Herbert when he was in the Tower."

"He wouldn't have wanted to see me."

"Do you really imagine that *Mew* will want to see you?"

"No, but that is just it. I suppose I want to say that I pity his fate, and tell him that I will pray for him."

"You could pray for him anyway," Cecil pointed out.

"I know, but still, may I see him?"

"You would find it a harrowing experience. Have you really told me why you are so anxious for it?"

"I think," I said huskily, "that if I am to continue to work for you, I should fully understand what I am doing. I can't bring myself to attend the execution, but please allow me to see this man before his last day dawns."

I could see that Cecil was still suspicious, but at length he said, "I will allow you five minutes. No more."

Cecil escorted me to the Tower himself. He introduced me to the Lord Lieutenant, repeating his orders that I should have only five minutes in Mew's cell. "I will go with her and remain close at hand. I understand the man is not thought dangerous, but he has cause to regard Mistress Blanchard with . . . a degree of dislike," said Cecil in his driest voice. "The turnkey should be nearby, too."

"So shall I be, since the visitor is a lady," said the Lieutenant of the Tower, gazing down at me. He was a tall man and I did not reach his shoulder. I could see that he, too, was puzzled by my request. "And the gentleman gaoler will also be with us. The man is chained, of course. We can remain in the doorway, Sir William."

The Lieutenant had a modern and comfortable house within the Tower walls. He lived in luxury, from the fragrant rushes on the floor to the embroidered wallhangings, to the silver dishes and goblets in which we were served on arrival with ginger-flavoured cakes and white wine. The basement cells of the Tower of London were quite a contrast.

A frightening contrast. The steps which lead down to them are a warning of what lies ahead. A turnkey, a short man with a strutting walk, led the way, followed by the dignified figure of the gentleman gaoler in his scarlet uniform, with myself, Cecil and the lieutenant behind. There were a few thin slit windows at first, admitting bright streaks of daylight, but as the steps went below ground level, the only light came from a few flambeaux, thrust into wall sconces. Our misshapen shadows prowled on the walls. It was cold and our footsteps echoed. So did the clank of the heavy keys attached to the gaoler's belt. He remarked over his shoulder that these cells down here weren't used that much.

"Most prisoners are 'igher rank and get tower rooms and servants. We bring 'em down 'ere to scare 'em into answering questions—that's what the basement's mostly used for. It's not that usual to 'ave the likes of this one down 'ere, all the time, like."

"That's true," said the gentleman gaoler. "The Tower is supposed to be for men of position. A dishonest clockmaker is not," he added in tones of fastidious disapproval, "what I am accustomed to."

"He's in the Tower because of the stature of his crime," said Cecil. "It's the crime that entitles him to be here, not his social standing. Take heart. He won't be with you for much longer."

"Oh, 'e's no trouble," said the turnkey cheerfully, pausing to light us round a corner. "Except that 'e seems to 'ave lost 'is appetite. Can't get 'im to eat, nohow. Pity. 'E'll be too weak to last long when 'e goes on show."

I shuddered, wishing I hadn't come, and knowing, too, that I couldn't have lived with myself if I had stayed away.

We went on to the foot of the steps, turned left and came to a massive, iron-studded door with a torch in a wall sconce above. Our guide selected a key and pushed it into the lock.

"I shouldn't think," said Cecil in my ear, "that your lock-picks would have much effect on that. It must be ten times bigger than anything they're meant for."

"I'm sure you're right," I said, feeling instinctively at my hidden pocket and its contents. I was in no mood for pleasantries.

The turnkey swung the door open and stepped in.

"Visitor for you, Mew! A pretty lady, too. Ain't you the lucky fellow?" He moved aside and beckoned me forward. "'Ere you are, then."

"We'll all be just here," said Cecil, "but take care."

I went in. The cell was small and it reeked, of ordure and sweat. A barred grating, high up in one wall, cast a faint daylight into the room. Against the wall furthest from the door, Mew was curled up tightly on a straw pallet, his knees drawn up to his chest as if in a desperate attempt to protect the vitals which must soon be exposed to the executioner's blade. When the turnkey announced me, the only response was a moan.

"Mr. Mew?" I said, hesitantly. I went over to him and stood there nervously, longing to get this over, to get away. I put my hand on his shoulder. He shuddered under it, but then looked up at me. His eyes were feral with fear. He was more like an animal than a human being.

"You!"

He sat up slowly, as though movement were difficult. Despite the gloom, I could see the untrimmed hair hanging limply round his ears, and when he put up a hand to push it out of his eyes, a chain clanked. He was very thin and his bony wrists were shackled to chains which hung from the wall above the bed. He could move a few steps from the bed but no more. He had adequate clothes and rugs—he was clearly not going to be allowed to die of lung congestion—but everything was filthy and he smelt.

I had wanted to dress plainly for this visit, but I could hardly go about with Sir William Cecil and the Lord Lieutenant of the Tower, looking like a beggarwoman. My gown and kirtle were unpretentious, thin summer-weight wool, brown over pale yellow, but there was embroidery on my kirtle and sleeves, and my farthingale was quite wide. I felt tastelessly overdressed.

Mew was waiting for me to say something. I must speak.

"Mr. Mew, I . . . I had to do as I did, but I grieve to see you or any man in this state. I came . . . I came to say that I crave the mercy of God for you, and a swift end to your pains. I will pray for you."

"Am I supposed to thank you?" Mew enquired. "Well, I'll need prayers. That's true enough."

"You shall have them, I promise."

I hesitated, and then I held out my right hand and grasped his, just for a moment. My skin crawled at the feel of his cold, damp palm, and the healed burn scars across my own palms momentarily throbbed at the pressure. I released him, trying not to be too quick about it.

With a faint attempt at sangfroid, he added, "Sorry I can't offer you anything in return. You don't need *my* prayers."

"You could tell me something," I said. "You could tell me what it was that Dawson overheard at Lockhill. He listened at doors, didn't he?"

"Oh, him. Yes. Damned, prying, snooping . . . Jennet saw him. Putting his ear to the door of that back room where they used to hear mass. She told me. She was just gossiping. She didn't know I was one of the people in the room. Crichton was the other."

"So she heard *you!* What were you saying? I'd like to know—to understand."

"Does it matter?" He shrugged and then answered anyway. "I was trying to make Crichton see that the scheme was stupid. It all depended on Wilkins believing in it, but sooner or later he'd see it was no good and realise how we'd cozened him into it. Wilkins is a fool, but he'd be a bad enemy if Mary Stuart ever did get on to the throne and he had power again. I wanted to *stop* the idea, but they wouldn't listen. I prayed Mason would kill himself in that gliding thing and then I wouldn't have to be afraid of him finding out about the music box any more. I encouraged him to build it."

"I expect I'd have felt the same," I said. "Thank you for explaining. I really will pray." I began to back away. His voice stopped me.

"Mrs. Blanchard."

I paused. "Yes?"

"The music box I gave the Queen. Does she still have it? Does she ever play it? It was exquisite." In Mew's tremulous tones were an echo of former pride. "I've never made anything so pleasing. Does she listen to it?"

"No," said Cecil, from the door, cutting across the lie I was about to tell. "She does not. Your box has been destroyed, Mew, and no other like it will ever be made. It was a fair invention, but you have tainted it for ever."

"But I did take a music box for my daughter," I said. "You remember? She still has it and plays with it."

"Does she? Thank you, Mrs. Blanchard," Mew said. Cecil almost pulled me out of the cell. "That man, if you recall, is a murderer. He nearly got rid of you! And Dale! I wish," said Cecil, "that I knew what all this was truly about. Were you really so anxious to know what Dawson discovered?"

"I was curious, yes. And I have been clearing my conscious, Sir William."

"And is it now clear?"

"As much as possible, yes."

"You make very little sense," said Cecil crossly.

On a bench under a sycamore tree overlooking the river, I sat with Cecil. Thamesbank House lay behind us, and in front of us the grass stretched down to the sunlit river. It was a windy sunshine: there were wavelets on the sparkling water and the tree above us tossed in the gusts. On the grass, Meg played with the Henderson children. Bridget was watching the game and sometimes joining in. It was a pity, I thought, that the Mason children could not share this well-ordered household. When I had made my farewells to them, the girls had all cried, and so had I. I missed them.

Meanwhile, Cecil was talking to me.

"I came to tell you something, Ursula. You were aware, of course, that Mew was to be executed a week ago?"

"Yes. *Was* to be executed?" I enquired. "I have not heard the latest news, I'm afraid."

"Had you been at court, you would have heard. The Queen has been generous with her leave of absence."

"I fell ill, Sir William, while visiting Meg. Today is my first day up."

"Indeed? What was it? A fever?"

"A fever and a series of sick headaches. I am prone to them, unfortunately. But what of Barnabas Mew? You said he was to be executed—does that mean that the execution didn't after all take place? He was reprieved?"

"No. He died in convulsions, possibly from fear, before he came to Tyburn. Shortly after your visit, in fact."

"Really? A merciful escape, I suppose."

"Yes. Something strange," said Cecil, "was found when Mew's cell was cleared out. I was informed of it this morning. Hidden among the rugs on his bed was a little glass phial, empty except for a drop or two of some dark liquid. According to the Lord Lieutenant of the Tower, who passed the information to me, a single tiny leaf was stuck at the bottom of the phial—a little needle-shaped leaf such as the yew tree bears. The inference is that the phial contained yew tree poison. One wonders how Mew could have come by it."

"Indeed yes. How extraordinary," I said.

"You believed, did you not, that the poison which was meant to kill you and nearly did kill Dale, was a brew made from yew foliage?"

"I think it possible, yes. Yew twigs were found in Crichton's room."

"The means to make the poison would be easily come by, of course. Anyone might have done it. Mew had various visitors. You were one. There were also different gaolers at different times, officials who came to question him, chaplains bringing religious comfort."

"And gaolers," I said, "are notoriously willing to be bribed."

"Quite. It's a mystery," said Cecil, "and I daresay it will never be solved." He rose to his feet. "Are you returning to court soon? There will be work for you. Lady Catherine Grey, the Queen's cousin, has been behaving oddly. She is very often not where she ought to be, and has been seen in places—rooms, courtyards, gardens, here and there in the royal residences—where she has no business to go. If challenged, she always has an excuse, but she had been involved in intrigue before, as you and I know. We thought you might like to undertake the task of watching her."

"I shall return to court tomorrow, Sir William," I said.

"Does her musical box still amuse Meg?" Cecil rose, brushing a few sycamore leaves from his doublet.

"No," I said. "Meg is a child, after all. The box lasted a fortnight and then she broke it."

"And you told Mew she was still playing with it, to comfort him? You really are the most extraordinary creature," said Cecil. "Until tomorrow, then. I hope your recovery continues smoothly. Take care of yourself."

He disappeared into the house, and I remained sitting on the bench, hoping that I really would feel equal to taking up court life again in the morning.

It was true that I had had a sick headache after my visit to the Tower, but it had only lasted a day. I had woken, the day after that, to another kind of pain.

At Lockhill, I had had one night with Matthew, just one night. During our brief married life the previous autumn, I had guarded against conception, with the aid of a vinegar-soaked sponge, but at Lockhill I had simply never thought about it. And one night had been enough, or too much.

Not that it mattered now. The shock of seeing Mew in his condemned cell, which had brought on the blinding headache the following day, had also brought on the miscarriage the day after.

Matthew's child would have been a considerable complication in my life, but the strength of my grief surprised me. How I would endure the court, how I would hold up my head and smile when I felt as though the world had ended and my spirit had been torn in pieces, I did not know.

I could do nothing, I thought, but rest against whatever satisfactions I had. I had penetrated the Lockhill plot, and I had done what I could for the pitiful Mew. My hidden pocket had that day contained more than just my lock-picks: I had used my body and my wide farthingale to hide my movements from the watchers in the doorway, and when I took his hand, I had pressed the phial into it. It had been more effective than prayer, although I had kept my word about that and spent an hour on my knees for him, that same evening.

I rose from the bench and strolled down the path towards the river, moving carefully. I was still bleeding, although it was lessening now.

What could Catherine Grey be up to? She had been caught out in serious delinquency in the past. It ran in her family. Her mother, a niece of old King Henry's, had been as ambitious a schemer as the world had ever seen. Catherine's sister, Lady Jane Grey, had been their mother's pawn and her end on the blcok should have discouraged any ideas Catherine might harbour, of plotting against the Queen. However, I had reason to know that the warning hadn't been entirely effective.

Catherine had had a good, sensible friend in Lady Jane Seymour, but it was that same Jane Seymour who had lately died. She had always been frail. Catherine now had no one to give her good advice.

If I were to shadow Catherine Grey at court, though, I would have to be careful. She didn't like me. It would be quite a challenge, but I ought to take it up, not just for the pay, but for Catherine's own sake. If she were really doing something stupid, I might, if I were quick enough, be able to deflect her before she put her neck at risk.

Smiling at Bridget and the children as I passed them, I made my way to the landing stage and stood looking down into the water. Here, close to the bank and sheltered by the jetty, it was calm despite the wind, and I could see the reflection of my own face. I did not really resemble Elizabeth, for she had light red hair and golden-brown eyes, while my hair was black, and although my eyes were hazel, they often looked dark. However, my face was pointed, like hers, and like her I had a naturally pale skin. As I gazed at my gently rippling reflection in the water, it struck me that my face, like Elizabeth's, resembled a shield. It was certainly no guide to its owner's nature.

No one, I thought, would see in me a woman who had picked locks and hunted criminals. They would not see the woman who only recently had secretly plucked foliage from the Henderson's topiary, and then asked to spend the night at Thamesbank, and sat up into the small hours, stewing the green yew needles over the hearth in her bedchamber.

I had that night done violence to something in myself, even though my purpose was not murder, but mercy. Even then, something else had been at work. In asking to see Mew, I had made an opportunity to satisfy my curiosity over what, precisely, Jackdaw had overheard at Lockhill. Thinking of that, I recoiled from myself with distaste.

It wouldn't do. If I were to pursue my curious calling further, I must make what terms I could with its darker side.

Elizabeth had called me tender hearted, but was I? Perhaps Matthew was right: perhaps deep within this heart of mine, there was a point of ice.

That could also be true of Elizabeth. Perhaps she could not otherwise be a Queen, and carry out a ruler's work. Perhaps my work required it, too.

Matthew, my dear, my very dear, my lost one. If ever we meet again, will you recognise me? Or will this work of mine change me into something beyond your understanding?

I think it may well change me into something that no man, ever again, can truly love.

It *was* my work, though. It seemed to be part of my nature. I had only to think of Catherine Grey, of having a new task ahead of me, and at once my tired spirits lifted.

Yes, I was strong enough. I would go back to Hampton Court in the morning. And go about my business.

HISTORICAL NOTE

In the course of this book, I have stretched a few historical points, but not beyond the bounds of possibility.

Bishop de Quadra's secretary Borghese really did betray his master. In 1562 (the year after the action of this book), he passed on to Cecil information about a very serious intrigue in which de Quadra was involved. For all we know, he may have been passing on smaller pieces of information earlier than that.

The musical box was not actually invented until the late eighteenth century and first appeared in Switzerland. It was developed from the watch mechanism, and to begin with consisted of a disc set with steel pins, which tapped against a fan of tuned teeth as the disc revolved. The cylinder type of box, in which the pins were set round a barrel and tapped against a comb of tuned teeth, was first invented in the early nineteenth century.

Nevertheless, clock mechanisms were quite well developed by the time of the first Elizabeth. A clock which chimed the quarter hours was built for Wells Cathedral in 1389; by 1488 pendant watches, which would strike the hours, had come into existence. On

New Year's Day, 1571, the Earl of Leicester presented Queen Elizabeth with a ruby and diamond bracelet with a clock set in the clasp—in other words, a valuable wristwatch.

The Renaissance and Tudor periods were times of great intellectual expansion. New lands were discovered, new trade routes opened, new commodities imported. Along with all this, fresh ideas and inventions sprang up everywhere. The cylinder musical box is not essentially very complex, and it seemed to me not impossible that an Elizabethan inventor with a fertile imagination might, perhaps with the image of a spinet keyboard as a starting point, arrive at the concept without the intervening stages of the Swiss watch and the flat disc.

It also seemed quite conceivable that an Elizabethan inventor should experiment with a glider. The concept of flight had fascinated mankind for centuries. Leonardo da Vinci was much intrigued by it, although his ideas never developed very far, and someone might have been inspired by him into investigating further and carrying out a few experiments, even to the point of beginning to perceive, dimly, the principle of the airfoil section . . .

My imaginary inventor's glider fails, of course, and his musical box is consigned to the dustbin of history as far as the Elizabethans are concerned, because it is tainted by association with treachery.

However, these inventions *could* have been conceived in the sixteenth century and after all, this *is* fiction. Let's imagine what might have been. Let's have fun!

Fiona Buckley

2354

FIONA BUCKLEY
TO SHIELD THE QUEEN

A brilliant historical mystery
that will transport you to
the glamorous, gaudy, and
very mysterious court of
Queen Elizabeth I.

Available from Pocket Books

...and be sure not to miss

FIONA BUCKLEY
THE QUEEN'S RANSOM

from Scribner

History and
mystery
come together
again.

POCKET BOOKS
PROUDLY PRESENTS

Queen's Ransom

Fiona Buckley

Coming soon in hardcover from Scribner

The following is a preview of
Queen's Ransom. . . .

Sir Robin Dudley, Master of the Queen's Horse, had broad shoulders and swarthy good looks, a dashing taste in doublets, and a great deal of personal charm. I was a young woman of only twenty-seven and I ought to have found him attractive.

Instead, I detested him.

He wasn't a kindly man, for one thing, and I appreciated kindness. The uncle and aunt who saw to most of my upbringing had so conspicuously lacked it.

And for another thing, Dudley came of a family so fiercely ambitious that his father and one of his brothers had lost their heads for plotting against their sovereign, and Robin once came near to plotting against her himself.

Queen Elizabeth knew this perfectly well, but remarkable individual though she was, in this respect she was the one who was conventional, while I was not. Dudley's masculine beauty entranced her and at twenty-eight, not much older than I was myself, she was not yet hard enough to have that handsome head and that muscular set of shoulders separated by the executioner's ax. She and Robin were not lovers, but he was still her favorite.

There were those who looked on her liking for him with a sentimental eye; for instance, Sir Henry Sidney, who had married Dudley's sister. Well, Sidney had the virtue of kindness but in him it sometimes went too far. As Sir William Cecil, the Secretary of State, once said to me in a private fit of exasperation, Sidney was too sweet-natured for his own good and every now and then his intelligence drowned in the sweetness like a wasp in a jam pot. "On this business of the Queen and Dudley," Sir William said furiously, "Sidney is a simpleton."

The majority of the council members were not simpletons and they were anxious. My immunity to Robin's attractions was useful to them. For although I was outwardly just a Lady of the Presence Chamber, I also took a wage from Cecil for (among other tasks) keeping an eye on Sir Robin Dudley and reading his correspondence whenever I got the chance. As a way of earning a living, it sometimes hurt my finer feelings, but somebody had to do it, for Elizabeth's sake.

I should be honest, though. I owe Robin something. In 1560, eighteen months after Elizabeth took the throne, I came to her court as a widow with next to no money. My husband was dead of the smallpox, and I had a small daughter to rear. I entered the risky but remunerative world of spying through an errand that Dudley asked me to do, and because of that, I was thereafter able to pay for the clothes and education that would give my little Meg a chance in the world.

Then, in 1562, quite by chance, and without ever knowing it, he could be said to have saved a life that was dear to me. But for Dudley and his ambitious skul-duggery, there would have been no royal inspection of the Tower Treasury that March, and the result could well have been tragedy.

It was to be an informal royal inspection of the Treasury in the Tower of London. The Queen would be accompanied by Sir Robin Dudley, by his brother-in-law Sir Henry Sidney, by her favorite ladies, including Lady Katherine and myself, and by selected guests such as the French and Spanish ambassadors. There was to be no ceremony.

This meant in practice that Sir William Paulet, the treasurer, and Sir Richard Sackville, the undertreasur-er, and a horde of minions spent days in advance in the Wardrobe Tower where the bulk of the treasure was housed, lining shelves with black velvet, burnishing choice items with soft cloths, arranging them on stands that would display them to advantage, and laying strips of blue carpet to provide Elizabeth with a pathway 'round the display.

It also meant that within the Tower enclosure, the informal escort for the royal party consisted of the lieu-tenant of the Tower, the gentleman porter, three yeomen warders, Sir William Paulet, Sir Richard Sackville, two gentlemen from each of their house-holds, and two trumpeters, who went ahead to announce the Queen's approach. There were a couple of page boys in attendance, too, to run errands, hold doors, and pick up anything that was dropped, and the whole business had been carefully rehearsed half a dozen times over the previous morning.

Rehearsal was needed, though, because the occasion was unusual. Having once been imprisoned in the Tower, Elizabeth disliked the place and rarely visited it, splendid though it was, and is. It would be better named the Towers, plural, for it contains any number of them. There's the White Tower, which is the keep in the middle; there are towers dotted all 'round the huge encircling walls and over the gatehouse; and there's the Wardrobe Tower, standing alone at the southeast corner of the keep. After a brief pause to take wine in the lieutenant's lodgings, and a side excursion, as it were, to inspect the Queen's jewel house and admire her regalia and her personal gold and silver plate, we set about the serious business of the day, which began with the gold and silver bullion ingots in the basement of the Wardrobe Tower.

"Please take care on the steps, ma'am. They're steep," Paulet said anxiously. Paulet himself was elderly and had rheumatic joints. He didn't come down with us. Sackville, however, though middle-aged himself, was fitter and acted as guide. Flambeaux in wall sconces lit the way as we descended. Dudley, just behind the Queen, kept a hand under her elbow. Sidney stepped down lissomely, but the French ambassador almost tripped, and muttered a Gallic oath under his breath, while short, dapper De Quadra murmured a warning to his colleague that the stairs were worn in the middle. The flambeaux threw misshapen shadows that glided over the stone of the walls, and although the staircase was dry, there was a river smell about the place. It was cold.

I didn't like it any more than Elizabeth did. It reminded me too much of an earlier visit I had made to the Tower to see a condemned man. My work could send men to their deaths, and sometimes accusing faces appeared in my dreams. In some ways, I, too, needed to be harder than I was.

We crowded into a torch-lit underground vault where ingots of precious metal were stacked like firewood along one wall. Elizabeth, oh so casually, asked Sackville what the total estimated value of the ingots came to, and then repeated the answer in Spanish and French for the benefit of the two ambassadors, apparently out of courtesy, but in reality to make sure they'd got it right.

Listening to this piece of dulcet political maneuvering, I thought, once again, how weary I was of intrigue and how glad I was that I would soon be on my way to France, free for a while to keep my nose out of other people's business. Indeed, I seemed lately to have lost my skill in investigation. I would gladly have left the court forever, except that I needed the money for my darling Meg. And if disenchantment with intrigue wasn't my only reason for going, well, the other was foolish and I wouldn't confess it, even to myself.

We climbed back to the daylight and up some more steps, easier ones this time, into a chamber where sunshine streamed through tall, slender windows to sparkle on the treasures so carefully arranged there. This was better. We moved along the azure carpet, marveling at spectacular sets of gold and silver plate, silver spoons with exquisite chasing, salts and candlesticks, gemmed boxes and figurines, ceremonial arms and armor . . .

Elizabeth had beckoned the ambassadors to her side and without any prompting from Paulet or Sackville, and was artlessly telling them the history of this and that, dropping in further references to the extraordinary value of the items.

"In an emergency, they would be sold or melted down, of course, but as you saw, our stores of bullion should make that unnecessary. We can keep these works of art and thereby honor the skill of the craftsmen . . ."

Dudley had drifted away from the Queen and was talking to one of Sackville's gentlemen, commenting on a recent court scandal. ". . . the girl was a perfect fool. There she was, as pregnant as a waxing moon, with no proof of her marriage because the so-called husband was abroad; she'd lost the document he gave her that acknowledged her as his wife; she didn't know the name of the clergyman who married them, and the only witness died last year. . . ."

"I know who he means." Sir Henry Sidney had moved to my side. "Personally, I pity her. A silly girl—but she was deep in love and I daresay she believed that she was married."

"I know who she is, too," I said. "And I pity her as well, even though I don't like her very much."

But Dudley clearly had no sympathy for her at all. As I said, unlike his brother-in-law, he was not kindly.

And because the girl who was so obviously not an object of his concern had once figured importantly in one of the intrigues that were so much a part of my life, the thought of her was like that descent into the treasury basement, bringing back insistent memories that I didn't want.

Once, I had had an alternative to this life of intrigue. The smallpox had killed Meg's father, my first husband, Gerald Blanchard, but I had married again. I had been in love and it should have been a good match, but a matter of conscience had forced us to part. Nowadays, I used my former married name, that of Mistress Blanchard, and I kept Matthew's wedding ring in my jewel box and wore instead the one Gerald had given me.

And that was that, I said to myself fiercely. I had made my choice. I was a wantwit even to think about Matthew these days. My life was here at court and although I was about to go away for a while, I knew I must return in due course and go on with my work and be grateful that I had it. Be content with that, Ursula . . .

". . . and here," said Paulet, leading the way to the next array of exhibits, "we have ceremonial weapons and mail. This corselet, heavily embossed, and inlaid with a pattern of enamel and gilding, is of German manufacture—it was made in Nuremberg, to be precise—and this one . . ."

The shelves and tables on this side were set out with ornamental breastplates and helmets, swords and curved Oriental scimitars, their hilts and scabbards all sparkling with gems. Sir Henry and I found ourselves in the company of Sir Richard Sackville. He was stiff in manner, and had an affected habit of using turns of phrase left over from the last century, but I liked him. He did not know of my work for Cecil and the Queen (few people did; not even Sir Henry, who was so high in Elizabeth's confidence), but both he and Paulet knew quite a lot about my background, for they knew the man for whom Gerald had formerly worked.

"Since good Bishop de Quadra is among us," Sackville murmured, "we thought it wisest not to enlarge upon the means by which some of these objects came hence. But that corselet there may interest you, Mistress Blanchard." He pointed to the expensively adorned affair from Nuremberg. "Made in Germany it may have been, but it was ordered for the armory of the Spanish administration in Antwerp. It's one of two thousand corselets taken from thence by divers tricks and strategems, and brought across to England."

"Where are the rest of the two thousand?" inquired Sir Henry with interest.

"We shall see them as the last part of this visit," Sackville said. "Weapons of all kinds and a great store of gunpowder were also taken from that same Netherlands armory and brought hither, and they and the other corselets lie in the vaults beneath the White Tower. There was not room enough for them here." He smiled at me. "Mistress Blanchard may well know more of how they were brought out of the Netherlands than even I or Sir William Paulet."

"Really?" said Sir Henry. "I knew you had lived in Antwerp, Mistress Blanchard. Gerald Blanchard was in the service of Sir Thomas Gresham at the time, was he not? But surely you didn't spend your time there stealing gunpowder and corselets."

"I didn't steal them myself," I said. "But Gerald did."

Gerald and I had lived in Antwerp for a nearly a year, as part of Sir Thomas Gresham's entourage. Gresham was a financier employed by Elizabeth to improve her credit and raise loans for her abroad. He had interpreted this brief somewhat liberally.

"Gerald helped Gresham to—er—obtain weapons and armor and other valuables from the Netherlands and get them to England," I said. "Not always—not even usually—with their owners' knowledge or consent." No, we had better not let De Quadra realize where they came from.

"You must have had an exciting time in Antwerp," said Sir Henry, amused.

He was quite right. Gerald's work had included finding people who could be bribed or blackmailed into lending keys and forging requisitions in order to get valuables—ingots, plate, armor, all manner of things—out of storage. Sometimes, Gerald took temporary charge of the filched goods. More than once, we had had consignments hidden under the bed in our lodgings, awaiting a ship or a better hiding place until a suitable ship was in port. It had indeed been exciting.

I glanced around the display. The Queen was now examining a sword with a spectacular hilt, encrusted with cabochon emeralds and rubies, and the French ambassador, in conversation with the lieutenant, had strolled back across the room to look once more at the gold and silver plate. With Sackville and Sir Henry still at my side, I followed them, wanting a second look myself. Sackville had jolted my memory. Yes, of course. That fine set of gold plate was one I had seen before. Gerald had taken me to see it aboard the ship that was to carry it illicitly away from Antwerp. And just before the smallpox struck, there had been another splendid consignment . . . I scanned the table and moved along it. But none of those items seemed to be on view.

"That isn't all the plate from Antwerp, is it?" I asked. "I take it that the rest is stored somewhere, like the corselets?"

"Oh no. We keep all the plate together, here," Sackville said. "It is so very beauteous. As you see, we have had stands made on which to set it out. Why do you ask?"

It had been two years ago. That particular consignment had rested, briefly, in our lodgings while Gerald checked it over. I had helped him, writing down a list of items as he dictated them, before he and the manservant took them away to be stowed, not under anyone's bed, not that time, but under the floor of a rented warehouse. The rent had been paid for five years in advance and the agreement contained a clause forbidding the owner to enter the property until those years were up.

I could still hear Gerald's voice in my head, dictating that list. As a child, I had shared my cousins' tutor, and he had made a great point of training his pupils' memories. I could recite verse by the furlong, and carry a shopping list of thirty or more items in my head with ease, after hearing them told over just once. I could remember almost word for word what Gerald had said, and besides, I had seen most of the items.

Slowly, as near as I could, I repeated the inventory.

"Item, one full set of gold plate, value approximately ten thousand pounds, including twenty-four drinking goblets, marked with the badge of a noble Spanish house, set in cabochon rubies and emeralds.

"Item, a golden salt, two feet high, shaped as a square castle tower, with a salt container under each turret and spice drawers below. Decorated with the same badge, set in rubies. Value approximately twelve thousand pounds.

"Item, a silver salt, with a fluted pattern and a chased pattern of birds and leaves around the rim. There is a hinged lid in the likeness of a scallop shell, beneath which are four salt containers that may be lifted out. Value approximately three thousand pounds.

"Item, sundry small costly ornaments, total value approximately seven hundred pounds.

"They're not here," I said. "But they were among the things that Gresham, well, sequestered, with my husband's help. Was some of the treasure from the Netherlands broken up—or melted down? Or sold?"

"One would hope not. Such exquisite artifacts should never be destroyed." Sir Henry was quite shocked.

Sackville, however, was nonplused. "Mistress Blanchard, I have never seen the items you describe, nor found them on any list. When were they sent to England? On what ship?"

"Gerald was arranging for a ship at the time when he fell ill," I said. "Come to think of it . . ."

His illness had struck suddenly and from the moment when I first knew what it was, I had thought of nothing except him and Meg and how best to care for them. I had had smallpox as a child, without my complexion being much harmed, but I would take no risks with Meg. In frantic haste, I had arranged other lodgings for her and her nurse; and, thank God, neither of them had caught it. I myself had stayed with Gerald, to nurse him and worry about him and at last to grieve for him. From then until now I had not thought, even once, about that hidden treasure. I hadn't even thought about it when I transferred Gerald's keys from his key ring to my own and noticed, vaguely, that the warehouse key, a distinctive affair in ornamental ironwork, was with them. I had meant to return it, but in the exhaustion and preoccupation of bereavement, I forgot. I was in England when I noticed the key again, and then trying to return it seemed like pointless effort.

It was only a key, after all. No one reminded me that it might unlock a treasure. Our manservant, John Wilton, had probably assumed that all arrangements for transporting the valuables were in hand. At least he had never mentioned it to me and I could not now ask him, for he, too, was dead.

The key was still on my ring; a souvenir of past happiness and nothing more.

"Come to think of it," I said again, "I doubt if those items ever left Antwerp. I expect they're still there."

I knew precisely where, too. When Gerald first rented the warehouse, he had shown it to me, and shown me the hiding place under the boards of the ground floor where, he hoped, not just one but a succession of consignments would rest. The first consignment had been the last, but I knew he had got it safely as far as the warehouse. It must still be where he hid it.

Well, it could stay there as far as I was concerned. I

wanted no part of it. It was just another symbol of the intrigue of which I was growing so tired, that even though France was now a country on the edge of civil war, and even though March was a terrible month for voyaging, I was prepared to travel there on family business just to get away for a while from plots and politics.

And to pass, perhaps, within a few miles of where Matthew de la Roche, my current husband, was probably living. Back it came, my longing for him, persistent and absurd.

I pushed it away. I would not try to see him and I didn't imagine he would want to see me. Matthew was gone forever and the sooner I accepted that the better.

Look for
Queen's Ransom
Wherever Books
Are Sold.
Coming Soon
in Hardcover
from
Scribner.